PHENOMENAL PRAISE FOR
THE HEADSMAN

"Read it at home alone, late at night. It will have you looking over your shoulder . . ."
—*The Daily Record* (MD.)

"Harvey goes a long way toward establishing his mastery of the horror genre with this engrossing thriller." —*Publishers Weekly*

"Guaranteed to keep the reader at the edge of the seat . . . terrifying."
—*New Bedford Standard-Times*

"Terror, titillation [and] mystery . . . well-done!"
—*Amarillo Globe-News*

"A suburban *Friday the 13th* for adults . . . a tidy little puzzle complete with clues, misdirection, and deftly hidden culprit." —*Kirkus Reviews*

"Dark secrets slowly emerge in this suspense thriller." —*Greensburg Tribune-Review*

"I was wondering whether the executioner was out of legend or actually one of the town's people. This kept me going, through each murder . . ."
—*Reading for Pleasure*

"Exciting!" —*De Land Sun News*

THE
HEADSMAN

JAMES NEAL HARVEY

JOVE BOOKS, NEW YORK

This novel is a work of fiction. Names, characters, places and incidents are either the product of the author's imagination or are used fictitiously. Any resemblance to actual events, locales, organizations or persons, living or dead, is entirely coincidental and beyond the intent of either the author or publisher.

This Jove Book contains the complete text of the original hardcover edition. It has been completely reset in a typeface designed for easy reading and was printed from new film.

THE HEADSMAN

A Jove Book / published by arrangement with Donald I. Fine, Inc.

PRINTING HISTORY
Donald I. Fine edition published August 1991
Jove edition / October 1993

ISBN: 0-515-11209-7

A JOVE BOOK®
Jove Books are published by The Berkley Publishing Group, 200 Madison Avenue, New York, New York 10016. "JOVE" and the "J" design are trademarks belonging to Jove Publications, Inc.

PRINTED IN THE UNITED STATES OF AMERICA

10 9 8 7 6 5 4 3 2 1

For Claudia, with much love.

Mind your mum
And give thanks for your bread
Or tonight when you're fast
Asleep in your bed
The headsman will come
And chop off your head

—*old English nursery rhyme*

ONE ···

The Return

1

Braddock High School was a pile of yellow brick, so ugly Marcy Dickens thought it would be better suited for a dog pound or the town jail. Just approaching it made her feel slightly ill, although she knew that was as much because she was a lousy student as it was due to the building's odd angles and its pukey color. And also she hadn't done her homework. As usual.

God. At least it was Friday.

Sometimes on a morning like this her mind shifted into another gear, and she imagined herself in some glamorous occupation. A rock star, maybe, or a movie actress. She'd be coming back for a brief visit, and the kids would be swarming around her limo as she got out, yelling her name and asking for autographs, and in the background Mr. Baxter would be watching. His face would have that constipated expression, his eyes little blue marbles behind the rimless glasses, and Marcy would know he'd be thinking that as principal of the school his whole year's salary wouldn't amount to what the famous Marcy Dickens gave out in tips. A lot of the teachers would be there too, of course, looking on with envy, really pissed that she'd not only made it but made it bigger than any of them could even dream about.

But it wasn't a limo she was getting out of now, it was a schoolbus. And the only person waiting for her was Buddy Harper, with grease under his fingernails and smudges of it on his windbreaker, his long brown hair flopping down onto his forehead. Like Marcy he was carrying books in one arm, and she was reminded that even though he spent every spare moment working on his beloved '79 Chevy, he got better grades than she did. Life was unfair.

She fell into step with him, and they joined the stream of kids moving slowly up the walk toward the school. Marcy said good morning and he grunted a reply. They'd been dating since the beginning of the school year, if you could call it that. Mostly their time together was spent groping in the back seat of the Chevy. Although once in a while they'd cruise over to Chelsea, the next town going east on Route 6, and take in a movie. There was a movie theater here in Braddock, which they also went to, but driving a few miles made it more fun, especially for Buddy. Anytime he had an excuse to wind up the Chevy he'd take it. He had it all charged up with stuff like high-speed cams, and headers, and a heavy-duty suspension, and a lot of other things Marcy didn't understand but which he was proud of. There were also a couple of roadhouses on the way where you could get served without showing I.D., and that was another good reason to get out of Braddock. You couldn't so much as go to the bathroom in this town without everybody knowing all about it.

Tonight would be more of a social event, however. There was the basketball game against Warren Falls, and afterward a dance in the gym. The Juggernauts would be playing, and they really weren't too bad. Four guys—lead guitar, rhythm guitar, bass and drums, and even though a lot of what they played was imitations of groups ranging from the Stones to U2, they had a big beat and enough amplified sound to make the walls shake.

And speaking of music, what was that? It sounded to Marcy like the Braddock High band, pumping out one of its crappy fight songs. She looked questioningly at Buddy, who shrugged. The band playing? At this time of the morning? Whatever for? But the thumping of the drums, the toneless bleating of the brass were unmistakable. Nothing else could sound that bad.

She looked up at the front of the building, and her suspicions were confirmed. The band was on the front steps, decked out in full regalia, looking like a bunch of Mexican generals with epaulets and gold braid dripping from their orange and blue uniforms. And the purpose of all this was instantly clear, as well. Taped to the wall above the front doors was a paper banner that read BEAT WARREN FALLS!

The cheerleaders were there, led by Marcy's friend Pat Campbell, with her long blond hair and her boobs pushing out the front of her white sweater with the orange *B* on it. And off to one side, sort of hovering, was Mr. Baxter, managing to seem pleased and snide at the same time. Which explained everything. This would be another of his brilliant ideas, intended to fire up enthusiasm and school spirit. What an absolute jerk.

The students were crowded around the steps, half-heartedly singing along with the band. Some of the younger kids were getting into it, however, urged on by the cheerleaders. Beside her Buddy suddenly launched into a loud braying of the song, startling her. Marcy realized an instant later that he wasn't singing the melody, but was blaring out the words to one note, like an idiot. "Fight on old Braddock, fight on brave Orange," Buddy intoned. "Braddock you are bound to win if you'll fight fight fight fight on." Marcy burst into laughter.

The pep rally went for another fifteen minutes or so, until she began to hope it would last all morning, the band playing and the cheerleaders going through the locomotive and a pyramid and a couple of other routines, but then the bell rang and suddenly this was just like any other Friday, more or less.

The band clumped its way through another fight song as the students climbed the steps, making way for the other kids to pass. When she went by Donny Lonzik, Marcy had to smile. Donny was playing one of those huge horns that wrapped around you—a sousaphone, she thought it was called. He was a fat guy and short, and even though it was a typical raw late-winter morning of the kind that passed for spring in this part of central New York State, Donny was running sweat, drops falling from his nose and chin as he huffed and puffed into the horn.

"Hey, Donny," Buddy called out. "You know your fly's open?"

Lonzik pulled away from the mouthpiece and a grin split his

face as he supplied the punchline to the old gag. "No, but if you could hum a few bars . . ."

They filed through the doors and into the school.

2

The first class of the morning was English, and it was a few minutes before everybody got settled after all the commotion. Marcy took a seat next to Pat, who was looking radiant. "Some whoop-de-doo."

Pat rolled her eyes upward. "Leave it to Baxter. He's such an asshole."

"Yeah." But Marcy wasn't fooled. The cheerleader loved all this stuff, holding center stage and with the boys' tongues hanging out as they watched her cavort in that tight sweater. Pat was her best friend, one of the few people that she could confide in, and yet she couldn't deny feeling envious at times like this morning, wishing she had hair like that instead of the mousy dark stuff she could never get to look like anything, and maybe a face that pretty. Not that Marcy was a dog. She wasn't, not by a long shot. When it came right down to it, she had almost as good a body, and she was two inches taller.

But somehow Pat put it all together in a way that Marcy couldn't. Blond hair, vivacious personality, a knack for wearing clothes. She also had the means to buy them; her father was one of the richest men in Braddock. Not that Marcy was poor. Her own father was president of a bank, and the Dickenses were one of the leading families in town. It was just that no matter how you looked at Pat, the sum total was terrific.

And if you wanted even more proof, all you had to do was look at her boyfriend. He was Jeff Peterson, captain of the basketball team, easily the prize catch of the whole damn school. He was sitting in the back of the classroom with a couple of his dimwitted buddies, his long legs stretched out into the aisle, cool and self-assured as usual. Some people thought he looked like a tall Tom Cruise, and while Marcy wasn't ready to go that far, she had to admit that with his lazy smile and his close-cropped dark hair he was pretty cute. She glanced back at him as she often did, pretending to be just casually looking around the room, making a mental comparison of Jeff and Buddy.

The bell rang to signal the beginning of the period, and Mr. Hathaway rolled into the room in his motorized wheelchair. No matter how many times she had been in his class, no matter how long he'd been a fixture in the school, the presence of this man never failed to make her uncomfortable. Part of it had to be that chair, of course. She'd never seen him out of it, and so it was as if it were a part of him. Instead of legs, he had wheels growing out of the bottom of his trunk. And instead of the sound of footsteps, he made a whirring noise as he moved around.

And that wasn't all of it. There were the broad shoulders, and the bony hands with the long fingers. And most of all, there was that face, with its swarthy complexion and the deep-set dark eyes looking out at you. Sort of accusingly, as if it was your fault. His gaze met hers now, and she looked away.

The truth was that this course was a pipe. All you had to do was read whatever Hathaway had assigned—or skim through it, even—and later discuss the material in class. No matter what you said, so long as you didn't make it obvious that you were bored, he would take your remarks seriously. And the exams were easy as well, all essay questions you could pretty much bullshit your way through if you had read at least a little of the stuff and then paid any attention to what had been said about it in the discussions.

What they had been studying for several months was work by American authors. *Moby Dick*, which Marcy couldn't stand, and then *Huckleberry Finn*—a kid's book, for God's sake, that Hathaway made a big deal of. And now for the past few days they'd been reading and then reviewing stories by Washington Irving, which was really going back into your childhood. The first time Marcy had heard that crap about the goofy school-teacher in Sleepy Hollow she must have been in the second grade.

"All right," Hathaway said. "Quiet down. I know you're all excited about the game and the dance tonight, but I want you to pay attention. You'll be tested on a lot of what we've been discussing here."

Some low-volume grumbling and rustling went on for a few moments, and then Hathaway asked Dick Heiser to summarize what they'd covered so far. As Heiser stumbled along with his answer Marcy listened for a while, and then as she often did when she was bored, she tuned out.

It was a habit she'd gotten into a long time ago, starting when her father would come home loaded and quarrel with her mother. Marcy was little then, and she didn't understand a whole lot of what was going on between them, what her parents were fighting about. She realized her mother was angry because her father had come home drunk, and that he was angry because her mother was angry. But there were other currents as well, which Marcy couldn't figure out. Her mother would yell, and her father would snarl, and then he'd pour himself another drink and the battling would become more intense.

And then Marcy would flick that little switch in her head that was sort of like the one on the TV, and she would be on a different channel, somewhere else. In fact, sometimes she would put herself into one of her favorite shows—"The Flintstones," for instance. Fred would be cavorting with Barney or with Wilma, and Marcy would be right there in their stone house with them, sharing their jokes and giggling and having a wonderful time.

Today when she switched channels she went to the dance that was scheduled to follow the game that night. She saw herself wearing her black blouse and her silver pants that Buddy said were so tight he could count the hairs, and she looked terrific. People turned to stare at her when she walked across the floor of the gym. Jeff Peterson was giving her admiring glances and Pat was friendly but obviously a little jealous, and when the music started Marcy just knew Jeff was going to ask her to dance.

"Marcy?"

It was so cool—dreamy, even.

"Marcy?"

Suddenly she heard sniggering. She snapped out of it. "Yes?"

Jesus, it was Hathaway. The laughter grew louder and her face flamed. Most kids found nothing funnier than someone else's discomfort, and the more embarrassed she became the more they relished it. Hathaway let the smirks and chuckles go on for a moment or two, and then he raised a hand to cut off the noise. His eyes were black and piercing but the rest of his face wore no expression whatever. Marcy squirmed in her seat as his gaze bored into her.

"I asked whether you thought Ichabod Crane's terror was justified," Hathaway said.

That sent her mind racing. *Justified?* First she had to remember what Ichabod had been terrified by to begin with. Ah, of course. He'd been chased by the headless horseman. The whole thing seemed like a crock to her, but that wasn't the issue. What concerned her now was coming up with an answer that would get Hathaway off her back. She decided a positive opinion would be the best one to give, because it would be the least controversial.

She cleared her throat. "Yes, I think it was. I mean, he was on that lonely road at night, and he thought he was like being chased by a ghost."

Hathaway pursed his lips, seeming to consider her answer. "All right, very good." Marcy felt a surge of relief. His gaze left her and swept the others in the room. "Anyone care to add a comment to that?"

The room was dead quiet. Nobody seemed anxious to volunteer a viewpoint, not even that kiss-ass Betty Melcher. Betty rarely missed a chance to brown-nose a teacher, but for the moment she was as mute as the rest of them.

"Betty?" Hathaway was looking at her. Which was something he did often. She always sat in the front row of the class, where she could give him a good view of her legs and where her low-cut blouses would show to best advantage.

This morning Melcher squirmed a little for his benefit, but she didn't offer a reply.

Hathaway glanced over the other students, and a note of cynicism sounded in his tone. "Surely one of you has a thought about this?"

The silence continued for several more seconds, and then it was rent by the sound of a long, piercing fart. Johnny Lombardi might have cut it, or maybe Billy Swanson. It came from somewhere in the back of the room, as loud and clear as a bugle call, and then the room erupted in shrieks of laughter. Buddy was sitting at the desk next to Marcy's. He stuffed his hand into his mouth and bent over, his shoulders shaking.

Hathaway's face darkened. It was sallow to begin with, even when he was calm. But now it looked like a piece of old leather. His brows hunkered down, a further clue to his anger, and when he spoke his voice cut through the titters like a knife. "Swanson!"

Billy looked up with a wide-eyed *who, me?* expression that inspired a few more choked-off laughs.

"Yes, you," Hathaway said. "What do *you* think about Ichabod Crane's fear?"

Swanson sat sprawled in his seat, one of his long arms hanging down at his side so that his knuckles almost touched the floor. He was a big tow-headed boy, left tackle on the football team. His usual manner was laid back and cool, and he slid into that protective covering now. "I think he got all wound up over nothing."

"That may be, but did he know it was nothing at the time?"

The class was enjoying this; a sparring match between the pupil and the teacher was in the offing, and it had little to do with "The Legend Of Sleepy Hollow."

Swanson became emboldened. He wasn't much of a student, but he was usually sure of himself when he'd formed an opinion. "He should have known. Anybody would fall for a stunt like that had to be stupid."

The teacher's tone took on an edge of sarcasm. "Then you believe most people would have thought it was just some sort of joke—a prank?"

A half-smile stretched the boy's mouth. "They would if they had any brains."

There were murmurs of amusement from the rest of the class. Hathaway seemed to be getting the worst of this, and it was apparent that he didn't like it. He studied Swanson for a moment. "Are you aware of our own legend, right here in Braddock?"

Swanson's smile widened. "What legend is that?"

Billy had to know damn well what the teacher was referring

to, just as Hathaway had to be aware that the boy was pulling his chain.

But the bearded man's face remained impassive. "I'm speaking of the headsman."

"Yeah," Billy said. "I've heard about it."

"A lot of people in this town believe it to be quite true." Hathaway let his gaze drift over the other students. "I'm sure you're all familiar with the subject."

Whispers passed through his audience, like the rustling of leaves in the wind. At the sound, the corners of the English teacher's mouth turned down. He had their attention now, but instead of seeming pleased, his expression was clearly disdainful.

"Yet I wonder," he went on, "if you know its origins. Probably not."

They waited as he closed his eyes in a dramatic show of thinking deeply about what he was going to say. Several seconds passed before he opened them, and several more before he spoke. "To begin with, the practice of execution by beheading is as old as civilization. It started when man learned to work copper, around 5,000 B.C. That enabled him to make edged weapons that were far superior to stone or flint. They were much sharper, much better suited to cutting through flesh and bone. And from that time on, a vanquished warrior or a criminal could expect to lose his head. Even the Romans, who were famous for crucifixion, actually preferred to behead their victims." He paused. "Can anyone tell us where else it was popular over the centuries?"

No one replied.

Hathaway's tone was dry. "The answer is . . . everywhere. In every country, and with every one of the world's leaders. Attila's horsemen carried opponents' heads on their lances as trophies. Charlemagne decorated his castle with them. So did Vlad the Impaler and Barbarossa. And Genghis Khan was believed to have beheaded as many as fifty thousand of his enemies. There was even a sport that got its start that way."

"I know," Betty Melcher blurted. "Polo!"

The teacher appeared surprised as well as gratified. "Very good, Betty. Tell us about it."

She sat up straight in her seat. "The tribesmen in Afghanistan played it. They'd take the head of one of their enemies and put it in a field and then they'd ride on their horses and try to knock the head over the goal line."

"Excellent."

Marcy felt like gagging. Little Miss Kiss-ass was scoring one of her own goals, as usual.

Melcher pressed her advantage. "The Afghans played it for hundreds of years, and when the British were there they picked it up. Only they used a ball instead of a head."

Hathaway was smiling at her. "How did you know that, Betty?"

"I saw it in a movie on TV."

He frowned. "Um."

"With Sean Connery and Michael Caine."

"Called *The Man Who Would Be King*. From a Kipling story. I was hoping you'd read it."

Melcher looked crestfallen. Marcy was elated.

Hathaway's dark eyes swept the class. "Then there was the French revolution, of course. The guillotine was used to behead the nobles and the bourgeoisie, and eventually the revolutionaries as well. But in most places the work was done with the ax."

His bony hands gripped the arms of the wheelchair. "In England, every community had its own headsman. The executions took place among the rich and the poor, the weak and the powerful. King Henry the Eighth had two of his six wives beheaded. And it wasn't uncommon for children as young as twelve to be put on the block for stealing a loaf of bread."

God, Marcy thought. How terrible.

"The English system of justice is different from ours," Hathaway said. "It decrees that the accused is guilty until proven innocent. A trial back then would take only a few minutes, and the offender would be condemned to death by the ax."

He's enjoying this, Marcy realized. Rolling around in it like a dog in a cowflop. What a sicko.

Hathaway shifted his heavy shoulders. "When the village of Braddock was founded, early in the eighteenth century, the settlers not only brought the custom with them, but they brought a headsman as well. When someone committed a crime here, he was decapitated. His head was chopped off."

The teacher paused, apparently gauging the effect his words were having.

Melcher tried again. "And the legend is that every so often, the headsman comes back."

Hathaway nodded somberly. "That's correct, Betty. Every few years, they say, the headsman returns to Braddock."

The room was quiet, and Hathaway's gaze moved back to Swanson. "So you see, we not only have the legend, but we know it was based on historical fact. It's quite possible that Washington Irving was familiar with the story, and perhaps was inspired by it. When you look at 'The Legend Of Sleepy Hollow' in that context, it's also easier to understand Ichabod Crane's fear, wouldn't you say?"

The tone of the boy's voice was arrogant. "I still think the whole thing's a lot of crap."

Marcy drew in her breath sharply. Whether he realized it or not, Billy was pushing it to the limit. If he went too far he'd be thrown out of the class. Hathaway was one of the few teachers in Braddock High nobody dared mess with.

But Hathaway surprised her by remaining unruffled. "You're entitled to your opinion, of course," he said to Swanson. "But in fairness to Ichabod, let's set up a hypothetical situation, closer to home. Okay?"

Billy shrugged, letting the audience know he'd won this little skirmish, but if Hathaway wanted to keep on looking like a horse's ass, then what the hell—he'd go along.

"Let's suppose," the teacher said, "you're out late at night, walking along a road right here in Braddock. It's a lonely road out in the country. You're out there all by yourself. Suddenly you hear footsteps behind you."

He leaned forward. "The footsteps come closer. You turn around, and there—standing directly behind you—is the headsman. Now be truthful. If that happened to you, wouldn't you be just a little fearful?"

Swanson grinned at having been given a perfect opening. It was obvious that he was in his glory now, in a position to show

everyone what he was made of and what he thought of
Hathaway and Washington Irving and the entire subject. "Nah.
I'd know it was all phony."

"Are you so sure? Think about it. What you see is a very big
man, obviously very powerful. He's dressed entirely in black.
He's wearing a hood and carrying a huge, double-bladed ax."

In spite of herself, a chill passed over Marcy. As long as she
could remember, and probably for as long as the town had been
here, Braddock's children had been frightened by the legend.
Parents used it to discipline their kids, telling them that if they
were bad, or if they didn't shape up and do as they were told,
or whatever, the headsman would come looking for them. He'd
be carrying that big ax, and the ones who were really naughty
would get their heads chopped off. Braddock's very own
bogeyman, lurking behind some tree or waiting to jump out of
your closet at night, swinging that awful weapon.

But hey, that was just so much nonsense. And you realized
it about the same time you stopped believing in Santa Claus.

"Well," Hathaway prodded, "what would you do?"

The grin on Billy's face widened. "I'd take the ax and stick
it up his dingus."

Hoots of laughter filled the classroom.

Still there was no change in Hathaway's expression. His eyes
glittered like onyx as his gaze once again ranged over the kids
in the room, but he said nothing until the giggling and chortling
died down. Then a tight, ironic smile passed briefly over his
lips. He turned the wheelchair around, its motor whirring, and
directed it toward the blackboard on the other side of the room.

Picking a piece of chalk out of the tray, he looked back at
them. "Since all of you seem to think this is some sort of joke,
I have a homework assignment for you."

A collective groan rose from the class.

The reaction seemed to please him. That's what he wanted,
Marcy thought. An excuse to jam it to us. He knows there's the
game tonight and the dance, and he wants to do what he can to
screw it up. Only a shit would give homework on weekends.

Hathaway held up the piece of chalk. "I want each of you to
write an essay on the subject we've been discussing. Apparently many of you believe Ichabod Crane would have been a

fool to react as he did when he was pursued by the headless horseman. So you're to write about how *you* would react if you found yourself in a similar situation. Describe how you would feel and what you would do if you were being stalked by the headsman right here in Braddock.''

There was an undercurrent of protest, but Hathaway ignored it, writing out the assignment on the blackboard. As if we couldn't understand what he'd told us, Marcy thought.

A few minutes later the bell rang, and the class was over.

3

The evening didn't work out the way Marcy had hoped. Braddock lost the basketball game by one point, 72 to 71, even though Jeff Peterson played as well as he ever had in his life, bringing the crowd to its feet again and again, sinking impossible baskets with his hook shot and setting up his teammates with dazzling ball-handling.

Pat had a big night as well. She looked sensational as usual in the white sweater, keeping the Braddock fans in a near frenzy as she paced the cheerleaders. But in the end it was all for nothing. Warren Falls was the winner, and what Braddock would have to concentrate on now was making the regional playoffs.

For Marcy the dance also fell a little short. She was smashing, all right, in her silver pants, but Jeff didn't ask her to dance, even though he and Pat sat at the same table with Marcy and Buddy.

The subject of Hathaway and the headsman came up when Jeff said he thought it would be a good idea to get dressed up in black and carry a big ax and go over to Billy Swanson's house in the middle of the night.

"You do that," Pat said, "and Billy's father'd be after you with a shotgun."

Jeff laughed. "The hell he would. If old man Swanson ever saw the headsman he'd have a heart attack."

"Well, who wouldn't?" Marcy said. "A lot of people around here really do believe that story."

"Oh, come on," Pat said. "Hathaway was just trying to get

everybody stirred up. He was pissed off because we laughed at him and because Billy made him look silly. I think he's a little nuts anyway."

"It's from oxygen starvation," Buddy said.

They looked at him.

"From driving too fast," he explained. "He gets that two-wheeler out on the interstate and gets it going so fast he can't breathe. Cuts off oxygen from his brain."

The others laughed at the mental picture of Hathaway flying down the highway in his motorized wheelchair, and that inspired Buddy to tell them about Mr. Baxter catching Joe Boggs smoking a joint in the men's room that afternoon. Buddy did an imitation of Joe sitting on the toilet and arguing that he was only answering nature's call and it was getting to a pretty pass at Braddock High when you couldn't even shit in peace. The incident had taken place that afternoon and Joe would probably be suspended.

And speaking of joints, Buddy said softly in Marcy's ear, let's go out to the car. They slipped out to where his Chevy was parked in the lot behind the school, and after about the second drag he began working on getting her silver pants off. But even though she was charged up from the excitement of the game and the dance, and the maryjane was making her head buzz, she held him off. That she'd save for later.

And she did. They went back in and danced a couple of times as the amplified foursome shook the walls. Marcy noted that the kids had become a little rowdier, which was to be expected as the night wore on. Some of the more daring girls were dressed in the latest far-out styles, ragged clothes with reflectors stuck on them, wearing their hair in exaggerated brush cuts standing straight up a couple of inches off their heads with white makeup on their faces, their eyes outlined with mascara. One of them had even dyed the left side of her head bright blue, but as far as Marcy was concerned that was going too far. The girl looked like one of those weirdos from London you saw on MTV.

After one especially strenuous workout on the dance floor Marcy and Buddy sat down at the table to catch their breath and Marcy saw that Pat and Jeff had taken off. It was getting late.

She finished her Coke and took Buddy by the hand and they left the dance.

There was a gravel road up alongside Powell's farm that was about as good a place to park as any, partly because nobody ever used it at night except kids like themselves and partly because you could get a good view of the moon, if there was one. Tonight there was, and a full moon, at that. They smoked another joint and then they got into the back seat and this time Marcy didn't resist Buddy when he tried to get her pants off; she helped him.

It wasn't the best place in the world to make love, with the narrow seat and with the armrest pressing against her head, and the night air cold on her naked skin, but it was better than nothing. She and Buddy had been able to use a real bed only a couple of times since they'd started going together—both occasions when her mother and father had gone out for the evening, which they didn't do often enough to suit Marcy.

Tonight she felt chilled and tired afterward, and even worse than that, she was suddenly uptight about being out here. Sitting in the dark in the back seat of a car on a lonely country road was making her think about Hathaway and his damned spook story. Buddy lit another joint, and when he opened the window to throw the spent match she thought she heard a noise somewhere. She jumped and then peered out into the darkness. The moonlight was casting odd shadows, and one of them looked as if it could be the figure of a man, crouched over.

Buddy pulled smoke deep into his lungs and blew out a stream. "Hey, what's with you tonight—you nervous or something?"

She took the joint from him and dragged on it. "Yeah, a little."

"Well, relax, will you? The night's young." His hand dropped to the inside of her thigh and squeezed.

She knew what that meant; in a few more minutes he'd be looking for another one. Most times that would be just fine with her, but tonight she *was* nervous. And uncomfortable about being out here. Again she looked out the window. The wind was blowing the trees around, and the shadows cast by their leafless limbs created strange patterns on the dark road. She pushed his hand away.

Buddy shook his head in disgust. "Aw, come on, Marcy. What is it, anyhow? That shit about the headsman got you shook up?"

"Maybe."

"That's all it is, you know. Just a dumb story people use to scare other people. Swanson was right about that."

"Was he? Then what made you think of it just now?"

He shrugged. "I don't know. Nothing, really."

"Maybe it's been on your mind, too?"

"Naw. I just thought that could be what's got you uptight."

"Uh-huh." It seemed colder now, and her back was stiff from lying on the narrow seat. She shivered, and asked Buddy to take her home. He grumbled, but finally pulled up his pants, and taking the joint from her in a small show of petulance climbed back into the driver's seat and started the engine. She got herself together and joined him in the front seat. They sat in silence as he drove.

4

Marcy's house was the only one she'd ever lived in. It was a large white Victorian on the south side of the village, in an area called Ridgecrest. The place was set back from the road and nestled under two towering oak trees that were probably the same age as the house. When she got home the wind had become stronger, and the moon was partially obscured by scudding clouds. Patches of rotting snow lay on the front lawn.

Buddy kissed her goodnight and said he'd call her tomorrow, and she shivered as she got out of the car and made her way to the house, hoping her parents were both in bed. They almost always were at this time of night, which was a small blessing. Her father was an early riser, one of the first to arrive each morning at the Braddock National Bank. How he managed, considering what he drank each evening, was more than she could understand. But that was his problem.

The interior of the house was in semidarkness, illuminated only by the light in the center hall. Her parents slept in the back bedroom on this floor, and her room was upstairs at the front of the house. Marcy was the only child in the family. Her mother had nearly died when she was born, and the doctor had been forced to deliver her by caesarean. Afterward the doctor had tied her mother's tubes. Marcy had often wished she had a sister when she was little, but now that she was older she realized if she had it probably would only have added to the stress. God knew there was enough of it around here as it was. She stepped quietly through the house and made her way up the stairs.

Once in her bedroom she shut the door and undressed, and then went into her bathroom, where she washed her face and brushed her teeth. Her pink cotton shorty nightgown was hanging from a hook on the back of the door. She put it on and got into bed and turned on the radio, tuning in WBDK, the local station. She listened to Phil Collins and then Paula Abdul without really hearing them. After a few minutes she switched out the light and a little while after that turned off the radio as well.

Outside the wind was really kicking up now, sharp gusts bending the limbs of the oak trees until the tips scraped against the roof like giant fingernails. On some part of the house a shutter was banging, and in the distance a dog howled. She pushed herself farther down under the covers. Maybe a storm was coming and they'd get more snow. She hoped not.

She had trouble dozing off, which was unusual for her. As hard as she tried to send her mind in other directions, her thoughts kept returning to Hathaway and the assignment he'd given them. What would she do if—

But it wasn't the assignment, was it? No, it was the mental picture his words had inspired. It was like a vicious little animal, struggling to get inside her head and her emotions and stay there. She kept pushing it back, shoving it away from her, refusing to acknowledge it, until she fell into a troubled sleep.

An hour later she found herself awake again. What had she dreamed? It was something terrible; despite the cold air in the room she was covered in sweat. She brushed her fingers against the skin between her breasts and felt the moisture there. Her head was hot and she couldn't think clearly.

A noise sounded somewhere below, like the heavy thump made by a man's footstep. She was instantly alert, her ears straining to catch the slightest sound.

And then she heard it again.

There was no mistaking it now—the sound *was* that of a footstep, and it was on the stairs below her bedroom. Even though she had closed the door, there was no doubt in her mind as to what she had heard. Her hand shot out to the lamp on her bedside table and she turned it on. Instead of reassuring her, the light that bathed the room seemed strange and distorting, as if she were looking through a faintly yellow lens that bent objects out of shape.

The noise sounded again. It was louder now, and she thought she also caught the rasp of air being sucked into a man's lungs and then exhaled. *Jesus Christ.* Was she still asleep? Was this all part of the same weird dream?

But she *was* awake, as much as she wished she weren't. What she was hearing was *real*. There were footsteps on those stairs, heavy footsteps made by a heavy man. He was coming up the stairs very slowly, one step at a time.

Could it be her father? No—he never came up here, especially at night; he was too loaded.

Buddy, maybe, playing some dumbass practical joke? He wouldn't dare. She'd kill him. Or Jeff? He was the one who'd suggested dressing up and—no, that was ridiculous.

So who—or what—was on those goddamn stairs?

She called out: "Daddy—that you?"

No answer.

It made no sense, but she tried anyway: "Buddy? Buddy Harper?"

Still no answer; only the sound of the footsteps reached her ears. She shrank back against the headboard, pulling the covers up around her neck, her heart pounding.

The footsteps stopped. For an instant she tried to convince herself she'd only been imagining this—that it was the result of that fool Hathaway planting an idea so deep in her mind it wouldn't leave her alone.

But then she heard the sound of breathing again, and realized that the reason the footsteps had stopped was because whoever it was had reached the landing and was standing there, just outside her door. She lay trembling, trying desperately to think of some way to protect herself. There was no lock on the door, but maybe she could barricade it. She could slip out of bed and steal across the floor to her dresser and shove that into place.

Which was foolish. She wasn't sure she could move the dresser at all; it probably weighed a ton. And even if she could move it the noise would be horrendous and a sure tipoff as to what she was attempting. And how did she know it would keep somebody from forcing the door anyway?

Maybe her chair would work. It was a plain, straight-backed wooden one, and she had seen people on TV jam a chair like that under a doorknob. She got out of bed without even rustling the sheets and tiptoed toward the chair. It stood on the far side of the room, only a foot or two from the door.

Once she got hold of the chair she'd have to be quick, she told herself. Grab it and stick it into position as fast as possible. And then she'd yell her head off. Her father might not hear her, but maybe her mother would.

A floorboard creaked under her foot. She froze for a moment, biting her lower lip. Then she took another step, praying it wouldn't create more noise. Only two or three more steps to go.

The door opened.

It didn't swing wide or bang open, but instead opened noiselessly and very slowly. It opened into the room, and because of the angle the landing was in shadow. She couldn't see who or what was there.

Her heart was hammering now and she couldn't breathe.

And her imagination was playing a horrible trick. It was making her think there was a man standing in the darkness looking in at her—a big man dressed all in black.

But it was no trick.

He stepped into the room, and the sight was her worst nightmare come to life. Everything was black, from his head to his feet. The eyeholes in the black hood were cut at an angle, so that his head looked like that of a giant cat. Or a devil. A black tunic covered broad shoulders and a deep chest, and his legs were encased in black tights. On his feet were black boots.

And his huge, black-gloved hands grasped the haft of an enormous, double-bladed ax.

Marcy opened her mouth to scream, but her vocal cords seemed paralyzed. As hard as she tried, she could make no sound. Her head was whirling; she was having trouble keeping her balance.

The man in black stepped toward her, and she raised her arms to ward him off. The back of a gloved hand smashed into her jaw and she sprawled to the floor. She looked up, cringing in terror, and at last she found her voice. A scream came boiling out of her mouth as he raised the ax.

5

Four miles northwest of the Dickens house, Karen Wilson stirred in her sleep. An icy wind blew through the open window of her bedroom and the covers were ruffled as if by an unseen hand. She turned and burrowed deeper under the blankets, drawn halfway into consciousness as a series of fragmented images appeared in her mind.

It was like seeing photographs in a light show, each strobeburst illuminating a scene or an object, impressions randomly appearing in brilliant flashes and then just as quickly retreating into darkness. She saw a shadowy figure, and after that a woman's open mouth, lips drawn back in a rictus induced by terror.

She saw huge hands wearing black gloves, and a black-hooded head. She saw eyeholes in the hood, slanted like the eyes of a demon. She saw thick, black-clad legs, and feet shod in black boots. She saw an ax with glittering double blades. She saw powerful shoulders in a black tunic.

She saw the ax raised high, saw a young woman scantily clad in a short pink nightgown lying on the floor, one hand raised in a feeble effort to protect herself. She saw the woman's eyes grow wider, saw the mouth screaming in protest.

She saw the axhead arc downward with terrible force, saw blood spatter in an explosion of crimson. She saw a black-gloved hand holding aloft the woman's dripping head as if in triumph. And then she saw the black boots striding away, smaller in each succeeding image, until they were gone.

Karen sat up in bed and turned on her reading lamp. Her heart was pounding and her breath came in shallow gasps, and her flannel pajamas were damp with perspiration. She looked quickly around the room, as if to reassure herself that she was where she should be, and that nothing was amiss. In the lamplight she made out her chair and her desk, its surface covered with knickknacks. The door of her tiny closet was open, revealing its overstuffed contents, her clothing jammed into every available inch. On the walls her posters were soft dabs of color, illustrations of Chamonix and Capri and Cap-Ferrat.

She glanced at the clock on the table. A little after one. She shivered, and after her gaze swept the room once more she turned off the lamp and slid back down under the covers.

Would she be able to sleep again tonight? Probably not. She didn't know what the images meant, or where they had come from, or where the action they revealed had taken place. But she knew that the horror she had seen was real. For a time she fought to keep the impressions from reappearing in her mind, but she remembered too vividly what she had seen.

Would she ever know what the images meant? It was impossible to say. Maybe what she had witnessed was not of the present, but had taken place a long time ago. She hoped fervently this would be the end of it, and that she'd be left in peace. Hours later she fell into a restless sleep, disturbed by dreams of a looming, black-clad shape, and an ax, and a young woman's head floating in space, the sightless eyes frozen wide in fear.

6

The blade gleamed softly in the lamplight. Only a few drops of blood still clung to its surface, standing in tiny crimson beads. He had always taken great care of the instrument, sharpening it until its edges were as fine as a razor's, polishing it for hours, and then covering it with the thinnest coating of oil. He wiped it now with a rag, restoring it to pristine cleanliness. Then he gripped the haft in both hands, turning the ax slowly, inspecting every inch of its great steel head.

What a work of art this was. Perfectly symmetrical, each of its blades the mirror image of the other. And balanced exactly, so that it didn't matter which edge struck when the ax was put to use. Both blades were equally efficient, equally capable of cleaving even the thickest, most muscular neck with a single stroke.

More than two hundred years old, the ax had been forged by a master craftsman in Hounslow, just west of London. No clumsy smithy that one, no heavy-handed forger of farm tools. On the contrary, its maker was an armorer who fashioned swords and daggers for noblemen, and pikes for the soldiers they led into battle.

As did a fine sculpture, the ax pleased the eye no matter from what perspective you studied it. The edges of its twin blades each described a gentle parabola, like the curves of a woman's breasts, or her buttocks. The mere sight of them never failed to produce a sexual response in the headsman, a stirring of desire.

As his fingers moved over the steel the feeling intensified, recreating some of the pleasure he had felt when he carried out tonight's execution. Once again he saw the terror in the girl's eyes, saw her mouth agape as cries of fear issued from her throat.

Ah, her throat. That slender column, white and delicate, with its arteries pulsing and its flesh heaving as it alternated between gasping for air and expelling screams. And the power he had felt when he looked down on it—as if he owned all the world and controlled every living creature in it. With his unerring eye perfectly coordinated with the massive muscles of his shoulders and his arms and his back, he had swung the ax with explosive force. And at the exact instant the blade struck, precisely when that exquisitely honed steel carried out the sentence, rending flesh and tissue and bone and tendons, spraying blood so that for a fleeting instant the air had been infused with a pink cloud, that was when his orgasm had burst.

And then he had been physically drained, but left with the deep satisfaction of knowing justice had been done. He had lifted the severed head with a sense of joy that was no longer hot and savage, but as cold as death itself.

He gazed at the ax fondly for a long time, losing himself in its beauty. Then through the window he saw that the night sky was turning gray; it would be dawn soon. With a feeling almost of regret that his work was done, he oiled down the steel with loving care and put the instrument away.

TWO

A State of Shock

1

Chief of Police Jud MacElroy pulled the patrol car out of the Dunkin' Donuts parking lot and turned into Water Street, driving slowly and carefully so as not to spill coffee from the foam cup in his right hand. He was a tall man, big-boned and rangy, and with his fleece-lined leather jacket he was a little cramped in the Plymouth. His cap was pushed back on his head, revealing closely trimmed black hair, and his ice-blue eyes swept the street as he drove.

It was Saturday morning, and he was restless. The previous night had been relatively quiet: a fender bender at the intersection of Main and South streets; a fight in the Pine Tree Inn that had resulted in a drunk spending the night in Braddock's jail; a domestic argument in a house on Belden Street. And that was it. Usually there was more action than that on Fridays.

Not that he consciously hoped for trouble. On the contrary, Jud was easygoing and friendly by nature, and he sincerely believed a cop's job was to keep the peace. Violence was to be avoided if possible, and mediation was better than hard-assed confrontation anytime. He knew his attitude didn't square with that of some of the men under his command, who liked to see themselves as Rambos in a war on crime. But at far as he was concerned, there were enough problems in running the department and coping with whatever mischief came along without stirring up more.

On the other hand, there was also a desire to prove himself. He'd been on the force eight years, having joined directly after

24

a hitch in the army, where he'd risen to the rank of sergeant in the MPs. A year ago he'd become chief when his predecessor, Emmett Stark, had retired. That was just after Jud's thirtieth birthday, and his elevation to the top had caused envy and even outright jealousy among a few of the other cops, some of whom were senior to him by many years.

But what the hell, that was human nature, wasn't it? So he could live with it, and in the meantime he'd try to justify the town fathers' faith in him by doing as good a job as possible, and by making improvements in the operation without alienating anybody in the BPD.

From Water Street he turned into Maple Avenue, and as he tooled along in the blue-and-white he noted the traffic seemed a touch heavier than usual. But that was typical of a Saturday, he reminded himself, with people shopping and running errands.

As he approached a corner he saw two black guys moving around a car parked on the opposite side of the street. He eased over to the curb and sat watching them, sipping his coffee. There weren't many blacks in Braddock, and those who did live there were mostly hardworking citizens who kept their noses clean. There was a fair amount of grass trade among them, but probably no more than what went on with the whites, especially the high school kids. At least there was no crack problem. Not yet, anyway.

The black men seemed young, in their early twenties, he would guess. Both wore windbreakers, and one of them had a flattop haircut. The other guy had on a baseball cap. Neither of them paid any attention to him, and he couldn't tell whether they knew he was there or not. The car was an older sedan, a grayish Pontiac. As he watched, the one wearing the cap walked around to the rear of the car, digging into his pants pocket and pulling out a set of keys. Then he bent over and opened the trunk.

So it was nothing, Jud thought. Car thieves do not use keys, nor do they mess with aging clunkers. He continued to sit there with his engine running, however, as the two guys went about getting a jack and a spare out of the trunk.

And now what? Watch people change a tire? He knew the

truth was that he was just dragging his feet, delaying going on in to his desk at the stationhouse and facing the stack of paperwork that inevitably waited there to greet him. Maybe it was just habit ingrained by years of patrolling the streets and roads that ran through and around Braddock, maybe not. But he had to admit he missed this part of the job. Reluctantly he swallowed the last of his coffee and stuffed the cup into the small plastic garbage bag on the floor. Then he dropped the Plymouth into gear and slipped out into the stream of traffic.

He'd gone about a block when the radio came to life. The dispatcher was Tony Stanis, whose style was usually a bored monotone. This morning, however, Stanis sounded so excited he could hardly get the words out. "Car Five, Car Five, go to Three-twenty Ridgeview Drive on a Code One. Repeat, Three-twenty Ridgeview Drive on a Code One."

MacElroy snapped to full alert. Code One? That was a homicide. He snatched up the mike and waited as Five—driven by Bob Kramer—acknowledged. Then he hit the key. "Tony, Chief MacElroy. Code One?"

"Affirmative, Chief. Just came in."

"Who is it?"

"It's a kid—uh, seventeen-year-old female. Name, Marcy Dickens."

"That Ed Dickens' daughter?"

"Right."

"Perpetrator?"

"Unknown. Not at the scene."

Jud switched on the cruiser's flasher and siren and skidded the car into a U-turn, scaring the shit out of the driver of a van in the oncoming lane. Jud could see the guy's eyes popping as he jammed on the van's brakes.

Jesus Christ. Dickens was president of the Braddock National Bank. His daughter was an only child. Jud felt heat course through his neck and shoulders as his body pumped adrenalin. He whipped the car in and out of the stream of traffic until he came to Pemberton Road, a narrow blacktop that would take him to the Ridgecrest area. He turned into Pemberton and increased his speed.

He pressed the transmitter button again. "Tony, Chief MacElroy. Who called it in?"

"A neighbor. Mrs. Keevis."

"What happened?"

"Don't know. The neighbor said the girl was dead and Mrs. Dickens was hysterical."

"Her husband wasn't there?"

"I don't think so."

"Call the bank. See if he's in his office. If so, tell him to get home. And send an ambulance to the house."

"Right, Chief. Wilco."

"I'm on my way there now. Also send another car." He dropped the mike back onto its hook and tried to concentrate on his driving.

A homicide.

And the daughter of one of the town's leading citizens.

Killings were rare in Braddock, and when they did occur it was usually when somebody got into a bar brawl and ended up with a knife or maybe a bullet in his chest. Or now and then a family dispute went over the edge. A few months ago a carpenter who lived out toward Norristown had come home drunk and punched his wife around. When he finally wound down and flopped into bed she got out his 12-gauge and shoved it into his ear, giving him both barrels. The case had not yet been tried; maybe it never would be. Meanwhile she was free on bail and living at home.

But more often sudden death in these parts was the result of an accident. People would smash themselves up in cars, and farm workers would get tangled up in their machines. Tractors were especially lethal, with a nasty way of flipping over backward and crushing careless drivers. And just the previous fall a fourteen-year-old boy had fallen into a grain loader and suffocated. Accidents happened all the time, and the cops went out and swept up the mess.

But homicide was something else again.

The Plymouth's speedometer needle was touching eighty. Jud passed another car, just getting back into his own lane before a stakebed loaded with logs blew by in the opposite direction. You better back off, he told himself, or they'll be shoveling *you* into a body bag. But he didn't. Instead, he squeezed a little more out of the cruiser, until he was barely able to hold it on a sweeping left-hand curve, the tires squealing over the howl of the siren and the suspension chattering on the rough surface of the road. He went over the brow of a hill, and when he got to the bottom and the road flattened out Ridgecrest lay just ahead of him. He slowed down and made the turn into Ridgeview Drive.

As he approached the Dickenses' home he saw Five parked in front of it. The house was painted white and was set back between a pair of towering oaks. It was a big place for a family of three, but then Ed Dickens was a prominent man in Braddock and appearances were no doubt important to him.

When Jud drew closer he saw a half-dozen people gathered together on the front walk. Neighbors, probably. A couple of the women seemed to be crying. He slid to a stop behind the other patrol car and turned off his engine and the siren and lights, then climbed out and hurried up the walk.

He recognized several of the onlookers, knowing them by sight if not by name. One was an old man who'd worked for years in Swanson's hardware store, and that one's name he did know. It was Art Ballard. They made way for him, and as he passed they stared at him with that dumb, frightened look people get when there's some kind of big trouble—an automobile accident or a drowning or a fire.

He went up the front steps and across the porch to the front door, rapping on the knocker and then trying the doorknob. The door was unlocked; he opened it and walked in. From somewhere inside he could hear a woman sobbing.

Jud had never been in the house before, but he'd passed it often enough. Braddock had no really elegant section, just a few big places like this one scattered through it, some of them built a hundred years ago or more, in the days when a sawmill and paper manufacturing business had flourished just outside the town on the banks of the Nepawa River. He was standing now in a wide hallway with deep carpeting and blue-and-white papered walls. A stairway led to the floor above, but the sobs seemed to be coming from down here, from one of the rooms off the hall. He went into the room.

Apparently this was the living room. It looked a lot more formal than what Jud was used to seeing around Braddock. There were two sofas and groupings of chairs and a desk and a marble fireplace and tall windows with drapes that came down to the floor. Helen Dickens was sitting on one of the sofas.

Jud had met her a few times, but he wasn't as well acquainted with her as he was with her husband. She was on the heavy side, with stringy brown hair and a face that might have been pretty when she was younger, but that had become bloated from age and maybe too much booze and rich food. At the moment it looked even worse, her nose red and her eyes swollen from crying. She was holding a handkerchief to her mouth and shuddering.

Kramer was standing beside her and seemed to be awkwardly trying to comfort her. The cop didn't look too great either, Jud thought—his skin was pasty and his expression looked as if somebody had kicked him.

Jud raised his eyebrows questioningly, and Kramer replied by pointing upward. Jud nodded and left the room, heading for the stairs. He took the steps two at a time, instinctively putting his hand on the .357 Magnum Smith & Wesson in its holster on his right hip. When he reached the upstairs hallway he saw several doors, one of them standing open. He made his way to it and looked into the room.

Dear God. Sitting on a dresser top, facing the door, was Marcy Dickens' head. The eyes were staring straight at him.

2

Death was no stranger to Jud MacElroy. He'd seen plenty of it in the army and in his eight years on the cops. And a mangled body was nothing new, either. He'd encountered them torn apart, disemboweled, crushed, blown to pieces, ripped every which way. And often enough over the years so that he could almost take the sight of one in stride. Horrifying, but part of the job. Something you'd seen before and knew you'd see again.

This one, however, was a different experience. Somebody—or some *thing*—had deliberately and savagely cut the head off what had been a healthy, pretty teenage girl. And judging from the horror frozen on her features, she had known what was happening to her. For all his experience, he felt like puking. He took a deep breath, and then tried to look objectively at what he was seeing.

The head was resting on a white dresser scarf, in a pool of dried blood. The rest of the body lay on the floor, on its back, wearing a short pink nightgown that was twisted around the waist. The legs were sprawled apart, the arms flung out to the side. A rug under the body was discolored by a large dark stain, and blood had seeped out from the rug onto the surrounding floorboards as the body had exsanguinated.

Jud immediately thought of sexual assault, but there was no way to be sure of that until an autopsy was performed. Moving very carefully so as not to disturb anything in the room, he stepped to the body and crouched beside it.

From what he could see, there were no signs of a struggle on her flesh—no cuts, no bruises. The skin was as white as goat's cheese, without even the usual dark spots from cyanosis. That would be because so much of the blood had drained from the corpse. No wonder the rug and the floor were such a mess; the human body holds six quarts of the stuff, and that was a hell of a lot of blood.

He glanced around at the rest of the room. No evidence of a fight anywhere else, either. The furniture seemed all in place, nothing overturned or broken.

He stood up and stepped to the dresser. Up close, he saw that the girl's eyes were glazed, the pupils dilated. Their wide stare was exaggerated because the eyeballs had been distended, as if from a blow. It looked to him as if her head had been severed with one swipe. From a sword, possibly, or an ax. The neck was sitting in the dried blood, but he could see the wound well enough to confirm his hunch; the edges of the cut were clean, not ragged as they would have been if the killer had used a knife or some other sharp object to saw through the tissues and the spinal column.

Jud was about to turn away when her hair caught his attention. It was dark brown, almost black, and the ends were stuck in the viscous pool. On top of the head, however, the strands were tangled and sticking up. Whoever had done this must have picked up the head by the hair and set it on the dresser top. A picture of the act came into his mind and again he felt his stomach turn over.

"Holy shit."

He turned to see two more cops, Dick O'Brien and Charley Ostheimer, standing in the doorway and peering into the room. Jud hadn't heard their siren, if they'd used it, and hadn't heard them come up the stairs, so deeply immersed had he been in his thoughts. O'Brien was an oldtimer. Ostheimer had been on the force only a year. But it was O'Brien who'd spoken.

"Don't come in here yet," Jud said. "You bring a camera?"

O'Brien was gaping at the headless body on the floor. He swallowed. "It's in the car."

Jud felt a twinge of embarrassment for the girl, her legs spread, the black pubic patch in full view. "Go get it," he ordered.

Ostheimer hurried down the stairs and Jud stepped out into the hall. "Anybody call the coroner?"

The older cop looked sheepish. "Naw, Jud—we just got out here quick as we could."

"All right," Jud said. "I'll take care of it. Ambulance here yet?"

"Yeah, it was right behind us. I told 'em to wait outside."

"Okay. You and Ostheimer start taking pictures. Nobody else is allowed in here until the doc gets finished. And for Christ's sake be careful, will you? Don't touch anything. We'll need the state guys in this and I don't want to hear a lot of crap from them."

As Jud made his way downstairs in search of a phone the front door burst open and Ed Dickens stepped into the hall. Jud had been dreading this; he slowed down as he got to the bottom of the stairs. Dickens looked stunned and frantic at the same time. His usually immaculate topcoat was rumpled, his tie was askew. His dark hair was disheveled. He started to push past and Jud stopped him by grabbing both his arms.

The banker struggled. "Let go of me, goddamn it."

Jud hung on. "Ed, listen. Don't go up there. You hear me? Don't."

Dickens went on trying to pull free. "But Marcy—I've got to—"

"No," Jud said. "Stay down here. You can't do anything for her now."

That registered; Dickens' body sagged. He stared at the chief. "Then it's true? She's dead?"

Jud nodded and released him, and Dickens buried his face in his hands. "Oh my God," he said. "Oh my God."

Jud let him cry, putting an arm around his shoulder. After a minute he said to him, "Your wife needs you. She's in the other room there."

Dickens drew back, making an effort to get himself together. He pulled a handkerchief out of his back pocket and wiped his eyes. When he looked at Jud he thrust out his jaw. "What happened—who did this?"

"We don't know who did it. We're just starting our investigation."

"But what happened—how did she die?"

There was no way to soften it; he'd know sooner or later. "She was decapitated."

Dickens flinched. "Jesus."

"Yes."

"Who could have done such a thing? Marcy didn't have any enemies—she was just a kid. You think it could have been a burglar?"

"We don't know, Ed. Please go to your wife now, will you?"

Dickens directed his gaze up the stairway for a few moments, and then he straightened up. He shook his head once and turned away, walking slowly down the hall and into the room where Helen Dickens was.

There was a telephone on a table near the front door. Jud went to it and called police headquarters. He got Sergeant Joe Grady on the line and told Grady to call Doc Reinholtz, the coroner, right away. Also to call the New York State Police barracks at Franklin and ask them to send a homicide investigation team.

"What about a medical examiner from Memorial," Grady asked. "To assist Reinholtz?"

"Yeah, call for one."

"And the county attorney?"

"Notify him too." Jud knew Grady was subtly needling him by asking about procedures that would be standard practice under the circumstances. It was Grady's way of reminding Jud that Grady had been a sergeant in the BPD longer than Jud had been on the force.

But Jud refused to let this kind of petty shit get to him. "Any news media contact you, dust 'em off," he went on. "Tell 'em there'll be a statement later. Also send more cops out here. I think we'll get a lot of rubbernecking." He hung up and went down the hall to the room where the Dickenses were.

When he walked in, Ed Dickens was sitting beside his wife on a sofa, holding her hand. She wasn't crying any longer, but was staring glassy-eyed at the floor, clutching the sodden handkerchief. Dickens had removed his topcoat and it lay over one of the chairs. Bob Kramer was still standing there, looking even more uncomfortable than he had earlier.

Jud motioned to Kramer and when the cop came over to him he inclined his head toward Mrs. Dickens and spoke in low tones. "She tell you anything?"

"No."

"All right. Go on out there on the porch. Don't let anybody near the house unless they have business here. No newspeople. There'll be more cops to help you in a little while."

When Kramer had left, Jud took off his cap and approached the couple. "Excuse me," he said to Helen Dickens. "I know this is very painful for you, but I need to ask you some questions."

Ed Dickens started to protest, and Jud said, "It could help, you know."

Before Dickens could reply, his wife said, "It's all right. I'll try."

Jud took off his jacket and dropped it onto the carpet along with his cap. He pulled a chair closer to them and sat down, taking a small spiral notebook and a ballpoint from the pocket of his uniform shirt. "Mrs. Dickens, I understand you discovered your daughter's body?"

She nodded, continuing to stare at the floor.

"What time was that?"

"About nine o'clock. I called her a couple of times, and she didn't answer. I don't like her to sleep too late. Saturdays she has things she's supposed to do for me."

He noticed she was speaking as if the girl were still alive. "And so you went up to her room?"

Helen Dickens' head came up, her puffy eyes widening and her mouth dropping open, as if she was living the shock of the discovery all over again. A low, tortured wail erupted from her throat.

I don't blame you, lady, Jud thought. I don't blame you a goddamn bit.

She was shuddering again, stuffing the handkerchief into her mouth, while her husband tried to console her.

This isn't going to work, Jud thought. She's in no shape to tell me anything.

But Helen Dickens surprised him. She struggled to get herself under control, speaking with obvious difficulty. "Yes. I went up there."

"Had you noticed anything wrong in the house? Anything out of place, any sign there might have been an intruder?"

"No, nothing."

Jud didn't know what the coroner would say about the time of death, but considering the condition of the body and the dried blood it was apparent Marcy Dickens had been killed sometime during the night. "When was the last time you saw her, before this morning?"

"It was—at dinner last night. We ate early, because she was going to the basketball game and the dance after."

"Did she go to the game with anyone?"

"Buddy Harper."

"Harper. That Peter Harper's son?"

"Yes. He came by and picked her up at about seven-thirty."

Peter Harper owned a drugstore on Main Street. Jud vaguely recalled his boy was a teenager who liked to fool around with cars. "Were they going together? Seeing each other often?"

"Fairly often, yes."

"Was she dating anyone else?"

"Not for several months."

"And before that?"

"A few different people, nobody special."

"So the Harper boy was the first one she'd ever gone steady with?"

Before his wife could answer, Ed Dickens said, "They weren't going steady. They were just dating."

"They were going steady," Helen Dickens said.

"What about some of her other friends?"

"She runs around with a crowd of seniors at the high school. Pat Campbell, Jeff Peterson, Alice Boggs, Billy Swanson, people like that."

"Any of them ever get into any trouble that you know about?"

Both parents were quiet for a moment, then shook their heads.

Jud made some notes. He looked up. "Don't be offended by this, but I'm sure you know a lot of kids drink these days, and smoke pot. Could you tell me if Marcy did either of those?"

"I think she drank a little beer now and then," Helen Dickens said, "but that's all."

"No dope of any kind," Ed Dickens added. "I'm sure of that."

Jud nodded. "Okay. What time did she get home, do you know?"

"I think around twelve," Helen said. "We were in bed, so I'm not positive. Our bedroom is downstairs, at the other end of the house."

"Would she have come in the front door?"

"Yes."

"Is it usually locked?"

"I always lock it before I go to bed. She has a key."

"Was it locked this morning?"

"Yes. I unlocked it when I got the paper off the front porch."

"Did you hear any noises during the night, either of you?"

Both shook their heads.

"What time did you leave this morning, Ed?"

"Usual time. Eight o'clock. We're open until noon on Saturdays, as you know."

"Yes. Did anything seem out of order to you around the house—anything at all?"

Dickens thought about it. "No. Helen made coffee for me and I had that and some juice and toast and then I left."

"Was your car in the garage?"

"Yes. I went out the back way."

"Door locked?"

"Yes. I remember unlocking it. It has a snap bolt that sticks. I keep reminding myself to put some oil on it. That's how I remember it was locked."

"Uh-huh, okay. Over the last few weeks, or months even, do either of you recall Marcy having any problems you were aware of?"

Helen Dickens shrugged. "She's had a few with her school-work sometimes. I don't recall anything else bothering her."

"Over that time, did you ever notice anything different about her personality—any change in her moods, for instance?"

"She has her ups and downs," Helen said. "Like any kid. But most of the time she's pretty happy."

"No period of time when she seemed unusually down, or withdrawn?"

"No," Helen said.

Jud looked at Ed Dickens, who again shook his head.

There was a knock on the door jamb, and Jud looked around to see O'Brien standing there. Jud excused himself and went out into the hall.

"We covered it good," O'Brien said. "Took three rolls."

"Okay. Tell Ostheimer to stay up there on the door. You start a check on the house. Look for any sign of forced entry, footprints near the windows, anything like that." He reminded himself that O'Brien was an old hand. "You probably know the routine better than anybody."

"Yeah," O'Brien said. "I do." He turned and went back up the stairs to give Ostheimer his orders.

When the cop had left him, Jud again called the stationhouse on the hall telephone and this time told Grady to have the Harper kid picked up and brought in for questioning. He hung up and went back into the living room.

The Dickenses remained sitting on the sofa, their faces wearing the same blank, stunned look. Jud told them to stay in the house, but not to go upstairs. He explained that the state police would also want to question them. Then he thanked them for their cooperation.

"I'm very sorry about your daughter," he said, knowing how awkward he sounded. "And I'm sorry you have to go through all this, I really am."

He felt stupid and clumsy, but he didn't know what else to say. Jud had no children, wasn't even married, but he could imagine what this was doing to them. He was also aware of the process: first the blinding shock, and when that wore off, there would come a bitter, empty agony that wouldn't leave them. As soon as he could, he'd find out who their family doctor was and call him. He stuffed his notebook and pen back into his pocket and left the room, putting on his cap and jacket.

He had guessed correctly; the crowd out front had grown to several dozen people. Shit—that would make it harder to question the neighbors. There were two more cops out there now, and they had strung a rope between a telephone pole and a tree near the road in an effort to hold back the gawkers. As Jud stepped off the porch he saw the coroner speaking to one of the cops, who let him pass. Jud met him on the walk.

Reinholtz was a small man, gray-haired and with a mustache. He squinted at Jud through gold-rimmed glasses and spoke in a high-pitched voice that made him seem younger than his age. "What the hell happened here, Chief?"

Jud described what he'd seen in Marcy Dickens' bedroom, and Reinholtz shook his head again. Jud could imagine what the doctor was thinking; he knew Reinholtz had a couple of daughters himself, and one of them had to be about Marcy Dickens' age.

"What's it look like?" Reinholtz asked. "Was there a robbery?"

"I don't think so," Jud said. "Nothing's disturbed in the house, at least that Mrs. Dickens was aware of."

"Think he raped her?"

"I don't know. Like I said, I didn't see any signs of a fight."

"Yeah, okay. The autopsy'll tell us. I better go have a look." He went on up the walk toward the house.

Jud turned his attention to the onlookers, most of whom were eyeing him curiously. He spotted Art Ballard, the old man he'd passed on the way in and walked over to him. "Hiya, Art."

Ballard nodded. "Hello, Jud." His face was rosy from the cold and his nose was dripping. He was wearing a cap that said Caterpillar on the front and there were wisps of white hair sticking out from under the cap.

Jud lifted the rope and beckoned to Ballard to duck under it. Then he guided the old man to a place near one of the oak trees, out of earshot of the others.

"You live near here, don't you, Art?"

"Just down the road there. The gray house."

"How'd you hear about this?"

"I was out front, puttin' back one of my storm windows. Glass was cracked, 'n' I fixed it."

"Yeah. So what happened?"

"So Helen Dickens, she come out her front door yelling. Lucy Keevis there, lives in the house next door, she heard her too. We both run over here and Helen was hysterical about what'd happened to Marcy. Lucy called the police right away. After that Lucy stayed in the house with her until the cop got here."

Jud made a mental note to question Mrs. Keevis later. "Let me ask you, Art. You see anything unusual in the neighborhood last night—maybe a stranger, or anybody who might have caught your attention? Have you seen anything like that?"

Ballard's eyes were rheumy, a watery green. "Oh, he was here, all right. No doubt about that."

Jud was startled. "Who was, Art?"

The green eyes narrowed. "The headsman, of course. He's come back."

3

Jud had been at the Dickens house almost two hours when the New York State Police inspector arrived. He said his name was Chester Pearson and he carried himself with an I'm-in-charge-here manner. He looked about ten years older than Jud, as broad as the chief but not as tall. Under his prominent nose a thick mustache sprouted, and he wore no hat on his bushy black hair. He was in civilian clothes, a raincoat over a brown tweed jacket and a white buttondown shirt with a red-and-white striped tie.

In the hallway outside Marcy Dickens' bedroom Jud recounted to the detective what he'd seen and learned so far, including his questioning of the Dickenses and several of the neighbors. Inside the room the coroner and the M.E. assisting him had finished their preliminary examination and the two-man ambulance crew had put the corpse into a rubberized bag and was trussing it onto a gurney. People from the State Police Crime Scene Unit were dusting for fingerprints and taking blood and fiber samples.

Pearson listened impassively until Jud finished. Then he said, "Okay, Chief. Don't sweat it. We'll be setting up in town here while we run our investigation. Or at least I will, along with Corporal Williger, my assistant. The CSU'll be going to Albany so the lab can run checks on what we get here. In the meantime, you say the girl had a boyfriend who took her to a dance last night?"

"Yes. The kid's name is Buddy Harper. I'm having him picked up for questioning."

"Good. He was the last one to see her alive, right? Except for the killer. So maybe they're one and the same. I'll want to talk to him right away."

"Sure. But I—"

"Yes?"

"Nothing. Coroner says he'll see to it the autopsy is done as soon as possible," Jud said. "Probably tomorrow."

Pearson fingered his mustache. "Yeah, I spoke to him. We'll cover that, of course. No need for you to be there."

Jud felt a touch of annoyance, but he put it aside. "We'll start interviewing the girl's friends, and my men will see if we can get a line on strangers in the area or a tip on anybody talking about planning a burglary."

"Uh-huh. You better go light on the questioning. Too many people doing interviews can cause a lot of confusion. Anything comes your way, report it to me, of course. But leave the rest of it to us. Okay?"

"Sure. But there're a few things I'll want to look into myself."

"Before you do, check with me. We'll work out of your headquarters, so what I'll need from you is an office with a separate phone line. You can set that up for me first thing."

Jud wanted to ask if he'd require maid service, but he bit his tongue.

"You got a good motel around here?" Pearson inquired.

"There's a Howard Johnson on Route Six," Jud said. "Isn't too bad."

"All right."

Jud wondered if Pearson was expecting him to make reservations. If he was, fuck him. The more he saw of this guy the more he realized having him around was going to be a strain.

The ambulance attendants wheeled the gurney bearing Marcy Dickens' body past them and one of the Braddock cops gave them a hand getting it down the stairs.

Doc Reinholtz came out of the room then, along with a resident from Memorial County Hospital who acted as assistant medical examiner. Pearson and MacElroy turned to them.

"Interesting," the assistant said. "I never saw one like that before." His name was Porchuk and he looked like a college kid, wearing a blue V-necked sweater over a white shirt, carrying a ski jacket in one hand and an equipment case in the other. Jud wondered just how many homicides he had in fact seen.

"Took her head off with one whack," Porchuk went on. "Had to be from an ax."

"That's what I thought," Pearson said. He looked at Reinholtz. "You agree with that, Doc?"

"Yes, I do," Reinholtz said. "There was just the one clean wound. No sign he hit her more than once. I'll make a more detailed examination when I do the autopsy, of course. But for now I'd say yes. One blow, and from an ax."

Pearson's assistant, Corporal Mark Williger, had trailed them out of the room. He was also in plainclothes, taller than Pearson and not as husky, but about the same age. Below his thinning sandy hair his features were bland. He spoke up. "I think we've got something else says it was an ax. Come take a look."

The four men followed Williger back inside. After taking samples, the State CSU cops had cleaned the blood off the floor. Williger squatted beside the stained rug the girl's body had been lying on. He pointed. "See here? This cut is in a straight line through the rug. Now look underneath."

He flipped the rug aside. In the floorboards was a clearly defined mark about six inches long that appeared to have been freshly made. "The blade was curved," Williger said. "That's why the cut's deeper in the middle than at the ends. You see it?"

Pearson bent down and ran a finger along the depression in the wood. "That's an ax cut, all right." He straightened up. "He cut her head off while she was down here on the floor, and then he put her head on the dresser."

Brilliant, Jud thought.

Pearson turned to Williger. "Good work, Mark. Be sure you get pictures of it."

Williger rose, looking pleased. "Will do."

Reinholtz glanced at Jud. "You turn up anything so far?"

MacElroy shook his head.

"We're taking over the investigation from here on in," Pearson said to the coroner. "We'll be working out of police headquarters. Any questions, or information you have, get in touch with me or with Corporal Williger here."

"Okay, sure," Reinholtz said. He looked down once more at the cut in the floor and then at the other men. "I've got to get back to my office and make out my report. Thanks, gentlemen. I hope to God we can get this thing put away in a hurry." He stepped past them.

"I'll walk out with you," Porchuk said. He raised a hand to the others. "See you at the autopsy." The two men left the room.

Pearson turned back to Williger. "Go on down to police headquarters. See if NYSPIN has anything to match this M.O." NYSPIN was the New York State Police Information Network. Law enforcement agencies throughout the state were linked to it by computer.

"I had one of my men do that," Jud said. "Nothing fit this."

"Oh? Double-check it, Mark," Pearson said. "And see if you can get anything by running down known sex offenders."

Jud was about to tell him he'd done that too, but then he thought, the hell with it. Let Pearson find out for himself.

"I'm going to stay here awhile," the inspector said to Williger. "I want to talk with the girl's parents. You go ahead." The corporal left the room.

"Excuse me, Chief."

Jud turned to see Kramer standing in the doorway. "Yeah, Bob?"

"There's a TV crew out there, and some reporters. They want to ask some questions."

"Tell 'em no statement yet," Jud said. "The investigation's just getting under way."

"Hold on a minute," Pearson said. "It's always smart to cooperate with the media. They can be helpful, if they're handled right. And there's nothing wrong with good PR, either. The citizens want to know the police have things under control." He glanced at Kramer. "Tell 'em I'll be down to talk with them shortly."

Kramer looked at Jud, who nodded. The cop turned and went back toward the stairs.

"You can come along, if you like," Pearson said to Jud.

"There's one thing you ought to know," Jud said.

"What's that?"

He'd debated getting into this, but he thought he at least ought to clue Pearson in before the news people jumped on it. "There's an old legend in this town. According to the story, the early settlers had an executioner who did his work with an ax. A headsman. The legend says that every so often, he comes back to Braddock."

As he spoke, he saw a glint of amusement appear in the inspector's eyes. But he went on with it. "There was another homicide here twenty-five years ago, never solved. Woman named Donovan was decapitated. People said it was the headsman who did that one, too. You can bet they'll be tying this murder to the same legend."

Pearson brushed his mustache with a fingertip. "So what are

you suggesting, Chief—we say we're looking for a ghost with a big ax?"

Jud felt his face get hot. "I'm just telling you something I thought you ought to know about before they start firing questions at you."

"Questions don't bother me," Pearson said. "Even screwball questions. So thanks for tipping me off, but I can handle anything they throw out. When you've been on the hot seat as long as I have, you learn to deal with that stuff. What was it Harry Truman said? If you can't stand the heat, stay out of the kitchen."

I'm beginning to wish, Jud thought, you'd stayed the hell out of Braddock.

"Which reminds me," Pearson went on. "I'll give these guys from the media the answers to whatever they ask. It's better that way—keeps the crossfire down to a minimum. And you can tell your men that, too. There's just one official spokesman on this case, and that's me. Understood?"

"Yeah," Jud said. "Understood."

"Good. And speaking of your men, I may need to borrow a few of them, preferably the brighter ones."

"I don't know that I can spare many people," Jud said. "Like I told you, I want to run a sweep for vagrants or any strange characters who might be around, starting right away. But I'll do what I can. How do you want to use them?"

"Legwork, mostly. Also some interviews with the girl's contacts."

"I thought you said—"

"I know what I said, Chief. But I'll handle it, okay? The essential thing is to get this investigation organized fast. As far as I'm concerned, your rounding up a bunch of bums is a waste of time. You know why? Because in about eighty percent of homicide cases, the perpetrator turns out to be somebody the victim knew well. In the end, all you're dealing with is just another asshole. Which is why I want to talk to the boyfriend. You follow me?"

"Yeah," Jud said. "I do."

"Good. What do you know about him, by the way?"

"He was in her class at the high school. Comes from a good family. Father owns a drugstore here in Braddock."

"Uh-huh. You need a warrant?"

"No. I'm sure he'll be cooperative."

"Okay, good. Now let's go downstairs so I can get the media squared away."

"Yeah," Jud said. "Let's do that."

4

The news people were on the porch, crowding around the front entrance. When Pearson and Jud stepped out the door, the first thing Jud noticed was that the reporters seemed to have their own pecking order, with the TV crews at the top. Two guys with video camcorders on their shoulders were in the front row, and standing with them were two TV commentators, one male, the other female, holding microphones. The crews were from Syracuse and Albany. Braddock had no TV station of its own.

The second thing Jud noticed was that his girlfriend, Sally Benson, was among the other reporters. Which surprised him, because what Sally usually covered for the *Braddock Express* was more in the line of weddings and meetings of the 4-H Club. She smiled when she caught sight of him and he nodded to her, feeling a little self-conscious about being the center of attention. Most of the other newspeople were strangers. He assumed that like the TV crews, they were also from out of town.

As soon as Jud and the inspector appeared, the red lights on the camcorders went on, and the reporters all started asking questions at once.

Pearson raised both hands and made a quiet-down motion, and when the noise abated he said, "I'm Inspector Chester Pearson of the New York State Police. I'm in charge of this investigation. We've just started our work, but I'll answer any questions I can."

The male TV reporter shoved a mike toward Pearson. "Inspector, what can you tell us about the victim?"

The detective cleared his throat. "The deceased was a young

woman named Marcy Dickens. Age seventeen. She was a student at Braddock High School."

Jud glanced sideways at Pearson. He sounds like one of those dipshit characters in a TV cop show, he thought. He wondered if Pearson watched those programs too, and decided he probably did.

"Is it true," the reporter asked, "her head was chopped off?"

Pearson's face was somber, his tone grave. "The victim was decapitated, yes."

"What with?"

"The preliminary examination indicates it was a sharp object."

Jesus Christ, Jud thought, could it have been done with a dull one?

"What kind of object?"

"We're not sure."

"Was it an ax?"

"We don't know," Pearson said.

As soon as he got the words out, the reporters all started yammering again. The guy who had been doing the questioning put one hand behind him and signalled frantically for them to shut up. When they quieted down a little, he said, "We understand Braddock once had a public executioner who used an ax to carry out his—ah—duties."

"Is that so? I wasn't aware of that."

Jud glanced sideways again. Pearson seemed to be enjoying this. Probably getting his rocks off over occupying the lime-light.

The reporter pressed on. "A lot of people in Braddock believe the executioner—the headsman—is still around, and that he may have been responsible for this killing. What's your reaction?"

"I think it would take a lot of imagination to come up with an idea like that."

The others were rumbling once more, and the TV reporter tried again to draw Pearson into making a controversial statement. "But if this girl's head was chopped off, don't you think that's a possibility, and wouldn't you want to investigate it?"

"We're investigating all possibilities," Pearson said.

One of the reporters yelled, "If the headsman didn't do it, who did?"

Before Pearson could respond, more questions erupted, and the crowd pressed in on him. The TV reporter gave up in disgust, while the detective went on fielding inquiries.

Watching this, Jud decided he'd had enough. As he turned away, he saw Sam Melcher striding up the walk, approaching the house.

Melcher was the mayor of Braddock, and the owner of a successful insurance and real estate business. His daughter was also a senior at the high school. He was almost totally bald, but despite the cold he wore no hat on his shining pate. He was staring at the commotion on the porch, and as he caught sight of Jud he frowned. He ascended the steps and took MacElroy's arm, drawing him aside.

The mayor made an effort to keep his voice down, but its tone was a rasp. "Chief, what the hell has gone on here? Who did this, for God's sake? What have you found out?"

"At this point we have no idea," Jud said. "The state police are running the investigation. That's Inspector Pearson over there, talking to the media."

Melcher glanced again at the swarm of reporters around Pearson, and then his gaze swung back to fix on Jud. "That's fine, and I'm glad you've got their help. But I want to tell you something. This is the most shocking thing that could happen. Marcy Dickens wasn't just a nobody. Her family are some of the best people in this town. To have her murdered like this, in cold blood, is just, just—*unthinkable*."

Jud was well aware that people often have strange reactions in times of crisis, but Melcher's attitude was hard to fathom. He was angry, which was certainly understandable, but his manner made it seem as if he were holding Jud responsible not merely for solving the crime, but for not having prevented it.

"Now goddamn it," Melcher grated, "what are you *doing* about it?"

Jud wished the man would calm down. "We'll do everything we can, Sam. But as I told you, Inspector Pearson is in charge. You know we don't have detectives in our department."

Melcher looked at Jud as if he were some strange species of animal. He thrust out his lower jaw. "Let me remind you that the reason we appointed you chief of police was because we wanted a go-getter. Somebody who'd bring young blood and energy to the job. Leadership, do you understand? I personally went all out pushing for you to get it. And what I expect now is for you to do your job the way you're supposed to do it, and not try to shove responsibility off onto somebody else. Do I make myself clear?"

Jud felt his gorge rise, but he kept his face from showing it. "Sure, Sam. Very clear."

"I hope so," Melcher said. "My advice to you is to get this terrible thing cleared up *fast*." He stopped and looked at the door. "Are Ed and Helen in there?"

Jud nodded.

"Anybody with them?"

"Just one of our police officers."

Melcher shook his head. "Poor, poor people." He shot one more black look at Jud and went into the house.

The chief glanced over at Pearson, who still seemed pleased by the attention the media people were giving him. Damned if I do, Jud thought, and damned if I don't. He left the porch and strode down the walk toward his car.

There were more rubberneckers pressing against the rope than there had been earlier, and a number of cars were driving slowly past the house. The sky had become overcast, and there was almost no wind. It was a sign of snow coming, and Jud hoped fervently they wouldn't be hit by another storm. Sitting in the middle of the snow belt, Braddock usually caught anything that blew up east of Buffalo, and late winter was the worst time. But maybe they'd have some luck for a change. Then again, squinting up at the leaden clouds, he doubted it.

"Jud!"

He turned to see Sally hurrying toward him. Her face was flushed with a combination of the cold air and the excitement, and her dark hair tumbled to her shoulders in loose waves. Her polo coat was open and he could see her breasts bobbing under her white blouse as she half-walked, half-ran to where he was standing. She was, he thought, a very good-looking young woman.

She put her hand on his arm. "Are you okay?"

He felt self-conscious again, aware that some of the onlookers were staring at them, and he gently removed her hand. "Yeah, I'm all right. How come you're on this?"

"Maxwell told me to cover it." Ray Maxwell was the owner and publisher as well as the editor of the *Braddock Express*.

Jud nodded. "That's a break for you."

"I suppose so. But I feel more like crying than anything else. What a horrible thing to have happen. It's just ghastly."

He thought of what he'd seen on the floor of the bedroom and on top of the dresser. "It is that."

She bit her lip. "I'd like to ask you some questions, but I wouldn't want anyone to think you were favoring me because we're friends."

"No, neither would I." He suddenly realized this was the first time they'd mixed business into their personal relationship.

"Maybe I should go to your office when you get back there."

"Same problem."

"Okay, then—see you tonight?"

"Yeah," he said. "That would be better. It'll have to be late, though."

"Fine. I'll come over." She turned and hurried back toward the other reporters, who were still gathered around Pearson. Watching her go, it occurred to Jud that she looked just as good from this angle as she did from the front.

He waved to the cop who was holding the crowd back and got into his cruiser. As he started the engine and pulled away, he thought back to how the morning had begun. A quiet Saturday, and now he had a feeling he was in for more problems than he ever could have imagined.

THREE ....
Fearful Impact

1

Karen Wilson awakened at dawn with a blinding headache. The images she'd seen during the night had been burned into her mind, and her sleep had been a jumble of nightmares, giving her no rest. She got out of bed and stumbled into the shower, feeling as if she'd been hit over the head with a hammer. Getting dressed took great effort, and when she left the house the cold outside air only made her feel worse.

By the time she'd driven to Boggs Ford, the car dealership where she worked as a secretary, she could hardly see. Carrying a paper bag containing coffee and a bran muffin she'd bought at the luncheonette down the street, she picked up the newspaper lying in front of the showroom and unlocked the door. Once inside she turned off the alarm and put her breakfast and the paper on her desk, then took off her coat and hung it in a closet. She returned to her desk and sat down, wishing she could turn around and go home.

But she couldn't. She needed this job, and as it was she often had trouble concentrating on her work when she was having one of her bad spells. When that happened she was apt to be forgetful and make mistakes. And when it got really bad, when she was afflicted by one of these migraines—or whatever they were—and she experienced a vision, she could hardly function.

That was when she fully expected Charley Boggs, who owned the dealership, to fire her. But he'd always looked the other way when she had her problems. Which wasn't so hard to understand, as she thought about it. She was an attractive young woman with an exceptional body, and although Boggs had never come right out and made a direct pass, Karen had caught him staring at her often enough, when he hadn't thought anyone would notice. She had no illusions about him; he was undoubtedly just biding his time.

She opened the bag and took out the container of coffee and the muffin. After removing the cap from the Styrofoam cup she sipped the black liquid, finding it steaming hot. She closed her eyes, and despite her resolve not to let the images return to her consciousness, she suddenly recalled them once more: the black hood, the glittering ax, the woman's face contorted by fear. And finally the dripping head held high in a black-gloved hand.

She shuddered, and opening a drawer got out a bottle of aspirin. She shook two tablets out of the bottle and stepped over to the water cooler, where she swallowed the aspirin and chased the tablets with a cup of water.

Back at her desk she seemed to feel a little better. It was just after eight o'clock, her usual arrival time, and she always enjoyed these few minutes of peace before the day's activities began. This was Saturday, the busiest day of the week. But she'd have enough time to eat her breakfast and glance through the morning edition of the *Express*.

As it had been recently, the news was mostly bad. The front page carried a story about a running battle between Moslems and Christians in Lebanon, and another about a train wreck in China that had killed more than a hundred people. Still another reported that the U.S. economy was in decline. That one took the view that the president was to blame, which irritated her. The problems went back years. Was the president supposed to just wave a magic wand and make everything wonderful again?

There was also the story about another B–1 bomber crashing in Nevada with the loss of five crew members. This was the second fatal crash of an air force jet in the past month.

She turned the page. A semitrailer had overturned on the interstate. The truck had been carrying crates of oranges from Florida, and the cargo had scattered all over the highway, causing cars to slip and slide as they ran over the fruit. Some of the vehicles had collided as drivers lost control. But the damage was relatively minor, and the truck driver was only slightly bruised. ORANGE CRUSH, the headline said. Karen smiled and turned to an article about the town's plans for issuing municipal bonds to finance an overhaul of the water system. She finished her muffin as she glanced through the story.

And then she saw the piece on a missing child.

At first she tried to skip over it, deluding herself that she hadn't really noticed it, that it didn't concern her. But her gaze was drawn to the story as if by a magnet. Resignedly, she read the article.

The boy was eight, the oldest of three children in a family that lived out on the Norrisville road. Their name was Mariski. The father was a machinist. The boy, Michael, had been missing since Thursday afternoon, when he hadn't returned from school. He'd gotten off the bus at the usual stop, and the driver recalled seeing him trudge up the hill toward his home. He never arrived, his mother said. No one had seen him since, and there was no clue as to his whereabouts. A search party had combed the area Thursday night and again on Friday, with no success.

Karen sighed. It was a sad story, and she could imagine how frantic that poor family felt. But it was with a sense of relief that she finished the piece and turned her attention elsewhere. At least it hadn't reached out to her, as those things sometimes did, projecting images, terrible revelations she wanted not to know about.

The ability to receive those messages in the form of a vision had been a curse since childhood. Sometimes the images were as plain and clear as photographs in an album, leaving no doubt whatever as to who was involved and what had happened. And at other times she saw only unexplainable fragments, as with the hooded man with the ax. And at still other times, such as in the case of little Michael Mariski, she received nothing at all.

Where the vision came from, or why she had been singled out to carry this awful burden, she had no idea. But it haunted her, and sometimes tortured her, and she'd been trying to escape from it all her life.

Her eyes focused on an announcement that the Jaycees were

giving a dinner dance three weeks from now. Maybe Ted would ask her to go. And then again, maybe he wouldn't. The relationship had been so strong for a time, but then she'd gone through one of her spells, and her dark moods and her withdrawal and her headaches had presented a side of her Ted didn't understand and that she couldn't explain.

"Hi, Karen."

She looked up to see Ed McCarthy approaching, pulling off his heavy tweed overcoat, his face ruddy from the cold outside air. "Oh, good morning, Ed. I didn't hear you come in."

"Geez, if I'd known that I would've snuck up on you."

She laughed. He was a good guy, friendly and open, easily the best salesman Boggs had. He was always leering at her and making suggestive remarks, but she knew it was nothing but a good-natured running joke between them. Ed was happily married, the father of two little girls, and Karen considered him a friend.

He hung up his coat and then came over to half-sit on the edge of her desk. "How you doing?"

"Not bad for a Saturday morning." Which was the truth. Her headache was easing up, and with any luck the spell would be leaving her. Just the thought of that buoyed her spirits. "How about you?"

"Terrific. I sold two cars yesterday, and I think I'm gonna close another one today. That's if I can get this guy off his ass. He's one of these fence-straddlers. His old car is a 'seventy-five Dodge and it's falling apart, but you'd think buying a new one was gonna cost him a million bucks. He's been hemming and hawing for a month. Can you believe it?"

"What makes you think he'll come through today?"

"His old lady's coming with him, that's why. He wouldn't be bringing her along unless he was ready to move. I'm gonna sell him that metallic blue Taurus four-door. It's loaded, and I'm giving him a good deal. And besides, ladies like blue."

"Good. Hope you sell him."

"Can't miss."

It must be great, Karen thought, always to be that optimistic. "How's everybody at your house?"

"They're fine. Jenny's got a cold, but outside of that they're okay. Few more weeks and the kids'll have spring vacation. I'm gonna drive to Florida, to see my mother in Tampa."

"Wonderful. Wish I were going down there."

"Hey, you mean it? I'll leave Jenny home, take you instead."

She smiled. "When I go to Florida, it won't be with you and a car full of kids."

A booming voice said, "Well, everybody looks bright and chipper this morning."

They turned to see Charley Boggs walking toward them from the showroom. Boggs was short and overweight, and as usual he was wearing one of his garish sports jackets, this one a bilious green plaid. He was carrying his topcoat over his arm. They said good morning to him as he approached.

Boggs glanced at his watch. "Where's Morrow and Guzik? It's after eight-thirty."

Jack Morrow and Fred Guzik were the other two salesmen. "Should be here any minute," McCarthy said.

"Better be," Boggs muttered darkly. "I'm not running this place for the fun of it. Those two clowns want to work for Boggs Ford, they better get humping."

He's in his executive mood, Karen thought. Ready to pound the desk and kick ass. The jerk.

Boggs pointed to the overflowing in-box on her desk. "Gotta get those invoices there, Karen. And the customer orders. Also I want the repair bills to go out. Bookkeeping was late getting 'em ready, damn it."

Karen looked at the box. As if she didn't know what her job was, or that she had to get this work out today. "Sure, I'll take care of it."

He marched through the outer area and into his office, closing the door behind him. Ed McCarthy glanced at Karen and rolled his eyes, holding his hands palms-up.

The front door opened and a middle-aged couple stepped into the showroom.

McCarthy jumped to his feet and hurried toward them, beaming. "Ah, Mr. Colvis. Good morning. And this must be Mrs. Colvis. How are you, ma'am? I'm Ed McCarthy. It's nice to see you both."

Colvis was a little guy, wearing a tan storm coat and a cap.

His wife was about twice his size, and she squinted at Ed through eyes narrowed to slits. She had on a woolly coat that made her look as if she were inflated.

Just behind them came Morrow and Guzik, the errant salesmen. They'd probably been sitting around in some diner together, having breakfast and shooting the breeze, Karen thought. And now the day was underway; it was time to go to work.

There were some factory orders she'd finished typing yesterday that needed Bogg's signature. She might as well get those out of the way. Picking up a stack of papers, she left her desk and went to his office, knocking on the door.

"Come in."

She went inside and closed the door behind her. Boggs always insisted on that, saying his office was private and that he didn't want customers to think they could just go barging in on him whenever they might feel like it. She stepped over to his desk and put the orders down in front of him. "Would you sign these, please?"

While he busied himself with the stack Karen stood beside the chair and looked around the office. The wall behind him was covered with pictures of Boggs with celebrities of one kind or another. There was one of him with Senator D'Amato, and another of him with Senator Moynihan. There was one with Cardinal O'Connor, and one with some New York Mets player, and one with Governor Cuomo. There was also one of him with a woman who looked like Faye Dunaway, but Karen wasn't sure. How had a sleaze like Boggs managed to get his picture taken with people like that? It was amazing. And it was also a clue as to why he thought so highly of himself. To him, the photos would be proof that he was a man of importance.

She glanced at his desk. There was a portrait of him there with his family, in a silver frame. His wife looked very much like Charley, round-faced and impressed with herself, and there were his two teenaged kids, a boy and a girl. Her gaze drifted to Boggs, and to her surprise he wasn't looking at the papers she'd given him, but at her.

He smiled. "How's it going with you, Karen honey?"

The smile was oily, and it made her uncomfortable. "Fine. It's going fine. They all signed?"

He ignored the question. "You know, I've been thinking about you."

"Oh?"

"Uh-huh. I like you, Karen. And I'm real pleased with your work."

"That's good. I'm glad you are." Her instincts told her to just scoop up the orders and get out of there. But she didn't.

"Yeah. I think you're a great gal. And you know, you could have a real good future here. You could move up, see? Get to be like my assistant."

She made no reply, which Boggs apparently misunderstood. The smile widened. "That'd mean a big jump in salary, lots of perks. Why don't we have dinner some night soon, talk it over, hmm?"

She froze. His hand had slid up under her skirt and was stroking the back of her thigh. Before she could yell or run or belt him it moved higher and squeezed her buttock.

Now she did move. As hard as she could, she chopped the edge of her left hand against the inside of his arm. With her other hand she slapped his face. The blow knocked him back in his chair, his cheek reddening, his mouth opening and closing like that of a fish. She left the orders where they were and hurried out the door, slamming it behind her.

There were more people in the showroom now; all three salesmen were busy with customers. But no one seemed to notice her. Which was a good thing; her face was burning with anger and embarrassment. She went back to her desk and sat down, struggling to get her emotions under control.

Damn that fat fool anyway. Why the hell couldn't he leave her alone? After this fracas he'd be sure to fire her. And then what? She'd have to go job-hunting again, start all over somewhere else.

It wasn't that jobs were so hard to find—especially for a good-looking girl with a college degree who didn't want a high-level position. It was just that she felt so different from other people—and so vulnerable. She'd been through a whole string of jobs since she'd graduated from Shippensburg, usually losing them when one of her spells came over her. And now the thought of going through the process again was depressing. She took a deep breath and let it out slowly. Whatever would happen would happen. She'd just have to cope with it. For now she'd do her work as well as she could, and if Boggs fired her, so be it.

The morning newspaper was still lying open on her desk. She picked it up and was about to toss it into the wastebasket when her gaze fixed on the story of the missing Mariski boy. As she looked at the words they blurred, and then the newspaper and the desk seemed to dissolve away, and she was no longer sitting at her desk at Boggs Ford, but was somewhere suspended in space, in a place without walls or dimensions, as if she were floating in limbo.

A series of images appeared. She saw a pond with marshy edges, grayish brown cattails rising from the spongy ground. The water of the pond was a dirty iron color and there was a thin sheet of ice covering part of the surface. A stone wall ran along one side of the pond, and beyond the wall was an old barn, its red paint weathered and one of its walls collapsed from rot. She saw a brown corduroy jacket and a mop of brown hair and battered high-top shoes. She saw pale flesh and staring opaque eyes.

"Karen?"

Startled, she looked up, feeling as if she'd been abruptly roused from sleep, jolted out of a strange dream. Charley Boggs was looking down at her.

He smiled, the same oily stretching of his mouth. "Here are those orders, honey. All sighed. Let me have the other stuff when you get to it, okay?" She nodded dumbly, and he turned and strode toward the showroom, greeting a customer with his hand extended.

Karen looked at the newspaper again, staring at the story of the missing boy. After a moment she swept it into the wastebasket. She felt like crying, like getting up and running away from here. But the truth was, she couldn't run away. Not ever. Because this thing, this vision—whatever it was—would always be with her. Wherever she ran, it would be there. She could run away from here, but she couldn't run away from *it*.

Now the question was, what should she do next?

In her heart of hearts she knew the answer, and she dreaded facing it.

2

The kid looked as if he expected to be hanged. His thin face was pale and drawn, and he was chewing nervously on his lower lip. He had on washed-out jeans and a zippered jacket over a chambray shirt, with grease stains here and there. There were traces of grease on his hands as well, and his fingernails were edged with black. So it's true he's a car nut, Jud thought, just like I was at that age. Kramer had brought him to the chief's office, and was standing behind him.

Jud leaned back in his chair. "Come on in, Buddy. Have a seat." To Kramer he said, "Thanks, Bob. We're gonna have a talk. You can leave us in here and shut the door."

The cop did as instructed, and the boy sank down onto one of the chairs opposite Jud's desk. He had brown hair that hung down on his forehead, and every now and then he'd toss his head a little to get the hair out of his eyes.

Jud stretched. It was only mid-afternoon, but he was tired and hungry and he knew he had many hours to go before he'd get out of here. What a bitch of a day this had turned out to be. He picked up his phone and told the cop on the desk not to put through any calls until Jud told him otherwise. He hung up and looked at the boy. "You want a Coke or something?"

"No, thanks."

"Don't think we've ever met, have we?"

Buddy chewed his lip. "No."

"But I know your dad," Jud said. "I guess everybody in town does."

"Yeah."

"He's had that drugstore a long time, hasn't he?"

"It was my grandfather's first. He started it."

"Any others in the family? Brothers or sisters?"

"Sister's ten," Buddy said.

So much for getting him to relax. But he'd keep trying. "Just the two of you?"

"That's right."

There was a bulletin board on the wall beside Jud's desk. Tacked to it, along with departmental notices and the tour assignments and a list of often-used phone numbers, were several Wanted posters. The boy's gaze flicked over the board and then fixed on the posters. When he realized Jud was looking at him he dropped his eyes.

"Pretty tough news today," Jud said.

Buddy didn't reply.

"You must be plenty shook up."

"Yeah."

"You two were good friends, right? You and Marcy?"

"Uh-huh."

"You took her to the game last night, and the dance?"

"Yes. I already told the other officer all about it. Inspector Pearson?"

"I know you did. I'm sorry you have to go over the same ground with me, but this investigation is important. I'm sure you understand that."

The kid mumbled that he did.

"So you took her to the dance, right?"

"Yes."

"Tell me about it."

Buddy shrugged. "We went in my car, and then after I took her home."

"Straight home?"

He hesitated. "No. We went up by Powell's farm and parked for a while."

"How long were you there?"

"I don't know. Maybe half an hour, an hour."

Jud wondered if Pearson had picked that up. "And then you took her home?"

"Yes."

"What time was that, when you got to her house?"

"Around one o'clock."

"Anybody up, could you tell?"

"I don't think so. House was pretty dark."

"You go inside with her?"

"No. She went in by herself."

"You sure about that, Buddy? Maybe you went in too, and the both of you sneaked up to her bedroom, huh?"

"No, I swear to God."

"But you did sometimes, didn't you? Went up to her room?"

He shook his head emphatically. "No. Honest. Marcy was afraid to do anything like that. If her father ever caught her he'd—"

"Yes?"

"She was afraid."

"You notice anybody around the neighborhood? Maybe on foot, or any strange cars?"

"No. I didn't see anything."

Jud got to his feet and came around from behind his desk, taking a straight-backed chair beside the one Buddy was sitting in. He knew kids had a strong built-in reluctance to speak freely with any adult, let alone a cop. So Jud would have to push him a little. He kept his tone mild, his manner offhand. "How long were you and Marcy going together?"

The boy shifted in his seat. "Six months or so."

"Since the start of the school year?"

"Yeah, I guess so."

"How'd you get along?"

"Okay. Fine."

"Ever fight or argue?"

"Once in a while, I guess. But never anything serious."

Jud put one foot up against the edge of his desk. "Sure you don't want a Coke or something?"

"No, no thanks."

"Who are some of the others in your crowd?"

"Excuse me?"

"Your other friends. People you see a lot of. Jeff Peterson's a pal of yours, isn't he? And Billy Swanson?"

Buddy's face took on an expression of wariness. "Yeah, I guess so."

"Also Pat Campbell, right?"

"Uh-huh." It was obvious he was wondering who'd been talking about him to the chief of police, but he didn't ask.

Jud took his foot off the desk and looked at the boy for a few seconds before he said, "Understand you and your friends like to smoke a little pot, now and then."

Buddy's face reddened, but he kept silent.

"Probably buy the stuff from one of those characters that hang around the school, right?"

"I don't know anything about that."

"You don't? I think you do. But let me explain something to you, okay? You're here because your girlfriend was murdered last night. That's what I had you brought in here to talk about. I don't know whether you had anything to do with it or not, but you can be sure I'm going to find out."

Buddy swallowed. "I told you, I don't know anything about it. I dropped her off and then I went home."

"Maybe so. But even if that's true, there's a lot you could tell me that could be helpful. So I'll make a little deal. You tell me anything I want to know, straight out, no bullshit, and I won't give you any grief on what you or your friends smoke, or stick up your nose, or whatever."

Buddy chewed his lip.

"You have my word on that," Jud said. "But if you don't buy it, if you decide you don't want to help me find out who killed Marcy, then I'm going to give you a very hard time. Starting with an investigation into drug involvement."

The kid looked up, his eyes suddenly wide and frightened. "I don't—"

Jud cut him off. "Buddy, I've already got some other people who'd be willing to talk about it." Which was crap, but the boy wouldn't know that. "So you make the decision. Now, how about it?"

Buddy cleared his throat. "Could I have that Coke?"

"Sure. You sit tight while I go get us a couple." Jud got up and left his office, closing the door behind him.

The Coke machine was at the end of the hall. Jud took his time going down to it, and when he got there he stopped to chat with a cop who'd just come off his tour. The guy's name was Dennis Delury. He was one of the younger officers, with about three years on the force.

Jud fed quarters into the machine. "Buy you a Coke, Dennis?"

"Sure, Chief. Thanks."

When a can rumbled out of the chute Jud handed it to him and put more change into the slot. "How's it going?"

Delury popped the top of the can. "Okay. Some guy in a truck ran a woman off the road out on Route Five. Car went into a tree."

"Yeah," Jud said. "I heard it come over the radio. She all right?"

"Split her forehead open when she hit the windshield. But she'll be okay. We took her to the emergency room and called her husband. She's gonna stay in the hospital overnight, though."

"Uh-huh." Jud collected the two cans of Coke he'd come for and turned away. One busted head on a Saturday was something he'd settle for anytime. But it was still daylight. Later on there would be plenty more activity.

"Say, Chief?"

He turned back. "Yeah?"

Delury seemed a little uncomfortable. He glanced over his shoulder, and then lowered his voice. "That state detective, Pearson?"

"What about him?"

"Just now when I was going to my locker, he said he wanted to talk to me."

Jud waited.

"He asked me if I wanted to work on the Dickens case."

"And what'd you tell him?"

"I told him sure, but it had to come from you."

"No problem," Jud said. "They're gonna need some help, and I said I'd work something out. I'll tell you when we get a plan together. Okay?"

"Yeah, okay. I just thought you should know."

"Fine. See you later."

Jud made his way back down the hall to his office, passing several more cops as he went. They ran double shifts on Saturdays, and the place was busy. Jud nodded and said a word or two to each of the people he passed.

Goddamn it. This thing was hardly getting started and already he was being sandbagged. Pearson had not only come in here and shoved him aside, but the inspector was now in the process of fucking up the department's morale. Which was only one of the problems Jud was facing. The mayor had made it very clear who would be held responsible for breaking this case, no matter what the state cops said or did. Melcher had climbed all over him. Was anything ever easy?

He entered his office and nudged the door shut, then handed Buddy a Coke.

The boy opened the can and took a long swallow. He wiped his mouth with the back of his hand. "Thanks."

Jud sat down at his desk and drank some of his own Coke. When he put the can down he said, "So what'd you decide?"

The boy was still hesitant, but Jud could see he was also scared.

"You know, there's another way of looking at this," Jud said. "You liked Marcy a lot, didn't you?"

His voice was barely audible. "Yeah, I did."

"So you want to see whoever did it get what's coming to him, right?"

"Yes. Sure." There was anguish now on his features. He leaned forward, and the words came tumbling out. "But I swear I don't have any idea who did that to her. I don't know anything about it. All I did was take her to the game and the dance. Afterward I took her home. And that's all. When I heard about it this morning, I—" His voice broke, and his eyes filled with tears. He clenched his fist and shoved the knuckles against his mouth. "Oh, Jesus—"

Jud waited for a minute or so while the boy got himself together. "I understand. All I'm asking is for you to help find out who did it. Now what about it—will you help me?"

Finally the boy nodded, still fighting the tears. "Yeah, I will. I mean, I'll do anything I can."

"Good. So anything I ask you about what went on with Marcy and her friends—your friends—you tell me. Even if you don't know it directly. No matter what I ask you about, no holding back. If you know, you tell me. Agreed?"

The kid nodded. He wiped his eyes with the back of his hand.

Jud opened the bottom drawer of his desk and took out a box

of Kleenex. He shoved the box across the desk and Buddy pulled out one of the tissues and blew his nose into it.

"Just one thing," Buddy said.

"Yes?"

"Could all of this be—you know, private?"

"Absolutely. Anything you tell me I keep strictly confidential. Like I said, you have my word." He stood up, and leaning across the desk extended his hand. Buddy shook it.

Jud sat down. "You said you went with Marcy about six months, right?"

"Yes."

"Were you making it?"

Buddy chewed his lip.

If he keeps it up, Jud thought, he'll have it bleeding.

"Yeah," Buddy said.

"Were you her first?"

"I—no."

"Where there many other guys before you?"

"I don't think so."

"How many, do you know?"

"I think just one."

Buddy seemed more nervous than ever, tossing the hair out of his eyes and twisting in his chair. But he got his answer out. "Ron Carpenter."

"Basketball player at the high school?"

"He was. He's in college now. Freshman at Hamilton."

"Yeah, I know who he is." A tall, gawky kid, father was an accountant. Jud could picture him in his mind. "She tell you that?"

"No, but I knew. They went together last year, when he was still at Braddock."

"Did she keep in touch with him?"

"No. I'm pretty sure."

"Last night," Jud said. "When you and Marcy went parking?"

"Yeah?"

"Did you make it then?"

The color came up in the kid's face. "We—yes."

"Tell me something. She ever worry about getting pregnant?"

"No."

"Ever tell you she might be?"

"No. She was on the pill."

"Did her parents know that?"

"Her mother did."

"How'd she seem to you last night—was anything bothering her?"

He thought about it. "Uh, yeah. One thing, kind of."

"Like what?"

"Like—well, this may sound nuts, but she was worried about the headsman."

"She *what*?"

"Well, not him exactly. See, it came up in English class yesterday morning. Mr. Hathaway wanted us to write a paper on it over the weekend. Marcy was p.o.'d about it. She said the story gave her the creeps."

Jud was flabbergasted. "You mean the whole class was discussing it?"

"Yes."

"And what was said about it?"

Buddy shook the hair out of his eyes. "A lot of kids said they thought the story was a crock."

And a lot of their parents think the exact opposite, Jud thought. "Go on."

"So Mr. Hathaway didn't like them making fun of it. That's why he said we had to write the paper."

Jud's tone was dry. "I don't think anybody will be writing one now."

"I know I won't," Buddy said.

Jud's thoughts were racing. If the story of the headsman was in the front of a lot of kids' minds, could somebody have gotten carried away with it? Or maybe something had started out as a joke, and then got out of hand? The power of suggestion was very strong, especially in teenagers. And despite what Buddy had said about kids not believing the legend, there was the almost hypnotic attraction it could have for them.

He looked at the boy intently. "Was anybody talking about

it after the class? Either about the headsman or the paper you were supposed to write?"

"Yeah, a lot of us were. Mostly like, you know—joking."

"Anybody in particular?"

"No, we all were. Everybody thought Hathaway was a shit for giving us the assignment."

"Yeah." Hathaway was the paraplegic Vietnam vet who used a motorized wheelchair. Drove a Chevy sedan with a handicapped permit attached to the sun visor. Jud occasionally saw him around town and had spoken to him a few times.

The chief drained his Coke and put the can aside. "How many kids in that class?"

"Twenty-five or so."

There was a yellow pad and a ballpoint among the papers on Jud's desk. He passed them to Buddy. "I want you to write down the names of everybody who's in it. Take your time, and don't leave anybody out."

While Buddy worked on it, Jud opened a desk drawer and took out a notepad and another pen, then made notes on what he'd been told. It would be tough to run all this down with a small department that already had a heavy workload, let alone one that had been depleted by having to lend some of its people to the state police. Maybe he should just tell Pearson to stick it up his ass, use his own troops. But that didn't make much sense either. With the mayor and the rest of the town expecting progress fast, their chief of police could hardly fail to cooperate with the state investigation team.

It took the boy several minutes to finish making his list. When he put the pen down he returned the pad to Jud.

"This everybody?"

"I think so."

Jud glanced down the scrawled list of names. Many of them were familiar to him; they included a number of families who'd been in Braddock long before the chief was born. He placed the pad on his desk and looked at Buddy. "Okay, that's fine. There anything else you want to tell me—anything at all?"

The boy tossed the hair out of his eyes. "Nothing I can think of."

Jud stood up. "All right, Buddy. You can go now. But remember, we made a deal."

"Yeah. I'll remember." He got up and walked to the door.

"Just one thing," Jud said.

Buddy had his hand on the doorknob. He looked back.

"Think about all this. Think hard. Anything comes to your mind that might interest me, you call. I'm not here, leave a message. Got it?"

"Yeah. Got it." He opened the door and slipped out, closing the door behind him.

Jud looked again at the list of names on the yellow pad. Then he sat back in his chair. The best thing that could happen would be for the cops to pick up the guy who'd killed Marcy Dickens and find he was a drifter. Somebody from somewhere else—anywhere else—and somebody they could build a good case on. Good enough to put him away forever. Or at least for twenty-five years, which was how they defined forever in the state of New York nowadays.

But if it was somebody from one of the old families who were important in Braddock, then that would be another thing entirely.

3

News of Marcy Dickens' death flashed through Braddock as fast as people could spread the word. They telephoned friends and neighbors, stopped each other on the street, brought it up at stores and restaurants and at gas stations. The talk was different from ordinary gossip, because it was tinged with fear.

"You hear about the Dickens girl—Ed Dickens' daughter?"

"No, what about her?"

"Headsman chopped her head off."

"What? When?"

"Last night."

"The *headsman*? Jesus, you sure?"

"God's truth. Went into their house, went right up to her room and chopped her with his ax. Took her head clean off."

"They sure it was him?"

"Oh, yeah. Some of the neighbors saw him. Big fella, all in

black. Police won't let anybody talk about what they saw, though. I hear he came out of the house carrying that ax and just disappeared. One minute he was there, next minute he was gone."

"What was the girl up to?"

"Nobody knows for sure. Except maybe the cops. People say it was drugs. Ran around with a wild bunch."

It was early afternoon when the story reached Boggs Ford. Karen Wilson had just come back from lunch when she overheard the salesmen talking about it. A customer had told Fred Guzik, who told Jack Morrow and Ed McCarthy, who told anyone they could find who hadn't heard.

Karen listened to the recounting, and was stunned. Her headache returned, and with it the nausea and an overwhelming sense of dread. She turned away, refusing to be drawn into the discussion. Trying desperately to shut the subject out, she stayed at her desk, busily taking data off the computer and typing customer correspondence.

As far as she was concerned, the less she knew about the murder, the better. As long as she could prevent her consciousness from receiving more information on it, she could keep it separate from herself.

Which was foolish, of course. Because the instant she stopped thinking about what she was doing, the instant she so much as blinked, the images returned to her mind. She saw the hooded man, saw the ax, saw the girl's severed head. And now she knew that the awful event hadn't taken place at some other time, somewhere far away. It had occurred here in Braddock, on the night the vision appeared. *Last* night.

So she was burdened with not just one terrible perception, but two: one of a hooded killer who struck with an ax, the other of a drowned boy whose family was suffering the agony of uncertainty.

There was nothing she could do about the first, but there was about the second.

She wished there weren't.

By the time Boggs closed for the night Karen was sick to her stomach and her head ached fiercely. She went into the ladies' room and soaked paper towels in cold water, pressing them to her forehead until she had her headache somewhat under control. Finally she put on her coat and walked out to her car.

What had she ever done to deserve this?

4

By early evening the cops had run a sweep of the town and the surrounding area that produced four suspicious characters. Three of them were drunks the police had pulled in on other occasions, harmless sots who panhandled nickels and dimes to get from one bottle of muscatel to the next. The fourth was a guy who said the world was approaching a cataclysm and they should repent. This one had long gray hair and a beard and smelled even worse than the winos. A check showed he had spent Friday night praying in the Baptist church on Wheeler Street.

Jud told Sergeant Joseph Grady to lock all of them in the drunk tank and let them go in the morning. At least they'd be out of the cold until then, and they'd get a couple of decent meals out of it. He didn't know where Pearson and Williger were; he hadn't seen them since that afternoon. He was glad Pearson wasn't around to say I told you so.

Jud had also questioned several more of the kids who'd been in class with Marcy Dickens, including Joe Boggs and Billy Swanson, but that had produced nothing of value either. There were others he wanted to talk to, but he'd have to get to them tomorrow.

It was a little before ten o'clock when he left the station-house. The action they'd get tonight—fights, car accidents, whatever—was yet to come, but he'd let Grady handle it. He wanted time to think and plan what he'd be doing on the Dickens case. The state police inspector might be in charge of the investigation, but there was no way Jud was going to just step aside and ignore it. Not as long as he had this job and lived in Braddock. Marcy Dickens' murder was the biggest thing that had happened here since he'd joined the force.

Every few minutes, it seemed, the picture of Marcy's severed head would come back into his mind, the features twisted in pain and horror, the eyes staring. He'd push it away, force himself to stop thinking about it, but then a short time later, without warning, it would be back.

So it was clear that what he needed to do now was call it a day and get out of here. It would help to relax over a couple of beers, maybe play his guitar a little.

The building that housed police headquarters was the town hall, an ugly red stone structure that had been erected in the nineteenth century. There was a parking lot behind it, and as Jud stepped out of the rear door and walked toward his cruiser he noted that the snow had begun falling in tiny flakes, a shimmer of white that could produce an accumulation of several inches. Snow was beautiful, but to a cop it was a pain in the ass.

He got a brush out of the car and swept off the windshield, thinking as he climbed in and started the engine that from October through April, living in this part of the world could be a drag. As he often did, he wondered what it would be like to work someplace like Florida or California. Sunshine, palm trees, bikinis. He could stand that.

His place was only two miles from headquarters, a three-room cottage he rented from an old lady who lived in a larger house down the road. After stopping to get his mail out of the box, he pulled into the driveway and left the car beside the cottage. As he walked in and turned on the lights he wondered if there was anything to eat.

The mail was all junk: bills, circulars, an L.L. Bean catalog. He dropped the pile onto the kitchen table and pulled off his leather jacket, draping it over a chair back. Then he peered into the fridge. Nothing much there to speak of, and he was hungry as hell, not having eaten since breakfast. He'd meant to get a hamburger or something but it had slipped his mind. There were some eggs, however; at least he could scramble a few of those. And there was also plenty of beer. Praise God.

He took out a can of Coors and popped the top, then drank half the can in one long swallow. It was ice-cold and prickled the back of his throat as he drank and it tasted wonderful. Carrying the can, he walked into the bedroom and set it down on his dresser, then stripped off his gunbelt and put it beside the beer. As he pulled off his clothes he realized his back and shoulders were stiff. Probably from the tension and from sitting on his butt. He stretched, and after that touched his toes a dozen times, which seemed to help.

The shower was blazing hot, and he stood under its needle spray for several minutes, soaping and resoaping his body. By the time he got out and toweled himself down the stiffness was gone entirely. He put on a flannel shirt and khaki pants and moccasins, and then he finished his beer and went back into the kitchen for another.

As he opened a fresh can, he heard tires crunch on the gravel driveway. He peered through the window and saw a car pull up behind his. Its lights went out, and Sally got out of the car and approached the house. She was carrying some things, but in the dim light he couldn't make out what they were. He went to the door and let her in, and she gave him a quick kiss as she stepped past and headed for the kitchen. He followed her.

The object in her right hand was a large pot, and the one in her left was a grocery bag. She put the pot on the stove and set the bag down on the counter. Then she unslung her shoulder bag and took off her polo coat, hanging them on a hook beside the back door.

Jud smiled. "What's this, a rescue mission?"

The range was an old-fashioned gas model, and as she fired it up she spoke over her shoulder. "It sure is. I was afraid you might starve."

"Don't want that, do we?"

"I certainly don't. I'd rather have you all nourished and full of energy."

He stepped close behind her and cupped her breasts in his hands. "So I can shovel snow?"

She put her head back so that her cheek was against his. "That wasn't what I had in mind."

He turned her around and kissed her, and as her mouth opened and her body pressed against his he felt himself respond. His hands moved over her, and he was conscious of her warmth and the fragrance of her and the way her mouth tasted. Desire rushed through him like an electric current.

"You'd better let me get this ready," she whispered, "if you want to eat dinner tonight. You do want to eat dinner, don't you?"

"I'm thinking about it."

She smiled, and pushed him away. "First things first. Why don't you make me a drink?"

"Sure. Bourbon?"

"That's fine."

He got a bottle of Wild Turkey out of a cupboard and filled a glass with ice and whiskey, handing it to her.

"Cheers," she said, and sipped some of it. She waved at a chair. "Make yourself comfortable while I get this going. I made it earlier. All I have to do is heat it up."

Jud dropped into the chair. As he drank the cold beer he realized that until now he hadn't relaxed for an instant since morning. He was also aware that this was Sally's way of being supportive, letting him know she understood what he'd been going through. "I'm glad you came over," he said.

She fussed at the stove. "So am I."

"You write your story?"

"Yes, and Maxwell's giving it quite a play. Wait till you see the *Express* tomorrow, it's practically the whole front page. With a byline, too."

"Congratulations."

"Thanks. It's the first time he's let me cover anything important."

"That's great."

She was quiet for a moment. "I just wish it didn't have to be on a subject like this one."

"Yeah, I know what you mean."

"You do understand, don't you? On the one hand I'm horrified by what happened. But on the other, I'll confess that I'm thrilled to work on something this big. What's gone on here is mindboggling. My God, what a story."

"Sure, I can understand how you must feel."

The meal was ready in a few minutes. It was one of Jud's favorites, a thick beef stew with potatoes and carrots and peppers and onions, and she'd brought a loaf of French bread, which she heated and served with chunks of butter. She'd also made a salad of tomatoes, Bibb lettuce and mushrooms. He thought he'd never tasted anything better.

As they ate, she asked what progress the cops were making.

"Not much," Jud said. "Inspector Pearson's running the case, as you know. He just wants to use my force as gofers."

"Doesn't that gall you?"

"No end. And I'm also catching a lot of crap from other sources."

"Such as?"

"The mayor, for one."

She rolled her eyes. "Sam Melcher. I suppose he's howling because you don't have the case all wrapped up."

"More or less."

"That blowhard. I hope you ignored him."

"I wish I could. But as long as he's the mayor, I think it might be a good idea to be cooperative."

"Oh, I know. It's just that it's not fair."

"All part of the job."

"Have you questioned many people? Or has Pearson?"

"A few."

"How about Marcy's boyfriend—the Harper boy?"

He put his fork down. "Listen, anything I say about this is off the record, okay?"

Her eyes widened. "Since when is it wrong for a reporter to ask the chief of police questions about an important case? In fact, probably the most important case this town's ever had?"

"Hey, you know what I mean. I wouldn't want anybody to think I was giving you special treatment. So just be damn careful how you use anything I say. Don't write anything that would embarrass me or the department. Deal?"

"Deal. Now what about Harper?"

"What about him?"

"Come on, Jud. He was the last one to see her alive, and I know he was questioned all afternoon."

"The kid's clean, I think. Pearson interviewed him too, and he'll stay under suspicion and be questioned again. But I don't think he did it, or that he has any idea who did."

She thought that over. "You brought in other people too, didn't you?"

"Uh-huh. We picked up some vagrants." Jud finished the last of his stew, and as Sally served him another helping he told her about the sweep and how it had given them nothing worthwhile.

"What about the other kids—Billy Swanson and the rest of them?"

"Same thing. No leads so far."

Once more she was thoughtful for a time. "It's really awful, isn't it?"

"Yeah, it is."

"I mean, not just the murder itself. That was hideous. But the idea that whoever did it is still on the loose is terrifying, when you think about it."

"I'm sure that's all part of why Melcher's so upset. Tell you the truth, I don't blame him."

"Hey, it's almost eleven. Let's clear this off and catch the news."

They put their dishes into the dishwasher and then went into the living room. Jud turned on the TV, and they sat together on the sofa as they watched the broadcast.

The show was from Albany. It opened with a roundup of the national and international news, covering disasters from a fire in northern California to more fighting in the Middle East. When the local news came on, the lead story was the Dickens murder.

A reporter delivered an on-the-scene commentary, and Jud recognized him as the same one who had done most of the talking when he and Pearson had emerged from the house to speak with the press. Watching Pearson answer questions, Jud thought the inspector seemed even more pompous on the tube than he was in person. Jud was also acutely aware of how he himself looked, standing there like a dummy while Pearson spoke.

The reporter then said that people in Braddock were especially frightened by the crime because it revived memories of the headsman legend. As if to prove his point, that was followed by brief interviews with a number of the local citizens. Each of them said more or less the same thing, that the headsman was back and he'd chop off more heads before he was through.

When the piece ended, Jud turned off the set. "God—talk about sensationalism. All that shit about the headsman. That'll get people even more stirred up."

Sally was quiet for a moment. "Jud?"

"Yeah?"

"There's something I want you to see."

"What is it?"

"Let's go back in the kitchen, and I'll show you."

The went into the room and sat down at the table. She opened her bag and took out a manila envelope. "There was another murder, back in the sixties. People said that one was the work of the headsman, too. Are you aware of that?"

"Yeah, of course I am. But that was a long time ago, and as far as I'm concerned, it was the same kind of half-truth, half-spook story."

"You think so? The victim then was also a woman. And because I'm a good reporter, I went down into our morgue at the *Express* and got out the clips on it. I figured it'd make an interesting angle. I also thought you'd like to see the stories."

"You mean you put that stuff in the piece you wrote?"

"Hey, it's relevant, isn't it? And the murder was never solved. But wait till you read this. It's creepy, the way it's a lot like the Dickens killing." She opened the envelope and withdrew some yellowing scraps of newsprint. "Nowadays everything's on microfilm, of course. But at that time the paper was still keeping files by hand."

He took one of the clippings from her. It read:

WOMAN SLAIN IN AX MURDER
Braddock Resident Beheaded
Killing Recalls Legend of Headsman

Mrs. John Donovan, 29, of Cedarton Road, was found dead last night by her husband upon his return from a business trip to Albany. A housewife and the mother of the Donovans' six-year-old daughter, Mrs. Donovan had been decapitated. Her headless body was in the living room of their home, and signs of a violent struggle were present. Mrs. Donovan's head was missing, and no murder weapon was found.

Chief of Police Elwood McDermott, who is conducting the investigation, said the slaying appeared to have been carried out earlier that evening, and that the murder weapon probably had been an ax. This immediately inspired long-time residents of Braddock to conjecture that the infamous headsman had returned. The ax-wielding public executioner was employed here early in the eighteenth century, shortly after the village was settled. According to the legend, the headsman has returned from time to time and slain towns-people, then disappeared.

Chief McDermott said no suspects have been apprehended. He urges anyone having information on the crime to contact him at once.

Mrs. Donovan was the former Janet Cowles. Funeral arrangements have not been completed.

As Jud read the piece, he felt the hairs stir on the back of his neck. He looked at the other clippings. One of them was a background piece on Mrs. Donovan, and another featured opinions of the locals as to what had happened. Just as in tonight's telecast, the people interviewed said the murder was undoubtedly the work of the headsman. There were several other clips, the dates spaced some days apart, and each of them reported more or less the same thing—that no progress was being made in solving Mrs. Donovan's murder.

He laid the clippings on the table and lifted his gaze to Sally, who was eyeing him intently. "Was this all?" he asked.

"Yes. After I found those, I hunted for stuff on that killing or anything else that might have to do with the headsman, but I couldn't find anything. I asked Maxwell about it, but he said that's all there was. He grew up hearing tales about the headsman, of course, and he remembered the Donovan case well. In fact, he not only worked on the story, but he knew the family at the time it happened. He said the case was a sensation, and that everybody in Braddock was convinced the headsman had killed her."

Jud shook his head. "So you're gonna fan the fire on the headsman angle even more? You don't really believe it, do you?"

"Believe what—that Mrs. Donovan was beheaded and nobody knows to this day who did it? I certainly do."

"You know what I mean. About the headsman."

She paused for a moment. "The truth is, I just don't know. But I'll tell you one thing—when I found these old stories and read them it sent chills up my spine. And you know something else? I'll bet you had the same reaction just now. I'm right, aren't I?"

He opened his mouth and closed it. Then he said, "Okay, so I did."

"Sure. I thought so. Look—nobody with any sense believes ghost stories. That's for kids and bumpkins. But it's a fact that we've had two murders where people had their heads lopped off. *And that's just two we know about.*"

"What does that mean?"

"It means the legend had to start someplace. You saw what that piece said, didn't you, about the woman's death reviving the stories? I'm just sorry the *Express* doesn't go back further." She gestured at the clippings. "What about before that? What other killings might have taken place?"

He snorted. "Take it easy, will you? You're so hot for the headsman angle you're trying to convince yourself it's true."

"Okay, but what's your explanation—it's a coincidence?"

He got up and went to the fridge for another beer. "You want a drink?"

"Yes, please."

He made her a fresh bourbon over ice and handed it to her, then sat down again at the table and opened his beer. "You want to know what I think? I think that in each of these cases, somebody used the legend to make people think the murder was the work of the headsman. Each time it gave the killer a perfect way to screw up the investigation. It just added to the confusion. That's what I think."

"You might be right."

"Hell, maybe it was the same guy did both of them."

"Oh, come on. Over that span of time? Every twenty-five

years or so he commits a murder and now he's ninety and still at it? What is this—the George Burns murder case?"

Jud drank some of his beer. There were times when she could get to him.

She smiled. "You mad at me?"

"Moderately."

"Aw." She reached under the table and squeezed him.

He put his hand on hers. "You're really asking for trouble, aren't you?"

She brought her mouth close to him. "I certainly am." She fastened her lips to his in a warm, wet kiss. It lasted a long time, and when she pulled away a little she said, "That got the desired effect, though, didn't it?" and squeezed again.

Jud put his beer down, then took the glass out of her hand and set it down on the table. In one motion he scooped her off the chair and stood up, holding her in his arms. As he stepped toward the bedroom he said, "All right, smartass. Now you're really gonna get it."

She kissed his ear. "I hope so."

5

Jud lay awake a long time with Sally nestled close to him, her head on his chest. Usually after making love he was asleep in seconds, but tonight he kept seeing ghosts—Marcy Dickens, his imagined impression of Mrs. Donovan, and finally a vague picture of a dark, hooded figure brandishing an ax. Which was ridiculous, he told himself; he was as bad as every other fool in town who was hooked on the headsman bullshit. But the images refused to leave him alone.

He sent his thoughts in another direction, going over possibilities in the case, thinking out what he might do next. Running down more of Marcy's friends was a must, of course. Because regardless of what he might think of Pearson personally, the inspector was right about one thing: in the majority of homicides the victim and the perpetrator knew each other well. Jud had had that drilled into his head often enough, in MP and civilian police lectures and the reading he'd done, as well as in his own experience. Even in manslaughter cases resulting from saloon brawls, the combatants were usually acquainted.

But Buddy Harper? All Jud's instincts said no. He'd keep an eye on the boy, of course. Maybe work him over again, see if he could trip him up. But his gut told him Buddy was clean.

It was still possible, of course, that this had been a murder committed while another crime was in progress, maybe during a break-in. But that theory wouldn't fly, either. Nothing in the house had been disturbed, and there was no evidence of forced entry. The intruder apparently had gone directly to where he knew the girl would be sleeping, and then had killed her with such efficiency he'd left no sign of even a struggle, let alone a fight. Except for that cut in the floor, there'd been nothing. No—Marcy had been a target well known to her assailant.

He went back to thinking about Buddy then, working out a scenario that had Buddy going up to her room and Marcy telling him she was pregnant, threatening him. But that was flimsy; any kid who wanted an abortion nowadays could get one without much trouble. And besides, the autopsy would reveal a pregnancy if there was one, as well as determine blood type if there was a residue of semen in her vagina. And since Buddy had already admitted having intercourse with her earlier, what would that prove?

Jud tended to trust his hunch, that Buddy had told the truth, but that was all the more reason not to let himself overlook anything. Could there have been something else going on— maybe to do with drugs? Smoking was another thing Buddy was into, so maybe there was something there. There were a couple of small-time dealers in town, and it was about time the cops came down hard on them. Even if the police couldn't put together a case, they could make the bastards wish they'd gone into the ministry. Leaning on them would be worth it, if only for the satisfaction.

And Marcy's other friends—the ones he had yet to talk to? Jud knew a few of them. Pat Campbell was the blond cheerleader with the great body. She was also the daughter of Loring Campbell, probably the richest man in Braddock. Jeff Peterson was a star on the high school basketball team. And there were a number of others.

Then there was the murder weapon. He'd try to ascertain the type of ax the killer had used. If it had in fact been an ax. That was another thing to work on.

And what about the point Sally had raised in connection with the old story she'd dug up on the Donovan murder? Had there actually been other headsman killings before that? He'd check with the county attorney's office, ask them to pull out the records on the Donovan case. Braddock's police department couldn't have been too great back then, which might explain why the case had never been solved.

Emmett Stark could probably help, too. In all likelihood the retired chief would have some ideas. Jud would get over to see him, and soon.

The illuminated dial on the bedside clock read 2:10. As gently as he could, Jud eased Sally's head off his chest and down onto the pillow, thinking as he did that once she was asleep he'd have to fire a gun to wake her up. He got out of bed and stepped over to the window, moving the shade aside and peering out to see if it was still snowing. He couldn't tell; it was too dark out there. He went to the closet and got out a robe, putting it on along with a pair of slippers. He left the room, quietly closing the door behind him.

In the living room he took his old Gibson acoustic out of its case and sat down on a straight-backed chair. He tuned the instrument, holding an E chord while his long fingers picked the strings. He didn't have the best ear in the world, but he could play fairly well for somebody who was entirely self-taught. Well, not entirely; he'd listened to James Burton and Chet Atkins by the hour. And also to Merle Travis and B.B. King. And most of all to his number-one favorite, Willie Nelson.

The encouraging thing about Willie was that he didn't seem to have that much talent either. He was only a fair guitar player, and his voice had that reedy twang. But put that together with his ability to write country songs and deliver them as if he'd opened a door in his heart, and he could knock you down. Not that Jud would go so far as to compare himself to Nelson, but he'd certainly learned a lot from listening to Willie's records.

He picked aimlessly for a while, strumming slowly and just

practicing chord changes, C to B flat, G to A, then increasing the tempo, feeling his fingers grow nimble. The sound of the guitar had a clean, clear quality in the quiet of the room.

After that he slowed it down again and sang a chorus of "Georgia," imitating Willie, and followed it with "To All the Girls I've Loved Before."

Then he sang one of his own:

> Listen to the wind
> Listen to the wind
> Telling me the things I ought to know
> Telling me the way it was
> With lovers long ago
> Listen to the wind
> Listen to the wind
> I can hear the words that ebb and flow
> Softly now reminding me
> That love will come and go
> Listen to the wind
> Listen to the wind
> Now I know which way the wind will blow

As the notes died away he wondered if the song was any good. The melody was all right, he thought, but maybe the lyrics were just a touch pretentious. He couldn't imagine Nelson or Chet Atkins using a phrase like *ebb and flow*, but what the hell, he needed the rhyme. And anyhow, nobody but himself would ever hear it. Sometimes he thought about taping a few of his songs and sending them to somebody. A record company, maybe, or a singer. But he knew he never would.

We all have our secret dreams.

And come to think of it, that might be another song idea. If it was, he'd work on it sometime.

He picked aimlessly at the strings for a while, his thoughts wandering through all the things he had to do tomorrow. It would be good if the snow would quit; that was one more problem he'd just as soon not have to deal with. He suddenly felt tired, as if all the weight of the day had at last come down on him.

He put the guitar away and went back into the bedroom, taking off his robe and tossing it over a chair. The air in here was frigid. He slipped in beside Sally, smiling to himself as he noted she didn't so much as stir. He moved close to her warm body and put his arm around her and in seconds he was asleep.

four ··
On Thin Ice

1

On Sunday morning Karen slept late, even though she'd gone to bed early the night before. In theory Saturday nights were for going out on a date and having a good time, maybe to dinner and then later someplace where you could have a few drinks and dance. And if the guy was somebody you really liked you might end up making love.

At least that was what Saturday nights were supposed to be for. And when she was seeing Ted Barton they had been, for a while. Until her moodiness and the headaches had turned him off. So last night had been just like any other; she'd had dinner at home with her grandmother and afterward she'd gone up to her room and read. She was still miserable and it was a relief to go to sleep.

This morning she looked out and saw the new-fallen snow. The sun was shining and the snow blanketing the ground and hanging from the tree branches was dazzling white, so bright it hurt your eyes to look at it. But as beautiful as it was, the sight failed to lift her spirits. She felt dull and logy, and the prospect of sitting around all day with nothing special to do was depressing. In an effort to pick herself up she took a bath and washed her hair, and by the time she'd finished blowdrying it she was feeling a little better.

She put on gray flannels and a white blouse and her blue lambswool sweater and went down to the kitchen. Her grandmother was sitting at the table reading the Sunday paper when Karen walked in; the old lady looked up and said good morning and Karen returned the greeting, bending down and kissing her forehead.

Her grandmother's eyes were magnified by the thick lenses of her hornrimmed glasses. With her slim body and her hair dyed a soft honey color it would be hard to guess her age, although Karen knew she was in her seventies. She'd been a widow since Karen was a small child; Karen couldn't remember her grandfather at all. He was a civil engineer, she knew, and Karen's mother had been their only child. After her death Karen had come to Braddock from Shippensburg, where she'd grown up, to make a new start. She got along with her grandmother well enough, although sometimes the old lady's opinions got on her nerves. And her grandmother had an opinion on everything.

"There's fresh coffee on the stove," the old woman said. "And some Danish in the oven."

"Fine. Smells good." Karen got a cup and saucer out of the cupboard and poured coffee for herself. "Care for some, Grandma?"

"No, thanks. I've had three cups already this morning. Any more and I'll get the jitters. You sleep well?"

"Very well." She cut herself a slice of the pastry and put it on a plate, then sat down at the table. When she bit into the warm Danish she realized she was hungrier than she'd thought.

"This murder," her grandmother said, "it's just ghastly."

Karen froze.

The old lady shoved the front section of the *Express* toward her. In large black type the headline read:

BRADDOCK TEENAGER SLAIN
DAUGHTER OF BANKER DECAPITATED
LEGEND OF HEADSMAN REVIVED

There was a photo of a pretty darkhaired girl and the story covered most of the front page.

Karen suddenly lost her appetite. She had known what the girl looked like even before she saw the picture. Her voice was a whisper. "How awful."

"It was on the TV last night, but you were already up in your room. Whole town's going crazy over it."

Karen read through the story quickly, an icy lump forming in her stomach. All of it fit, all of it confirmed what she'd seen in those horrible images two nights ago. The vision had come to her precisely when the attack occurred—when the monster had stood over the helpless girl and swung that huge ax.

She studied the girl's features. The face seemed so young, so full of hope, so charged with excitement. Here I am, the expression seemed to say, at the very beginning. Ready and eager for life and all the good things it can bring me.

Instead it had brought her a hideous death.

"That poor kid," Karen said. "And her parents. God."

Her grandmother was watching her. "Isn't the first time, you know. You saw the rest of the story, about the headsman?"

"Yes, I read it."

"That last one was twenty-five years ago, but I remember it like it was yesterday. Same situation, too. The Donovan woman was a hell-raiser. Married and had a little girl, but she played around plenty."

Karen found the smug conclusion irritating. "Same situation?"

Behind the thick glasses her grandmother's eyes narrowed. "Come on, Karen—you know what these kids are like today. All they think about is sex and drugs. Wasn't just some accident that he picked her out."

"You think that's why it happened?"

This time the old woman didn't answer immediately. She seemed to be gauging Karen before she replied. Finally she said, "You may think that headsman story is just an old wives' tale, but a lot of people in Braddock know better."

Karen found it hard to breathe. "But what do *you* think?"

Again the old woman paused before answering. "I think there's a lot of evidence says it's true. Every so often, each time years apart, he comes back here. Somebody's been messing around, up to no good—*whack*. He takes their head off. You asked me what I think? All right, I'll tell you. That kid was into something, you can bet on it. And if the police ever come up with so much as a clue, I'll be surprised."

Karen read through the story again. It was by a reporter named Sally Benson, and the writing had a breathless quality about it. The article described in graphic detail how the girl's head had been severed, and how the murder weapon had unquestionably been a large ax.

When she finished reading it, Karen went through the rest of the paper slowly, as much to avoid getting into a further discussion of the murder as for any other reason. Most of what she read didn't register at all.

Until she saw a piece buried on one of the inside pages, next to an ad for an appliance sale. The headline said,

BOY STILL MISSING

The story wasn't much—a few lines on the Mariski child, more or less a rehash of what she'd seen yesterday. But reading it brought her an almost overwhelming sense of guilt. She pushed the paper aside and sat back in her chair.

As much as she dreaded it, what she had to do now could not have been more clear. Nor did she feel she had any choice. She got up and scraped the remainder of her Danish into the garbage pail under the sink, hoping her grandmother wouldn't notice. Then she washed her plate and her cup and saucer, drying them with a dishtowel before putting them away.

Her boots and her ski jacket were in the back hall closet. She got them out and put them on, then took her car keys from the hook next to the door.

Her grandmother looked at her. "Where you off to?"

"Just out," Karen said. "For a breath of air. Do you need anything?"

"Nope. Did my shopping yesterday."

"Okay, back soon." She went out the back door and down the snowy steps to the driveway.

2

Karen's car was a gray Escort, bought at dealer cost from Boggs Ford. She took a broom out of the trunk and, after sweeping off the snow, got into the car and drove out to the address she'd seen in the paper. The roads had been cleared, and driving was no problem.

The house was the type that was sometimes called an expanded cape, meaning one story with rooms added in what had been the attic. It had green shingle siding and white trim and needed paint. There was an apple tree in the side yard with a tire swing hanging from one of its lower limbs, and a couple of junky cars were parked in the driveway.

The drive had been plowed out, and mounds of fresh snow were heaped on both sides. Pulling into it took all the courage she could muster. She parked her car behind the others and made her way to the house, following a shoveled path. When she got to the front door she hesitated, instinct telling her to turn around, go back to the car and get out of here, mind her own business. But as much as she wanted to, she didn't do it. She knocked on the door.

The woman who opened it probably wasn't much older than Karen, but she already had that worn look you saw on wives who had borne too many children too fast and had worked too hard and worried too much and knew the future didn't hold a lot to look forward to. She had on a cotton dress with a ratty sweater over it and her brown hair was tied in a bun. A tiny, half-naked child with a pacifier in its mouth was clinging to her leg and staring up at their visitor. The child appeared to be a boy, but it was hard to tell.

"Are you Mrs. Mariski?"

"Yes."

"My name is Karen Wilson. I—wanted to talk to you about your son. The one who's missing?"

"What about him?"

"I think maybe I—" She had been about to say, "know where he is," but she couldn't put it that way. And besides, she wasn't sure. "May I come in?"

The woman moved aside, and Karen stepped past her, into the living room. Newspapers littered the shabby furniture, and toys and assorted debris lay on the floor. There was a bicycle leaning against one wall and the TV set had crayon streaks on the face of the tube. Another child, this one a girl a few years older than the little boy, came into the room, looked at Karen in surprise and ran out again.

Mrs. Mariski closed the front door. She picked a pile of papers off a chair and added them to the heap on a table. "Sit down," she said. "Take your coat?"

"No, thank you." Karen sank onto the chair and unzipped her jacket.

Mrs. Mariski pushed more papers aside on the sofa and sat on it, the child still clutching her leg. "What about Michael?"

Karen had thought about how she'd handle this, but now she couldn't get the words out. Or at least have them make sense without her sounding like some kind of a nut. Which was probably how she'd be seen anyway. She took a deep breath. "I'm really sorry about your son. But I think I might be able to help find him."

"How?"

"I—have some ideas as to what might have happened to him."

"What kind of ideas?"

"Did he ever go skating after school?"

"Oh, lord. We went all over that with the police. Right now he don't even have skates. He had a pair, but he outgrew them. And he never cared much about skating anyhow."

"Is there a pond near here?"

It might have been the intensity in Karen's voice. Whatever it was, Mrs. Mariski glanced at her curiously. Then she turned her head toward the rear of the house and yelled, "Phil? Come in here, will you?"

She turned back to Karen. "I want my husband to hear this."

A moment later a man came into the room. He was dark-skinned, with receding black hair. There was a beard shadow on his jaw, and he was dressed in blue work pants and a gray shirt. Mrs. Mariski introduced him to Karen and he sat down beside his wife on the sofa.

"She says she knows something about Michael," Mrs. Mariski said.

Philip Mariski looked at Karen. "You know where he is?" The way he asked the question made it sound aggressive.

"No. That is, I just thought—maybe I could help."

His expression turned to one of suspicion. "What makes you think so?"

"I—intuition, maybe."

"You from around here?"

"I work at Boggs Ford," Karen said, knowing how irrelevant that sounded. But she wouldn't try to explain what had led her to come here; that would only make it worse. "I was asking Mrs. Mariski if your son ever went skating."

"I told her Michael don't have skates," Mrs. Mariski said.

Mariski cocked his head as he looked at Karen. "Okay, so what's the point?"

"Is there a pond near here?"

"No."

Karen's heart sank. You damned fool, she berated herself.

"There's Kretchmer's," Mrs. Mariski said.

Her husband glanced at her impatiently. "That's a couple miles away."

"Did he ever go over there?" Karen asked.

"I don't think so," Mariski said.

"Do you know the pond well?" she persisted.

"Yeah, I guess so. I know where it is, been by it enough times. But if you think he was fooling around over there, forget it."

"Why?"

"Because old man Kretchmer's been known to chase kids with a shotgun. Michael wouldn't go anywhere near the place."

Karen again felt foolish. But she'd come this far, and maybe there was a chance. "So you know what it looks like?"

"It's a pond," he said. "That's all—a pond beside a pasture. Kretchmer uses it to water his cows."

"Would you show it to me? Drive over there with me?"

Mariski continued to hold his dark eyes on her. He was quiet for a few seconds. "Look, lady. I don't know you, and I don't know why you're here. Our son's lost, and we been out of our minds worrying. We got everybody looking for him. Cops, Boy Scouts, you name it. If you're guessing he fell in a pond, I think you're wrong." His voice rose. "But if you know something about where he is for Christ's sake, tell us."

The child holding onto Mrs. Mariski's leg began to cry and she shushed him.

"I don't know," Karen said. Her voice grew small. "I just think I might have an idea."

Before Mariski could respond, his wife said, "Go with her, Philip. She wants to see it, take her over there."

He looked as if he might let go with another outburst, but instead he abruptly stood up. "All right, you want to go, come on."

He put on a mackinaw and they went in Karen's car, Mariski directing her along the narrow, freshly plowed roads. Except for telling her which way to turn, he said nothing. The sun was high now, its rays reflecting brilliantly from the drifts and the snow-blanketed fields.

The pond was as he'd said, simply a small body of water in a low place beside rolling pasture land. Karen parked the Escort on the road and she and Mariski got out of the car.

The pond was about fifty yards away, its surface glistening under a coat of white. At one end was a haphazardly built stone wall. Karen raised her hand to shield her eyes from the sun's glare and peered up the slope on the far side of the pond.

Standing on the crest, as she'd known it would be, was an old barn. Its snow-covered roof sagged, and its weathered sides showed traces of red paint. Part of the wall at one end had collapsed from rot.

Karen looked at the barn and then back at the pond. She turned to Philip Mariski. "I think," she said, "you ought to tell the police to look in there."

3

The photograph in the newspaper was a good likeness of Marcy Dickens, but her face in the picture only faintly resembled what it had looked like the last time he saw her. Here she was bright-eyed and happy, her mouth stretched in a dazzling smile, the set of her chin exuding confidence. A perfectly content, dumb little bitch.

What he remembered were those same features twisted into a mask of fear. The eyes had bulged out then, so that he could see the whites all the way around the pupils. The lips had been drawn back, but to express horror, not joy. And the mouth had been wide open, to release the screams.

The headsman studied the picture for a long time. It was pleasurable for him to look at it, because it helped him relive the moment when she had lain helpless on the floor at his feet and watched him raise the ax. It brought back the excitement, the sense of power, the thrill when steel met flesh, when that white throat became a burst of crimson.

And then, finally, looking at it returned to him the exquisite sense of fulfillment.

Later he used a razor blade to cut out the photograph. Not all of it; he sliced away only the head. Then he tacked the scrap of paper onto a board above the secret place where he kept the ax. He contemplated it, pleased by the way it looked against the old, hand-planed slab of chestnut.

The photograph wasn't as satisfying as the girl's head itself would have been, but it would do for now. He'd had a good reason for leaving the head in her room after he'd executed her.

It had had precisely the effect he'd wanted.

4

When Jud awakened, the first thing he was conscious of was the smell of bacon frying and coffee perking. The second was the sound of Linda Ronstadt coming from the radio in the kitchen. He got out of bed and stretched, then went to the bathroom. When he came out he put on his robe and followed his nose and his ears.

Sally was at the stove, scrambling a pan of eggs. She was fully dressed, wearing the white blouse and the checked skirt she'd had on the day before. She looked up as he approached and smiled at the expression of disappointment on his face.

He drew her into his arms. "Is it that obvious?"

"Uh-huh."

"Well, you don't have to be in such a damn hurry."

"Sorry, Chief. I've got work to do."

"Um." He kissed her nose and sat down at the table. Usually when they'd spent the night together they'd have breakfast and then go back to bed for a time, especially on a Sunday. No matter how good it had been the night before, making love the following morning was even better. But here she was, all ready to go. He decided she was getting too ambitious.

A minute later she set a plate of bacon, eggs and toast in front of him, along with a mug of coffee. She sat opposite him and raised her own mug. "Cheers."

"Aren't you going to eat anything?"

"I had a piece of toast."

He ground fresh pepper onto his eggs and took a bite, realizing as he did that he was ravenous. Which was nothing new; he was hungry most of the time, and breakfast was his favorite meal. Or one of them, anyway.

The eggs were delicious. He looked at her. "That isn't enough for you."

She sipped her coffee. "It is if I want to keep my figure."

That wasn't something he wanted to argue about, and anyway, it was too early in the morning to think of a snappy rejoinder. "What's all this work you've got?"

"I have to write another piece for tomorrow's edition."

"More about the headsman?"

"More about the Dickens murder. But sure, I'll refer to the headsman."

He groaned.

Sally put her cup down. "Jud, there are a couple of things you just have to accept. As terrible as this case is, it's also a great opportunity for me. I've tried to explain how I feel about it, and you said you understood."

"Yeah, I know. I just wish you'd tone down the part about the headsman."

"That may be how you feel, but there's also another way of looking at it."

"Which is?"

"Which is that the newspaper business is just like any other. If you want to succeed, you have to compete. Can you imagine a story about the murder that didn't touch on that angle?"

Grudgingly he admitted he couldn't.

"And can you imagine what the out-of-town papers will be doing with it?"

"Yeah, I suppose I can."

"I promise you, they'll make their coverage as lurid as possible. And those papers are all for sale here in Braddock too, right alongside our hard-charging little *Express*."

"So?"

"So I'm going to do the best job I can. If I didn't, Maxwell would put somebody else on it, or else he'd write the stuff himself. And I'll give him that much—he knows how to sell newspapers."

"Uh-huh."

"That's another reason why I dug out the clips on that old Donovan murder. I'll bet my story is the only one that hits on it. And every bit of a competitive edge will help."

"All right," he mumbled, "you made your point." He shoveled more eggs into his mouth and spooned blackberry jam onto his toast.

She watched him eat for a moment, and then stood up. "I've really got to go. I'll try to call you later."

He got to his feet, wiping his mouth with a paper napkin. "See you tonight?"

"I don't think so. There's too much going on." She put on her coat and slung her bag over her shoulder.

"Sally?"

"Yes?"

He stepped close and again put his arms around her. "Last night was great."

"Can I quote you?"

He grinned. "On that, sure. But not on anything else."

She kissed him lightly. "Chief, you're too much."

And then she was gone.

5

When he finished his breakfast he put his dishes into the dishwasher and turned it on. Then he went into the bathroom and shaved and showered. Less than ten minutes later he was dressed and the bed was made, a trick he'd learned in his army days. He strapped on his gunbelt and put on his jacket and cap and left the cottage.

The fresh snow was several inches deep and his driveway hadn't yet been plowed, although he had a standing deal with the Exxon station on Water Street to get to him first after a storm. For a moment he thought about using his own car, a Chevy Blazer that was parked in the shed. But there were snow tires on the cruiser, and after he'd swept off the car he had no trouble backing out. Obviously Sally had had no difficulty either. On the way to headquarters the town looked like a Christmas card, clean and white and with the tree branches bending under the new-fallen snow.

When he entered the stationhouse he saw that Pearson and his corporal were already there, occupying the office Jud had turned over to them. A couple of uniformed state troopers were in with them as he passed, and so were two of the men Jud had lent them. He didn't stop to chat; if the inspector needed anything Jud would hear about it soon enough. He went to the coffee urn in the locker room and poured himself a steaming cup, then walked to his own office.

The usual stack of reports lay on his desk. He looked at the pile of paper with distaste and, after hanging his jacket and cap on a peg, sat down and leafed through the reports. These were carbons of officers' handwritten write-ups of the previous day's activities. The formal versions, typed into the computer by a clerk, would be printed and distributed later and Jud would never look at them. It was a part of the job he detested, knowing that if he did it all by the book he'd spend most of his time drowning in a sea of paper.

He was always intensely interested to know what was going on, but he would much rather have gotten his information verbally from the cops involved. Which of course wasn't always possible. So he scanned the carbons and grumbled, thinking to himself that if a small-town operation like this was bad, what must a big one be like? After reading each report he jotted his initials on it and then dropped it into his out-box.

The reports were predictable. On a stormy Saturday night you got the exact opposite of a clear one: fewer altercations in public places, more domestic disputes in private homes. And far more accidents on the roads. There had been plenty of those, most of them of the minor-damage-and-slight-injury

variety. One had been serious, however; a truck had turned over
on Deer Hill and the driver's legs had been crushed. But there
had been nothing the police couldn't handle. If there had been,
he would have been called during the night.

The door opened, and he looked up to see Joe Grady entering
the office, carrying a load of Sunday newspapers. Grady was
stocky and red-faced, and his heavy black brows made him
look as if he were perpetually scowling. He'd made sergeant
years before Jud joined the force, which undoubtedly had a lot
to do with the resentment toward the chief he managed only
partially to hide.

Grady laid the newspapers on Jud's desk. "You seen these?"

"No."

"The shit really hit the fan. Look at this stuff." Grady
pointed to the one on top, the front page of the *Braddock
Express*.

Jud saw Sally's byline almost as soon as he saw the headline.
He read through the story quickly. Just as she'd told him, she'd
played up the headsman angle heavily, and there were references to the Donovan case.

Included in the stack were papers from other cities as well,
including Syracuse, Albany and Binghamton. He didn't read all
the coverage, but he got enough from the headlines and the lead
paragraphs to see that they'd treated the story pretty much the
same way. Reporters must all be stamped out of the same mold,
he thought. And then felt a twinge of guilt as Sally returned to
his mind. Just as she'd predicted, hers was the only piece that
referred to the old Donovan murder.

He shoved the stack away and sat back in his chair, looking
up at Grady. The shadow of an ironic smile was playing about
the sergeant's mouth. "Nothing turned up around the Dickens
house?" Jud asked.

Grady leaned against the wall. "No, nothing. No footprints,
no sign anyplace of forced entry. And this morning I talked to
Williger. Only prints they got were the family's."

"Uh-huh. Anything from NYSPIN?"

Grady gestured toward a computer printout lying among the
other papers on Jud's desk. "Nothing worthwhile. They still
haven't come up with an M.O. like the one we're looking for."

"Anything else?"

"Yeah, the mayor phoned. Wants you to call him."

"What's it about—he after a progress report?"

"I think more than that. He said there was gonna be a meeting."

"Oh shit."

Grady's tone was dry. "Members of the Town Council. Our leading citizens."

Jud sighed. "I'll call him."

"Okay." The sergeant turned to leave. "I got things to do. You need anything, I'll be here."

Jud looked through the reports on his desk for a few more minutes, knowing he was deliberately delaying making the call to the mayor. Finally he flicked through the Rolodex for the number and then called it.

Melcher said he wanted Jud to get together with him and several other men to discuss the Dickens case. Jud was to be at the mayor's home at 3:00 P.M.

After he hung up he debated what he'd do next, finally deciding to pay a visit to Emmett Stark. It would be good to talk with the former chief; Stark was one of the few people in Braddock—maybe the only one, for that matter—who would understand the situation Jud was in, the pressure he was under. And it was a good bet Stark would have some insights on the Dickens case as well.

Jud was about to call the old man when the door opened and Chester Pearson walked in. He shut the door behind him and took a chair opposite Jud's desk, a grave expression on his fleshy face.

Okay, Jud thought. Here comes trouble in a hundred-pound bag.

"I thought we had an understanding," Pearson said. He was looking natty as usual, wearing a tweed jacket—a gray one, this time—and a blue-striped tie.

The more Jud saw of this peckerhead the less he liked him. "On what?"

"On this investigation. The Harper boy tells me that after I talked with him, you had him in and went over all the same ground. You were questioning some of the Dickens girl's other friends as well."

"So?"

"So I told you, I'm running the show. It doesn't help to have you working at cross purposes. Any interviewing to be done, my people will do it. Or I'll do it myself. What you have to realize is, working on a homicide case like this takes a lot of experience, a lot of training. To put it bluntly, I don't want you fucking things up."

It would be nice, Jud thought, to hang one right in the middle of that fat nose.

But he didn't do it. Instead he said, "Look, Inspector. I still head the department here. I also live in this town, and I know damn near everybody in it. I'm not going to just walk away from this case. Not when there are things I can do that might help break it."

"You have something specific in mind?"

"Yeah, I do. For one, I think that old Donovan homicide ought to be looked into."

A corner of Pearson's mouth curled derisively, an expression that was becoming familiar. "I've already done that, Chief. Yesterday I called the county attorney at home. He went to his office and got out the records. Called back with a complete report. The husband's whereabouts at the time of the murder were verified, and there were no other suspects. It was almost surely committed while a burglary was in progress. Apparently the perpetrator killed the woman and then took off."

"Is that right?"

"I'd say so, yes. I'm sure the case stirred imaginations around here, just as this Dickens homicide has done. But that kind of hysteria is common, especially in a small community. People get carried away."

"Uh-huh."

Pearson studied him. "Let me make something clear to you. I have no objection to your contributing where you can. But I want you to recognize a chain of command. Anything you do, you talk to me ahead of time. If I think it's a good idea, fine. I also want to be kept fully informed of your activities, and anything that comes your way. You stick with that, we'll get along just dandy."

Jud couldn't resist. "And if I don't?"

Pearson's face hardened. "If you don't, I'll have a talk with my superiors in Albany. This case had drawn a lot of attention, if you haven't noticed. The state certainly doesn't want to be embarrassed by local people who refuse to cooperate."

Oh shit, Jud thought. There are times when it just doesn't pay to argue. He set his jaw and forced himself to keep his mouth shut.

Pearson apparently misread the silence. He stroked his mustache with his forefinger. "You think it over, Chief. I'm sure you'll see it makes sense to do things my way. Better for you, too, in the long run. Right?"

Jud said nothing.

The inspector got to his feet. "See you later."

When Pearson had gone, Jud curled his right hand into a fist and slammed it down onto his desk.

6

The Braddock police records had been stored by the department's IBM on computer disks starting in 1982. Before that they'd been kept by hand, and there were cabinets filled with the files that covered the previous ten years. Anything earlier than that was stored in a basement room. Jud took a set of keys with him and went down the stairs.

The room was dingy and low-ceilinged, its only illumination coming from a naked overhead light bulb. The space was jammed with dusty wooden boxes containing the old records, none of them in any particular order. In addition to the boxes stacked on the floor, there were shelves along the walls bearing an assortment of junk: confiscated weapons ranging from pistols and long arms to knives and hatchets; stolen items that had been recovered by the cops but never claimed; picks, jimmies and various other burglary tools.

He spent an hour pouring over the files, which were a mess of yellowing paper. As he'd expected, the reports were sketchy and sloppily kept, some of them no more than penciled notes.

They went back not merely years, but decades. The earliest file was labeled 1922.

But there was nothing from the mid-nineteen-sixties. He went through the records box by box, folder by folder, but he was unable to find so much as a single scrap from that period. Finally he turned out the light and, locking the door behind him, went back upstairs.

When he returned to his office he telephoned Emmett Stark. The old chief said to come on over, he'd just made fresh coffee.

7

The farmhouse was on Watchhill Road, off Route 5, a fifteen-minute drive from town. It was an old two-story white frame structure, and Stark had lived there for as long as Jud had known him. The driveway had been cleared, and Stark's Jeep with the yellow snowplow on the front was parked near the barn.

When Jud left his car a dog came out of the barn and growled at him. The animal appeared to be a cross between a hound and some other large breed, maybe a Rotweiler. It barked and snapped, straining against a chain around its neck that was fastened to a thick wooden post, and Jud was glad the thing wasn't loose. The barking triggered a hullabaloo from other dogs confined to a pen some twenty yards or so away. Jud went up the front steps to the house and stamped snow off his feet. Before he could knock on the door Stark opened it and told him to come on in.

It pained Jud to see how much the old man had aged since the last time he'd paid him a visit. Stark's once-robust body was now bent over. His gray hair was thin, and behind his wire-rimmed spectacles his eyes were watery. When he shook hands his grip had little strength.

But he was obviously pleased to see Jud. He smiled broadly. "So how you doing?"

"Okay, I guess."

The smile faded. "I expect you want to talk about the Dickens homicide."

"Right."

"Hell of a thing."

"Yeah, it sure is."

After hanging his visitor's jacket and cap on a clothestree in the hall Stark led Jud through to the kitchen, where he poured mugs of coffee for them. Then they went into what the old chief called his workroom.

As he always did when he came in here, Jud had to admire the way it was organized. There was a worn leather sofa at one end of the room, with a table in front of it on which a small TV set rested. A bottle of bourbon and a pair of glasses stood on a lamp table within easy reach, and the wall beside the sofa held built-in bookcases. In one corner there was a pot-bellied woodstove, and running along another wall was a workbench with a fly-tying vise and equipment for hand-loading ammunition. Opposite the bookcases were racks holding rifles, shotguns and flyrods, and above those were two mounted heads, a handsome eight-point buck and a black bear with teeth exposed in a snarl. Stark had everything important to him right at hand.

There were two high wooden stools in front of the workbench. With some difficulty the old chief climbed onto one and indicated the other to Jud. "Don't mind, do you? I been working on a Royal Coachman, and I hate to quit now. Anyhow, helps me think."

Jud sat on the stool and inspected the fly in the vise. A bracket above it held a magnifying glass, and he could see that the lure had been expertly fashioned from bright bits of feather and nylon, bound with thread and glue. It was set on what he judged to be a number-four hook. As he watched, Stark picked up a pair of needle-nosed pliers and a tool that looked like a jeweler's pick and resumed his efforts with the delicate touch of a surgeon.

"Won't be long before I'll be using this," the old man said.

Jud drank some of his coffee. It was very strong and tasted fine. "Feels like forever to me."

"Winter's always that way. You think it's never gonna end, and then all of a sudden it's trout season."

"I guess that's true." Jud set his mug down. "This homicide has the town in an uproar."

"So I see. Been on the TV and in the Sunday papers and everybody in Braddock's talking about it. Any leads?"

"No."

"Then you're getting some heat, huh?"

"Oh, yeah. The mayor's been all over me, even though I called in the state and they sent a detective team."

"Anybody I'd know?"

"An inspector named Chester Pearson and a corporal Williger."

Stark was squinting through the magnifying glass, teasing a piece of red fuzz into place on the shank of the hook. "Nope. Don't know 'em. How they making out?"

"All right, I guess. Pearson's kind of an ass-buster."

"Lot of those state guys are. Think they know every fucking thing."

"That's Pearson, to a T."

"Uh-huh. So let 'em take over. Get His Honor off your back."

"I'm trying, but it's not working too well. As far as Melcher's concerned, I'm responsible no matter who's in charge."

"Yeah, that figures. The way Sam sees it, he and his pals own Braddock and everybody in it."

"They give you a bad time when you were running the department?"

"You bet they did." He looked up at Jud and smiled briefly. "But I never let on just how much of a bad time. Those guys're always looking for ways to bend things, you know? Everything's got to get done so it's to their benefit."

"So I'm beginning to see."

"How's the investigation going, so far?"

Jud gave him a rundown on what had transpired from the time he picked up the dispatcher's call on Saturday morning.

Stark went on with his work as he listened. Then he said, "You stop and think about it, you can see why Sam and his friends are so upset. Not only is Ed Dickens one of them, but they've got plans for this town. A thing like this murder is a black eye. That's a hell of a thing to say, with what happened to Dickens' daughter and all, but it's the truth."

"What kind of plans?"

Stark shrugged. "I don't know the specifics, but I hear Sam and Dickens and Bill Swanson and some of the others are trying to attract some big company to locate here."

Jud was incredulous. "A big company? In Braddock?"

"Mm-hm. Don't hold me to that. Like I said, it's just something I heard. But you know, if they could do that, there'd be a lot of money coming in here. And the people who run the town are the ones who'd benefit the most, right? That's pretty obvious. Just think of what it'd do for real estate values alone."

"And for somebody who's in that business. Like Sam Melcher."

Stark nodded. "Exactly. The last thing they want now is a lot of notoriety. Bad public relations."

"Bad everything. But I sure feel for the Dickenses."

"Yes. That part's terrible. Losing somebody in your family is one of the worst things could ever happen to you." Stark put his tools down and looked at Jud. "I thought when Martha died I'd go out of my mind. Even though I figured I was prepared for it. She had cancer, you know."

"Yes, I know."

"Took three years for her to go. Hell, I'm still not over it. Don't guess I ever will be."

"Chief, what do you think about this case?"

Stark pursed his lips. "Same thing you do, I suppose. Somebody who knew that kid wanted to kill her and did. Planned it all out and used the headsman story as a cover. Now every dingbat is saying we got a monster who's come back here to punish sinners. All that's gonna do is make it harder to run down. Which is exactly what whoever did it wanted. People'll be scared shitless and spreading rumors all over the place."

"What about that old case back in the sixties—the Donovan killing?"

"Don't know much about it. Happened before I came to Braddock, so all I know is the stories I heard. But that stuff about the headsman had to be pure bullshit. Probably the same thing happened then that's going on in this case—somebody used it to confuse things. Or maybe it wasn't even intended.

Maybe the guy cut her head off and then people just jumped on the headsman idea."

"You ever see the records on the case?"

"Nope. Be worth a look, though. Although I can't say you're gonna find nice clean files going back twenty-five years. In those days the department wasn't much on records and procedures."

"I did look. There was nothing there. Not only on that case, but whole years were missing."

"Huh. Not surprised. Woody McDermott was chief then. He was some character. Not only a drunk, but stupid."

Jud smiled. "You ever wish you were back in harness?"

The older man's lined features registered surprise. "You serious? I looked forward to retiring for years. Not that police work's so bad. At least it's never boring. Or hardly ever. The political shit's what I couldn't take."

"I can understand that well enough."

"I'm sure you can. You know, I'm proud of you, Jud. I knew when I took you on, right out of the army, you'd be a good one. And when I retired, there was nobody better qualified to be chief, even as young as you were. The politics, all the crap you get, that's just something you'll have to learn to live with. But do I miss it? No indeed. Now I got time to do the things I like to do." He looked at the trout fly and then back at Jud. "Only thing I wish is that the old lady was still around to enjoy it with me."

"What about your son?"

Stark brightened. "Alan? He's been pestering me to move out near him and his family. Lives in Arizona, did you know that?"

"Yeah, you told me."

"And I think I just might do it. Got no reason to stay around here, and I sure as hell wouldn't miss the winters."

Jud laughed. "Sometimes I think about that myself." He stood up. "Thanks for the coffee."

Stark walked him to the front door and waved as Jud went back out to his cruiser. The dogs again barked madly as he pulled out of the drive.

8

At a little before three, Jud drove to the mayor's house. On the way he thought about what Chief Stark had told him concerning the possibility that a large company might be moving into Braddock. The benefits that would accrue to the town—and especially to Melcher and the other civic leaders—were obvious. But what would be the attraction to a firm that might consider coming here?

On an overall basis, business had been static for years. There was no skilled labor force that amounted to anything, except for the people who worked for Loring Campbell's company, which manufactured engine gauges and other instruments for aircraft and marine installations. Braddock Airport was small, with one runway and only a couple of hangars. The winters were long and the town was in the middle of nowhere.

On the other hand, there were some positive aspects. Land was cheap, and there was plenty of it. There was the rail line, and the throughway was nearby. Expanding the airport would be a simple project. The state capital wasn't all that far, and neither was such centers as New York City and Boston. Maybe it was a possibility, at that.

Sam Melcher's house was one of the few in Braddock you would call elegant. It was a sprawl of fieldstone and white clapboard on ten well-tended acres and filled with the antiques Sarah Melcher collected. The Melchers had three children, Jud knew—one girl in the class Marcy Dickens had been in at the high school, and two older daughters in college. They were also one of only a handful of families in town that employed a maid.

Several cars were parked in the circular driveway when Jud arrived. He pulled the cruiser in behind them and went on up to the house.

The maid met him at the door, a friendly black woman who took his cap and jacket and deposited them in a closet in the foyer. Then she led him through to where Melcher and the others were waiting for him. As he passed the living room he heard what sounded like a group of women talking, and surmised that the mayor's friends had brought their wives along.

The meeting was in the library, a large, high-ceilinged room with a fireplace at one end where logs were crackling. The furniture was formal, groupings of richly upholstered sofas and chairs, and tables and a desk that appeared to be antiques. Bookcases ran from the floor to the ceiling, and there was an oil painting of a horse over the fireplace. When Jud walked in Melcher shook his hand and waved toward the group of men assembled there. "I think you know everybody."

Jud did. Loring Campbell was tall and slim, an athlete who took pride in his reputation as one of the town's better tennis players. Bill Swanson was even taller, a one-time fullback at Cornell whose son was considered a sure bet to follow him there. Buddy Harper's father was also in the group; Peter Harper looked much like his son, except that his hair had mostly disappeared. Seeing him made Jud think of the discussion he'd had yesterday with the boy. He wondered how Harper was taking the attention the police were giving his son. The fourth guest was Charley Boggs, red-faced and overweight, the owner of the most successful automobile dealership in Braddock.

All of them were wearing sports jackets and ties, and all of them had glasses in their hands. Jud exchanged greetings with each man, and Melcher asked if he'd care for a drink. Jud said he'd have a beer.

There was a bar set up on one side of the room. Melcher stepped over to it and returned with a tall pilsner glass filled with amber liquid. He handed it to Jud and the men raised their glasses and wished him luck.

Jud drank some of the beer. It was an imported brand, he realized. German, probably, different from what he was used to.

Despite his effort to appear cordial, Melcher was obviously tense. "Sit down, Jud."

Jud did, in a chair beside the fireplace, looking at the others and waiting to hear what they had to say.

The men settled onto chairs and sofas. Melcher led the discussion. "Ed Dickens couldn't be with us, of course. He and

Helen are just devastated. Marcy was their only child, you know. Losing her was a terrible thing."

Of course Jud knew. He was as sensitive to the tragedy as any of them, maybe even more so. And yet despite Melcher's strained attempts to be hospitable, the mayor was talking to him much the way he had the previous day, as if the homicide was somehow Jud's fault.

"The reason we wanted to see you here, instead of in a formal Council meeting at the town hall, was that we wanted to keep this private," Melcher said.

Campbell spoke up. "Nothing against you personally, Chief. But we're trying to hold down the rumors."

Jud fixed his gaze on him. "Rumors about what?"

"About the murder and who might have committed it."

Melcher leaned forward. "Jud, we're going to be completely frank with you, the way I know you'd want us to be."

He wished they'd stop fucking around and come out with it.

"I'm sure you remember there was some controversy when I appointed you chief after Stark retired," the mayor said.

Jud made no reply.

"A lot of people thought you were too young," Melcher went on. "They thought you didn't have enough experience for the job."

Jud waited.

"And to tell the truth," the mayor said, "maybe they were right. I don't want you to think we're reacting hysterically to this murder, but we're going to have to have some action on it, and fast."

For Christ's sake, could this be for real? As calmly as he could, Jud said, "May I say something?"

"Yes, of course."

"That's why you're here," Swanson said.

He took his time, telling him not to lose his temper, to play it cool. "The homicide occurred Friday night. Today is Sunday. The investigation is going as quickly as possible. We haven't even had an autopsy yet. And as you're also aware, I'm not in charge—Inspector Pearson is."

"I've spoken to the inspector," Melcher said. "He's told me you haven't been as cooperative as he'd like you to be."

Despite his resolve, Jud felt the heat come up his neck and spread through his face. "Hey, what is this? The state's running the investigation. What I'm trying to do is help as much as I can. First you're telling me it's not going fast enough, and now you're saying I'm not doing my part. What do you want from me?"

"What we want is for this thing to be cleared up as quickly as possible," Melcher said. "That's what we want. Whatever it takes to get it done, we're going to see that it happens."

Boggs cleared his throat. "Chief, don't blame this on the mayor here. All of us feel the same way. If this case is too much for you to handle, we're just going to have to bring in somebody who can do the job."

"Somebody from where?"

"Inspector Pearson can give us some help on that."

Jud got it then. What Pearson was doing was setting up a way to cover his ass. If the investigation didn't produce results, it would be because Braddock had a rinky-dink police department led by an incompetent rube who couldn't give the inspector the necessary assistance. Not because the state police investigation team wasn't doing its job. *Jesus Christ.*

"We know you're trying," Harper said. "Buddy told me about your questioning him."

"Did he?"

"Yes, he did. But you can't believe one of Marcy's friends was responsible, can you?"

Everybody has his own interests uppermost, Jud thought. "I don't know who was responsible," he said. "That's what we're trying to find out."

Swanson said, "If I can make a suggestion, I think you ought to be looking at the criminal element in town, and not go around embarrassing a lot of people who couldn't have had anything to do with it."

Jud looked at him. "In other words, I shouldn't have questioned your boy."

Swanson reddened. "Seems to me you were wasting your time and getting those kids upset for nothing."

Before Jud could reply, Melcher broke in. "What we're telling you is that the investigation has to move forward, and fast. And at the same time, you ought to be moving in the right direction, not in a way that would simply make more trouble. You have to realize a lot of people here are terrified. This could have a very damaging effect on the community."

Jud thought of the talk he'd had earlier with Emmett Stark. The old man had called this one. Get the case cleaned up and quickly, they were saying, because it's bad for business. But while you're about it, don't step on the wrong toes.

Loring Campbell said, "I'm sure you can understand our concern."

"I understand very well," Jud replied. He put his glass down on the table beside his chair and stood up. "If that's it, gentlemen, you'll excuse me. I've got work to do."

They mumbled awkward goodbyes, and Sam Melcher led him back to the front door. Jud put on his jacket and cap and told the mayor he'd do his best. Then he left the house. There was a bad taste in his mouth, and it wasn't from the beer.

9

Billy Swanson waited until his parents' Cadillac pulled out of the driveway, then telephoned Alice Boggs. She told him her folks had just left, also on their way to visit the Melchers, and that her brother Joe had gone out earlier. Billy said he'd be there in a few minutes and hung up.

He let out a whoop and pulled on his varsity sweater, the heavy white cardigan with a big orange *B* on it. He was proud of the sweater, wore it on all but the coldest days instead of a parka or a ski jacket. He'd always been a big kid, a good head taller than anyone else in his class all the way through school, but it wasn't until his junior year at Braddock High that he'd come into his own.

That was when the baby fat had disappeared, when the roly-poly softness gave way to muscle and he went from JV cannon fodder to first-string left tackle at BHS. Suddenly his name began to appear in stories on the sports pages of the *Express*, and people began to notice him, treat him with respect. He wasn't just Bill Swanson's kid any more; he was

Billy Swanson, the lineman scouts from Colgate and Bucknell and even Penn State had come to look over.

Not that he had much of a chance of going to one of the real football powers. His old man had played at Cornell, and was bound and determined that was where his son would be going as well. Billy's marks weren't all that great, and neither were his SAT scores. But football would get you a long way in the world of academe, and the coaches at Cornell had expressed strong interest. He'd know soon whether he'd be going to Ithaca this fall to play for the Big Red.

But whether he wound up there or somewhere else, the fact was that Billy had carved out an identity for himself. And so the varsity sweater was a lot more than a way to fend off the wind; it was a badge of honor, a signal to the world that its wearer was his own man.

He drove the Bronco to Alice's. It was a clunky kind of machine, half-truck, half-station wagon. The good thing about it was that when you put it in four-wheel drive it would go anywhere, even in deep snow. The bad thing was that you had to be a contortionist to get laid in it. Even with the back seat folded down to make a deck, you couldn't stretch out comfortably. He would much prefer something that was either jazzy to drive or practical for sex, instead of a bucket like this that didn't cut it in either direction.

On the other hand, he was lucky to have a late-model vehicle he could almost call his own. A lot of kids had cars, but few got to drive new ones. Except for when his mother needed it, which wasn't often, Billy took the Bronco to school. So for the most part it was a pretty cool deal. Still, if he had a choice he'd probably go for a van. That would be sensational. Something with an eight-speaker sound system and a back that converted into one huge bed.

When he arrived at the Boggs home, Alice took him down into the basement playroom, where a fire was burning on the hearth and Whitney Houston was pouring out of the stereo. Billy had been hoping they'd go straight to her room, but she was tense and nervous, which wasn't like her at all. She went over to the small refrigerator under the bar and got Pepsis for them, and they sat on the sofa opposite the fire.

Alice had her hair done up in a ponytail and she kept twiddling the ends in her fingers. "It's the most awful thing I ever heard of in my life. Marcy was one of my best friends. I just can't imagine that happening to her."

"Yeah." He didn't even want to think about it, along hash it over. He'd been picked up by the cops yesterday and taken to the station for questioning by the chief of police, for Christ's sake, and that had blown his mind. The chief hadn't seemed like such a bad guy, but Billy wasn't about to get chummy with a cop. MacElroy had asked him over and over again about how well he'd known Marcy and had they ever dated, and a lot of other shit, including whether he smoked grass. All Billy had done was dodge and weave, in essence telling the cop nothing.

Because the truth was he didn't know anything about Marcy's death, not anything at all. On Saturday morning he'd been as shocked as anyone else when he heard about what had happened to her. He'd seen her with Buddy at the game and later at the dance and that was it.

After that he'd taken Alice to Greasy Pete's for hamburgers and they were there with a bunch of other kids for a couple of hours and then he'd taken her home and they'd made it right here on the sofa. Not that he'd told the chief that last part, or any of the other personal stuff MacElroy was digging for. The chief had even asked him about the discussion in English class with that shitbrain Hathaway, when they'd gone on about the headsman. It was amazing.

On Saturday he and his buddies had talked about the murder until they'd exhausted the subject, and even though Billy remained as morbidly fascinated by Marcy's death as anybody else in town, he certainly hadn't come over here this afternoon to go into it. Especially when Alice's folks had gone out and given them a clear shot like this one.

But she wouldn't leave it alone. "The wake's tomorrow night at Morrison's." That was the largest and most prestigious funeral home in Braddock.

"Uh-huh."

"You're going, aren't you?"

"I guess so."

"I hear the casket'll be closed, though."

"Really?" He'd been to one wake, when his grandfather had died some years earlier. Billy had been ten or eleven at the time, and he remembered thinking as he viewed the body that the waxy figure lying on the satin cushions didn't look like his grandfather at all. To Billy it had seemed more like a dummy, with its face painted and the mouth twisted a little to look as if there was a hint of smile. That was the only dead person he'd ever seen, and he had no desire to see another one. As far as he was concerned, a closed casket was a good idea, no matter who was inside or what the circumstances of death had been.

Alice twiddled her ponytail. "But that's only right, don't you think? I mean, they couldn't have it open. If they did, they'd have to, you know—*reattach* her head. Oh God, it's so awful."

"Sure," Billy said. "Better for it to be closed."

"The funeral's on Tuesday."

"I know."

"I hope they catch whoever did it soon."

He drank some of his Pepsi. "Me too."

"Billy?"

"Yeah?"

"Do you believe it? That the headsman really came back?"

"Aw, that's bullshit." The fact was, he didn't know what he believed at this point; all he wanted to do was to get her out of this mood, get her thoughts going in another direction.

But she kept after it. "Well, if he didn't do it, who did?"

"I don't know. Maybe some wacko who was trying to rob their house."

She was quiet for a moment, staring into the fire. "I don't know what I'd do if that thing ever came near me."

He didn't reply. Alice had on a blue oxford-cloth shirt and jeans. It looked to him as if she wasn't wearing a bra under the shirt. He put his hand on her back casually, and rubbed it a little. He couldn't detect a strap, which meant no bra. He felt himself stir.

She continued to look into the flames. "You know something else that was weird?"

"No. What?"

"The way Hathaway was talking about it in class on Friday."

"Uh-huh." He kept up the stroking motion, but tried to make it seem as if he were doing it absentmindedly.

"Did you mean it—what you said?"

"About what?"

"That you wouldn't be scared if you saw the headsman?"

"Oh, I might be a little, at first. But like I told Hathaway, I don't believe in crap like that. If I saw somebody coming after me dressed up that way I'd bust him in the mouth."

"Yeah, but somebody with a big *ax*?"

"An ax or anything else." He liked the idea of casting himself in the role of hero, warming to it as he spoke. "I'd make him wish he'd picked on somebody else, you can bet on that."

Alice continued to gaze fixedly at the flames. "I wonder what he's gonna say now."

"Who?" He moved his hand around the side of her body, continuing the stroking motion as his fingers touched the curve of her breast.

She seemed not to notice the exploring hand. "Hathaway. It'd be just like the jerk to say I told you so."

"He probably realizes what a horse's ass he made of himself."

"Maybe. But I still think it was weird that he was talking about the headsman, and then the same night Marcy was killed."

"Yeah." His hand closed gently, and he rubbed his thumb against her nipple. He was aware that he had produced an iron-hard erection.

Alice slowly turned toward him. "You know something?"

"What?"

"You're getting me excited."

Jesus, he certainly hoped so. He pulled her tight against him and mashed his mouth against hers. Her tongue was hot and slippery and he felt as if he was ready to explode.

She pulled away a little and there was urgency in her voice. "Come on, Billy. What are you waiting for?"

He fumbled with the buttons on her shirt. The hell with going upstairs. Once again, the sofa would do just fine.

five ··
Not Always What They Seem

1

On Monday the *Express* ran another front-page story on the case, with a banner headline that read:

TEENAGER'S MURDER FANS
HEADSMAN LEGEND

The byline was Sally Benson's. Jud read the piece and sighed. She'd opened the article with another account of the Dickens killing, and then had gone into the headsman legend and its origins. There were grisly descriptions of how the executioner had lopped his victims' heads off, interwoven with references to the kinds of crimes that had resulted in such punishment in the old days.

Jud suspected a lot of the story had been created in Sally's mind; she had no more idea than he did as to what actually had gone on back then. What she had written was largely what she'd imagined it had been like. Or what she thought would most titillate her readers.

The piece also contained quotes from Inspector Pearson but none from Jud, although it did refer to the police picking up vagrants and other suspicious characters and not finding a suspect. And just as in the TV coverage, there were interviews with local citizens, along with their pictures. It seemed to Jud the people interviewed had been chosen on the basis of their absolute belief in the headsman and his guilt in Marcy's murder.

It also seemed Sally had outdone all the other papers in providing sensational coverage of the case. Job or no job, big opportunity or not, he wished he could put a bag over her head until this damned thing was cleaned up. What was as galling as any of it was that Grady pointedly avoided making any reference to the article. The effect was to make Jud all the more aware that Sally had added fuel to the fire. In that sense, the headline to her story was entirely appropriate.

The telephone rang. He pushed the papers aside and answered it. The voice on the other end had a down-home twang that was deceptive. "'Morning, Chief. George Ternock here."

"Hello, George." Jud sat up straight at his desk, as if erect posture would make him more alert. Ternock was a shrewd lawyer, and when you dealt with him you were well advised to pay attention. "What can I do for you?"

"You can stay off Buddy Harper's back."

He could picture Ternock sitting with telephone in hand, dark eyes cold beneath his shock of white hair. "Are you representing Buddy, George?"

"The Harper family have been my clients for a long time. Three generations of them. Do you have a charge you want to bring against the boy?"

"He's not charged with anything. All I did was have him in for a talk. He was one of the last people to see Marcy Dickens alive, which certainly made him important to the case, and maybe a suspect."

"Ayuh, and that's reasonable. But now you've had two cracks at him, and that's enough."

"I had him in once, George."

"So did Inspector Pearson, which makes two times he was questioned. The boy's under a lot of strain, without the police adding to it. Marcy's death was a terrible shock to him."

"It was to everyone."

"So if you have anything further you want to ask him about, you better have a good reason."

"An unsolved homicide's a good reason, isn't it?"

"Certainly is. But disrupting the boy's life amounts to harassment, and you have no right to do that. You have

absolutely nothing to indicate he was inside the Dickens house
that night, do you?"

Jud wondered if Ternock was probing and decided he wasn't.
The lawyer didn't bluff, and he didn't operate on hunches.
"Like I said, George, we're not charging him with anything."

"Of course you're not. There's nothing to charge him with."

"That's true for the moment, anyway. But even if it is, we
may need him as a material witness at some point."

"That'll be up to the county attorney," Ternock said. "Not
you. First a case has to be presented to a grand jury."

"I understand that."

"In the meantime, I'll expect you to let the boy get on with
his life. His parents are quite upset with all this, as you'd
imagine they would be."

"I know they are. I've spoken with his father."

"So he told me. Let me point something out to you, Jud. You
should keep in mind that after you break this case, if you do,
you'll want to go on being an important part of the community.
Wouldn't do to rub people the wrong way. Braddock is a small
town."

There it was again. Ternock was being more subtle than the
group at Sam Melcher's home had been yesterday, but not
much. Certainly the message was the same. *Do your job, solve
this dirty problem, but respect the station of those above you.*

"Do I make myself clear?"

"Yes, George. You do."

"Good. I wish you luck in your investigation." There was a
click and then the hum of the dial tone in Jud's ear.

2

In the afternoon Jud drove over to Dr. Reinholtz's office for a
copy of the coroner's report and also one on the autopsy, which
had been conducted that morning. The doctor was brisk and
businesslike, but despite his manner and his jaunty bowtie there
was a touch of sadness about him that Jud caught. Which was
certainly understandable. Reinholtz had been a doctor in this
town for decades; there was hardly anyone he didn't know, and

a great many of the locals were his patients. That probably had included Marcy Dickens.

Reinholtz confirmed it. "I delivered her, you know."

"No," Jud said. "I didn't know."

"Oh, yes. Saw her through measles and flu, and a broken wrist when she fell off her bike. She was about seven when that happened. Great kid. Had her whole life ahead of her."

"You confirm what killed her?"

"I'd say a blow from an ax, just as we suspected."

"Couldn't have been from some other kind of weapon?"

"It's possible, but I don't know what it would have been. Had to be very sharp and very heavy. Sliced her larynx and severed her spine at the fifth cervical vertebra. Death was almost instantaneous."

"What do you mean, *almost* instantaneous?"

Reinholtz shrugged. "When someone's decapitated, the brain stays alive for a few more seconds."

Jud felt a crawling sensation at the back of his neck. "Let me get this straight. Are you saying she was conscious *after-ward*?"

"Probably. But only until the blood drained away and the brain was deprived of oxygen. That would have been just a moment or two later."

"So in other words, she could have thought about what had happened to her? After her head was separated from her body?"

"She could have had an impression, yes."

"Holy Christ."

The doctor waved a hand impatiently. "For all practical purposes, she died instantly."

Not quite, Jud thought. Not quite. He was silent for a minute or so, numbed by what he'd learned. Then he shook himself out of it. "You find any sign of a struggle?"

"Just one. There was a bruise on the underside of her jaw."

Jud hadn't noticed it when he saw the body, but that probably was because of the way the head had been sitting on the dresser. "What caused it, could you tell?"

"Could have been a lot of things. A club, or a fist."

"But fresh?"

"Yes. Inflicted at the same time."

Jud tried to picture it. "Sounds as if he knocked her down, then swung the ax."

"Probably, yes."

"What about time of death?"

"Between midnight and two A.M."

"You find anything else?"

"There was semen in her vagina. We don't have a lab report on that yet, but I expect it'll be confirmed. She must have had intercourse not long before she died."

Jud thought of his talk with Buddy Harper, and another idea came into his mind. "You think she was raped?"

"No, although it's hard to say, under the circumstances. Wasn't altogether forcible rape, anyway."

"How do you know that?"

"Condition of the mucous membranes in the vaginal tract. When a woman is sexually excited in a normal situation, she's lubricious. The juices flow, the penis slides. But when she's frightened and angry, as in a rape, she's dry. Even if the rapist uses some kind of lubricant, which would be unlikely, there can be damage. So what happens is, there are abrasions and sometimes even tears in the tissue. I found no evidence of anything like that."

"So rape is out."

"Not altogether. She could have been threatened, and then submitted without putting up resistance. But I don't think so. She had intercourse, but in my opinion she wasn't raped."

"Uh-huh."

"She had a boyfriend, right? The Harper kid?"

"Yes."

"Okay, so that could explain the semen. Inspector Pearson said they'd want a DNA analysis, and that'll give us the answer."

"How reliable is that?"

"Very. Before we had it, all the lab could tell you about a semen sample was blood type. Which made it pretty general. But now semen's as good as a fingerprint, because the DNA can be identified. DNA is deoxyribonucleic acid—the basic chromosomal material that reveals somebody's hereditary pattern. Chances are something like one in ten billion that any two people would have the same DNA fragments. So you can positively identify somebody a female had sex with."

Jud again thought of Buddy. The boy had admitted that he'd made it with Marcy that night, so the test would only confirm what Jud already know. But what if she'd been raped after that?

"Let me ask you, Doc. This DNA test—would it work if she'd had intercourse with two guys?"

"You mean if there was semen from two different people?"

"Yes."

"Sure it would. The test would distinguish between them and still identify both. What made you ask that?"

"Nothing, I was just curious. When will you have the results?"

"Tomorrow morning. I'll call you as soon as I get them."

Jud thanked him and went back to his own office. What he wanted to get going on now was questioning more of Marcy's friends. One of the unfortunate side effects of trying to conduct an investigation in a small town was that you couldn't say good morning to someone without everybody else knowing all about it, but that couldn't be helped. A little later on he'd go over to the high school. He looked at his watch. It was still early; he flicked through the reports on his desk.

One of them caught his eye. Philip Mariski had called yesterday and insisted the cops drag Kretchmer's pond. Jud wondered why that had come up now. He noted that Grady had agreed to look into it. Jud made a mental note to stop by the pond before going to the high school.

3

An ambulance and a police car and three other vehicles were parked beside the road when Jud arrived. He pulled up behind the cruiser and got out, looking across the snow-covered field at Kretchmer's pond. He could see a boat on the pond with several occupants in it and a small group of people standing at the water's edge.

He trudged through the snow to where the onlookers were gathered. When he got there he saw that the men in the boat had used poles to break up the ice on the pond. He recognized

Philip Mariski among the people in the group on the shore and nodded to him. Overhead the sky had turned leaden once again and there was a threat of more snow in the air. A slight wind was blowing out of the east and it was raw and cold and Jud turned up the collar of his jacket.

As he watched, the men in the boat poled the vessel toward the shore. One of them was a cop, Charley Ostheimer. The other two were men who worked for Braddock's department of public works. They were silent and grim-faced, and as they came closer Jud saw something lying on the bottom of the boat, covered by a blanket. When they reached land the men got out and lifted the bundle from the boat. An ambulance attendant raised one corner of the blanket.

The boy's face was bloated, but not as much as it would have been, Jud realized, if the water had been warmer. The skin was pasty white, the lips blue. His eyes were half-opened slits in the swollen face. Philip Mariski pushed close and groaned, then turned away. The men carried the small body to the ambulance.

Mariski walked alone to his car, a battered Chevy sedan. He bent over the roof of the vehicle and buried his face in his arms, his shoulders shaking. Jud went to him and stood by, wishing there was something he could do to ease the man's pain and knowing there wasn't.

After a minute or two Mariski pulled himself erect. He got a bandanna out of the back pocket of his blue work pants and blew his nose loudly. He noticed Jud standing near him and shook his head.

"I'm sorry," Jud said. "I'm really sorry."

Mariski's eyes were redrimmed in his dark face. He wiped them with the bandanna, then blew his nose again. "She knew," he said. "She *knew*."

"Who knew what?"

"That woman. That goddamn woman. She knew where he was. She knew he was drowned in there. She knew right where to look."

"What woman?"

"Said her name's Karen Wilson. Works at Boggs Ford. I'm telling you, she *knew*."

4

Driving to Braddock High, Jud thought about what Mariski had told him. He'd never heard the woman's name before, he was reasonably certain. And with the emotional state Mariski was in, Jud couldn't be sure that what he'd said about the woman's visit to his house was accurate. But he'd check it out when he had time. He parked his cruiser in front of the school and approached the building.

As he made his way up the walk he thought about his own schooldays. He'd gone to Norwich High, not so many miles from here, in a town even smaller than Braddock. At that time he was sure he'd either become a guitar player or a professional athlete. The idea that he'd wind up as a cop, let alone chief of a smalltown police department, had never occurred to him.

But then he'd learned the hard way that he'd never be able to hit a curveball at a level above Class C, and that put an end to seeing himself as another Mike Schmidt. And his work with the guitar had gone no further than playing with a few pickup groups. The most he'd ever made in one night was twenty dollars in a bar, trying to be heard above the loud talk and clinking glasses.

So when he'd gone into the MPs after basic training it was like backing into a career almost without realizing it was happening. As it turned out he had an aptitude for police work, and he liked it. Which was more of an advantage than many young guys had, especially the ones whose lives seemed to just drift along in no particular direction.

While he was in the army his father died of a stroke, and a year after that pneumonia took his mother. His father had been a foreman with a construction company, a big rough guy who drank too much and got nasty when he was loaded, but who was capable of gentleness with Jud's mother. Maybe he was afraid of her; Jud was never quite sure. The only time the old man had shown much interest in Jud was when he had been playing ball, but even then there hadn't been a whole lot of communication.

There was one other child in the family, Jud's older brother

Roger, who had gone out to the West Coast and was now an electrical contractor in Oregon. He was married and had a son, but Jud had never seen his sister-in-law or his nephew. He spoke to his brother once a year, in a telephone call on Christmas day.

After his parents died Jud began to take life a little more seriously, at least to the extent of thinking about what he was going to do. He figured as long as he was in police work and enjoying it, he might as well stick with it.

At the time of his discharge from the army he realized he'd need an education. So right after he'd signed on as a rookie in the BPD he enrolled in an adult program at one of the New York State University branches. Even applying his army credits, it had taken seven years of hard work to get a degree through the courses he'd taken on a catch-as-catch-can basis. But when he made chief of the Braddock force it seemed for once he'd really put it all together.

Until the Dickens case had flipped a quiet Saturday morning upside down. Now he had a feeling he could be walking blind-folded through a minefield.

The Braddock High principal was David Baxter. Jud went to him first, out of courtesy. On his way to Baxter's office the kids he passed in the corridors were wide-eyed at seeing him. There couldn't be doubts in anyone's mind why he was there; all anyone in Braddock was talking about was Marcy Dickens' murder.

Baxter was a little guy with a prissy mouth and beady eyes behind steel-rimmed glasses. He was polite enough, even unctuous, when Jud entered his office. He asked the chief to sit down and offered coffee, which Jud declined.

It was terrible, Baxter said, about the Dickens murder. The students were stunned and grief-stricken, and so was the faculty. The school would be closed tomorrow to show respect for Marcy, so that anyone who wished could attend the funeral. In all his years with the Braddock educational system, he'd never seen a tragedy like this. True, they'd lost students to accidents of various kinds, especially in automobiles. But murder? And especially one as bizarre as this? It was unheard of.

It was also unfortunate that so many people in Braddock believed the headsman legend, he said. That wasn't at all healthy, in his opinion. No rational person should swallow such an absurd story. But still—it was strange, wasn't it, that the poor girl had been decapitated? And with an ax, at that. How was the investigation coming along, by the way?

"We're looking at every possibility," Jud said. "The reason I'm here today is to get a better understanding of what Marcy was like. I thought it would help to talk to some of her friends."

Baxter squinted through his glasses. His voice dropped a few levels. "You think one of them might have been responsible?"

"Not necessarily. I'm just getting background information." Jud was used to people angling for information. "Preliminary fact-gathering, you could call it."

The principal seemed a little disappointed. "There are so many difficulties with our young people today. Very little discipline at home, you know. That's the main thing. Parents don't seem to care what their children do so long as they don't have to get involved. That's one reason we have such a drug problem, in my opinion. It's just about impossible for us to control it. And frankly, Chief, I wish your force would be a bit tougher in that area."

"We're doing the best we can," Jud said. Baxter was like a lot of other people he knew. Ready to point out that drugs were a blight, and just as quick to say that solving the problem was somebody else's responsibility. "Maybe a better drug education program in the schools would help."

"Oh, I agree. We're trying to get more funding for just that purpose. Both from the federal government and the state. But all politicians do is talk. There's very little action."

So here we go round in a circle, Jud thought. It's still everyone else's fault. "Getting back to Marcy."

"Yes?"

"What was she like as a student?"

The principal pursed his lips before answering. "Above average, I would say. Not on the honors list, but close to it. Did her work, got it in on time. I went through her transcript after you called this morning, and also talked with a couple of her teachers. By and large she was doing a good job, academically.

Liked history quite a bit, I understand. Her weakness was math."

Mine too, Jud thought. "How about her personality—what was that like?"

"Sunny and cheerful, most of the time. A willing participant in classroom discussions. Quite articulate, and not afraid to express herself."

"I understand they were discussing the headsman in her English class on Friday morning."

Baxter's jaw dropped. "Really? I wasn't aware of that. Let's see, that would have been Mr. Hathaway's class."

"Yes."

"Strange that would come up. And on that day, of all days."

"Struck me as odd, too."

"Although that old story has always been part of the local lore. Perhaps that might explain it."

"Maybe."

"Uh, would you mind my asking how you learned that?"

"Some of her friends mentioned it. Seemed to me to be an unusual coincidence."

"Yes, I should say so. Indeed it was."

"Anything else you can think of that might be helpful for me to know?"

Baxter thought about it. "I'd take a good hard look at that drug angle, if I were you. No telling what might have been going on there."

"Uh-huh." Nothing specific, Jud thought. Just some vague implications. No wonder the students at Braddock High were so contemptuous of this little prick. "I'm sure she had plans for college?"

"Oh, yes. Had applications in at Hamilton, Colgate and Rochester. She was waiting for acceptances to arrive, as a number of our students are at this time of year." He shook his head. "What a pity."

"Thanks for your help, Mr. Baxter. I appreciate it."

"Certainly, Chief. Anything I can do, you be sure to call on me. You said you wanted to speak with some of Marcy's friends?"

"Yes. Can you tell me where I'd find Pat Campbell? I'm told she and Marcy were close."

"Of course. Just give me a minute or two." He swung his chair around to face a PC on the table behind him. He keyed the machine, and true to his word he had the information a few moments later.

He turned back to Jud. "She's in American History this period." He looked up at the electric clock on the wall. "It'll be out shortly. She has physics after that, but we'll have her excused."

"Is there a place where we can talk?"

"Absolutely. There's a small conference room just two doors down. You can use that if you like."

"Fine," Jud said. "I'll wait for her there."

On the way out of Baxter's office it occurred to him that the last time he'd had a talk with a high school principal was when he was a student himself. He'd been called in after an argument with another kid that had escalated into exchanged punches. Jud had been nursing a black eye, which was humiliating.

It was funny the way some things stayed with you.

5

Pat Campbell was as Jud remembered her—a knockout. Her blond hair was long and slightly wavy and she looked at him with big blue eyes and he couldn't help but notice what she did for her sweater. When he did he wished he were seventeen again. There were comfortable chairs in the conference room and she and Jud sat opposite each other. She crossed her legs, and from this perspective she looked even better.

"I'm really sorry about Marcy," he said, feeling awkward.

The blue eyes immediately filled with tears. "It's horrible." Her voice was very small. "We were friends since the first grade. I can't believe this happened."

"Sure. I know how you feel, believe me I do. And I'm sorry to have to ask these questions, but it's important, okay?"

She took a tissue from the pocket of her skirt and wiped her eyes. "Yes, okay."

"You say you and Marcy were friends for a long time. Did you see much of each other outside of school?"

"Oh, yeah. Sometimes we studied together, and a lot of times we'd stay over at each other's house."

He wanted to help her relax, get her talking. "I guess she had a pretty good sense of humor, from what I hear."

"Marcy? She could be a riot when she wanted to. You'd be with her five minutes and she'd have you laughing. That's why everybody liked her so much. One of the reasons, anyway. She was really a nice person all around."

"Did you double-date much?"

"Oh, sure. She was going with Buddy Harper. I guess you knew that?"

"Yes, I've spoken with Buddy."

"And we used to go out together once in a while."

"How did they get along, would you say?"

"Fine. They were real close."

"They ever fight?"

"Fight? Oh, I guess so. I mean, they'd have their squabbles now and then, but nothing serious."

"You're dating Jeff Peterson, right?"

"Yes."

"I understand you and Jeff were with them at the dance Friday night?"

"We sat at the same table."

"When you were together, did the subject of the headsman ever come up?"

"Yeah, it did. See, we had a discussion about it in English class that morning. The teacher—Mr. Hathaway—brought it up. We were studying Washington Irving and he talked about how Braddock had its own legend."

"Did Marcy participate in that?"

"Yeah, as a matter of fact she did. I don't remember what she said, though. A lot of people talked about it."

"And then you got into it again at the dance?"

"Yes. We were making jokes about it."

"What kind of jokes?"

"Oh, like kidding around about how somebody ought to go over to Billy Swanson's house with a hood on and scare him."

"Why Billy Swanson?"

"Because in the class that morning he was saying he didn't believe the headsman story. I think he made Mr. Hathaway mad. Hathaway was like cool about it, but you could tell he was pi—I mean, you could tell he was angry."

"I see. You and Marcy used to confide in each other, didn't you?"

"Sure, all the time."

"She ever tell you she was worried about anything, or that anything was bothering her? Anything important?"

She was quiet for a moment. Then, "This is confidential, right?"

"Of course. Anything you tell me is."

"I think—she had problems with her father."

"What kind of problems?"

"Well, like, he drank a lot."

"Yes?"

"And sometimes when he did, I guess he was pretty mean to her."

"Mean to her how? Did he ever hit her?"

"Sometimes she—hinted at it. I don't know for sure, but I think sometimes when he was drunk, he might have."

"That's pretty serious."

"I know it is. But she never would have said anything, if there wasn't something going on."

"She never really came right out with it?"

"She was ashamed. I knew that. But at the same time, she needed to tell somebody. Even though she wasn't all that specific, I knew what she was getting at."

So it was possible Marcy had been abused by her father. Who was one of Braddock's most respected citizens. And there was no way of proving it. In fact, even this kid who was telling him about it couldn't swear it was true. And yet if it were, wouldn't that make Ed Dickens—

Jud told himself to go slow, to think it through. "Any other problems you know about, with anybody else?"

"I don't think so."

"She ever worry about getting pregnant?"

Pat colored slightly. "That's awfully . . . personal."

"I know it is."

She looked at the floor.

"Listen, Pat. I told you, anything you say will be kept confidential. All I'm trying to do is find out who killed her. You want to help with that, don't you?"

Her gaze met his. "Yes, of course I do."

"Then what about it—did she ever worry about that?"

"She did, you know, at first. But then she went on the pill and it was okay."

"When was that?"

"Last year."

"When she was going with Ron Carpenter?"

She seemed startled. "How did you know about that?"

"I know about a lot of things. It's part of my job. Who else was there besides Carpenter and Buddy?"

"Nobody."

"You sure?"

"Yeah, I am. If there was, I would've known it. She had to really care about somebody, you know? And with Ron and Buddy, she did."

So Buddy had it right. Marcy's lovers had been only two young men. But then again—"She ever talk about anybody else she might be interested in?"

"Yeah, sometimes."

"Who, for instance?"

"Oh, there's a guy who's a sophomore now, at Brown. His name's Bob Waltham. Marcy always thought he was pretty cute. But he goes with Tracy Adams."

"Yeah, I know him. Who else?"

"Nobody. Except I knew she was . . ." Her voice trailed off and she looked away.

"Yes? You knew she was what?"

"I knew she was interested in Jeff."

"Oh?"

"Uh-huh. I mean, she never talked about it, but I could tell. The way she looked at him, the way she acted around him."

"Did he know it?"

"I'm not sure. Probably."

"You never discussed it with him?"

"No, never. I didn't want him to think I was jealous. And besides, she was my best friend."

"In your opinion, how heavily was she into drugs?"

A change came over her. The blue eyes hardened, and her chin came up. "I don't know anything about that. As far as I could tell, she never touched anything."

"Not even a little pot, now and then?"

"I told you, I don't know anything about that. So the answer's no."

There are some people you get farther with by not pushing too hard. He sensed she was one of them. Even though she was just a kid, there was a streak of intransigence not far beneath that pink and blond surface. And anyway, he'd already learned a number of things from talking to her.

He stood up. "Thanks, Pat. I'll be talking to you again. I'm sure you want to get back to your classes."

She smiled. "Nope. They're over for the day."

6

The air in the gym was warm, maybe close to eighty degrees. With only a handful of onlookers in the stands the place seemed cavernous, much larger than on a game night, when the fans would pack every inch of space and the noise would be like rolling thunder. Now the shouts of the practicing players and the thump of balls bouncing off the lacquered floor and the fiberglass backboards echoed hollowly. Jud took off his jacket and draped it over his arm, leaning against a wall as he watched.

Peterson was easy to spot. He was a good-looking kid, even-featured and with short black hair. He wasn't the tallest member of the team, but he was easily the most graceful. He took a rebound and passed, then moved downcourt, running with long strides that were deceptive; he was moving faster than he seemed to be. The ball came back to him and when he cut and accelerated he blew past the defenders for an easy lay-up.

Watching him, Jud could see why there was talk of Jeff going to one of the Big East teams on a scholarship—Syracuse or Georgetown or maybe Seton Hall. He and Billy Swanson were probably the best athletes in the school.

Braddock's basketball coach was Fred Walsh. He'd been at BHS forever, or at least for years before Jud had joined the police department as a rookie. A lanky man with thinning red hair fringed with gray, Walsh was wearing sweatpants and a T-Shirt with WILDCATS printed on it. A whistle hung from a lanyard around his neck, and every few minutes he'd blow the whistle and run the team through another play.

At one point he caught sight of Jud and walked over to where he was standing. "Hey, Chief—want to shoot a few?"

Jud smiled. "Not today. Wouldn't want to make your kids look bad."

"We'll take a chance."

"Some other time, Fred."

"Anything I can do for you?"

"I want to talk to the Peterson boy for a bit."

"Sure." Walsh didn't ask why; he didn't have to.

"You got a place that might be a little private, where we could be alone?"

"How about my cubbyhole?" the coach offered. "Go through the locker room and shut the door. After the kids are out of the shower I'll send Jeff in there. Shouldn't be long, practice is over for today."

Jud thanked him and walked through the door under the stands that led to the locker room. It was even warmer in there than in the gym, the benches strewn with pieces of clothing and equipment and more of it hanging in the open lockers. The shower room was at one end of the area and apparently some of the kids were already inside. Clouds of steam were rolling out the door and Jud could hear shouts and laughter over the sound of water pounding onto the tile floor. He walked to the opposite end of the room to a door bearing a sign that said COACH and went into the tiny office, closing the door behind him.

There was a battered gray metal desk in the room, and shelves along two of the walls held a variety of junk—old basketballs and team photos from years past and sweatbands and an alarm clock. On another wall was a bulletin board with team rosters and newspaper clippings tacked to it. Jud sat down at the desk and waited, dropping his jacket and cap onto the floor and wishing it weren't so damned hot in here.

Peterson came in a few minutes later, his face still flushed from the workout and the shower, his wet black hair combed back. He had on an open-necked white polo shirt and jeans and he seemed at ease.

Jud shook hands with him and told him to take a seat. "How's it going, Jeff—think you'll make the finals?"

The kid smiled. It was apparent that he was used to being asked about basketball and how the team was doing. "We've got as good a chance as anybody. The other night against Warren Falls we just blew it. We're a better team than that. I hope we get to play them again."

He wasn't cocky, Jud realized, just confident. And much more self-assured than most kids his age. "You were with Marcy Dickens after the game, right? You and Pat?"

The boy's face clouded. "Yeah, we sat at the same table with her and Buddy."

"Terrible thing, what happened to Marcy," Jud said. His manner was relaxed, but he was watching Jeff closely.

"Sure was. I hope you catch whoever did it."

"Oh, we will. Sooner or later we'll get him." That sounded good, but Jud wondered just how much truth there was in it. Thus far the police, including Pearson's team, hadn't come up with a single lead. "You seen Buddy since then?"

"Yeah, I was with him for a while Saturday night. He's plenty shook up."

"Sure. He tell you I talked with him?"

"Yeah, he did."

"How'd he and Marcy seem to you when you were with them at the dance?"

"Okay, I guess. Nothing unusual."

"Anybody else with you?"

"Joe Boggs and Tina Ferrell part of the time."

"How about Marcy—how was she?"

"Fine, I guess. Nothing out of the ordinary. Except—"

"Yes?"

"Except maybe she wasn't as, like, happy as she usually is."

"Why would that be, do you know?"

"No idea."

"What did you talk about, do you remember?"

For the first time in the conversation, Jeff seemed uncomfortable. "Yeah. And it was kind of strange. We were talking about the headsman. It came up in English class that morning, and at the dance we were joking about it."

"So Buddy told me. Odd coincidence, huh? When you think about how Marcy died."

"Yeah, it was."

"I understand your teacher brought it up that morning."

"Hathaway." Jeff shook his head. "What a spook."

"Why's that?"

"I don't know. The guy's just—peculiar. And you know something? This morning he never said one word about Marcy. Nothing. Everybody in the school was talking about it, all the kids and the teachers. They're really upset, you know? Mr. Baxter announced school's closed tomorrow so anybody who wants can go to the funeral. But Hathaway never said a word. It was like it never happened."

The English teacher's part in all this had struck Jud as more than a little strange as well. It'd be interesting to learn more about Hathaway's apparent preoccupation with the legend of the headsman—whether the reason for it was as simple as his drawing an analogy to what the class had been studying. *The power of suggestion.*

"Where'd you go after the dance, Jeff?"

"Greasy Pete's."

"Lot of other kids there?"

"Oh, yeah. Billy Swanson and Alice Boggs, Joe Lombardi, Betty Melcher, quite a few."

Lombardi was one of Jeff's teammates. "How long were you there?"

"Maybe an hour or so."

"You drive your car?"

"Yes."

Jeff had an old Ford convertible, Jud knew. He'd seen him driving it around Braddock. "What time did you take Pat home?"

"Pretty late. Around two."

"You go in the house?"

He shifted in his chair. "Yeah, for a while."

That figured. The senior Campbells would likely have been in bed by then, which would have given Jeff and Pat a chance to be by themselves. "What time did you leave?"

"Uh, three, three-thirty."

"And then?"

"And then I went home."

According to Dr. Reinholtz, Marcy had died between midnight and 2:00 A.M. Unlike Buddy Harper, Jeff could prove where he'd been until much later than that on Sunday morning. "Let me ask you, Jeff. Anything happen that night, anything you might have thought about later you think I ought to know?"

"Like what?"

"Like anything. If there is, tell me. It'll be confidential, just between you and me."

The boy was silent for a moment, then shook his head. "No. Honest, I can't think of anything."

"All right, Jeff, thanks. Anything you happen to think of that could interest me, anything at all, you let me know."

Jeff said he'd do that. He left the office, obviously glad the interview was over.

After he'd gone Jud sat there for a few minutes, thinking back over their conversation. It was the damnedest thing, but he had the distinct feeling he was close to something. The trouble was, he didn't know what. He wondered if it were true, that he'd learned something but hadn't recognized it, or if police work was doing to him what it did to so many cops: getting him so nutty he saw hidden motives everywhere, shadows behind the shadows.

He looked at his watch. Classes had been over for some time, but he still might catch Hathaway. He picked up his things and left the coach's office, aware that his uniform shirt had become damp with sweat.

7

Jud asked directions to Hathaway's classroom, but when he got there the English teacher had left for the day. There was a phone booth in the hallway near the front doors of the school, and he went to it. Hathaway was in the book; Jeff called the number and said he'd like to have a talk with him.

Hathaway's manner was coolly distant, but he told the chief to come to his apartment. It was in the Keeler building, he said, at the south end of Main Street. Jud drove the cruiser, arriving less than ten minutes after he left the high school.

The building was one of the newer ones in Braddock, a project developed by Sam Melcher's real estate company. There were stores on the street level and a suite of dentists' offices at the rear, and the upper two floors contained apartments. Hathaway's place was on the top floor. Jud rang the bell and a moment later the door opened and he was looking down at the teacher.

The man's face was broad, and his clipped black goatee and his mustache made his jaw seem even wider. Hathaway extended a hand. Jud shook it, then followed the motorized wheelchair as it whirred and turned, leading him from the small foyer into the living room.

The decor was pleasant enough, but Jud quickly perceived that everything had been arranged so it could be reached from a sitting position. The bookcases and shelves, the pictures on the walls, everything was at a lower level than normal. From a point about five feet from the floor on up to the ceiling, the walls were bare. The furniture in here was modern, and not to Jud's taste. Everything seemed as if it had been designed to look at and not to sit on. He took off his jacket and dropped them onto a chair.

Hathaway gestured toward a sofa and swung the wheelchair around to face his visitor as Jud sat down. He smiled with his mouth, but not his eyes. "Like some coffee, Chief, or a drink?"

"No thanks," Jud said. "I just want to ask a few questions."

"About Marcy Dickens, I assume."

"Yes."

"What a tragedy. Somehow you just don't associate that kind of violence in a sleepy little town like Braddock."

"No, you don't. I understand she was a student of yours."

"That's correct."

"A good student?"

"Average. Nothing outstanding. She did her work most of the time. But that was about it. Like a lot of kids nowadays, school didn't seem very important to her."

He had big hands, Jud noted. Broad shoulders, a deep chest. Probably worked out with weights in order to keep his upper body in shape, stuck in that wheelchair all the time.

"Her death must have given you quite a shock."

Hathaway's eyes were so dark you couldn't tell what color they might be. It seemed to Jud they sat back in the teacher's head and looked out at you. "It certainly did."

"She was in class Friday morning?"

"Oh, yes."

"Did she participate in the classroom discussion?"

"I think so. I seem to remember her answering a question."

"What kind of material have you been covering?"

There was a hint of condescension in Hathaway's reply. As if a cop wouldn't know one book from another. "American authors, at the moment. Melville, Twain, Washington Irving."

"I see. How many classes do you teach?"

"Five altogether. But just one in senior English. That one is supposed to be for our better students, which is laughable."

"Why is that?"

"Because we don't have any better students. They range from ordinary to dull."

Jud smiled. "Must be tough, trying to get pupils to respond when there isn't much interest."

"It can be frustrating, yes."

"You've been at Braddock High a long time, right?"

"Almost twenty years."

"In the Vietnam War, weren't you?"

"Yes. I was in the infantry."

"What outfit?"

"Three Hundred Sixty-fourth Regiment."

"Where were you when you were hit?"

"Mo Duc. I was a platoon leader and we were on a reconnaissance patrol. A mortar round landed near me."

"Rough."

"Actually I was lucky. Could easily have been killed, of course. As it was, my spinal column was permanently damaged, but—" he patted the arms of the wheelchair "—I can still get around quite well."

"So I see."

"Were you in the service, Chief?"

"MPs, but on the other side of the world. Two years in Frankfurt."

"So you got to see some of Europe."

"Yes. I did all the traveling I could. France, Italy, Switzerland. It was a good deal."

"I'm sure it was."

There was a barely restrained bitterness about this guy, Jud decided. Which was understandable. From the waist down he was nothing but bone and shriveled tissue. He couldn't walk, couldn't cross his legs, couldn't even feel it when he wiped his ass. And worse of all, he couldn't screw. Who wouldn't be bitter? Especially when so many Americans had regarded Vietnam soldiers as criminals, had shunned even the ones like Hathaway who'd come out of it shattered in mind or body or both.

The teacher's eyes were fixed on him. "Must be quite a contrast, living in Braddock after seeing some of the more sophisticated parts of the world."

"It has its compensations," Jud said. "Police work here is a lot better than in some other places."

"I can imagine."

"Yeah. I wouldn't want to have to deal with what cops run into in New York or Detroit, places like that."

"No."

He's anxious to get rid of me, Jud thought. Trying to seem casual but wishing I'd get the hell out of there. And he never mentioned the one thing I know his class was talking about on Friday. "In school the other morning?"

"Yes?"

"Did the subject of the headsman come up?"

Hathaway's eyes seemed to narrow for a fraction of a second. "The headsman? Oh, you mean the local legend." He smiled. "Braddock's favorite ghost story. I think it may have. We were discussing 'The Legend Of Sleepy Hollow.' That's by Washington Irving. There are some parallels between the two."

"I'm familiar with Irving's work," Jud said dryly. Having this guy talk down to him was beginning to get on his nerves. "Did you think back to talking about it in class when you heard about Marcy's death?"

"I suppose I did. Actually I was too stunned by her murder to dwell on any connection. And then again, the headsman business is nothing to take very seriously, is it? I imagine every town has one or two ghosts in its closet. People love to invent variations on the bogeyman. It's almost a tradition in any society. And a lot of the stories have become classics. Not just Irving's, but many others. 'The Pied Piper of Hamelin,' 'Frankenstein'—they're all variations of the same theme."

"Uh-huh. What was said in your class on Friday about the headsman—was there a lot of interest?"

The small smile reappeared at the corners of Hathaway's mouth. "As I told you, Chief, there isn't really a lot of interest in any of the class discussions at Braddock High. I think my students were more concerned with the basketball game that night and the dance that was to follow it."

"So no one said much about it—about the headsman?"

"No. Just some scoffing by the boys."

"Which boys?"

"I don't even recall."

"I see. Well, I won't take any more of your time. Thanks for seeing me."

"It was a pleasure, Chief. If there's any way I can help you, be sure to call on me."

"Fine, I may do that." He stood up. "Don't bother about seeing me out." Jud collected his jacket and cap and put them on, then shook Hathaway's hand. The man's grip was firm and dry, and this time Jud thought he detected callouses. He turned and left the apartment.

On the way back to police headquarters he made a mental note to contact army records. That was another thing he'd learned about this job: it paid to check out details. And there was something about Hathaway that just didn't feel right. Jud didn't know what it was exactly. But there was something. Taking a closer look was one more thing he'd add to his list.

8

Frank Hathaway sat motionless for a long time after the police chief had gone. How many times in his life had he encountered such people—officials in organizations ranging from the army to Braddock's town government, who took themselves and their silly little positions so seriously? Even the uniform MacElroy wore was reminiscent of comic opera, with its visored cap and its epaulet-shouldered blouse and fancy gold badge.

And the pistol, heavy and ominous in its black leather holster, probably a .357 Magnum at least, as if the larger the caliber the more important the man who carried it. But what would happen if the chief were to come up against a really powerful foe? With all his confidence and his cocksure faith in himself and his enormous gun, what would he do if he were actually face to face with the headsman?

Would his reaction be the slightest bit different from that of one of those idiot high school students? How contemptible that the man could go huffing and puffing as he conducted his bumbling investigation, when if he ever were to bring it to a successful conclusion, he'd probably die of fright. Weren't they so much alike, Chief of Police MacElroy and that oafish Swanson boy?

Swanson had been so obvious. He'd spewed out his infantile expressions of courage not because he didn't fear the headsman, but because he believed he'd never confront the monster, and therefore could show contempt for him. He could display bravery for the benefit of his cronies and those little pussies who sat in the classroom and crossed their legs and squirmed.

The girls were the worst. They teased Hathaway with impunity, believing that even though he looked like a man and spoke like one he was a non-threatening cipher. Fools, all of them. Vain, pitiful fools.

Hathaway glanced at the window. It was growing dark outside; the long winter twilight was fading. He touched the controls on his chair and propelled himself to a wall switch, flicking on the lamps in the room. From there he rolled to the bank of windows and closed the blinds. He was hungry, but he wouldn't bother to fix dinner until he'd relaxed and enjoyed himself for a time.

From a cupboard in the kitchen he got out a bottle of Johnnie Walker Red and poured himself a stiff drink over ice. He went back into the living room and opened the cabinet on which the TV stood.

There were a number of video cassettes in the cabinet. He rummaged among them until he'd made a selection, finally settling on a special favorite. He turned on the TV and the VCR and shoved the cassette into the machine. In a moment an image loomed onto the screen, a scene showing the tanned bodies of nubile girls surrounding a young man. The girls were all young and beautiful. They caressed the young man's naked flesh and teased him and stroked him and then began a series of acts that inflamed Hathaway to watch. He sipped whiskey and sat back in the chair, his eyes riveted to the screen.

six ....

A Sixth Sense

1

Olson's Diner was on Water Street, a block south of Boggs Ford. When Jud walked in at midmorning he saw people he knew, a couple of hardhats and some farm workers. He nodded to them and exchanged a word or two before sitting down on a stool and asking for a cup of coffee.

The waitress was fat and jovial and even though she was busy she fussed over him a little, asking how he was feeling and how things were going as she placed a cup before him. It was warm in here and the windows were steamed over. He unzipped his jacket and pushed his cap back on his head as he sipped the coffee.

The young woman came in a few minutes later. Jud guessed who she was from the look of uncertainty on her face and the hesitant way she approached him. He was sure he'd never seen her before.

"Chief MacElroy?" Her voice was low-pitched and pleasant.

"Yeah, hi. You must be Karen Wilson. Sit down." He indicated the stool next to his.

She took it, unbuttoning her gray cloth coat.

It was strange that he didn't recognize her, for two reasons. One, he thought he was familiar with just about everybody in Braddock, at least by sight. Two, she was pretty. And there weren't that many young women in this town who looked that good. She had long, dark brown hair with reddish glints, a true chestnut color, and green eyes set far apart. Her chin was on the

139

squarish side and she carried it at an angle that suggested stubbornness or pride or maybe both. She also had a good body, from what he could see of it under the coat.

The waitress came by and she ordered coffee.

"I don't think we've ever met," Jud said.

Her expression was guarded. "No, we haven't."

"You from around here originally?"

"No. I grew up in Pennsylvania."

"Oh? Whereabouts?"

"Shippensburg. What did you want to see me about?"

Okay, so she was a little uptight at being invited to have coffee with the chief of police. Jud had suggested it to make their meeting easier on her, figuring that to an observer it would seem casual, that they'd simply run into each other by accident. He hadn't wanted to call her in to the station or visit her at her job; that would have made it too big a deal, when all he really wanted to do was to thank her and to satisfy his curiosity. So he'd called and asked her to meet him here.

He tried to reassure her. "I just wanted you to know I appreciate your help in finding the Mariski boy."

To his surprise, that only seemed to make her more tense. "I really wasn't much help at all."

The waitress returned and set a cup of coffee on the counter in front of the young woman. There were two little plastic containers of cream on the saucer. Karen set them aside.

"It meant a lot to the parents," Jud said. "It was terrible for them to lose their son, of course, but at least they were able to know the truth."

She didn't look at him, but kept her eyes on the cup of steaming coffee. She touched it with both hands, not raising it from the saucer. It seemed to Jud her fingers were trembling slightly.

"You don't mind my asking," he went on, "I'd like to know how you realized where he was."

She didn't respond, and for a moment he wasn't sure she'd understood him. But then she replied, her voice so low he could barely hear her over the babble of conversation in the diner. "I just guessed."

"You guessed?"

Her lips compressed, and she bobbed her head.

"You mean that all the places he could have gone, all the things that could have happened to him, you just guessed he'd drowned in a pond a couple miles from his house? A pond his family says they never knew him to go near?"

She looked up then, fixing him with a defiant stare. "Kids often go places they shouldn't, and they like to fool around on the ice. It seemed to me the pond would be a good bet."

Jud sipped his coffee. It was his third cup of the morning, but it tasted good to him, better than the stuff the cops brewed in the locker room at the stationhouse. Oddly, everything Karen Wilson had said thus far had done more to pique his curiosity than to satisfy it.

He put the cup down and returned her gaze. "How did you happen to pick Kretchmer's as the place to look? There are plenty of other ponds and lakes around here."

Tiny pinpoints of anger flared in the green eyes. "Why—did I do anything wrong?"

He spoke quietly. "Hey, of course not. I told you, everyone is grateful for your help. I'm just curious. Philip Mariski said you didn't even know where Kretchmer's was—he had to tell you how to get there. But he said you were certain that's where they'd find his son."

"And I told you it was just a hunch. I wasn't certain at all. I—just thought it was a possibility . . ." Her voice trailed off.

The air in the diner suddenly felt even warmer. It was obvious now that she was hiding something, and Jud thought he understood what it was. "You knew, didn't you?"

"What?"

"I said you knew. You knew just where to look. Isn't that true?"

Color rose in her cheeks, and for a second or two he thought she might snap at him or even get up and walk out. But he could see that instead she was struggling to regain control of herself. He turned his face away, wanting to give her a chance to calm down.

The waitress moved along the counter and stopped opposite him. She smiled. "Get you anything else?"

"No thanks. All set just now."

"You need anything, just yell." She stepped away.

"I'm sorry," Karen Wilson said.

Jud glanced at her. "No problem. Sorry I upset you."

"It's—hard to explain."

"I'm sure it is. But I'd like you to try."

She picked up her cup. This time Jud was sure of it, her hands were trembling. It looked as if she might spill the coffee, but again he saw her force herself to regain her poise. Her hands steadied, and she drank from the cup as if she was proving to herself she could do it. She carefully returned the cup to the saucer.

He tried again, gently. "But you did know, didn't you?"

This time her reply held none of its earlier truculence. "I told you the truth. I didn't know. I had a feeling. An impression. And that's all I had."

"An impression. Was that like a dream or some kind of a picture in your mind?"

The green eyes narrowed. "What makes you think that—that I saw a picture in my mind?"

"Look, Miss Wilson. Karen. Okay if I call you Karen?"

"Yes."

"From time to time, people claim they have the ability to see things, to know them in a kind of—extrasensory way. Sometimes they call it a sixth sense. Sometimes they say it's just a feeling. Other times they say they actually see things in their minds. They see people or places, just as if they were looking at photographs. I think you know that, don't you?"

"I—yes. I know it."

"Is that what happens to you?"

"You think that's how I came to believe the Mariski boy had drowned?"

"It's possible, isn't it?"

Her features continued to register suspicion. "What do you know about that kind of thing?"

"Not much. What little I do know comes from my experience as a police officer. Not that I've ever personally encountered anybody who had that sense or ability. But I've heard of cases where a psychic"—he saw her bristle and quickly

corrected himself—"where gifted people sometimes volun-
teered to help the police."

"I'm not gifted."

"I didn't say you were. I just asked whether you had some
kind of sixth sense or something that made you think that's
where to look for the boy."

"I told you, all I did was try to help. It was just an
impression I got when I read in the newspaper about how he
was missing. It just seemed sort of logical to me. Okay?"

"Sure. But let me ask you, has anything like this ever
happened with you before?"

There was the merest flicker of hesitation before she
answered, but Jud caught it. "Sometimes I have hunches, but
that's all. They never amounted to anything before this. Now if
you'll excuse me, I have to get back to work."

"Okay. But again, thanks. You were a great help, and I know
it took courage for you to come forward."

That might have had some effect, but it was hard to tell. She
got off the stool, gathering her coat around her. "Thank you for
the coffee. Goodbye."

"'Bye, Karen." He watched her walk out of the diner. She
really was very pretty. And wound up so tight she seemed ready
to fly apart.

He turned back to his coffee. The waitress had returned, and
before he could stop her she topped off his cup.

When she stepped away he thought about Karen Wilson.
Whatever went on in her head, whether she really did have
some kind of extrasensory perception, he could only guess at.
But one thing was indisputable: She had led Philip Mariski to
the exact place where his son's body lay entombed in icy green
water. For a moment he toyed with the idea of asking her for
help in the Dickens case, but then he put it aside. After her
reaction to his questions, he could imagine how she'd respond
to such a proposal. But maybe at some point he'd figure out a
way to approach her. It was worth a try. Hell, anything was.

He put a tip on the counter, paid his check and left the diner.
He had some things to look into at the BPD, and then he'd
attend Marcy Dickens' funeral.

2

When Karen got back to the dealership, Charley Boggs was
standing near his office door looking at some papers. He
glanced up and smiled, watching appreciatively as she took off
her coat and hung it up.

She ignored him. Just as she did Ed McCarthy when he made
some joke about going out for a roll in the snow. She sat down
at her desk and mechanically went through the process of
typing some orders on the computer, only half-conscious of
what she was doing.

Damn that cop. Why couldn't he have left her alone? And
how had he known about the strange ability she'd been cursed
with—the sixth sense? He'd even called it that. He'd known
how she saw things other people couldn't. Known it as if he'd
been able to look inside her head and see some of the dark
secrets she kept hidden there.

But the real fault wasn't the police chief's—it was hers. She
was the one who had this weird faculty. She was the one who
could receive a vision, whether she wanted to or not.

But what could she have done—let the Mariskis go on
suffering when at least she could offer them the scant comfort
of learning what had happened to their son? Hadn't she done
the right thing after all?

Of course she had.

But that was a fact she hated to admit, even to herself.
Because if acting on what she knew about the Mariski boy was
right, then wasn't she also obliged to act on what else she
knew?

She shuddered and forced herself to type faster—struggling
to free herself from the thoughts that were tugging at her like
demons deep inside her mind.

3

What gave a song its true spirit was the melody even more than
the lyrics. And also the rhythm and the chords you put under it.
If it was like most country music you just strummed in two or

four beats to the bar and kept it simple, never using more than about three chords throughout. Which was why so much of it sounded alike. When you heard the opening bars of a song for the first time, you knew just about to the note how it was going to go. You wouldn't know the lyrics, but the chords would tell you where the melody was headed and how it would get there.

So what Jud always tried for was a surprise now and then, going for a seventh, say, or a minor chord when the ears of an audience would be expecting the phrase to resolve with a major. They wouldn't know that's what they were expecting, couldn't define it, but instinctively that would be what they'd feel they were going to hear. And then when it came out a little differently it would make the song just that much more interesting.

At least that was the theory. He'd never tested it in front of an audience, because the few times he'd played in front of one had been in saloons where the customers were too drunk to realize what was going on and wouldn't have cared if they had. But it was nice to fantasize about people watching and listening, pleased by his songs and his playing.

He did it now, sitting by the dying fire in the living room of the cottage, the clock on the mantel showing 1:30. He had his legs crossed comfortably and the Gibson felt natural and easy in his hands. He picked out a four-bar intro, using a variation on the melody he'd created, and then went into the song.

> Got a pair of itchy feet
> Just can't stay at home
> When I see a pretty gal
> It makes me want to roam
> I love to wander
> Love to wander
> But in my heart I'm always true
> And I'll come back to you
> The grass looks so much greener
> On the other side
> One thing you can count on Babe
> You know I never lied

I love to wander
Love to wander
But in my heart I'm always true
And I'll come back to you

"Can I depend on that?"

He turned to see Sally leaning against the doorway of the room, her arms folded. A knowing smile was playing at the corners of her mouth. He was surprised, because it was rare for her to wake up during the night, no matter how much noise he made. Her hair was tousled and she was wearing one of his shirts, the tails hanging down almost to her knees.

"Hi." He continued to pick out the melody, modulating from E-flat to F when he got to the chorus. "Can you depend on what?"

"That in your heart you're always true? Seems to me every time a guy picks up a guitar he sings about how he screws around a lot but it's okay, eventually he'll come back to his dearest love. And she'll be so thrilled to have him back she won't care."

He grinned. "That's life, isn't it?"

"Not hardly."

She might have a point, at that. And beside, tomcat themes were pretty much of a cliche in country songs. Maybe he ought to be going for more originality in lyrics, as well as in the melody and chords. He put the Gibson back into its case. "You want a drink?"

"Maybe just a little one." She came over and sat down in the chair beside his as Jud got up and went into the kitchen.

He was back a minute or two later with a short bourbon for her, a can of Coors for himself. She was looking at what was left of the fire, and when he handed her the glass she continued to stare at the embers. There was no other source of light in the room and the glow was soft and warm on her skin. He sat down beside her and drank some of his beer.

"Jud?"

"Yeah?"

"I want to say something, but I don't want you to make fun of me. I want you to take it seriously."

"Okay, go ahead."

She sipped a little of her whiskey. "Suppose it was true."

"Suppose what was true?"

"The headsman. Suppose he was for real."

He looked at her. "Hey, you can't—"

"Now wait a minute. I don't believe it either, but hear me out. We know that two hundred years ago, Braddock had a professional executioner who beheaded people. Anybody committed a crime or was considered a sinner, off with their head."

"Go on."

"Then over the years, other people died the same way. Their heads were chopped off, and there was never any explanation of who killed them. Except one. People said the headsman had come back. There was the Donovan killing. And now it's happened again. Marcy Dickens is dead, and she was beheaded by a powerful man who did it with an ax."

"Apparently, yes."

"This time there's you and your police force, and the state cops with their lab and all their modern technology, and what are the results? Just like the other times. You don't even have a lead, any of you."

"That doesn't mean we won't have. Something'll break, sooner or later."

"Will it? How can you be so sure? Maybe nothing will turn up, just like with the Donovan case. Then this one'll go down the same way. Marcy Dickens, age seventeen. Homicide committed by person unknown. Murder weapon, an ax. Never found. And that's all—until sometime in the future, when it happens again."

He swallowed some of his beer. "Where does that leave us—tough shit, Marcy, you ran into the wrong ghost?"

She tossed her head impatiently. "No, damn it. That's just my point. I'm not saying he's real. What I am saying is that you and Pearson and all your cops have been going in just one direction. You acknowledge the killer chopped Marcy's head off, but you say it couldn't have been the headsman. That's impossible."

"Okay. So?"

"So maybe that's exactly what he wanted. He knew the cops

would never take that idea seriously. But if you did, then as a
police officer, as a professional, wouldn't you go about your
investigation differently?"

"Look, let me point out something. In police work, you learn
that most felonies get solved one of three ways. One, you get
a tip from an informant. Two, circumstantial evidence leads
you to a perpetrator. Three, the bad guy makes a mistake. Gets
caught red-handed. Or sometimes he confesses, either to the
cops or to somebody else who tells the cops, which gets us
back to number one. In most cases, by far the majority, it's the
tip that breaks it."

"Does that mean all you do now is sit back and wait?"

"No, of course not. You have to run down every possibility."

"Okay, then let's say the killer really is the headsman. How
are you doing to run *that* down?"

He finished his beer and set the can down on the hearth,
trying to be patient. "I don't know."

"Exactly. You see what I'm getting at? I'm saying, why not
start out with the premise that it's true, that the headsman really
did kill Marcy. Even if you didn't believe it, wouldn't that
make you think about this whole thing differently? Maybe take
you in some whole new direction?"

"Maybe."

"Then why not try it? Why not use your procedures to run
him down just the way you would any other killer?"

He snorted. "Because if you're right, you can forget about
police techniques. What procedures do you use to track a
ghost? Do you try to use an informant? Or go after him on the
basis of circumstantial evidence? Evidence of what? Does the
guy evaporate into thin air? Does he go back to the dead and
stay there until it's time to return here? Is that what you try to
track?"

"Um. I see what you mean."

"Right. Mrs. Donovan was killed over twenty-five years
ago. Before that? Who knows? All we have are a lot of stories
that've been handed down."

"Yes. Well." She finished her drink and stood up. "I'm
cold."

He got out of his chair and put an arm around her. "Good."

"Good?"

"Sure. That's a problem I can do something about."

As he led her back to bed, one corner of his mind was turning over the beginning of an idea. Maybe her train of thought wasn't so crazy at that. Maybe it had triggered something he'd want to look into. The only trouble was, he was almost afraid to learn whether it was true.

4

The shrill pealing jarred him out of sleep, but he couldn't figure out what was causing it. On the second ring he realized it was the phone. He fumbled the receiver off the hook and pulled it into bed with him. The digital clock read 4:12. "Yeah?"

"Chief, it's Stanis."

"What's up?" He still wasn't awake.

"We got a suicide."

That cut through the haze. "Who?"

"Art Ballard. That old man lives near the Dickenses?"

Jud sat up in bed. "When?"

"Few minutes ago. His wife said he shot himself. Sorry to call you, but—"

"Yeah, it's okay." It was a standing rule that in the event of any violent death in the town, the BPD was to notify its chief immediately. "You send a car out there?"

"Yeah, Delury. I sent an ambulance, too."

"All right, I'm on my way."

He put the phone down and got out of bed. As he did Sally stirred in her sleep, burrowing deeper under the covers. Jud dressed in the semidarkness, the only illumination in the room coming from the face of the clock. The air was icy cold. He moved as quickly and as quietly as he could, and within minutes he was out the door and into the cruiser.

Sally's car was parked behind his in the driveway, and he had to inch around it as he backed out, hoping he wouldn't get stuck in the drifts. When he made the street he accelerated quickly but didn't bother with the siren or the flasher; the roads were pretty well deserted at this time of the morning. It took several minutes before the heat came up in the car, and he wished fervently he had a cup of coffee.

Art Ballard a suicide? Jud could see his face, with its network of blue veins, the nose dripping from the cold, wisps of white hair blowing in the wind. And most of all he saw the rheumy eyes burning with conviction as Art told him the headsman had returned to Braddock. What the hell could have driven the old man to shoot himself?

When he got to the house he saw lights in all the windows of the small gray frame structure. Car Three was parked out front. The ambulance and the coroner had not yet arrived. Jud got out of the cruiser and went up to the front entrance.

For the second time in less than a week, Jud found himself going into a home where sudden death had occurred in the middle of the night. But this time he didn't have to ask where the body was. What remained of Art Ballard was not far from the door, lying on the floor in a pool of blood. A Winchester pump shotgun lay beside him.

Delury wasn't in sight; Jud assumed he was with Mrs. Ballard.

If he hadn't known who it was, Jud would never have been able to identify the corpse. The old man apparently had shoved the muzzle of the shotgun into his mouth and pulled the trigger. His lower jaw was still intact, but that was the only part of his head that was. The rest of it had been blown completely away, and pieces of bone and tissue had exploded onto the wall. The gaunt frame was dressed in pajamas and a frayed blue robe. A pair of scuffed leather slippers were on the feet.

Dennis Delury came around the corner, and when he saw Jud the young officer said he'd been in the kitchen with Mrs. Ballard. Jud told him to go back and stay with her; he'd be in there later.

Jud heard a car drive up, and looking out the window saw Doc Reinholtz leave his sedan and approach the house. Just behind the coroner came an ambulance.

Reinholtz shook his head when he greeted Jud. He shook it again when he saw the body. Then he put his bag down onto the floor and took off his overcoat and his hat and dropped them onto a chair before kneeling beside Ballard's corpse.

"He another one of your patients, Doc?" Jud asked.

Reinholtz sighed. "Looked after him and Ethel for years."

"Did you treat him for anything lately?"

"No."

"How was his health in general?"

"I'd say fairly good. Oh, he had a few problems. Bad back, for one thing. And a little rheumatism now and then, 'specially in wet weather."

"But nothing serious?"

"Nothing serious enough to make him blow his head off, if that's what you mean."

"That's what I mean," Jud said.

The front door opened and two ambulance attendants with heavy jackets over their whites came into the room and stood gaping at the mess.

"I'll just be a few minutes here," Reinholtz said to them.

He turned back to Jud. "Whatever was bothering him wasn't his health. If there was anybody in the family I'd say might have done something like this, it would have been Ethel, not Art. She's got a kidney problem that gives her a lot of pain. You talk to her yet?"

"No. I'm gonna do that now."

"All right. When I'm through here I'll look in on her."

"They have any family around here, do you know?"

"Nope. The children are all grown with kids of their own, all of 'em living out of state. I think Ethel has a sister, though. I'll call her, let her know."

"Okay," Jud said. "I'll go see how Ethel's doing." He left the room.

Ethel Ballard was sitting at the kitchen table, drinking coffee with Delury. She was wearing a pink flannel robe. In stature, Art's widow was the opposite of her late husband. She was heavy, almost obese, but her features were small and childlike. Even her hair seemed incongruous; its white strands had been tinted blue.

She looked up when he walked into the kitchen. "Hello, Jud."

He put his hand on her shoulder. "Ethel, I'm sorry."

"Ayuh. There's a fresh pot of coffee there on the stove. Help yourself. Mugs are in the cupboard."

As Jud moved to get himself coffee, Delury stood up. "I'll be in the other room, Chief." He picked up his coffee mug and put it into the sink, then left.

The mugs had cartoon characters on them: the Seven Dwarfs. Jud picked out a Grumpy and filled it with coffee before sitting down across from Ethel Ballard. The surface of the table was covered with red polka-dotted oilcloth and its cheerful color seemed out of place under the circumstances. It was warm in the kitchen and Jud unzipped his jacket and put his cap down on a nearby chair. He looked over at her, trying to gauge her emotional state but not succeeding. It could be that she was actually this tough, but it could also be that she was simply numb from shock. "You have any warning this was coming?"

"No. You ask me, it was a dumb damn thing to do. We were going to get out of here, you know. Sell the house and move to Jacksonville. Art's got a cousin lives down there."

"Why do you think he did it?"

She fixed him with a steady gaze. "I don't know. He didn't have any troubles. Not big ones, anyway. If he did I would have known about them."

"He was pretty upset, wasn't he, by the Dickens girl's death?"

"Oh, yes. We all were. But for Art it was a lot worse."

"Why was that?"

Her small eyes were like bits of blue china. They gleamed as she spoke. "Because he saw the headsman."

"You believe that, Ethel?"

"Believe it? Of course I believe it. He told me about it. Saw him plain as day. So maybe he was afraid. But he didn't have no reason to be."

"Why is that?"

"Because Art was harmless, that's why. Never hurt nobody. Worked all his life in Swanson's Hardware, let Bill Swanson walk all over him. Just the same way Bill's father did when he was alive and running the place. They do that to you, you know."

"Who does what?"

"All of 'em. They treat you like dirt. Not just the Swansons, either. The whole crowd that runs this town. It's like they own it, and the rest of us just work for them. But Art never caused no trouble, not to them or anybody else. Whatever they dished out, he took it."

She drank some of her coffee. "One time he went two years without a raise. He knew the store was making money, too, both of them years. But you think he had the guts to tell Bill Swanson he should get a little jump in his lousy salary? Not Art."

"Why was he afraid of having seen the headsman?"

"I don't know. I told you he didn't have no reason to be. The headsman, he only kills people who've done something bad. Somebody who's committed a mortal sin."

"You think that's what Marcy did?"

The blue-china eyes narrowed. "Could be."

Jud wondered if the old lady might know something of value. "Did you see much of Marcy?"

"Enough. Watched her grow up from a baby. She was a nice kid until she got mixed up with that bunch at the high school."

"What happened to her after that?"

"'Bout what you'd expect. She got into dope and sex, staying out all hours of the night. And those parents of hers let her get away with it, too. Let her do just about anything she pleased. It's what comes of having too much money, thinking you're better'n everybody else."

"She was seeing the Harper boy, did you know that?"

"'Course I knew it."

"Was there anybody else?"

"Not since last year. Buddy and her, they was together all the time."

"You said Art told you about seeing the headsman. What did he tell you about it?"

She fiddled with the handle of her coffee mug. "Art was up that night. He had a bad back, and a lot of times it kept him awake. Friday night, sometime around one o'clock, he got up and went downstairs. He was gonna read or maybe watch TV

in the living room. Before he turned the lights on, he looked out
the window and saw him."

"What did he see, exactly?"

"It was clear that night, and there was a moon. Art said he
looked down the road toward the Dickens house, and when he
did he saw a man come out the front door. There was a light
someplace downstairs in the house, and when the man walked
past the window Art got a look at him. He said it was a big man,
dressed all in black with a hood on his head and carrying an ax.
It was the headsman, no doubt about it."

"And then what?"

"And then nothing. The headsman was gone, and Art didn't
see him again after that. Art stayed up until it got light out.
Then he come back to bed."

"Why didn't he call the police?"

A faint smile crossed her face. "Can you picture that? Hello,
Officer, I just saw the headsman running around outside. They
would've said he was ready for the looney bin."

She had a point. "Did he tell you what he'd seen?"

"No, I was still asleep. Later on he did, after Helen Dickens
found Marcy's body. He said he told you, too."

Jud was about to explain that he hadn't taken Art literally
that morning, but she already knew that. Saying anything more
about it would only make him look more foolish. "After that
did he bring it up again?"

"Oh, yeah. Couple times. He said he wondered who was
next."

"He tell anybody else?"

"I don't know. Don't think so, but I could be wrong. Art
wasn't a big mouth, though. Wouldn't be like him to go around
blabbing. And like I said, I think he was afraid, even though he
didn't have no reason to be. He was just poor old dumb Art
Ballard." Suddenly the blue eyes filled with tears.

Jud felt awkward and helpless. There was nothing he could
say or do at this point to make her feel any better; only the
passage of days and weeks and months would ease the pain,
and even then much of it would stay with her. *Time heals all
wounds.* But does it?

He got up and patted her shoulder. Then he picked up his cap and went back into the living room.

The ambulance crew had removed the body, but what remained behind was a godawful mess. The floor was covered with blood, and the wall looked as if somebody had heaved a bucket of gore at it. Bits of tissue and hair and other human detritus were stuck to it, and the surface was pocked from birdshot.

Doc Reinholtz said it was a simple case of suicide; he'd have a report out later that day. And there would be no autopsy; he told the ambulance crew to take Ballard's corpse to the Garavel funeral home. And that was about it. He left the room, going into the kitchen to offer Ethel Ballard what comfort he could.

Jud then told Delury to give him a hand, saying they'd do what they could to clean up the room. It was against regulations for cops to be doing that kind of thing, but Jud didn't give a damn. He didn't want Ethel Ballard to have to do it, and he didn't want her to have to tell somebody else to, either. He and Delury found a broom closet in the back hall with a bucket and rags in it, and they worked on the wall and the floor for a good hour. When they finished the marks in the plaster were still there, as were some of the stains on the floor, but altogether it was better than it had been.

When he left the house Jud thought about his discussion earlier that night with Sally. Did the headsman really exist? To anybody with any sense, that was ridiculous.

And yet Art Ballard had seen him.

5

Jud figured there were two possible sources of information on Braddock's history. One was the public library, the other was the museum. Both were run by the same man, a one-time Utica college professor named Paul Mulgrave. The reason Mulgrave was able to hold down two jobs at once was that each was a breeze. The library was a small, sleepy operation that discouraged its use by young people in a number of subtle ways, chiefly by not keeping an inventory of items they'd be interested in, such as record albums and videocassettes, which

libraries now offered routinely. Instead, it catered to older
citizens, who found it a pleasant place to pass the time reading
and dozing at its long wooden tables. And the museum was
open only occasionally. Since both the library and museum
depended principally on public financing from the town's
coffers, it wouldn't do much good to complain about the
shortcomings of either one. It was expensive to run such things,
you'd be told, and Braddock's finance committee was not noted
for throwing money around.

Jud parked in front of the library and went inside. It was a
one-story red brick building, apparently of the same vintage as
the town hall. The librarian at the desk was a thin, gray-haired
woman who reminded him of a teacher he'd had as a kid: stern,
foreboding and dried up. She peered at him through wire-
rimmed glasses as he approached.

Her voice was appropriately quiet. "May I help you?"

He took off his cap and opened his jacket. "Afternoon,
ma'am. I'd like to see Paul Mulgrave, if he's around."

She looked at the gold badge on his shirt. "I'll see if Mr.
Mulgrave is in. Who shall I say is calling?"

"My name is MacElroy. I'm the chief of police."

Keeping her eyes on him, she lifted a telephone and spoke
into it, her voice now even softer. When she put it down she
said to Jud, "Mr. Mulgrave will be with you shortly."

"Thank you." Talk about formality. You'd think he was at
the White House, trying for a visit with the president. He
turned, holding his cap behind him, and looked around.

There weren't more than a half-dozen people in the place, as
far as he could see. One old guy was nodding off at one of the
tables, and now and then he'd bite off the end of a snore and
wake himself up. A woman was sitting at the same table,
frowning at his antics. It would have been simple enough for
her just to get up and move, but probably not as interesting.
Instead she sat and glowered at the source of the noise.

A sign over one of the shelf sections said NEW FICTION.
Jud stepped over and looked at the backs of the dust jackets. He
thought he recognized a couple of the titles, but he wasn't sure.
Reading was an activity he both enjoyed and constantly
promised himself he'd do more of, but somehow he never got

around to it. What with his hours, all he seemed to want to do when he was home at night was watch the tube and play his guitar.

Another librarian came by, carrying an armload of books. This one looked even more spindly than the one at the desk. Jud watched as she put the books onto shelves, wondering why it was necessary to have these two women plus Mulgrave working here. Or not working here. There couldn't be enough for one person to do, let alone three.

He heard a footstep behind him and turned to see Paul Mulgrave coming forward with his hand extended and a smile on his broad face. Mulgrave was a tall man with a full head of gray hair and an ample gut that his brown tweed jacket couldn't quite hide. He spoke in a stage whisper. "Chief MacElroy. Nice to have you here. How can we be of service?"

Jud shook the hand. "Hello, Paul. There a place we can talk?"

"Of course. My office. Come this way."

He followed Mulgrave to a door on one side of the main room. They went through the door and down a hallway, and now the man spoke in a normal tone. "Don't think I've seen you for a while. You don't get to the library very often, do you?"

"No, not often," Jud said. "Just come in now and then to check on whether you're hustling pornography."

For an instant Mulgrave looked stunned, but then his face relaxed in a wide grin. "We have it all in a special cabinet. Same way the video rentals keep their X-rated tapes."

It was a nice counter, he had to admit. There was only one video rental store in Braddock, and Jud had been trying to force the scumbag who ran it to get rid of his porno tapes, but without success. As long as he kept them separated from the rest of the stock and swore that he rented them only to people over eighteen years of age, there was no legal way to stop him from doing business in the stuff.

And for that matter, what people looked at in the privacy of their homes was their own concern. That was one good thing about the proliferation of VCRs; it had taken the play away from porn moviehouses. Braddock had had one of those, too, but it had closed several years ago after the boom in videotapes had stolen its business.

Mulgrave led the way into his office. The room was about twice the size of Jud's shoebox at the BPD, and comfortably furnished with an old mahogany desk and a couple of leather chairs. There were even paintings on the walls. A window looked out on a snowy field with hemlocks scattered across it, and beyond the trees you could see a few houses.

Mulgrave waved at one of the chairs and took the other one himself. "Now then, what can we do for you?"

"I'm interested in doing a little research," Jud said. "On what Braddock was like in the early days when the first settlers were here."

"I see. Interested in anything in particular, or just the history of our charming little town in general?"

"Mostly I want to know things about my own line of work. What kind of police activity went on here then, things like that."

The tip of Mulgrave's nose was darker than the rest of his face. Jud wondered if he was a boozer, and decided he probably was. He was also obviously homosexual, but Jud had always been tolerant of gays—as long as they didn't try to recruit young boys. "We've had a number of people in here asking for books of that kind over the past few days," Mulgrave said. "Quite an upsurge in interest, you might say."

"That so?"

"Yes. Frankly, I think what they really want to know more about is the legend of the headsman. Could that be what you're curious about as well?"

"Could be."

"Horrible tragedy, that poor Dickens girl dying that way."

"Yes, it was."

"I do hope you're able to bring that to a satisfactory conclusion, and soon."

"So do I."

"This business of the headsman. Amazing, isn't it, the way it fires the imaginations of people here?"

"Maybe," Jud said. "But it's also understandable."

"You think somebody decided the legend would make a good *modus operandi?*"

Mulgrave's use of the term exhibited an air of superiority. As if he'd studied a subspecies and learned its language.

"I haven't come to any conclusion. I'm just looking at all the possibilities, anything that could give us a direction to follow."

"I see. Well, I'm afraid you're not going to find much here."

"Why is that?"

"To begin with, there is no history of Braddock per se. I suppose no one ever considered the community important enough to devote a book to it. As far as references to it in broader works are concerned, such as histories of the war between the English and the French, there are a few of those. But what volumes we have are out right now. As I said, there's been a lot of interest. And anyway, as far as I know only one or two of them makes any reference to our famous—or infamous, I should say—headsman, and he's only mentioned in passing."

"And that's it?"

Mulgrave looked pleased with himself. "That's it. But I'll be happy to round up what we have just as soon as I can. I'll let you know."

"What about the museum?"

The expression on the narrow features changed slightly, as if the librarian hadn't expected the question and found it distasteful. "The museum?"

"You're the curator, aren't you?"

"Yes, of course I am. But I don't know if anything on the subject might be there. Also the place is rather untidy at the moment. Last year we were expecting the town to give us funds for renovation and updating, but the money never came through. Unfortunately we'd already started the work, so we just had to suspend everything. As a result, a lot of our materials and exhibits are somewhat disorganized. It's only open a couple of days a week, you know—also due to a lack of funds. And only a part of it is open to the public."

"But you say there might be something there that has to do with the headsman?"

"I said I don't know. Tell you what—I'll drop in some time

in the next day or so and see what I can find for you. Not today, though—I'm much too busy."

Yeah, Jud thought, you look it. "Wouldn't take but a few minutes. Why don't we take a run over there now? My car's right outside."

Mulgrave still hesitated, but then he shrugged. "I suppose we could do that, if it's that urgent."

"It'd save time, as long as I'm here," Jud said. He stood up. "Better wear a coat. It's chilly out."

6

The Braddock Museum was housed in what was believed to be the oldest structure in the area. Its main claim to fame was that General Braddock had lived there the winter before he died. It was on the west side of the village, a three-story sprawl with leaded windows and dark siding and a steeply pitched roof. The architecture of the original section clearly derived from a style brought by the early settlers from England, but it was also obvious that a number of additions had been made to it over the years. The result was a polymorphic hulk with chimneys and gables and cupolas and wings that wandered off in various directions. It was, Jud thought, incredibly ugly.

He parked the cruiser in front of the building and he and Mulgrave walked up the narrow shoveled path to the front entrance. Mulgrave hauled out a heavily laden keyring and fumbled with it until he found a key that unlocked the massive door.

The interior certainly went with the outside, Jud thought. Even when Mulgrave turned on the lights the place seemed dark and gloomy. It also smelled bad. The odor was one of dampness and decay, of stale air and ancient dust. It was cold in here as well, and they kept their coats on. No central heating, Mulgrave explained. Only a few electric units, which didn't do much to relieve the chill. He didn't bother to turn any of them on.

"I don't know if I've ever been in here," Jud said.

"No? Then you must let me give you a little tour." Mulgrave was wearing a trenchcoat festooned with flaps and buckles and straps. He turned the collar up and thrust his hands deep into the pockets. "This is the oldest part, built somewhere around seventeen-twenty. At that time the English were at war with the French, who wanted to claim this territory for themselves, and they also had to contend with Indians. The tribes around here were friendly to them at first, but the English were rather duplicitous. They made promises, but since they were making them to half-naked savages they saw no reason to keep them. So the Indians first came to distrust them and then to hate them. They were always at each other's throats."

"Which tribes, do you know?"

"Onandaga, mostly. But there were Siwanoys in the area as well. Anyway, that's why the walls are so thick. Double-thick, actually, with a layer of stones and dried mud between the wooden outside and inside walls. Quite unusual method of construction at that time. Most colonial homes had no insulation, you see, which is why they were so drafty. But because the British commander lived here for a time it was well fortified, and that also insulated it."

"Couldn't prove it by me," Jud said.

Mulgrave smiled. "Not worth it to try to warm the place up since we'll only be here a short time. On days when it's open we use the heater and several of the fireplaces. Makes it quite cozy. The walls also work well the other way in the summertime. They keep it cool. This is the drawing room we're in now. Some of the furniture is actually original. That chair, for example, and several of the tables."

Jud glanced at his surroundings. The area looked less comfortable than a dentist's waiting room, and not nearly as friendly. The walls had been painted dark green, and a number of portraits hung on them. The men in the pictures wore their hair long, tied behind their necks, and they reminded Jud of hippies he'd seen in the sixties. The furniture was stiff and ungainly and there were only a few small rugs on the old wide-board floors. The most interesting feature of the room was the fireplace, which was a good eight feet across.

Mulgrave led him into another room. "This was the main dining room. The table's original, and it could seat fourteen. There's a smaller dining room off the kitchen, less formal."

"That for the servants?"

"No, that one was used mostly as a breakfast room. The staff ate in the kitchen. Those end chairs you see are called bowbacks, and they're rather rare. To bend the wood that way the cabinet-makers had to soak it in water and then heat it, and the process took quite a while. The kitchen's this way—let me show you."

The fireplace in here was even bigger than the ones in the living and dining rooms. Iron pots were hanging inside it.

"They did all their cooking in here," Mulgrave said. "After the British were gone, the place was run as an inn. Travelers from Pennsylvania or New Jersey and other places occasionally passed through the village on horseback or by coach, and they'd stop over here for a meal and a night's lodging. Sometime in the nineteenth century that fireplace was covered up, boarded over. Then a huge iron woodstove was set right in front of it, with a chimney pipe running into the old flue. When we restored the place we pulled out the stove and sold it to a dealer in Binghamton. It was a shame to lose it, but it wasn't authentic, you see."

"Yeah, I do see." What he also saw was that Mulgrave intended to keep him wandering around in here until his balls froze and he wouldn't be able to think of anything but getting out and going someplace that was warm.

"There's an interesting room over this way," Mulgrave said. "It's less formal than the drawing room, and it's believed the general's wife used it to do crewel and write letters in."

Jud could see his breath in the icy air. "That's fine, Paul, and I appreciate your showing me around, but what I really want to see is anything that had to do with the headsman. I've heard you have some pictures, or drawings, or whatever. Is that true?"

"Pictures? We may have a few things. I'm really not sure. If we did, they'd be in one of the storage rooms. As I told you, we were starting some renovation when the town decided it would be too expensive. So a lot of things are upside down. Might take a long time to find anything."

"That's okay," Jud said. "Let's have a look."

"Yes. Well. If you'll follow me, please."

They went down a hallway to a door leading to a steep staircase barely wide enough to admit a man. They made their way up to the second floor, and Mulgrave stepped along another hallway, stopping before a locked door. He got the keyring out again, and as he was fumbling with the lock it occurred to Jud that it would be easy to get lost in this building. The tiny windows were spaced far apart and set with old-fashioned glass so thick and blurred you could hardly see through them. Combined with the narrow passages and the dim light that made it doubly hard to get your bearings. You could drift from one room to another and not know where the hell you were.

Mulgrave finally got the lock undone and pushed the door open. He touched a wall switch and an electrified sconce cast a pale glow into the gloom. From what Jud could see, the room was filled with haphazardly stacked boxes of various sizes and piles of framed pictures leaning against the walls.

"If there's anything," Mulgrave said, "it might be in here."

Jud inched his way past a stack of boxes. "Great. Let's see what we can find."

"Very well."

It was obvious that Mulgrave was annoyed by the chief's insistence, but at this point Jud didn't give a shit. He was cold and running out of patience with this fatuous asshole. Courtesy was all well and good, but if the guy didn't get it on pretty soon Jud would shake him up. He bent over the pictures in the nearest pile and began pulling them away from the wall one at a time.

All of them were paintings or drawings, no photographs. And all seemed to be quite old. They showed a jumble of subjects, done in media ranging from ink to watercolors. Mostly what they depicted were village scenes: people riding in carriages or strolling on the street, a church, children ice-skating, a woman with a basket of flowers, a pony drawing a cart. There were also still-life renderings of fruit and game and floral arrangements.

But there was nothing remotely like what he was looking for. He went through three of the piles, looking at more pictures of early times than he'd ever hoped to see, while Mulgrave went through still others. But when he finished, all Jud had to show for his efforts were fingers that had become red and stiff from the cold. He looked over at Mulgrave. "This all there is?"

"I'm afraid so. The problem is that nothing is organized properly, as you see. We're going to set up a computerized system, and that'll be a big help. But of course, all those things take time and money. Doesn't do to be discouraged, though. I'm sure the finance committee will come around eventually."

"What's in the boxes?"

"Mostly things that have been donated," Mulgrave said. "Household items, clothing, things of that sort."

"Mind if I look inside some of them?"

"Not a bit. You're welcome to see anything that interests you."

Jud turned to the nearest carton and opened it. Inside was an assortment of junk that somebody most likely had finally gotten around to cleaning out of an attic. They're probably debated whether to consign this stuff to the museum or the town dump and decided on the museum. There were bowls and cups and a couple of cracked plates, some moldy books, a shawl, a rolling pin, a grater, a doll with frizzy yellow hair and one eye missing, other odds and ends.

Mulgrave was watching him. "Lot of history in these boxes. Every one of them tells you a story of a family, often spanning several generations. A lot of it's worthless, of course, but once in a while we come across a gem. Last year we got a wonderful coin collection, really quite valuable. We had a numismatist from New York look at it, and he said it could bring thousands at an auction. Not that we'd ever sell it, of course. But sorting all this out is really a tremendous amount of work."

I'm sure it is, Jud thought. But it'll keep you and whoever else you'll have working on it busy for years. You can fuss and fiddle and screw around and go to meetings of the Braddock Historical Society, and between this and that library you can stay occupied until it's retirement time.

Jud opened another box, finding this one's contents also a jumble. He did come across one curious item, however. It was a slim, cast-iron stand with an object shaped like a human foot on the raised end. He lifted it out of the box. "What's this?"

"A shoemaker's last," Mulgrave said. "The foot comes off, and the shoemaker had a whole set of them he could replace it with, each of a different size. That was in the days when all footwear was made by hand, one shoe at a time. Machines weren't in widespread use until the late nineteenth century."

"Interesting." Jud dropped the last back into the box. "How many other rooms like this are there?"

"About a dozen. Some of them with more things in them than others."

Jud looked at the unopened boxes. All right, he thought. You win, for the time being. "Might be better to come back another day, at that."

Mulgrave pursed his lips. "Very well, if you'd rather. If you'll let me know when you want to come, I'll see the heat's on early, so that the place is a little more comfortable."

"Fine, I'll do that." Jud shoved his hands into the pockets of his jacket and followed Mulgrave as the curator turned off the light and left the room. They retraced their steps down the steep stairway to the first floor and headed for the front hall. As they passed a door Jud asked idly, "What's in there?"

"It was the general's study originally," Mulgrave replied. "We've been working on restoring it." He continued walking as he spoke.

Jud stopped before the door. "Mind if I look inside?"

Mulgrave glanced back. "Sure you want to do that now? I'm getting a bit chilly myself at this point."

"Yeah," Jud said. "It'll just take a minute."

They keys came out again, and more fumbling ensued until the door at last swung opened. Mulgrave stepped back and Jud peered into the room. It was small, with little inside beyond a leather-topped desk and a leather wingchair beside the small corner fireplace. It was even darker in here than in the other rooms, with only one tiny window high in the outside wall. There was a brass lamp on the desk. Jud stepped over to it and turned it on.

Hanging on the wall over the desk was a painting showing a company of foot soldiers led by an officer on a handsome black horse. It occurred to Jud that things hadn't changed all that much over the years. The uniforms were different and horses had been replaced by jeeps, but the dogfaces still marched while the brass traveled sitting down. Of course nowadays there was the mechanized infantry, but when the trucks stopped the soldiers still had to get out and make their way on foot.

He turned away and saw that there was a low bookcase beside the door. Hanging above the bookcase were more paintings. They were a matched set, and there were six of them. Jud realized they were arranged sequentially. He stepped over for a closer look.

The first showed a man down on his knees with arms extended, a soldier on either side holding him by the wrists. Facing the prisoner were several men dressed in fancy uniforms that suggested they were high-ranking officers.

When he looked at the second painting, Jud caught his breath. It showed soldiers dragging the prisoner onto a low wooden platform on which an executioner was standing. The executioner was a tall, burly man dressed from head to toe in tight-fitting black clothing. There were black boots on his feet and black gloves on his hands. His head was covered by a black hood with eyeholes cut on a slant. In his hands was a huge, double-bladed ax. Near his feet, on the floor of the platform, was a block and a basket.

It was eerie, seeing this. For all his scoffing at the legend, and as crazy as he knew his reaction was to the old painting, Jud somehow felt he was face to face with his quarry for the first time. He stared at the ominous figure for a minute or so, taking in details of the man's clothing, his posture on the platform, and especially the ax.

It was apparent how well the weapon had been designed to serve its purpose. Its blades were curved much more than the blade of an ordinary wood-cutter's tool, and together they made the axhead quite large. It would have to measure well over a foot from the edge of one blade to the edge of the other. And the man who wielded it would have to be very powerful. Looking at the ax, Jud wondered if the curve of those blades would match the cut in the floor of Marcy Dickens' bedroom.

He studied the other four paintings in the set, one at a time. The next one showed the prisoner on his knees again, praying this time, as the soldiers and the headsman watched. A crowd of onlookers was visible in the background. In the next, the condemned man was lying on his back with his head on the block, and the executioner was raising the ax. Then came the moment when the blade sliced through its victim's throat, and it was spellbinding to Jud to see the expressions on the faces in the audience—expressions not merely of horror, but also of perverse joy.

The last of the set was equally striking. And perhaps more revealing of the emotions of the principals in this tableau than any of the others. In this one the soldiers were carrying the basket off the platform, the executed man's head visible in it, while his decapitated body lay on the floor, the block drenched with blood from his severed neck. And now the arms of the audience were raised in a salute to the headsman, who was responding with a wave of his hand, as if in triumph.

Jud glanced at all of the paintings once more, feeling a surge of excitement. He suddenly realized Mulgrave was standing behind him. Jud turned to him.

"Sorry," the curator said. "I'd really forgotten all about these. Matter of fact, they probably shouldn't even be displayed."

"Why is that?" Jud had his own ideas, but he was annoyed that Mulgrave had conveniently overlooked their existence. He was curious to know how Mulgrave would explain it.

"For one thing, they're ghastly. They're so—graphic. Quite a horrible portrayal. I certainly don't think a public execution is suitable subject material to be included in a display of the town's heritage. Especially in light of what's happened here recently. I think it might stir up the worst kind of interest. We seem to have enough sensationalism at present."

"I agree with that." Jud gestured toward the pictures. "But how could you just forget about these?"

Mulgrave was standing with his hands pushed deep into the pockets of his trenchcoat. His nose appeared redder than ever, but the cold probably was also contributing to that. "I suppose because I never thought much about their content. They were just a matched set of paintings that made a nice grouping in here. And anyway, I didn't choose them; one of the ladies who works on the restoration committee is in charge of that kind of thing. Also I must remind you that we have several thousand items here in the museum. I really can't keep all of them at the top of my mind, you know."

Jud looked at the pictures once more. It was true that they were of good quality; that was apparent at a glance. They appeared to have been done in a combination of ink and watercolors. As if they'd first been meticulously drawn and then the color had been added later. The action depicted was like what you'd see in a newspaper or magazine if a photographer had covered the event.

He glanced at Mulgrave. "I'd like to borrow these, if that's okay."

The curator seemed startled. "Oh, I don't think we can do anything like that. Even though their content is terrible, I'm sure they're quite valuable. It would be a tragedy if anything ever happened to them."

There'll be a bigger tragedy, Jud thought, if you don't stop dicking around. "What are you telling me, Paul—I can't take them? You gonna force me to get a warrant?"

"Oh no, no—that won't be necessary. I take it you think they could help with your investigation."

"They might, yes."

"Well, then. In that case I'll agree to your taking them. I assume you'll handle them with great care and keep them in a safe place. Also I'll need a receipt."

"Sure. No problem."

"Let me get something to wrap them in. I'll be right back." He left the room.

Just took out a ballpoint and his pocket notebook and scribbled out a receipt. When Mulgrave returned, carrying what looked like an old bedsheet, Jud carefully took each painting down and wrapped the set in the cloth. Carrying the bundle, he followed Mulgrave back to the front door.

The visit to this depressing old dump had been worth the effort after all.

7

The following day Jud was busy with routine departmental work, spending most of the morning catching up on it. He went through the papers on his desk, then talked at length with Joe Grady. The sergeant filled him in on what Inspector Pearson and Corporal Williger had been up to, which consisted mainly of questioning Marcy Dickens' classmates. From what Grady told him, Jud gathered that so far the staties had zilch.

After that he went out for a hamburger, stopping in at the McDonald's on South Main. He took a copy of the *Express* with him and read it as he ate. There was another of Sally's bylined stories in the newspaper, and reading it gave him indigestion worse than anything a Big Mac could produce. The piece contained not one scrap of new information; it was all innuendo and quoted rumor, interspersed with allusions to the headsman legend. Jud stuffed the paper into the garbage receptacle along with the remains of his lunch and left the restaurant.

He'd driven one of the unmarked cars simply because it was handy, and as he was getting back into it he glanced out at the street and saw Loring Campbell drive by in a gray Buick station wagon, headed south.

That was odd. One of the things the industrialist was known for was the flashy cars he owned. His red Porsche was the envy of every kid in Braddock, as well as many adults. The station wagon was probably one of Empex Corporation's company cars. Why was Campbell driving it, and where was he going in the middle of the day? The Empex offices were in the opposite direction, and if he'd wanted to go to the throughway he would have been going east.

All of which probably could have been explained easily, and would have made perfect sense, if Jud had had the answers. Moreover, where Campbell went and what he drove was none of Jud's business.

But Jud was a cop. And he was curious.

He wheeled the Plymouth out onto the street and turned in the direction Campbell had gone.

The Buick was some distance ahead now, moving at a good clip as the street became Old South Road. There wasn't too much traffic to contend with, and Jud had no trouble keeping Campbell in sight. There was one car between him and the station wagon, which made for good tailing. Even if Campbell were to check whether he was being followed, it was extremely unlikely he'd spot Jud. As a further precaution, Jud took off his cap and laid it on the seat beside him.

At the intersection of Route 23 Campbell turned right, which took him in a southwesterly direction. The other car turned the opposite way, leaving no vehicle between the police car and the Buick. After that Jud hung back, letting Campbell run a few hundred yards ahead.

Route 23 was the road leading to Claremont, which was the first town past the county line. As they entered the outskirts the highway became busier, and after a mile or so there were several vehicles between Jud and the station wagon. Along this stretch the roadside was dotted with gas stations, used-car lots and fast-food joints.

It had become more difficult to keep an eye on the Buick, but as he approached the town Jud saw the car turn off the road and pull into a motel. He slowed down as he drove by the place. It was a one-story layout, dingy in its weathered coat of yellow paint. A sign out front said THE MAYFLOWER. He went on by, then made a U-turn and came back.

When he turned into the drive he saw the Buick parked in front of the motel's office. Campbell wasn't in sight; he must have gone inside. Jud pulled into an open slot in front of one of the rooms and shut off his engine. He slumped down in his seat and watched the door of the office.

Minutes passed, and then Campbell emerged and got back into the station wagon. He wheeled it down to one of the rooms at the far end of the motel, parked the car and went into the room.

Jud made himself as comfortable as he could, keeping his eyes on the door Campbell had entered. He knew he'd have a while to wait, but he had a hunch it wouldn't be too long.

A half hour later Jean Harper drove into the entrance. Jud would have recognized her by the car alone; Jaguar sedans were far from common in this part of the world. Moreover, hers was a distinctive metallic green. He watched as the car stopped, giving its driver time to get her bearings. Then the Jaguar turned and moved slowly down to a place close to where the Buick station wagon was parked.

She got out of the car and quickly made her way to the door Campbell had entered. She had on a slouch hat and her coat collar was turned up, but there was no mistaking the swing of the hips and those long, beautifully turned legs. Keeping her head down, she knocked on the door. When it opened she slipped into the room.

Jud sat still for several minutes, mulling over what he'd seen. One thing was apparent: Mrs. Harper's reputation was founded on more than mere gossip. Another was that despite his precautions, Loring Campbell had hung his ass out by a mile. Jud had no way of knowing whether this information would ever turn out to be useful, but instinct told him there was a good chance that it might.

One of the things an experienced cop was never supposed to be was surprised. Yet Jud constantly found himself amazed by the things he stumbled across. And each time something like today's little discovery came to light, he wondered just how much more was going on that he didn't know about. He shook his head. As if Jean Harper and her family didn't have enough trouble.

He'd wait until Campbell and Harper left before he headed back to Braddock. There was one other thing he needed to do.

SEVEN ···

An Execution

1

The V-8 was running rough, and it seemed to be burning oil. It couldn't need rings, Buddy thought—he'd put in new ones only about four thousand miles back. And he'd ground the valves at that time as well. But there was a noticeable drop in power, and instead of showing its usual hard charge the engine just sort of farted along. What the hell could be the problem? It was exasperating.

At the same time, he was secretly pleased that the car needed work. Getting his hands dirty by grubbing around in the engine's innards was therapeutic for him, although he wouldn't have recognized the process by that term. To him the simple fact was that tinkering with the car was one of the few things he could do that could get his mind off Marcy and what had happened to her.

Maybe the only thing.

He pulled the Chevy into the barn and turned on the lights, then closed the sliding door and went about getting the car ready to work on. It was the middle of the evening, and he had plenty of time. He'd raced through his homework after dinner so that he could spend a few hours out here.

First he had to get some heat going. He had two electric heaters in here, and between them they threw out a pretty good blast, but the barn was so big they couldn't do much more than warm up the immediate vicinity. The old structure had been used for carriages originally, with stalls for horses on one side, and there was even some ancient hay still covering the floor of the loft. The ridge beam was a good twenty feet about the floor, and with all this space it was impossible to heat the place. On winter nights you could freeze your nuts off in here.

On the other hand, it was great to have so much room to work in. Nothing like an ordinary cramped garage, where you couldn't turn around without bumping into the wall. In here you had as much space as in any repair shop, and probably more than in most. He moved the heaters in close and turned them on. Then he rolled his tool car over to the car.

Illumination came from an overhead rack of fluorescent bars, which Buddy had rigged so it could be raised or lowered. He brought it down now so that it was about three feet above the front end of the Chevy. There was also a work lamp with a caged bulb that he could place wherever he wanted it.

He removed the hood from the car and set it aside, then attached the work lamp to a radiator support rod. Now came the procedure of working his way into the engine. For somebody with no feel for mechanics the job would have been a bitch, but to Buddy every bit of it was a pleasure. He had his own way of going about it, removing the air filter and the carburetor and laying them out on the bench in a distinct pattern along with the nuts and bolts and washers, all arranged so that he could have put his hands on any of them blindfolded. It was a good system, because it simplified putting the parts back together.

He stopped to light a cigarette, deciding as he did that it was too quiet in here. The only sounds were the wind whispering around the corners of the barn and the occasional rustle of rats' feet off in the shadows. His tape deck was on the workbench. He went to it and shuffled through his cassettes until he located a U-2, popping it into the machine and rolling up the volume.

He'd hung a pair of speakers on vertical posts about ten feet apart, and when the group's bass and drums and guitars blew out their big beat it made the tools and the other junk on the bench rattle and buzz. Which was another thing he liked about working out here; it was far enough away from the house so that he could make all the noise he wanted without his mother screaming at him.

She could be a very large pain in the ass at times, and he'd learned long ago that the only hope he had of getting along with her was in staying out of her way. She didn't approve of his smoking cigarettes—let alone dope—and she didn't like him spending so much time on his car, and she didn't like him drinking beer, and she hated his music.

He thought she'd also had a pretty good idea he'd been screwing Marcy, although she'd never challenged him on it. Maybe that was because she did a little messing around herself and suspected that he knew she did. He'd seen her at dances at the country club, flirting with people, dancing with men in a way that wasn't just being social. And he'd also seen her in unexpected places with some of those same men. Once he'd spotted her in a car with one of them, driving on a country road when she was supposedly out playing bridge, and another time he'd left school early because he'd come down with a stomach virus and just as he arrived home he saw someone pull away from the house. When he walked in she was flustered and he'd known why; guilt was written all over her face.

Nevertheless, most of the time she treated him as if he were a five-year-old who'd pooped in his pants. And he never knew when she might come charging in here, disapproving of whatever he was doing. Which was why sneaking up into the loft with Marcy had been taking a hell of a chance.

It made him sad to think about those times now. Marcy's death had been a terrible shock, by far the worst experience of his life. He'd seen her in nightmares ever since. In one of them she was naked, carrying her head before her in her hands. Her eyes were staring at him and her voice was a hollow rasp as she accused him of deserting her, leaving her alone to die. In another dream her head floated free in roiling clouds, and that time she had no eyes but only raw empty sockets and when she opened her mouth a snake darted out, its tongue flickering, and hissed at him.

In still another he'd watched as the headsman attacked her. Marcy was screaming in fear, her arms upraised to ward off the blow. The blade had slammed into her flesh, but it failed to cut through her neck and the headsman struck her again and again, hacking at her throat as blood erupted from her wounds. Buddy had awakened then, drenched in sweat, and had spent the rest of the night lying in his bed with the lights turned on, reluctant to go back to sleep for fear of experiencing another nightmare.

He let the cigarette dangle from his mouth as he worked, tilting his face to one side to keep the smoke out of his eyes. He removed both heads from the engine, placing them on the bench with care, and then examined the valves. None of them showed wear or excess carbon, but then he would have been surprised if they had. As he went on with his inspection his mind kept returning to Marcy and he tried to force her out of his thoughts but it was impossible. He kept seeing her face, hearing her voice, remembering the times they spent together, the things they'd done.

How could those dipshit cops think he might have been involved in her death? And as crazy as that was, it was only one part of the humiliation he'd been put through. Chief MacElroy had tricked him into admitting he and Marcy had been making it, and that Buddy and his friends smoked grass.

Well, so what, for Christ's sake? So did a lot of other people in high school, no doubt in every town in America. People had sex, and people smoked dope. Pussy Forever. In Pot We Trust. With all the crime that went on in the world, was that such a big deal? Marcy had been murdered, and this jerk was pumped up over whether they'd been in the sack together and whether they sometimes shared a joint. What a crock of shit. Why wasn't the cop out doing what he was supposed to do—tracking down the murderer?

The other guy, Inspector Pearson, had been a lot smoother, but Buddy hadn't had any trouble with him at all. Buddy had just played the part of the innocent shocked kid when the inspector had questioned him, telling him everything he wanted to know, cooperating to the max and revealing nothing. At least, nothing like what MacElroy had got out of him.

It was odd, but he had a distinct impression that the chief and Pearson were like oil and water. In fact, it seemed as if they didn't even talk to each other. He wondered why. Was it because one was a local cop and the other was state? Were they jealous of each other? Maybe they were both nuts.

He also wondered if the chief had revealed the substance of their talk to Buddy's father. MacElroy had assured him that anything Buddy said would remain confidential, but he knew better than to buy that kind of crap. That was what adults always told you when they wanted to screw you over, whether it was Mr. Baxter, the dearly beloved fuckhead principal of Braddock High, or a cop, or anybody else.

The trouble was, if Chief MacElroy revealed their talk to Buddy's old man it would go straight to his mother, and that would be something to worry about. Her first reaction would be to blow her cork, and then after that to think up ways to make his life miserable. She'd tell him he couldn't go out, couldn't drive his car, couldn't talk on the phone, couldn't see his friends, couldn't do any goddamned thing. She was an expert on what Buddy couldn't do. And learning that Braddock's chief of police had pried an admission out of him concerning his sexual and pot-smoking habits would be all she'd need.

She'd known the chief had questioned him, of course. After all, Buddy had been with Marcy that night, had been one of the last people to see her alive. In fact, his mother had actually shown some sympathy toward him, which certainly had been out of character for her. But if she ever found out what he'd admitted to MacElroy they'd have to scrape her off the ceiling.

So the chances were the chief had kept his word—for the time being, anyway. If he hadn't, Buddy would have heard about it by now. There was no way his father could have kept it to himself if he'd learned about it; Buddy's mother had the poor bastard trained so that he was afraid to take a leak without her okay. The old man was so pussy-whipped it was pitiful. If Buddy ever got married he'd be damned sure it would never happen to him—you could bet on that.

When he finished going over the valves, he took another look at the open block, and there, by God, was the problem. The head gasket on the right bank of cylinders was blown. No wonder the engine had been running like shit. He stamped out his cigarette and worked the gasket loose with a screwdriver. He grinned to himself, feeling a small sense of triumph at having located the trouble.

The tape ended, and the sudden silence was startling. The wind had become stronger, and it was causing some of the old boards and beams in the barn to creak. He wanted to put something else on; music was good company. But he was too busy at the moment, lifting the blown gasket off the studs. His fingers were cold, which wasn't helping any, and he couldn't get a decent grip on the greasy metal.

As he fumbled with it he heard a different noise, one he couldn't identify. He stopped for a moment to listen, and a few seconds later he heard it again.

It was the sound of a heavy foot stepping on one of the floorboards.

He turned, staring out from the cone of light that shone down on the front end of the car, but all he saw were shadows.

2

The headsman stood in one of the old stalls, every nerve attuned to his surroundings. There had been no animals housed in here for many years, and yet his nose detected the faint scent of horses. He smelled other things as well: rodent droppings, hay, rotting wood, the nests of barn swallows, rust on metal hinges. Good smells.

In contrast, the odors emanating from where the boy worked were an abomination, a blend of oil and carbon and gasoline that stung his nostrils like a swarm of nettlesome insects. But far worse than the smell was the insult to his ears—the raucous shrieking that poured from the boxes hanging on the posts. Voices sang childish, monotonous phrases, set to a frenzied rhythm that repeated itself over and over.

He raised the ax, taking pleasure in the feel of its smooth hickory haft, in the weight of its gleaming head and its superb balance. His breath came quicker, and his mouth grew dry from excitement. He slipped out of the stall and stepped slowly toward the boy who was bending over the front end of the car.

As he did, the cacophony from the speakers suddenly stopped. It left behind a void of silence, disturbed only by the wind. The headsman took another step, and then another. A board creaked underfoot, and the boy looked up, staring in the headsman's direction. The man in black stood still, knowing the youth's gaze could not penetrate the shadows. He waited for a time as the boy squinted and finally got up from the car's fender and wiped his hands with a rag.

Uncertainly, still peering out into the darkness, the youth made his way to the bench. He had a habit of tossing his head to get his long brown hair out of his eyes, and he did it now as he put the rag down and groped among the objects on the bench. When he found what he wanted he went to the tape machine and a moment later a new torrent of sound issued from the speakers.

The headsman watched, giving the boy time to settle down, to resume his work. Minutes passed, as the youth once more draped himself over the fender of the car. He was slender, the type who wouldn't mature physically for several more years. Not like some of his more athletic friends, who had already grown into robust manhood. His legs were long but thin, and his rump barely filled his faded jeans. Only his hands were man-sized. They were wide and meaty, with long fingers, and they dangled from his wrists like hooks.

It was surprising that such hands could be so deft. And it was unfortunate that this stupid little shit had wasted their potential. He might have become an engineer, or even a surgeon, with hands like those.

The boy was again deeply absorbed with the metal guts of his vehicle. A cigarette was hanging from his lips, and every so often he tossed his head and exhaled a cloud of blue smoke as he worked.

The headsman approached within a few feet of the car and paused, standing just outside the shaft of light. He was balanced on the soles of his feet, aware of the great strength in the muscles of his shoulders and his arms and his back. Behind him the roar from the speakers hammered against his body like a storm, but he ignored it.

As he watched the boy, the headsman planned his moves. It wasn't enough for a sinner merely to be beheaded. The experience of death would then consist only of the brief shock as the steel severed the neck. Pain would be so short-lived, so closely followed by unconsciousness, as to be almost a non-experience.

Instead it was much better for the guilty one to see death approaching, to imagine how it would feel at that moment when the instrument cut through flesh and nerves and bone, separating not only the head from the shoulders, but the living from the dead. That was why in France, in the old days, a person to be executed by the guillotine was often placed on the block face up, so the blade could be seen falling. It was said that to the subject, the huge knife seemed to take a very long time to travel downward, and that it was impossible not to watch its hideous descent.

It was for this same reason that the headsman's clients were forced to receive the blade while lying on their backs. It gave them an opportunity to *anticipate*.

He moved closer, holding the ax in his left hand and raising it so that the blades were at eye level. He leaned forward and with his right hand seized the young man's shoulder.

It was as if the boy had been jabbed with a firebrand. He jumped, twisting his head to see who had assailed him. His eyes were wide, and when they caught sight of the hooded figure they bulged in shock and fright. He struggled, but the headsman clamped him in a powerful grip, splaying him across the fender of the car. The boy was holding a wrench, and he writhed and bucked in an effort to bring it around so that he could strike the man in black.

His struggles were like those of a rat caught in a trap. The headsman tightened his grip, his thick, gloved fingers biting into the thin shoulder until the youth's mouth opened and a cry of pain sounded over the hellish music.

At that point the boy managed to turn onto his back, so that he was facing his attacker. He swung the wrench, but the headsman blocked the blow by moving the ax a few inches to the left, the tool clanging as it bounced off the steel blade and fell to the floor. The headsman slammed the boy back down onto the fender and drove a massive knee into his groin.

He heard a groan, saw the youth's eyes fill with tears of agony. The slender boy grew limp, and resistance flowed out of him like grain from a leaking sack. Shifting his grip to his victim's jaw, the headsman drew the youth away from the car and threw him to the floor.

For an instant it seemed as if he might somehow find the strength to regain his feet. He groaned again and tried to stand up. But the headsman sent a heavy boot crashing into his belly. The boy collapsed face down and lay sobbing for breath.

The headsman moved very deliberately. With the tip of his boot he rolled the youth over onto his back. He looked down at him, seeing the terror in his eyes, the expression of horror on his face. The boy's mouth was wide open, but no sound came out of it. He continued to clutch his gut as he stared upward, lips drawn back from his teeth.

The headsman stomped down on the boy's chest, paralyzing him. Then he rotated the axhead slowly, so that the youth could see the twin blades. He raised the instrument high in the air, holding it there for several seconds, as the boy's lips formed the word *no*.

The aiming point was the larynx. The bulge it made in the slender throat provided a perfect target. Not only would it guide the blade to a point midway between jaw and thorax, but striking it would ensure a clean cut between the vertebrae. His muscles tensed, and he raised himself up onto his toes.

With great force he swung the ax.

3

Karen sat in the bath for a long time, replenishing the hot water and feeling her muscles slowly relax. She still had a slight headache, but that was nothing new; she'd had one in varying degrees of intensity for days. And no wonder. The tension lately had been damn near unbearable.

There'd been the strain of the Mariski experience, and that had left her feeling as if somebody had used her as a football. Getting up the courage to go to that family and tell them what she knew had happened to their son had been so difficult she still didn't know how she'd done it. And as bad as it would have been under any circumstances, their reaction had made it much worse.

Mrs. Mariski had eyed her as if she were a freak—a creature compelled to tell lies. And her husband was at first suspicious and then disgusted, implying that Karen was out looking for a thrill, trying to involve herself in somebody's misery purely for the sensation. Or that she just wanted to be part of the excitement. He hadn't said it in those words, but that was what he'd seemed to think.

And then when she stood with him at the edge of the pond that morning, when she looked at the stone wall and the old barn and knew without any doubt about the awful bloated dead thing under the coating of snow and ice, he'd been so *angry*. As if it couldn't be true—but if by some crazy fluke it was, then it had to be her fault.

After that had come the meeting with the chief of police. He'd seemed like a nice enough guy, but his probing had frightened and intimidated her. He'd tried to cover his feelings, but Karen had sensed that he too thought she was some kind of freak. All of it had been hideous, and she hoped fervently she'd never be faced with a situation like it again.

But wouldn't she be? She'd had those terrible sightings of the man with the ax, and in a way that had been even worse. Still, she could rationalize that was different; they were just nightmares caused by awareness of the murder of that poor girl. Everybody was talking about how she'd been decapitated with an ax, and about the legend of the headsman. Those idiot salesmen at Boggs Ford had even made jokes about it. There had been news stories on TV and in all the papers, many of them going on about how this kind of thing had been happening in Braddock off and on for over two hundred years. So if Karen had been having nightmares after hearing and seeing so much of it, that was only to be expected.

Except for one thing.

She had seen the man with the ax *before* the girl's mutilated body was discovered.

As much as she tried to push it away, the truth sat there in the deepest corner of her mind, laughing at her like some evil troll who enjoyed torturing her. *Damn* it, why couldn't this power she had leave her alone? Why had she been singled out, as if she'd been given a special talent other people didn't have? A talent that instead of being something she could develop and be proud of, like a great voice or a gift for dancing, was hurtful and mean, showing her events she didn't want to see—events that were dark and horrible?

The thing had followed her all her life. When she was a small

child, she saw her kindergarten teacher, Miss Eggert, driving
her car at night on a country road. There was a horrendous
crash, with torn metal and smoke and blood running, and Karen
had screamed and screamed and even after her mother had
taken her into her parents' bed and let her spend the rest of the
night there, she had lain awake until dawn, listening to her
father snore, afraid to go back to sleep. And then in the morning
when her mother took her to the kindergarten class in the annex
of Hill Street School, there had been the shocking news that
confirmed exactly what she'd seen in her vision.

Most of the time the images weren't that clear. She would
see only fragments, bits of action or parts of objects, often
seemingly unconnected to actual events in her life. And there
had been periods when she'd gone for months or even years
without seeing anything. Even when important events took
place, milestones in her life. When her father left them, for
instance, when he just sort of slipped away one balmy summer
evening, leaving them with no money and no apparent way of
supporting themselves, she had neither sensed nor seen a thing.

And then during the years when she was growing up, the
hard years when her mother worked as an office clerk in
Shippensburg, the images had returned. Usually they were just
brief snippets or hazy impressions. But there had been another
kind of vision as well.

She was sixteen when the Collier boy had noticed her. He
was a year older, a senior in the high school they attended, and
by Karen's standards he was rich. He drove a red BMW his
father had given him, and his family lived in a stone and
clapboard house that looked just like one Karen had seen on the
cover of a magazine. His first name was Danny, and every girl
Karen knew wanted him for a boyfriend.

He'd asked her to go to the movies with him and she was
thrilled. She wore her new blue sweater that was a little on the
tight side, which pleased her because it showed off her newly
developed breasts and she was proud of them.

After the movie they drove out to a back road and parked,
and Karen let him kiss her and touch her in the first real
necking experience she'd ever had. He tried to go further but
she stopped him—that time. The following week when his

parents were out for the evening Karen went up to his room
with him and they spent two wildly exciting, blissful hours in
bed. She was in love then—blindly, madly in love. It made no
sense whatever, she was just a teenager, but if Danny had asked
her to marry him she would have done it. She'd never felt
anything like this; it was achingly wonderful.

Two days later she saw the images in her mind, as sharply
defined as in a color photograph. She saw Danny naked, and he
was with an older woman, a beautiful woman with dark eyes
and dark hair, and she was masturbating him.

Karen was shocked and then angry with herself. The vision
wasn't true this time. It wasn't real—it had nothing to do with
reality. She'd made it up, imagined it, and in doing so she'd
stained Danny. She'd made him dirty, and it was unfair of her
and she was ashamed. She promised herself she'd never again
permit such a filthy lie to enter her mind.

That Friday afternoon after school Danny drove her over to
his house for Cokes and to listen to records and he introduced
her to his mother. Karen had never met Mrs. Collier before but
she recognized her the instant she saw her. She was the
beautiful woman in Karen's vision. After that day Karen never
spoke to Danny again.

Eventually the vision had led to her leaving Shippensburg.
She hadn't been able to afford to go away to college but instead
had attended Shippensburg University as a day student. Which
wasn't so bad, but wasn't so good, either. Her mother tried to
make it as pleasant as possible for her, encouraging her to
invite friends to their shabby little apartment, but it was nothing
like the college life she'd always hoped she'd have.

The vision was with her off and on during those years as
well. Usually it was just a flash or an impression, but sometimes it was much more than that, and seeing the images took
its toll. She became moody and withdrawn, often hating
herself. Her friends drifted away, and even boys who were
hungry for the girl with the chestnut hair and the big jugs and
the great legs were put off when they found her glum and bitter
much of the time.

So when her mother died of lung cancer just after Karen
finished college, she had no reason to stay in Shippensburg.

She came to Braddock to live with her widowed grandmother
until she could afford a place of her own, hoping she could
make a fresh start among people who didn't know her,
believing a change of scene might even put an end to the
visions. But she learned soon enough that the one thing she
couldn't run away from was herself.

Tonight she felt she could stay in the bath for hours more,
luxuriating in the hot water and the suds, but it was already past
nine o'clock and there was a movie on TV she wanted to see.
Reluctantly she stepped out of the tub and toweled herself
down, shivering a little as the cool air touched her skin. She
went into her room and put on pajamas and a robe and slippers
and then went downstairs to the living room.

The house was small and simple but adequate for the two
women. In fact, compared to what Karen had grown up in, it
was opulent. Her grandmother apparently had already gone to
bed, which was unusual, because the old lady liked to stay up
late. Karen turned on the TV and tuned it to the channel
carrying the movie.

It was a Clint Eastwood picture, one of his Dirty Harry
stories, and it had just started. She liked Eastwood. He'd been
so handsome when he was young, and now that he was older he
didn't try to hide the lines in his face or his receding hairline
and she admired him for it. In a way middle age made him
seem all the more masculine. She wished she knew a man like
him—someone strong and dependable and uncomplicated, who
would be tender and understanding toward her.

Instead of the jerks she did know. Her romance with Ted had
definitely cooled—she was sure of it. Even though they'd
gotten along well enough at first, sharing many likes and
dislikes, enjoying each other's company, the relationship eventually had gone the way of all the others. She'd become tense
and irritable, often experiencing the headaches and the mood
swings that had plagued her for so long until he'd backed off.
Even the sex they'd enjoyed had become more of a routine than
a pleasure. She was sure now that she'd never hear from him
again.

A commercial came on—some dopey thing about how eating
Nabisco crackers would fill your life with love—and Karen

went out to the kitchen to get herself a glass of milk. Her weight was okay but it was too easy for her to put on pounds; she had to watch it.

She put the milk carton back into the fridge and as she did a sensation passed through her head. It wasn't painful exactly—not one of the smashing headaches she sometimes experienced—but more like a faint electric shock. She'd had them before, God knew, and she sensed what would happen next. She stood by the counter and closed her eyes, touching her temples with the tips of her fingers.

It was the man with the ax.

She saw him as clearly as if he'd been standing in front of her. He looked just the way he had the other times, monstrous in that black hood with the slanted eyes, and he was holding the ax in both hands. There was music, too—hard rock—and it was thunderously loud.

In a series of flashing images she saw him struggling with someone. There were bursts of light, and the fighting was violent. A young man with long brown hair strained and twisted in the headsman's grip. Metal glinted as the young man swung a tool of some kind at his assailant.

The headsman slammed the boy to the floor and as he did Karen caught a glimpse of what looked like the front end of a car. Then the images speeded up and the action was herky-jerky, as in an old-time movie. The headsman raised the ax and the boy's eyes were wide with terror and his mouth formed *No!*

The ax struck, and all Karen saw after that was blood. Torrents of brilliant red, splashing blood.

And then nothing.

She put her hand out to the counter to steady herself and as she did she knocked over the glass of milk.

Shit.

For a minute or so she couldn't move to clean it up or even set the glass upright. Her head hurt and she felt faint. She closed her eyes again and opened them. Her stomach was turning over, and she thought she might fall.

All of it—the terrible burden of knowing what she'd witnessed—came down on her like some huge weight. There were times in her life when Karen wanted to die, and this was one of them.

She forced herself to move, to get out a sponge and paper towels. Then she set about cleaning up the mess.

EighT ....
The Suspect

1

Jud arrived at police headquarters earlier than usual; it was only a few minutes past eight when he parked the cruiser in the town hall lot and went inside the building. He said good morning to Grady and the cop who'd just come off the midnight tour, and got himself a mug of coffee. Then he entered his office and hung up his cap and jacket before sitting down at his desk and going through the copies of the previous night's reports.

A guy in a pickup truck had hooked another driver's bumper in front of the Sears store on Main Street, and instead of simply exchanging insurance information these two characters had punched each other around. The investigating officer had issued summonses to both of them. It was funny, the way minor vehicle damage could get people so riled up they'd try to commit mayhem. Maybe it recalled primitive instincts, the kind of thing cowboys felt about their horses.

Whatever it was, people seemed to take on a whole new dimension of aggressiveness when they got behind a wheel. Put a guy in a driver's seat and he was ready to do battle if anybody as much as brushed him or even crossed his path.

There had also been one domestic squabble, but that wasn't much either: a guy who worked at Squam's Dairy came home drunk and found his wife had locked him out. He broke a window to get in and she called the cops. By the time a patrol car arrived the guy had passed out. The whole thing was resolved when the cop helped the drunk's old lady roll him into bed.

187

An altercation on Weaver Street had been more serious. Two young men had cut each other with knives in an argument over an issue that was unclear. The cops hauled both of them to the emergency room for a patch-up and then brought them in and booked them. They'd spent the night in separate cells.

That one caused Jud concern. Weaver Street was in the town's black neighborhood, and there had been reports lately of an increase in crack use. He'd look into it; if there was anything he didn't want boiling up in Braddock it was a crack problem.

Pot he could live with. There was no way it could really be controlled anyway—the stuff was cheap and available anywhere. And while smoking it no longer had the cachet it once had, when if you blew grass you were making some kind of political statement, using it was still considered hip by a lot of kids.

Coke was even less of a worry, chiefly because it was so much more expensive. Some of the more well-to-do young people in town could afford a toot now and then, but by and large its use wasn't all that common. As long as it stayed small-time and nobody got into trouble over it, Jud would leave it alone.

Of course, this kind of hard-headed acceptance was an attitude the cops kept to themselves. As far as the town was concerned, they were battling drugs tooth and nail, but as with any smalltown police force, that was so much bullshit. If they really tried to run down everybody who bought, used or sold an illegal substance, they'd never have time for anything else.

Crack, on the other hand, was another thing entirely. For only a few bucks you could buy a high that would take you over the moon, and while you were on it anything was possible. The national crime statistics showed skyrocketing increases in crack traffic and homicide, with a direct link between the two. The mere thought of a crack epidemic could cause Jud to break out in a cold sweat. And right on the heels of crack was this new thing from the West Coast, something called ice. Where the hell was it all leading to? And did he really want to know?

He initialed the reports and busied himself with paperwork. He'd pay the night fighters a visit later.

Grady came in after he'd been at it awhile. Jud pushed back

from his desk and told the sergeant to sit down. "How's it going, Joe?"

The big man slumped into a chair. "Not great. This guy Pearson is a ballbuster."

"Don't I know it."

"Him and the corporal, Williger, been driving us nuts. They got Kramer and Delury working for them, which makes us shorthanded, and they keep asking for more help. That's on top of their own guys."

"I'll talk to Pearson."

"Yeah. If you ask me, all they're doing is spinning their wheels. They been interviewing everybody who knew the Dickens kid, but they haven't come up with shit. Not one real lead."

"How do you know that?"

"Delury told me. They're just running all over telling the world how hard they work. Every time you turn around, Pearson's talking to the papers or the TV. You'd think the guy was running for office."

"Maybe he is."

Grady's mouth curled in an expression of disgust.

Jud gestured at the report on his desk. "These two guys who were carving each other up. Were they on crack?"

The sergeant shrugged. "Hard to say for sure, but I think so. One of them's been in a couple of times before. Stolen car, suspect in a convenience store burglary, shit like that."

"Okay, I remember now. I thought one of the names sounded familiar. You talk to them?"

"Yeah. It was an accident, they say. Like switchblades are for cleaning your nails."

"Let's stay after it. Maybe we can get something out of them. I sure don't want a crack blowup around here. We got enough to deal with."

"All right, will do."

Jud twiddled with a pen on his desk. It was strange, but he never felt completely at ease with Grady. The resentment over Jud's promotion was obviously still there. And in some ways it seemed as if it might be more than that. On the surface, Grady came off as just a big, stolid, hardworking cop who'd been on the job his entire life. He was streetwise and cynical, and like most police officers he was suspicious of anybody who came into his purview.

Grady had also caught enough crap from the town government over the years to be able to handle it; obviously he'd learned long ago that when the punches came your way you rolled with them. Jud depended on him and made it clear that the sergeant was his number-one man. He made it a point to defer to the older cop whenever he could and to treat him with respect. Yet the attitude was always there, so palpable Jud could feel it.

Grady stood up. "Anything else?"

"No, Joe. That's it for now."

There was a knock at the door and Bob Brusson stuck his head into the office. "Excuse me, Chief. We just got a call from Peter Harper. He says his son is missing."

"Buddy?"

"Right."

Christ. Jud looked at Grady, whose face was impassive, and then back at the young officer in the doorway. "What did he tell you?"

"He said the kid wasn't in the house this morning. His car was in the barn but he wasn't in his room. Harper wants you to call him."

"Okay, thanks." He reached for the phone.

Peter Harper answered on the first ring. The strain in his voice was apparent. "Chief, I think you'd better get over here right away. Buddy's gone."

Jud felt a tightening in his chest. "You sure?"

"Yeah, I am. His mother and I are worried sick something's happened to him. It's just not like him to take off someplace without saying a word to us. His car's here, too. And that's even more odd. If he was going to go someplace, you can bet he'd use his car."

"Okay, I'll be there right away. I know you're upset, but try to think about anything Buddy might have said or planned to do that might give you an idea where he is. Could be a simple explanation after all." He hung up.

Grady raised his eyebrows but said nothing.

Jud got up from his desk. "I'm going over to the Harpers'. Anybody's looking for me, give me a call." He reached for his jacket and cap and put them on.

"What about Pearson?"

Jud stopped in the doorway and looked back. "Yeah, I better let him know."

He went down the hall to the office he'd turned over to the two state police detectives, but neither of them was there. Jud told Stanis where he was going and said to let Pearson or Williger know what had happened.

"You want me to try to run 'em down?" the cop asked.

"Sure," Jud said. "Do that."

He hurried out the back door of the building and climbed into the cruiser. When he pulled out of the driveway his wheels kicked up gravel.

2

The Harper home was near the Nepawa River, a two-story gray colonial that Buddy's great-grandfather had built for his growing family. That was years before the opening of the drugstore; the old man had started a company to produce chemical fertilizer when that industry was in its infancy. When he died his son sold the company and opened Harper's Drug on Main Street, thereby blowing a great opportunity. But the son had lived comfortably enough, and had passed the store on to Peter, Buddy's father. Peter Harper had built it into a thriving business, more of a department store than a pharmacy.

There was an old-fashioned portico on one side of the house, and the drive went on out to a garage and beyond that was a barn. Jud parked in the drive and walked up to the front entrance. He knocked on the door and Peter Harper opened it.

Harper was close to fifty, Jud would guess, but his thinning hair made him look older. He'd earned a reputation as one of Braddock's better amateur golfers, and his name often appeared in the sports pages of the *Express*. He was almost always listed as a low-scorer in tournaments at the country club. He took Jud's jacket and cap and hung them in the front hall closet, then led him into the living room.

Jean Harper was waiting for them, and as always when he saw her Jud was struck by this woman's appearance. She seemed at least ten years younger than her husband. Her tawny hair hung to her shoulders in soft waves, and her green wool dress showed off the trim lines of her body. He couldn't help wondering what she'd say if he told her about the last time he'd seen her.

They sat facing each other, with Mrs. Harper nervously twisting a Kleenex in her fingers. Harper explained that when they'd called Buddy that morning there had been no response, which wasn't unusual—they practically had to blast him out of bed on school days. But this morning Harper had finally gone into his room and found the bed hadn't been slept in. Then he went out to the barn and saw his son's car sitting there with the engine opened up, where he'd obviously been working on it. But no sign of Buddy.

Harper clasped his hands in front of him. "That's when I really began to worry. If Buddy was going anywhere, you could be sure he'd drive his car. That Chevy means the world to him."

Jud nodded. "I asked you to try to think of anything he might have said or anything he might have been doing lately that would have some bearing on this."

Harper shook his head. "No, there's nothing I could think of that would explain it."

"Have you tried his friends?"

"I did," Jean Harper said. "I called several of the kids he runs around with, but nobody's heard a word from him. They sounded as surprised as we were."

"Did he take anything from his room, or the house? Like a suitcase, or extra clothes, or anything that could suggest he expected to be gone for awhile?"

"We thought of that," Peter replied. "But there doesn't seem to be anything missing. In fact, there was even some money he'd left on his dresser. It was just a few dollars, but you'd think if he planned to go anywhere he would have taken money with him, right?"

"Yeah," Jud said. "You'd think so. Tell me, how's he been

acting since Marcy's death? When I talked to him he was still in shock, of course. But since then?"

"He seemed numb for the first couple of days," Jean said. "Sort of pulled himself into a shell. Lately he's been better, though. At least I thought so. Didn't you, Peter?"

"I don't know. Or I guess so. Lots of times it's hard to tell what's going on in a kid's head."

"Beyond that, you notice anything unusual about the way he was acting, either of you?"

Peter shook his head, but his wife said, "Can this be between us? I'm worried about him, but I don't want anything I might say to lead to further trouble.

Jud could guess what she was getting at. "Of course. What is it?"

"Lately I have noticed something. In fact, I found it."

Both men looked at her quizzically.

"The other day I went into his room, and I decided to take some of his things out and put them in the laundry. He forgets now and then, and his clothes can get a little ripe. Anyway, what I stumbled across was his stash. He had a pretty good load of marijuana in a plastic sack. I knew what it was, or course. When I was in college everybody smoked it. I know a lot of kids do today, but I couldn't help wondering if maybe Buddy hadn't gone overboard. I left it there, and I didn't say anything to him. It wasn't the first time I'd come across something that suggested he was smoking it, but I was surprised at how much he had. So it was a problem I was trying to figure out how to deal with, and now I wonder if it could have something to do with his going off. Or whatever he's done."

"Jesus," Peter said. "I didn't know anything about that. You never told me—"

She cut him off. "I know I didn't. There are some things I handle better than you do, Peter."

Jud had a feeling she would have said more on that subject if he hadn't been there that morning to referee a squabble. "What did you do with it?" he asked her. "The marijuana?"

"I left it where I found it. Next time I looked, it was gone."

"Generally speaking, how do you get along with him?"

An ironic smile lifted one corner of her mouth. "Generally speaking, I don't. Peter leaves the responsibility for disciplining him to me, unfortunately. As a result I'm often not very popular."

They were on the verge of getting into it, Jud saw. Again he tried to steer the discussion in another direction. "You said he was working on his car last night?"

"It seemed so to me," Peter said. "I got home a little late, and when I put my car in the garage I looked out and saw lights on in the barn. He was often there in the evenings, so I didn't think anything of it."

"Were the lights on when you went out there this morning?"

Peter looked at the ceiling, then at Jud. "Come to think of it, yes. I remember turning them out as we left to call you, but when we got there they were on."

"I'd like to have a look," Jud said.

"Yes, of course."

They put on jackets and went out the back door, Peter leading the way, his wife following.

Jud brought up the rear. Walking behind Jean Harper he was again strongly aware of her physical presence. The long legs and the way she had of swinging her hips made it hard not to be. Studying her, he decided that taken individually her features weren't all that beautiful, but somehow the way she put everything together made her very exciting.

He'd heard the stories about her from time to time, but until he'd seen her slipping into Loring Campbell's room at the Mayflower Motel he hadn't paid much attention. He hadn't known whether the innuendoes were based on fact or jealousy. There weren't many housewives in Braddock who looked that good.

When they got to the barn the Harpers stood aside and let Jud enter first. One glance at the Chevy told him Buddy had indeed been working on it. The hood had been removed and the engine opened up. Both heads were lying on the bench, along with the air filter and the carburetor and other parts. A worklamp with a long cord was hooked into place in the engine compartment. He was about to step closer when he noticed the oil.

There was a large pool of it on the floor beside the vehicle.

Or at least there had been. Much of it had soaked into the
floorboards, but a viscous residue remained. It reminded Jud of
the blood he'd seen on the floor of Marcy Dickens' bedroom
and the living room of Art Ballard's house.

It was odd, but the mess seemed out of place here. The rest
of the area was reasonably clean and the workbench was well
organized. Tools were hanging in neat rows on a pegboard, and
the engine parts on the bench had been laid out in a pattern. An
open toolbox on a cart held a set of socket wrenches. Buddy
was obviously the kind of mechanic who liked to keep his tools
and his work in order. So why the oil, and where had it come
from?

He spotted a can lying on the floor, on the far side of the
workbench. It was a five-gallon container of the kind that
mechanics used to catch drain oil. This one was on its side, and
it was empty. Jud stepped over to it and nudged it with his toe.
There had been oil in it recently; some of the stuff was still
coating the inside, and a drop hung from the lip of the can. It
appeared that someone had knocked the can over, spilling its
contents. But if that was what had happened, why was the can
lying over here, several feet away? A better explanation would
be that someone had poured oil on the floor, either deliberately
or by accident, and then had tossed the can aside.

Why?

He walked around the Chevy, opening the doors and peering
inside, seeing nothing worth noting. When he came back to
where he'd been standing earlier, he noticed a wrench lying
under the front end of the car, as if it had been dropped there.

The Harpers had stood quietly by while Jud inspected the
area. He turned to them. "Did Buddy always work alone, or did
he sometimes have a friend over to help him?"

"No, he did all the work himself," Peter said.

"He wouldn't let anyone else touch that car," his wife added.

Before Jud could probe further, the sound of tires on the
driveway reached them from the direction of the house. They
looked up to see an unmarked state police Ford come to a stop
behind Jud's car. Inspector Pearson and Corporal Williger got
out. The pair came up the drive toward the barn and Jud and the
Harpers stepped forward to meet them.

"You must be Mr. and Mrs. Harper," Pearson said.

They acknowledged that they were.

"I'm Inspector Chester Pearson, New York State Police. I'm heading the investigation of the Dickens homicide. I understand your son is missing."

"That's right," Peter said. "We were just telling Chief MacElroy that he was out here in the barn last night, working on his car. But this morning he was gone."

Pearson sometimes had a flat way of speaking that Jud suspected was an affectation. "I interviewed your son after the Dickens girl was killed," the inspector said. "You know that, of course."

"He told us," Jean Harper said.

"Do either of you have any idea," Pearson asked, "where he might have gone, or why he left?"

They said they had none.

"I'm sure you realize," Pearson went on, "he could be in a lot of trouble if he's run off someplace. I told him at the very least he could be a material witness in the Dickens homicide."

Peter Harper cocked his head. "What do you mean, 'at the very least?'"

"I mean he was very close to her and one of the last people to see her alive. He was with her just before she was killed. The fact is, your son could also be a suspect."

Jean Harper flushed. "That's ridiculous. Buddy thought the world of Marcy. He was just shattered when she died. The last thing he'd ever have done would be to hurt her."

"That could be," Pearson said. "But if he had a clear conscience, why did he take off?"

Her voice rose in anger. "Take off? What makes you think that's what happened? Our son is *missing*, Inspector. If he wanted to take off, he would have driven his car. Which, as you can see, is right there in the barn."

Pearson glanced at the Chevy. "Yeah, and out of commission. What other vehicles do you have?"

"A Jaguar and a Ford station wagon," Peter Harper told him. "They're both in the garage."

Pearson turned to the corporal. "Will, go out to the car and call Braddock headquarters. Tell 'em to get out an APB with the kid's description. Have 'em contact the Lincoln barracks, too. We'll want to get it into NYSPIN. I'll call Lincoln myself as soon as I get back."

"Yes sir." Williger trotted back up the driveway toward the Ford.

"I think we ought to go in the house and talk," Pearson said to the Harpers. "There's a lot I want to go over with you."

Jud noted the inspector had tacitly cut him out of the discussion. Which was okay with him. Pearson was in charge, and besides, listening to him work Buddy's parents over was an experience Jud would just as soon skip. He told the Harpers the police would do everything possible to locate Buddy. Then he walked back to his car and drove as quickly as he could to headquarters.

3

When he got to the stationhouse, Jud gave Grady a quick recap of what had gone on at the Harper home and then went into his office, where a number of messages were waiting for him.

A reporter from one of the Albany papers had telephoned, requesting an interview. The mayor had called; Jud was to call him back. An attorney had called to register a complaint about the way his client had been treated by the Braddock police.

What client? Jud wondered. Ah, one of the duelists who'd spent the night in the can. Apparently he'd given the cops some shit and they'd slapped him around a little.

And Sally had phoned. That one he'd save until last; it would be the only pleasant one of the bunch.

But before returning any of the calls, he wanted to think for a few minutes. He got out a pad and doodled on it. The way he saw it, there were two possibilities. One was that Buddy Harper had run off, as Pearson seemed to think he had. That would sure as hell make the kid the prime suspect Pearson wanted to think he was. The other possibility was that something had happened to him. But what—an accident? Or worse? Jud decided to consider the runaway theory first.

Suppose Buddy had actually murdered his girlfriend. In the annals of crime there was nothing unusual about that scenario.

Lovers had been killing each other forever. Especially males killing females. The Chambers case came to mind, as well as the one involving that asshole on Long Island who'd strangled the girl and claimed it had happened during rough sex, copying Chambers' defense. So that kind of homicide was possible here, too. And if Buddy had panicked and fled, it was obvious that he was guilty and running away.

Except that with Buddy it was hard to come up with a motive that made sense. Marcy hadn't been pregnant, and the murder obviously hadn't taken place in a moment of rage, caused by jealousy or whatever, the way lovers' killings usually happened. Instead, this one had been thought out in advance. Whoever did it had gone to the Dickens house that night well prepared to carry out a plan. A plan to chop Marcy's head off.

His phone rang and Jud answered it.

"Chief, this is Brusson, at the desk. Young lady here says she wants to see you. Name is Wilson. Karen Wilson."

"I'll be right out." He hung up, wondering. Then he left his office and went out to the front of the station.

When he got there he was surprised by what he saw. Instead of the pretty young woman who'd joined him for coffee in Olson's diner, the girl standing at the desk looked worn, haggard. Her face was pale, and there were bluish pouches under her eyes.

Jud approached her. "Karen—you all right?"

"Yes. Is there somewhere we can talk?"

"Sure. Come this way." He led her back down the hallway to his office and asked her to sit down. "Sure you're okay? Want a drink of water or anything?"

She sank into the chair and shook her head. "No, thank you. This is going to be difficult."

He sat down at his desk. "Take your time."

"Can it stay between us? I wouldn't want anything I say to get out. There's my job, among other things."

"Sure. Go ahead."

She took a deep breath. "When I saw you in the diner the other morning? I didn't tell you everything."

He waited.

"Those . . . mental images you asked me about. It's true.

There are things I see, somehow, just the way you guessed. They're like pictures or scenes that come into my mind. It's happened for as long as I can remember. Ever since I was a small child."

"And that's how you knew where the Mariski boy was."

"Yes. I was very upset over that. On one hand I wanted to help that poor family. And on the other I didn't want to be involved. I didn't want anyone to know this thing about me."

"You were embarrassed by it."

"More than that. A lot more. It's been like a curse, always. Or not always. Sometimes I didn't see the images for years at a time. I'd think it was over, I didn't have them anymore. The visions, or whatever they are. But then they would come back. I'd see things again."

He sat quietly, listening.

"Sometimes they'd be just flashes. Most of the time I never understood them, couldn't connect them to anything or anyone I knew. I'd just—see something. And then it would be gone. But then there were other times, not very often, when I'd see someone I did know. And it was always—bad."

"You mean you'd see someone you knew in a bad situation?"

"Yes. Although sometimes I didn't know them. That little boy. I read the story in the newspaper, and then . . . I saw him."

"You saw him—how? What did you see?"

She looked down at her lap, and then back at Jud, the strain now more evident on her face. "I saw him as he was at that moment. Under the ice. Dead."

Jud felt an odd sensation, as if he'd been touched by a chill wind. "But how did you know where—"

"I saw the pond, and there was a stone wall and an old barn. When the boy's father took me to Kretchmer's, there they were. The pond, and the wall and the barn. Just as I'd seen them."

"And you'd never been there before—never driven by the pond before that?"

"Never." She was silent for a moment. "You should have seen how the Mariskis treated me. As if I were a freak."

"They were distraught," Jud said. "They didn't want that kind of information. They were still hoping."

"Yes, I understand. But anyway, that's not why I'm here."

From the hallway came the bustle of the station's activities, cops and others talking, moving about. But in Jud's office it had grown very still. He sensed what she was going to tell him next.

"The headsman," he said.

"Yes."

"What did you see?"

She clenched her teeth, and then seemed to force herself to speak. "I saw him. The night the girl died, I saw him. I saw him kill her."

He continued to sit quietly, watching her. But he could feel the electricity. He leaned forward, forearms on his desk. "Tell me exactly what you saw."

Again she breathed deeply. "There was this man. Huge. Dressed all in black. A black top, like a tunic. Black pants, black gloves, and a hood with slanted eyeholes in it. And he was carrying this big ax. It had a double head, with blades on both sides. Then I saw—it's hard to explain, but these things appear in flashes. I see these . . . pictures. Some of them aren't even complete. Just—pieces."

"It's okay, just go on."

"And I saw the girl. She was on the floor, screaming. The man stood over her and she was screaming and then he swung the ax." She shuddered. "Afterward he—"

"Yes?"

"He held up her head and put it down on something. A table top, or a dresser."

Jud tensed. Except for the cops and the coroner—and the girl's mother—no one had known that detail. Marcy Dickens' head had been placed on the dresser, all right; Jud would see it there, with the eyes staring at him, for as long as he lived. What this woman was telling him now was proof that she'd seen what had happened. It hadn't been an illusion formed in her mind by all the publicity the case had generated. And it wasn't something she'd made up, either as a result of hysteria or because, as Phil Mariski suspected, she was drawn to events like these by some macabre desire to be involved. She had *seen* what took place that night.

He continued to hold her in a steady gaze. "Then what?"

"Then nothing. It was gone. Afterward, the next day, I tried to convince myself it was nonsense, just another one of my creepy episodes. But then the story was in all the papers and on TV."

"At the same time you were struggling with the vision you'd had of the Mariski boy."

"Yes. And that made it worse. It convinced me that what I saw with the headsman was true. Not that I didn't know it was. But I realized I'd been trying to talk myself out of it." She dug a tissue out of her bag and blew her nose.

Jud waited for her to continue.

"Over these past few days I felt so . . . torn. I had nothing to base it on, really. Except these crazy experiences I've had. That's why I decided I wouldn't tell anybody."

"What changed your mind?"

Her eyes locked on his. "I saw him again."

For the second time, Jud felt an involuntary contraction of the muscles in his gut. "When?"

"Last night."

"What did you see?"

"I saw the headsman fighting with a young man. They were sort of wrestling, and the headsman had him by the throat. The young man tried to hit him with something shiny. A metal tool, or something."

Holy shit—the wrench.

"What did the young man look like?"

"He was slim, and he had long brown hair. There was loud rock music playing."

Now it was Jud's turn to conjure up a mental picture, and what he saw was Buddy, his hair flopping down over his forehead. "Go on."

"Then the headsman threw the boy down and—and—" She bent over, struggling to hold back tears.

"What happened then?"

"He kicked him. And then he—chopped him with the ax. There was all this blood. It was awful."

"What then?"

She shook her head. "That was all. I've been going out of my mind. I haven't been able to sleep or eat and I have this terrible headache. I keep feeling I'm going to be sick."

"Listen, won't you let me get you—"

"No. Thank you. All I want you to do is believe me and not let the news people get hold of me. I couldn't stand that. See, I know how crazy all this is. That's why it was so hard for me to tell somebody. But I kept thinking maybe I could help. Maybe I could help stop him from doing it again. But I know what would happen if what I've told you got out."

"It's okay. I won't let anybody know."

For a lot of reasons.

For one, if she really could help, he wouldn't want her to be ripped apart by the press and by the cops as well. God only knew what Pearson would do with something like this. And who was to say anybody would believe her anyway? More than likely she'd be labeled a nut, just as she feared.

But if she could use this thing she had, this *vision*, to help him, then he had to protect her. To say nothing of another angle that suddenly occurred to him: if it became public knowledge that Braddock's chief of police was relying on a psychic, or whatever she was, he'd look like a buffoon.

He sat back in his chair. "I'm glad you came in, Karen. It took a lot of courage."

Tears formed again in her eyes, and she wiped them away. "Are you? Thank God. I wasn't really all that sure about you, either."

"You thought I wouldn't believe you?"

"Yes. Or you'd think I was just off the wall, or something. But that morning in the diner you seemed to understand. A little, anyway. And you didn't try to push me. For somebody I didn't know, and a policeman at that, you were kind. At least that's the impression I got. So I finally decided to trust you."

"I'm glad you did. And now I'm going to tell you something. Last night a high school boy disappeared. He'd been working on his car in the barn behind his family's house. Marcy Dickens was his girlfriend."

She put a hand to her mouth. "Oh, God."

"Yes. His name is Buddy Harper. That name mean anything to you?"

"No. Wait—yes. Where I work—Boggs Ford? There's a Peter Harper who's a customer."

"His father. As you can imagine, the media will give the boy's disappearance quite a run."

"I'm sure they will."

"I want you to promise me you won't say anything about this to anyone."

"Don't worry, I won't. I promise."

"Where do you live, Karen?"

"Maple Street. With my grandmother. I came here from Shippensburg after my mother died."

"Does your grandmother know anything about this—ability you have?"

"No. My mother never said so, but I think she was always a little ashamed of me. Not that she knew all that much about it. I think it also scared her, just the way it did me. So she never discussed it with other people, never let on about it. Not to anybody, including my grandmother. All my grandmother thinks is that sometimes I have emotional problems. And that they give me headaches."

"I see. Is there anyone else?"

Jud saw the shadow of an ironic smile cross her face before she answered. "Some man, you mean? No. There's nobody."

He thought about what she'd told him. "Your vision. Can you tell when it's going to happen? I mean, do you have any warning?"

"No. It's always right out of the blue. And it could be any time of the day or night. But like I said, usually it's just a little piece—a fragment of something."

"Then you can't influence what you're going to see, can't will yourself to receive anything?"

"Never. There have been times when I tried, just out of curiosity, I guess. But I've never been able to do that. I'd think, what if I could make myself see something really valuable. Like tomorrow's newspaper. Or if I could see what was going on behind some closed door. But I couldn't. All I get is what comes into my head, and most of the time when it does happen I don't even know what I'm seeing."

"All right. I'm sure you know where I was going."

"Yes. But that's something I just can't give you."

"As it is you've been a great help."

"Have I really?"

"Yes, you have. I believe you."

Her shoulders slumped as if in relief. "I'm so glad you do. I was so worried about how you'd react. I wouldn't have been surprised if you'd—"

"If I'd what?"

"Nothing. But I'm glad."

He stood up. "I want to show you something."

He got out his keys and unlocked the closet behind his desk, then swung the door open. This was where he kept his personal files, along with anything else he wanted to secure. He reached inside and lifted out one of the paintings he'd bought from the Braddock Museum. It was the one that depicted the headsman waiting for his victim as soldiers dragged the condemned man onto the platform.

He turned and held it up so she could see it.

Her jaw dropped. "Oh, God. That's the man. That's exactly what he looked like."

"Exactly? Here, take a closer look." He passed the painting to her.

She studied it, holding the frame in both hands. "This is so strange. It shows him just the way I saw him. The hood, the eyes, everything. Even the ax is the same, with the double blades." She looked up. "Where did this come from?"

"A friend lent it to me. Is there anything you see in it that's different from what you saw last night? Anything at all about him that's different?"

She stared at the picture once more, then looked up. "No, nothing. Even his size looks right. Tall, husky."

"Okay, thanks." He took it from her and returned it to the closet, closing the door and locking it.

He stepped to where she was sitting and held out his hand to her. "Thanks, Karen. I really appreciate this very much."

She took his hand and shook it briefly as she stood up. "Is that it?"

"For the moment, yes. I want to think about what you've told me, and then I'll contact you and we'll talk some more. In the meantime, if you see anything, call me right away. Either here or at home."

"I will."

He scribbled his home number on a piece of paper and handed it to her. "It's in the book, but this'll make it easier."

She put the paper into her bag. "Okay. And Chief?"

"Jud."

She smiled. "Jud. Thank you. I feel so much better, just from talking about it. It's such a tremendous relief not to have to keep it all bottled up inside me."

"Here, let me show you out." He took her arm and led her back out to the front entrance of the station.

4

Inspector Pearson scheduled a press conference in the station house for 2:30 that afternoon. Grady asked Jud if it was about the Harper kid's disappearance, and Jud said it was. Why get the press into it at this point, Grady wanted to know. Jud told him to ask Pearson. Grady muttered that Pearson was a dickhead.

Jud went out for a sandwich a little before two, and when he got back there was a cluster of reporters at the outer desk, Sally among them. Some of the reporters he recognized from the conference held after the Dickens girl's body had been discovered, and from the sniffing around the press had done since. For them to get here this fast from Albany and Syracuse and Binghamton and wherever else they'd come from must have taken some doing. A couple of them greeted him and tossed questions at him, but Jud told them it wasn't his show, Inspector Pearson would be briefing them.

Promptly at 2:30 Pearson walked in, Williger trailing as usual. The guy was well trained, Jud thought. Pearson didn't even have to tell him to heel.

The inspector looked especially crisp this afternoon in his

gray tweed jacket and his white buttondown with a repp tie, red and black stripes this time. His mustache had been freshly trimmed and he'd combed his hair. All he needed was Ed McMahon urging the crowd to applaud. He stood with his back to the desk, and when the buzzing had quieted down he said he had an announcement to make. You could feel the tension; they were expecting to hear there'd been a break in the case, or maybe even that the cops had made an arrest.

Pearson cleared his throat. "We have a suspect in the Dickens homicide."

Predictably, that set off a roar of questions, and Pearson raised his hands and shushed them. When the reporters finally quieted down he said, "The suspect's name is Peter Harper, Junior, known as Buddy."

"Hey," somebody yelled. "Isn't that the boyfriend?"

This time it took even longer to stem the noise. Over the uproar Pearson said, "I can't give you information if you just stand here and shout. If you want to hear this, you'll have to shut up."

When they subsided once more, he continued. "The subject was a friend of Marcy Dickens, yes. He was with her the night she was killed. He was questioned extensively after the homicide, but not charged because of lack of evidence. Last night he disappeared from his home without advising his parents or anyone else we've talked to about his plans. At this point he is considered a prime suspect, and we've put out a nationwide alert for his arrest. Harper is seventeen years old. He has brown hair and brown eyes. Five eleven, a hundred forty-five pounds. He's a senior at Braddock High School. He could be armed and dangerous."

Not the questions came in a flood: *This guy's the headsman? You find the ax? Why'd he wait until now to take off? You got any other evidence? Has he been in trouble before?*

Jud stood in the corner of the room, and after a few more minutes of this he tuned out. There were a number of things he wanted to do now. One of them was to have Grady check the floorboards of the Harper's barn, see if he could come up with anything from that oil spill.

The other thing he wanted to do had first been suggested to him by Sally, an idea he had scoffed at at the time.

He told Grady what he wanted him to do at the Harper place, and then left the stationhouse via the back door.

NINE

Stalking

1

The editorial offices of the *Braddock Express* were only a few doors from police headquarters. Jud walked it, saying hello to people he passed on the street and seeing his breath appear in small clouds of vapor. The wind was out of the south, so maybe they'd be spared another snowfall for the time being anyway; he hoped so. He turned his collar up against the cold, but he could still feel the crinkling at the edges of his nostrils that told him the temperature was well below freezing. He could hear it under his boots as well, frozen bits of snow and ice crunching as he stepped along the sidewalk.

Ray Maxwell was in, and he greeted Jud with a smile and a handshake. The publisher was in shirtsleeves as usual, wearing his trademark bowtie. His gray flannel pants were held up by a wide leather belt with a western buckle made of silver and inset with turquoise. Maxwell's hair was touched with gray at the temples and Jud knew he was close to sixty, but his grip was strong and he had a way of looking sharply at you with his pale blue eyes, as if he were trying to read your thoughts.

"Surprised to see you," Maxwell said.

"Why's that?"

"Press conference going on, isn't there?"

"Not my show," Jud said. They were standing out in the open area where people were working. "Can we go in your office? I'll tell you about it."

"Got a better idea," Maxwell replied. "Let's go over to the Century Club. We can have a drink."

Jud smiled. "If it's off the record."

"Positively."

They went in Maxwell's station wagon. On the way Jud filled him in on Buddy Harper's disappearance and what Pearson was telling people from the press. Maxwell would hear it all from Sally Benson anyway, but that wasn't the subject Jud wanted to talk to him about.

The club occupied an old mansion at the north end of Main Street, constructed of the same red stone that had been used in so many of the town's buildings. It took less than ten minutes to get there from the offices of the *Express*.

A black man greeted them at the door and took their coats. Maxwell had put on a navy-blue blazer that added to his jaunty appearance, and he obviously was in his element here. Members of the Century boasted that it was the best men's club in Braddock, and they were right; it was also the only one.

As they walked through on their way to the bar they passed a game room, where two men were playing chess, and the main reading room, where several others were leafing through magazines and newspapers. Most of these guys were ancient, Jud observed. But if you could sit around here wasting time in the middle of an afternoon you had to be either rich or retired, and that eliminated most of the younger members.

It was also interesting that Maxwell prided himself on his fiercely liberal editorial positions in the *Express*, and yet membership in this place was like belonging to some organization from another age. Women were not allowed even to set foot in the building, and there had never been a black member. Before either of those policies could be altered, the directors had vowed, the club would be shut down. A lot of the town's political maneuvering was conducted here, and Jud knew that Sam Melcher's becoming mayor had been pretty much decided within these walls before the election ever took place.

The barroom had the ambience of an old-time saloon, with its dark wood paneling and beamed ceiling. Jud had been in here once or twice before, and it hadn't changed. It probably hadn't changed since the club was founded at the turn of the century, which was where its name supposedly came from.

The bartender smiled broadly when he saw them. "Afternoon, Mr. Maxwell. Chief."

"Hello, Arthur," Maxwell said. "I heard a rumor that you had run out of scotch whiskey and I thought I ought to come right over and check up on it."

Arthur's face grew serious. "No sir, that's not true. I'd like to have an opportunity to prove it."

"All right then, give me a double on the rocks."

Maxwell and the bartender burst out laughing, and Jud realized this had to be an old gag between them. Maxwell probably went through the same goofy-ass routine every time he came in here. Jud told Arthur he'd have a beer.

They sat at a corner table, the only people in the bar. When the bartender had served their drinks they touched glasses and drank, and the older man gave Jud one of his sharp-eyed looks. "You think Buddy Harper killed the Dickens girl?"

Jud put his glass down. "No, I don't."

"Then why do you suppose he ran off?"

"I don't know."

The blue eyes continued to bore in on him. "But there's something else on your mind, isn't there? Something else you wanted to talk about. What is it?"

"The headsman."

"Ah. The ghost of Braddock. You're probably angry because of all the play the press had given him. Including the *Express*. Gets people all riled up."

There was a barely disguised cynicism Jud sometimes observed in this man. It was another thing he found hard to reconcile with what the paper seemed to represent. He wondered if Maxwell was jaded from years of reporting on corruption and disasters and man's inhumanity to man, or if he was simply a hypocrite at heart.

"I do think it's wrong," Jud said. "But I don't think you plan to stop it, either."

Maxwell laughed. "You're right about that. It sells newspapers. And one thing I learned early on, it doesn't mean a goddamned thing how good a paper is if nobody reads it."

"The stories you ran on the Dickens homicide referred to an earlier murder back in the sixties."

"Janet Donovan."

"Yes."

"Did you cover that yourself at the time?"

"I certainly did."

"Did you know her?"

"Knew her, knew her husband, John. He was an insurance man. Father left him the business. John Donovan wasn't overly bright."

"And his wife—what was she like?"

Maxwell sipped his whiskey. "Pretty, and a terrible flirt. They belonged to the country club, and Helen and I used to see them there at the Saturday night dances. Janet was always beautifully dressed, in a sexy way. You'd see her with low necklines and slit skirts, things like that. She had a great body, and she loved to show it off. The joke was, if you wanted to get your rocks off, all you had to do was dance with Janet Donovan."

"Like that, huh?"

"Worse. She had affairs all over the place. John worked late a lot, trying to hold his business together. Or maybe he was trying to figure it out. But she didn't sit around waiting for him."

Jud drank some of his beer. It was draught, and its cold fresh taste was better than the canned stuff he was used to. "I tried to look up the case in our files. There was nothing there."

Maxwell smiled. "Not surprised. Woody McDermott was our chief of police back then. He went around half-bombed most of the time. Wouldn't know a murderer if one confessed to him."

"What about the state police?"

"At that time they didn't have a separate detective force, as they do now. All they had was troopers, and they rarely got involved in a homicide case unless it was related to something else they were working on. Not like today at all. You know how the state police got started in New York?"

"No, I don't."

"It was back in the twenties," Maxwell said. "They were formed by an order from the governor, for the purpose of stopping bootleggers from running booze down from Canada.

At least that was what he proclaimed. What he really wanted to stop was the criticism from the press over what a piss-poor job he was doing. There were so many liquor trucks they practically ran on schedules."

"So he probably had a piece of the action."

"Bet on it."

"Dirty politics. Not so different from now."

"Nope. The more things change, the more they stay the same. Or another way to put it is that times change, but people don't. The Volstead Act made a lot of folks rich, and a good many of them were politicians."

They finished their drinks, and Maxwell signaled the bartender for another round.

"According to the county attorney," Jud said, "there were never any arrests in the Donovan case."

"No. No arrests, but half the men in Braddock could have been suspects. After a while it all just blew over. Most of the idiots in our fair village really believed the headsman did it. They never took any other idea seriously. Everybody knew Janet had a whole flock of lovers, but do you think any of them were ever under suspicion? Hell, no. They could have had any number of motives, too. Yet all anybody talked about was that half-baked legend. The headsman had come back and chopped her with a big shiny ax. And you know why he did, according to them? Because Janet was a floozy. You see? Human nature again. It was *her* fault. She was a sinner, so the headsman punished her. Just the way he'd been doing for over two hundred years."

Arthur brought fresh drinks to the table and collected the empties. When he'd gone back to the bar Jud asked, "What happened to the Donovan family after that?"

"Oh, they stuck it out for a while, but John's business finally went down the drain altogether. They moved to Binghamton, and he got a job with another insurance firm there. I think the owner owed his father some favors, something like that. I heard he remarried, and after that I lost track of him."

"I see."

"And now tell me, Chief. What's this about? You think

there's a connection between the two cases, or have you started believing in the headsman, too?"

"What I see is that there were two homicides, years apart. In both of them the killer used the identical M.O. The victims were beheaded with an ax. The chances of that being a coincidence are pretty remote. As you've said yourself, the Donovan case was never properly investigated. I wanted to learn more about it."

As Maxwell drank his whiskey, his face became flushed. "If I were you, I'd be careful. There are some sleeping dogs there, and you know the old saying."

"Yeah, I do."

"You want to tread softly, that's all. Remember this isn't New York, or Philadelphia, or some other big city. You were made chief of police because you were a bright, energetic young cop. The town fathers believed you'd be hardworking and reasonably honest."

"Yes?"

"But they also believed you'd be smart enough to understand that a police force in a small community is a service organization. Your job is to keep the peace. Protect homes, fight drugs, drive out any bad elements that might spring up here. If a crime occurs, you're to run down the offender so that he's punished."

"Which is what I'm trying to do now."

"And that's fine. I'm just telling you to be careful while you're doing it."

Jud finished his beer and shook his head when Maxwell pointed to his glass to suggest another. "Let me ask you about something else, Ray. I heard a big company might be moving to Braddock. You know anything about it?"

Maxwell's eyebrows raised. "Where did you hear that?"

"Let's just say I picked it up. Anything to it?"

"I don't know. But if I were you I might consider that sensitive information. Speaking of politicians."

The implication was clear enough; Jud dropped the subject. "You said Janet Donovan had a number of lovers."

"She certainly did."

"Are any of them still living in Braddock?"

All jocularity disappeared from Maxwell's expression. "Jud, I told you—"

"Yeah, but are there?"

Maxwell drained his whiskey and set his glass down with an air of finality. "Not as far as I know. And now I'd better get back to work. I have tomorrow's edition to get out."

. The drive back was pleasant enough. They talked about the weather and how the winter hadn't been too bad after all.

2

When Jud got back to the stationhouse the afternoon was nearly over. The days were getting longer now; it wouldn't be dark for another hour at least. Spring wasn't in the air exactly, but it was no longer so far off. He thought of Emmett Stark and his trout flies. The old chief was right; the season would be here before you knew it.

There was a ruckus of some kind at the front desk. A fat, red-faced man wearing a sheepskin coat was yelling something at a cop, and Grady was telling him to calm down. They were trying to get information from him, but all the guy wanted to do was argue. Jud moved closer to the group. Brusson was on the desk and Bob Kramer apparently had brought the guy in.

"Fucking police brutality," the guy yelled. Jud saw that he was holding a handkerchief with blood on it. Under his left eye was a welt the size of a walnut, and he kept touching it with the handkerchief. There was a bluish cut in the welt, and after each dab with the handkerchief it would start to leak again.

When the guy caught sight of Jud he said, "You in charge here?"

"I'm Chief of Police MacElroy," Jud said. "What's the problem?"

Kramer said, "This man was—"

"Goddamn it," the guy yelled, "he asked *me*."

"Let him talk," Jud said.

Redface reduced his volume by a few decibels. "I was driving through town here and this dummy stopped me. Gave me some bullshit story about an accident. I wasn't in no accident. Then he hit me. He *hit* me, for Christ's sake."

Jud looked at Kramer. "What happened?"

Redface was yelling again. "Listen, are you going to pay attention to what I'm telling you, or—"

Jud turned to him and raised his hand, palm up. "Now *you* shut up, mister. I want to hear the officer's explanation." His gaze swung back to Kramer.

The cop said, "I got a radio call there was a hit and run on South Main. Late-model white Cadillac. Hit a kid on a bike and left the scene, headed north. I was on Route Five. I started down toward there and spotted the car. I chased it maybe a mile before I could pull it over. This character was driving. When I told him I was taking him in he resisted."

"Punched me in the fucking eye," Redface shouted. "Then he pulled a gun on me."

"We got a witness," Grady said. "Saw the accident." He turned around. "Would you come over here, please, ma'am?"

A woman was sitting on a bench. Jud hadn't noticed her when he came in. She was bundled up in a heavy brown coat and had a babushka tied around her head. She got up and came forward hesitantly, a frightened look on her face. Grady took her arm and guided her to where the others were standing.

"What's your name, ma'am?" Grady asked her.

"Doris Banazak."

"You live in Braddock?"

"Yes, on Birch Street."

"Where were you this afternoon, and what did you see?"

"I was on my way to the store. On South Main Street."

"Where exactly?"

"On the corner by Hillside Avenue. I seen a white car hit a boy on a bike. It was almost right in front of me. The car kept going a ways and it was dragging the boy and the bike. Then it stopped and this man got out." She pointed at Redface. "He pushed the bike and the kid off the bumper of his car and then he got back in and drove away."

"Oh, Jesus," the guy said. "That's crazy. I never hit no kid."

"What's your name?" Jud asked him.

"Victor Scalzo. I live in Ithaca and I was on my way there. This is all bullshit."

Jud looked at Grady. "What about the kid?"

"Ambulance took him to Memorial. He's busted up, but they think he'll make it."

"Who is he?"

"Name's Eddie Marcus. Father works for Purdy's Heating Oil."

"Yeah," Jud said. "I know the family. You notify them?"

"Yes. They're at Memorial now."

Jud then spoke to the woman. "Thank you, Mrs. Banazak. You've been a real help. The officers will want to get a statement from you."

He turned to Scalzo. "You better hope that kid is all right. As it is you've got endangering lives with a vehicle, reckless driving, leaving the scene of an accident and resisting arrest."

"How about assault on a police officer?" Kramer said. "He took a swing at me."

"Sure," Jud said. "Write that up, too." He left them, walking toward his office.

Behind him he heard Scalzo yell, "This is all bullshit, I'm telling you. Wait 'til I call my lawyer. It's bullshit, you hear me?"

And then Grady's voice: "You don't shut up I'll bust your other eye."

When he got to his office Jud hung up his cap and jacket and sat down at his desk, sliding the Rolodex over in front of him. He found the number for the Binghamton Police Department and dialed it. A cop answered and Jud told him who he was and asked to be connected to Chief Broadhurst.

When the chief came on the line he asked Jud how the Dickens case was doing. Jud told him about the Harper kid's disappearance, knowing Broadhurst would be seeing the APB on it anyway. Then he asked the chief if he could have somebody do a rundown on a family named Donovan. Jud told him about the earlier homicide, explaining that John Donovan had gone to Binghamton afterward. He'd worked for an insurance agency there but Jud didn't know which one. Broadhurst said he'd do what he could and that he'd call back as soon as he had something. Jud thanked him and hung up.

3

Billy Swanson put on his varsity sweater and drove the Bronco
to the Boggs house to pick up Alice. Her parents were at home,
and so was her brother, so Billy had no intention of staying
there. The plan was to go over to Pat Campbell's. Pat's folks
were out for the evening and her kid sister was spending
the night at a friend's, which would give them the run of the
Campbell house. Pat had called Alice earlier to give her the
word, and between them they had hatched the program. Jeff
Peterson would be coming over, and so would Johnny Lombardi and Betty Melcher.

Mrs. Boggs opened the door and made a little fuss over Billy
the way she always did, and then led him into the living room.
Mr. Boggs was sitting reading the newspaper. He looked up and
said hello, and then asked how the Bronco was running, which
was his way of showing his ceaseless concern for his customers. When Billy said it was fine he went back to his newspaper.

Mrs. Boggs sat down on a sofa and patted the cushion next
to her, asking Billy to talk to her until Alice came down. He
joined her on the sofa, hoping Alice would hurry it up.

Mrs. Boggs was one of those women who have a tough time
coping with the fact that they're no longer young, so they try to
make up for it by dressing as much like their daughters as
possible. It wasn't unusual; Billy had seen it with the mothers
of several other girls he knew. Mrs. Boggs even dyed her hair
the same shade of dirty blond Alice had naturally. He knew that
was true because Alice had told him so. She thought her
mother's antics were ridiculous.

Billy agreed. Mrs. Boggs' face was pudgy and it sagged, so
that you wouldn't mistake it for a kid's face even in the dark.
She also had a sag in her ass, and there was that dimpled fat on
her thighs. Billy remembered that from the times he'd seen her
around the pool at the Braddock Country Club last summer,
wearing a bikini even skimpier than Alice's. Nevertheless Mrs.
Boggs went around in tight sweater and skirts that came to just
above her knees, or else jeans that looked as if they were going

to pop at the seams any minute. Tonight she had on a sweater and a gray skirt.

When he sat beside her the first thing she asked was about Buddy Harper. "Has anybody heard from him? Has he been in touch with any of his friends?"

"I don't know," Billy said. Jesus. It was in the newspapers and on TV how cops all over the country were looking for Buddy, and here this assbrain wanted to know if he was sending postcards, or calling up to chat, or whatever dumb fucking thing she thought.

"It's all so terrible, isn't it?" Mrs. Boggs went on. "I feel so sorry for both poor families. Marcy was such a lovely girl, and I just can't imagine Buddy doing such a thing. It's just too ghastly to think about. But of course I don't believe he did it, do you?"

Billy mumbled that he didn't, wishing she'd get off the subject, or better still that Alice would get down here and rescue him. What was keeping her?

"You're too young to remember the last time anything like this happened in Braddock," Mrs. Boggs said. "In fact, you weren't even born. I wasn't much more than a child myself at the time."

The hell you weren't, Billy thought.

"There was this young woman who died the same way. Her name was Janet Donovan. You probably read the stories about it that were in the papers after Marcy was killed."

"Yeah, I did."

"She was a beautiful girl. And very social. I remember she had this red Buick convertible, and I used to see her driving it with the top down. My husband knew her too—didn't you, dear?"

Mr. Boggs' nose was still buried in the newspaper. He made a grunting noise and went on reading.

"But you know what everybody believed, don't you, at that time? They believed the headsman had come back to Braddock and cut Janet's head off. They really believed that's what happened. Can you imagine? Of course, the case was never solved, and so that might have had a lot to do with people feeling that way, but isn't that something? And now here we are years later with the same thing all over again. Doesn't it just give you the creeps?"

"Yeah," Billy said. "It's pretty spooky." And you're another one, he thought. You're getting your jollies just talking about it. You probably buy that headsman bullshit too. You're just like all the other dingbats Hathaway was talking about.

"Hi."

He turned to see Alice come bouncing into the room. Christ, it was about time.

Billy stood up. "Hi."

She was wearing a yellow cardigan over a beige dress and she looked pretty cute. He felt a surge of pride.

Alice waved to her parents. "See you guys later."

"Have fun," Mr. Boggs said from behind his paper.

Mrs. Boggs got up and walked to the front door with them. "Home early," she said to Alice. "Not a minute later than twelve. You know how I worry."

"Okay, ma. Don't get worked up about it."

"You can't blame me. Marcy's murder, and now Buddy running off, who wouldn't be concerned? Billy, you see she's home by then, won't you?"

"Yes, ma'am. Good night." It was a relief to get out the door. He went down the walk to the turnaround in front of the garage and climbed into the Bronco. He had the engine running before Alice got in, but he was still careful to back out of the driveway slowly. If he knew Mrs. Boggs she'd be watching them from the window. No sense getting her glands in an uproar if he didn't have to. As far as she was concerned, he was that nice young Billy Swanson, with good manners and even better morals.

It never occurred to him that Ethel Boggs might have memories of her own teenage years that would enable her to guess what was in Billy's mind or know what went on between him and her daughter.

As soon as they were around the bend he jammed his foot down and the Bronco lurched forward. As usual he wished the damned thing wasn't so stodgy. Maybe he could talk his mother into trading it in on one of the new Mustang convertibles with a 5-liter engine. Now there was a car that could haul ass.

4

The house was a contemporary, more daring in its architecture than any other in town, and Billy felt it went with Mr. Campbell's personality. Pat's father was head of the Empex Corporation, a company that produced engine gauges. It was one of the town's largest employers, with a bunch of government contracts, and Campbell's lifestyle was one Billy admired. He was an excellent tennis player, and his red Porsche cabriolet was by far the neatest car in Braddock.

When Billy and Alice arrived, the others were already down in the playroom. It was a large space with bleached oak paneling on the walls and a terrazzo floor that was great to dance on. There was a bar that was always stocked with soft drinks and a fridge full of junk food. At one end was a fireplace, with a pingpong table nearby. The opposite wall contained glass sliders that led out onto the terrace and the pool.

Pat was dancing with Jeff Peterson when they walked in. They had on a Gloria Estefan record, a new one Billy hadn't heard, and before he even took his sweater off he and Alice began dancing to it. Pat looked over, smiling and waving hello. John and Betty were sitting on a sofa in front of the fire, smoking a joint. Billy maneuvered his way over there, staying with the beat, and when he got close enough he reached out and deftly plucked the cigarette out of Lombardi's fingers. He took a deep drag and passed the joint to Alice, then took another drag before giving it back to Johnny.

He liked dancing with Alice—watching her move her body in time to the rhythm, her shoulders and breasts heaving and her hips jerking suggestively. She had her eyes locked on his and he sensed she was thinking the same kind of thoughts he was, relaxed and happy and a little excited too, knowing they'd all have a good time together and then later she and Billy would slip off to some place in the house where they could be alone and get it on. Pat had said her parents had gone to a party and wouldn't get home until late, which would work out just fine.

When the record ended Billy went to the fridge and got

Cokes for Alice and himself, and then all of them took pillows from the sofas and chairs and laid them on the floor near the fireplace. Pat put on more music, Whitney Houston this time, and they sat on the pillows and John passed out fresh joints.

"Hey," Jeff said, "anybody heard from Buddy?"

"You're as bad as my mother," Alice said. "She asks me that all the time."

Billy lit his cigarette and pulled smoke into his lungs. "She asked me, too. When I got to your house that's all she wanted to talk about. That and the crap about the headsman."

Betty Melcher was holding a joint between her thumb and forefinger. "Listen, don't be so sure it's crap. The more I think about it the stranger it gets. My mother was talking to a friend of hers about it on the phone last night and I heard what they were saying. That woman whose head was chopped off years ago?"

"Donovan," Jeff said.

Betty nodded. "Yeah, that's the one. My mother said a lot of things in that murder were exactly like what happened to Marcy. She said there was stuff in that one that never came out, and that a lot of people in Braddock would be plenty nervous if it ever did. Is that creepy? Jesus, the whole thing gives me goosebumps."

Lombardi slid his hand up under Betty's sweater. "Yeah, it sure does. Man, what a set of bumps."

She giggled and pushed his hand away.

"I think it's awful," Pat said. "The police aren't doing anything. I don't believe Buddy had anything to do with Marcy's murder. He never would've hurt anybody, let alone Marcy."

"I'm with you," Billy said. "You heard him after the police talked to him. He was shit-scared."

"How many others were there?" Jeff asked. "If the headsman's been chopping people for all that time, he must've whacked off a lot of heads. So how many others—anybody know?"

"Fifty-seven," John said.

"What?"

John doubled over laughing and Betty gave his arm a playful poke.

"Hey, really," Jeff persisted. "Anybody know anything about that?"

"No, but I know something else that's terrible," Betty said. John leaned forward. "Great—what is it?"

"You're going to think this is so disgusting," she went on. "I don't know if I should even tell you."

That brought a roar from all of them, as they urged her to divulge whatever she knew.

Betty tossed her hair and took a hit from the joint Jeff was smoking. She held it in, then exhaled a gray-blue cloud. "Dr. Reinholtz is our family doctor, you know? And he's also the coroner? My mother said they checked Marcy's body after the murder to see if the headsman had done it with her before he cut her head off—or maybe after."

"*After?*" Alice shrieked. "Oh, God—how gross."

"Ugh," John said. "I think I just might puke."

Betty laughed. "I told you it was disgusting."

It's weird, Billy thought. These girls were Marcy's friends, and at the funeral they were all falling down crying and carrying on like they were about to die from grief. Now here they were, playing it for laughs. And all because of some dogshit rumor. Lombardi had the right idea; it was enough to make you barf.

"You know what I think?" Alice said. "I think the headsman really did do it."

That triggered another round of jeers.

Billy waved his hand. "Come on, Alice. You can't really buy that crap."

"I'm just telling you what I believe, that's all. And it's what a lot of other people think, too."

"Then what happened to Buddy?"

"I don't know that, either. Maybe he knew the truth and it scared him, so he ran away. Or maybe he was afraid he might be next."

"Jesus," Billy said. "That's too much."

She looked at him. "You remember that morning in class,

when Hathaway was talking about the story of the headsman and you were sneering at it?"

"Yeah, and I still think it's a crock of shit."

"That was the same day Marcy died," Pat said. "Tell the truth, Billy. Didn't that shake you up, when you said all that stuff about how you weren't afraid of the headsman and then that night Marcy's head was cut off?"

Before Billy could answer Jeff said, "Yeah, how about it, William—I bet you had brown drawers after that."

Billy was damned if he'd get pissed. They were riding him just the way Hathaway had, but the hell with it. He was feeling too mellow, and besides, there was another subject he'd rather explore with Alice, in private. He took the roach from her and almost singed his lip getting one more pull out of it. He tossed it into the fire.

"Hey, the man needs a new smoke," John said. He pulled a fresh joint out of his shirt pocket and held it out, but Billy waved it away.

"No? How about you, Jeff?"

"No, man. I have to take it easy. I'm still in training."

Billy guffawed. "Training? You train on pot, beer and pussy."

"The breakfast of champions," John said.

Betty reached for the fresh cigarette and took it from him. She leaned over as he lit it for her.

"Say, Billy," Jeff said. "Remember what Hathaway asked you? So now what would you do, if the headsman snuck up on you, out of some country road in the middle of the night?"

"Same thing I said then. I'd take that ax and stick it up crossways."

Alice stood up. "Come on, Tarzan—let's go for a walk."

That was more like it. Billy got to his feet, taking her hand. Together they walked to the door that led from the playroom to the stairs.

Watching them go, Pat said, "Just don't use my mother's room. She'd have a fit."

5

The headsman stood in the shadows, watching. The wind was strong, whipping around the corners of the house and sending clouds of snow crystals swirling across the terrace. It clutched at the ancient black cloth of his tunic and pressed the hood against the back of his head, but he ignored it. The temperature was already below freezing and dropping, but he was oblivious of that as well.

Looking in through the large glass panels he saw the young men and women dancing, holding their bodies near each other and moving in a barely disguised simulation of the sex act. They jerked and twisted and bucked to the repetitive, monotonous rhythm of the music, facing each other and leering, pelvises thrusting.

After a time they sat down near the fireplace on pillows they had laid out on the floor. He couldn't hear their words, but he could see that they were laughing and joking. They got out more marijuana cigarettes and lit them, blowing clouds of smoke into the air as they giggled and stroked each other. Hands were cupping breasts, caressing buttocks, teasing nipples.

He saw the tall, blond-haired boy and the plumpish girl get up and say something to the others. There was an exchange of words among them and then more laughter. After that the boy and girl left the room.

He watched for a few more moments, and then he disappeared into the snowy night.

TEN ·······································
Betrayed

1

Chief Broadhurst sounded cheerful. "Got the story for you on that Donovan family."

It was early evening and Jud had been about to leave his office when the call came in from Binghamton. He had promised to take Sally out to dinner, a rare event. "Yeah, Chief—good. Go ahead."

"John Donovan, the husband of the woman who was killed? He worked for the Garrison Insurance Agency after he came here from Braddock. He remarried, stayed with Garrison until he retired. Died of a heart attack in nineteen seventy-nine."

Jud felt a stab of disappointment.

"Then his wife," Broadhurst went on, "the one he married after he came here, she got married again a year later. To a man who worked for the Oneida Glass Company. She died too, just last year."

"What happened to the daughter?"

"I was getting to that. Name was Joan Donovan. She was in a lot of trouble while she was growing up. Expelled from high school, and then her stepmother threw her out of the house. She was picked up a couple of times for shoplifting, also for soliciting. Finally hooked up with a black pimp and went to New York. That was the last we knew."

"Nothing more on her?"

"No. We had a sheet on her, but when she took off that was the end of it."

"All right, thanks anyway."

"Sure, Jud. Glad to help. How you doing with the headsman—anything new?"

"Not at the moment."

"We got a bulletin on that kid you told me was missing. The Dickens girl's boyfriend. Anything turn up on him?"

"No."

"Looks like he's your man, doesn't it?"

"Hard to say."

"We'll keep a sharp eye out for him."

"Thanks again, Chief. You've been a lot of help." He hung up.

Next he called the front desk and told the cop where he'd be that evening. Then he drove home for a quick shower and a change of clothes.

He put on a white shirt and a red tie, and his tan sports jacket, which he almost never wore. When he looked at his image in the mirror over his dresser he felt as if he was seeing a stranger. But he decided he didn't look all that bad, either. It was just that he wore the uniform so much of the time it seemed to be part of him.

Instead of the patrol car he decided to use his Blazer. Might as well make the transition to civilian complete. For tonight, anyway. He climbed into the machine and backed around the police car. Sitting high in the driver's seat also felt different from what he was used to. He put the Blazer in gear and drove to the offices of the *Express*.

Sally was at her desk when he walked in, typing rapidly on her word processor. She gave him a brief smile and went back to her work, saying, "Hi. Just gotta finish this. It'll only take a minute. Have a seat."

He sat down on a chair beside her desk and glanced around. The place seemed busy with the clicking of the office machines and people running around acting harassed. The *Express* put out only one edition a day, and he knew this commotion was a nightly occurrence as they rushed to get the next morning's paper ready.

It was funny, in a way, because except for the stir caused by the Dickens case and the focus on the headsman legend, there wasn't all that much to get excited about, as far as he could see.

There'd be the occasional accident, or dispute of one kind or another, but the rest of the local news was usually about church suppers and meetings of the Rotary Club. All the national and world news the *Express* bought from the wire services. So what was the big deal?

When Sally finished her typing she ran it off on a printer and gave the pages to Maxwell's secretary. Jud heard her say, "Be sure Ray sees this." Then she got her coat out of a closet and he helped her on with it.

As they went out the door he said, "That another one of your feature stories?"

"Yes, and it's terrific."

"You gonna let me in on it, or do I have to wait to get my copy?"

"No, I'll tell you about it. You remember the little boy who drowned in Kretchmer's pond? Name was Mariski?"

Jud's antenna went up. "What about him?"

They got into the Blazer, and as Jud started the engine and pulled away from the curb she said, "I had a tip on it today. I heard that a woman told the Mariskis where the boy's body was. The woman saw it in a vision."

Jud felt his stomach sink.

"So I called Mrs. Mariski and asked her if I could talk to her about it. At first she didn't want me to. But then I went over there, and she told me the whole story. How this young woman came to their house right out of the blue and told them exactly where the boy was. She said he was in Kretchmer's pond. And get this. The woman described the pond, even though she'd never been there. Is that strange?"

"Uh-huh."

"Well, don't you think it is? Mrs. Mariski said the woman didn't even know the name of the pond. She just knew that's where their boy was. Her husband didn't believe the woman. He thought she was a fake, just out to give herself some kind of a sick thrill—you know how some people are? If there's trouble they're fascinated. They want to get near it. They're like groupies, only what turns them on is disaster."

"Yeah."

"But Mariski was wrong. He stewed about it, and then

finally he called the cops and said he thought maybe the boy had been fooling around on the ice at Kretchmer's. You know the rest—they dragged the pond and found his body in less than an hour.''

"Um."

"Well, is that all you've got to say—just *um?* I think it's a great story. It's so odd, the way she knew exactly where to look."

"Is that the end of it?"

"Of course not. I'm too good a reporter for that. I called the woman right after I left Mrs. Mariski. Her name is Karen Wilson, and she works for Boggs Ford as a secretary. Came here last summer from Shippensburg. She had a fit when I told her who I was. Refused to see me. But I told her if she wouldn't talk to me I'd just run Mrs. Mariski's version of the story. So finally she agreed to meet me and discuss it. When I saw her, all she did was try to talk me out of it. Which was obviously her real reason for agreeing to see me. When I tried to pin her down she was very evasive, but I kept after her and she more or less admitted what Mrs. Mariski told me was true. But she kept trying to downplay it, telling me it was just a hunch."

"So? Maybe it was."

"Hey, whoever heard of anybody pulling off a thing like that with just a hunch?"

"Then how do you think she did it?"

"Maybe she's psychic. She knew because she received a message."

"A message."

"Oh, Jud—I don't believe in parapsychology any more than you do. And yet *something* came to her. Somehow she got some kind of a signal or something and she took Philip Mariski directly to where his son's body was. So whether you or I believe in telepathy, or extra-sensory perception, or anything else doesn't matter. That's what *happened*. It's strange, but it's also one great story."

They were approaching Armando's. It was an old country house the restaurateur had converted so that the first floor contained a bar, two dining rooms and the kitchen. He'd also had the exterior painted purple, for some unfathomable reason.

Jud wheeled the Blazer into the parking lot. As they got out and he guided Sally up the walk he wondered how long it would take her to come up with her next brilliant idea, knowing just what it would be.

"I tried to get more out of her," Sally said. "You know, background stuff. I asked her how long she'd had this ability, and if she'd ever used it for anything like this before. But she wouldn't tell me. Just kept brushing it all off."

He opened the front door and they went inside. Armando's was a popular restaurant, combining good food with a pleasant atmosphere. There were red leather banquettes that were cozy for couples to sit on side by side, which was one of the reasons he'd chosen it. As he checked their coats he saw that the place was crowded. Several people were ahead of them, waiting for tables.

Armando himself spotted Jud and moved toward them with a wide grin on his face and his arms extended. "Hey, Chief. It's good to see you. Welcome to my restaurant." He gave Jud a hug and then turned to Sally. "This your lady? Beautiful." He grabbed her hand and kissed it. She was wearing a red dress and a gold chain necklace and Jud had to agree she looked wonderful.

Armando stepped toward the dining rooms. "Come on, follow me. I gotta nice table for you."

He led them past the people who were waiting, and when they were seated he clapped his hands and a waiter scurried over. Armando told him to take the Chief's drink order and to make it quick, and after getting it the waiter hurried off.

"What's good tonight?" Jud asked.

"Everything. But the veal rollatini is very special."

"Great, we'll try it." He glanced at Sally. "Okay with you?"

"Sounds fine."

"Okay," Armando said. "You leave the rest to me. I'll take care of everything for you."

When he'd left them Sally said, "No wonder you like coming here."

"It's a nice place, and as you just saw, I'm famous."

"Not yet you're not, but you will be if you stick with me."

"The great writer?"

"Of course. And you knew me when."

The waiter brought a bourbon on the rocks for Sally, a beer for Jud. They touched glasses and drank, and she said, "The story I was telling you about? At first Maxwell was a little reluctant, too. But one thing about Ray, he'll run anything he thinks will sell newspapers."

"So I gather."

"But you wait and see, I wrote a really good piece."

"Can't wait to read it."

She missed the irony in his tone. "That's better. Be sure to let me know what you think. Which reminds me—there's something I wanted to ask you. Did Mariski tell the police anything about the psychic when he had you drag the pond?"

He stiffened. "I heard something, but I didn't pay much attention. It sounded kind of way out to me."

"So you didn't believe it?"

"Like I said, I didn't pay too much attention. The boy's body was recovered, and that was what counted."

Their first course arrived, angel's hair pasta tossed with basil and butter. When he tasted it, Jud realized how hungry he was.

"So that gave me another idea," Sally said.

Here it comes, he thought.

"Now don't tell me I'm crazy, but just listen to what I have to say, okay?"

He nodded resignedly, his mouth full of pasta.

"Why not talk to this Wilson woman and see if she can tell you anything about the headsman?"

"Mm."

"All right, I knew you'd say it was a little nuts, but think about it. What would you have to lose? Nobody'd have to know about it, either."

"Except you."

Her eyes widened. "Well, sure except me. I just gave you the idea, didn't I? Oh, I see. You're afraid of what I might write about it—is that it?"

"Something like that."

"Okay, look. I give you my word of honor, I wouldn't write anything that would upset anybody or hinder anything you were doing. Fair?"

"No."

"No? What do you mean, *no?*"

He put his fork down. "Listen. The case is tough enough as it is. Most of the people in Braddock already believe the headsman came back and killed Marcy Dickens. They don't even consider any other possibility."

"Except maybe that the Harper boy did it after all?"

"I don't think they pay much attention to that, either. As far as they're concerned, the killer was the headsman. So now, as if that wasn't bad enough, you want to write stories that say the chief of police is lighting candles and looking into a crystal ball or whatever."

"Oh, Jud—be reasonable. I still think it's a great idea, and for all you know it could be valuable to you. The fact is, she found that boy. You can't take that away from her, regardless of how you may feel about it."

When their entrees were served, Jud ordered a bottle of Chianti. The rollatini was everything Armando had said it was and then some. Jud never ate veal at home; it was too much trouble to fix. Steak was much easier. Couple of minutes under the broiler and there you had it. But this was superb. The veal slices were paper thin and very tender, rolled around a marvelously spicy stuffing. Along with them was a baked dish that combined zucchini with tomatoes and peppers and mushrooms, and on the side a tossed salad with gorgonzola dressing. There was also plenty of Armando's renowned homemade bread. Sally ate lightly, but Jud waded in like a trencherman.

She wasn't about to give up. After the waiter refilled their wine glasses she said, "How about this idea? And don't get mad, just hear me out. Suppose I promise not to write a thing about this angle until the case is broken?"

"So now you're off in a new direction? A few days ago you were telling me I ought to go on the assumption that the headsman was real."

"Hey, will you try not to be so pigheaded?"

"*Me?* I'm the one who's pigheaded?"

"You certainly are. I made that suggestion, if you'll recall, because it was the one idea you hadn't thought of."

"The answer is still no deal. I don't want to mess with some woman who claims to be telepathic and then have you write a story on it." He should have left it at that, but he didn't. "Even though you think all this could be your ticket to a great job on a big-time newspaper."

She thrust out her jaw. "Now that's not fair. I'm just trying to do the best I can. I'm a reporter, and this case is certainly the biggest thing I've ever worked on. No matter what happens, I'm going to make the most of it."

"Okay, take it easy. I understand." He tried to make small talk after that, staying away from the subject of Karen Wilson and the headsman altogether. But his mind kept churning the problem. If Karen suspected complicity between Sally and the cops—especially with Jud himself—he could forget about any further help from her. As it was, Sally's story in the *Express* tomorrow could stir up trouble. From what he knew of Karen Wilson, she'd be devastated. The thing she feared most was the possibility that the media would get a line on her psychic power and begin to exploit it. And now here was Sally leading the way.

The other side of the coin was almost as grim. If Sally were to learn about the time he'd already spent with Karen Wilson she'd accuse him of deceiving her. Which was just too damn bad. His job was to run a police department, not to worry about the interests of a newspaper reporter—even if she was his girlfriend. All that part of it did was complicate things further. Christ. Everyplace he looked, he saw hornets.

They refused dessert but had coffee, small cups of strong, rich espresso.

Karen put her hand on his. And then she turned his mood around with one sentence. "Now let's forget all these silly arguments and go to my place—I'll bet you have some interesting ideas of your own."

He grinned. "I do, and they're all obscene."

"Wonderful."

He signaled the waiter for the check.

2

Her apartment was on the top floor of a four-story building on Water Street. She'd told him one of the things she liked about living there was that she could walk to work, which she said was was good for her figure. He knew she also went through a lengthy routine of calisthenics each morning, and sometimes she put on a sweatsuit and jogged a mile or two before her shower and breakfast.

Whatever it was, the figure was terrific. She was full-breasted and her belly was taut and flat, her buttocks and legs smoothly rounded. Whenever he saw a layout in one of the skin magazines, he inevitably made a comparison of the girl in the picture with Sally, and Sally always won. But then, he was prejudiced.

He was feeling fine by the time they reached the apartment, full of good food and a little flushed from the wine, but most of all he was excited by the prospect of what was to happen next. He promised himself he'd take his time, make every move last as long as possible. No matter how many times he'd undressed her, going about it just this way, very slowly and deliberately, it never failed to get him so excited he felt like a kid going to bed with a girl for the first time in his life.

She put on some mellow, dreamy music and turned the lights down, and then she kicked the rug back from the parquet floor and folded herself into his arms. The music was awful—some saccharine thing with strings and a rippling piano—but the beat was right in sync with his mood. It was steady and pulsing and Sally pressed her body against his and moved with him as if they were joined together. By the time the music ended and he eased her into the bedroom he could almost taste her.

He started with the blouse. It was made of light, slippery material—silk, probably—and it fastened down the front. He turned her around so that he was tight against her rear end and as she felt him pressing against her she squirmed a little. He undid the buttons one at a time, starting from the top. The music playing in the living room drifted into the bedroom as fragile as smoke. He kissed her neck as he worked on the buttons, and she nuzzled him with her cheek.

When he got her blouse open he didn't pull it off but instead draped it back from her shoulders. He put his hands under her breasts, continuing to kiss her neck, moving his lips down to the hollow where it joined her shoulder. He held her like that for a long time, his hands barely moving, just enough so that she could feel him caressing her.

His fingers moved to the front of the bra, and he deftly unhooked it. Then her breasts were free and he was stroking them, his fingers lightly brushing over her nipples, feeling them grow erect. She'd begun to make little whimpering sounds in her throat, and he knew what that meant. He slipped the blouse away from her and tossed it to one side. It floated to the floor like gossamer.

Then she turned around again to face him, and her eyes had the wanton look he loved. They were half-closed, but he could see the fire in them. He kissed her hard then, her mouth opening to him and her tongue probing. She put her arms around his neck and stood on her tiptoes and he held her buttocks in his hands, feeling the tautness as she strained against him. She pulled back, and her fingers went to his belt buckle, fumbling to get it open.

They were standing at the foot of the bed. Jud pulled her bra away and flipped it to the floor. Then he placed both hands on her shoulders and shoved just hard enough to make her topple over. She lay on her back, the hungry expression on her face deeper now, and he unbuttoned her skirt and pulled it off. She'd kicked off her shoes, and that left only her pantyhose. He reached down and took hold of them by the waistband, peeling them off. When he drew them down to her buttocks she arched her back so that he could get them down, and as he pulled them off the fragrance of her came up to his nostrils and he could feel his pulse pounding in his temples. She lay before him, watching, and it took an effort to stay with the slow, steady pace.

He took almost as much time removing his own clothes as he had hers. She kept her eyes on him through every second of it, staring at the broad shoulders and the heavy pectoral muscles as the shirt came off. When he got down to his shorts, she raised herself up on her elbows for a better view. He pushed her back down again.

He began by kissing her. All of her. Her mouth and her eyes and her ears and her throat, her back and her buttocks. He kissed the soles of her feet and licked her toes until she shivered. Then he lay between her legs and buried his face in the hot sweet musk of her. His head was whirling now, his heart pounding as she writhed and moaned.

After that he had no concept of the passage of time or the exact order in which things happened. They went through a slow-motion ballet, sweat glistening on their bodies, twisting and turning, trading places, moving in the rhythm of love.

Later they lay quiet in each other's arms, warm and relaxed and content. When Jud opened his eyes he realized the music had stopped. The room was silent.

"Jud?"

"Mmm?"

"Do you love me?"

"Yes. Of course I do."

She snuggled closer and seemed to doze, as if his reply had reassured her, leaving her secure and happy.

Did he love her? Not just enjoy her company both in and out of bed, but really care for her with all the commitment the term meant? Absolutely. He had for some time, in fact had almost taken it for granted they'd be married, perhaps within the year. But the relationship suddenly seemed different.

Why?

It was because Sally was different, he realized. She was the same bright, enthusiastic, interesting young woman who'd dazzled him from the first time he'd seen her, but now she was showing him a dimension he'd never known existed. You could call it ambition, but it was more than that. What this case had provided wasn't just an opportunity to do well in her job; it had given her the chance to perform on a level much higher than probably even she had imagined she was capable of. And so her horizons had broadened, and she'd gained confidence. And she'd never again be the same person he thought he knew.

Then too, the momentous events of the last few days had

changed Jud as well. It was strange, the way you could work to
organize your life, thinking you had everything in hand, that
you were going in exactly the direction you'd set for yourself,
and then in an eyeblink something could happen to make you
see you had no more control over your fate than if you were a
speck of dust tumbling in the wind. And could also make you
see that what you'd been so rock-solid sure of wasn't necessarily true at all.

Just a short time ago he'd thought he had it made. Not only
was he doing work he enjoyed, but he'd reached a pinnacle that
made his success official. He was the chief of police in
Braddock, New York, an important figure in the community,
responsible for the protection of its citizens and highly respected.

So why did he suddenly feel this gnawing discontent?

It was because he'd been given a glimpse of the future and
what he saw was not the idyllic path he thought lay there but
something else entirely.

For one thing, he couldn't imagine Sally settling down after
this, going back to writing about gatherings of the Garden
Society and then later on dividing her time between that and
raising a family. Sooner or later she'd feel an emptiness that
would make her not only unhappy but bitter.

Even worse was the thought of his own prospects. Was he
really prepared to live the rest of his life being servile to people
like Sam Melcher and Swanson and the others—eventually
spending his winters the way old Chief Stark did, with nothing
to look forward to but the arrival of trout season?

Or had he come to understand that what he'd thought of as
reaching the peak of a career was in fact bumping his head
against a ceiling, and a low one at that?

The more he struggled with the questions, the more troubled
he was by the answers.

Sally nudged him. "Not going to sleep on me, are you?"

He chuckled. "You know me better than that."

She stroked him lightly and he felt himself respond. "That's
better," she said.

He turned to her and kissed her long and deeply, and in some
ways what happened then was even more satisfying than the

first time, because there was less urgency now, and he felt it could last forever.

Afterward he slept. And dreamt that a man dressed all in black was standing beside the bed, raising an ax high above his head. He awoke with a start and saw that the clock on the bedside table read 2:40.

Sally was in deep sleep. He slipped out of bed, taking care not to disturb her, and dressed quietly. In the dim light he could see her dark hair streaming out on the pillow.

He carried his shoes into the living room and put them on. Then he stuffed his tie into a pocket of his coat and left the apartment.

3

Karen Wilson stopped in at the luncheonette as she did every morning, ordering a black coffee and a muffin to go. She was in a hurry to get to her office, not knowing quite what she'd find in the pages of that morning's edition of the *Express*.

The reporter who'd interviewed her yesterday had been persistent, but also friendly and pleasant. Maybe she'd taken Karen at her word and hadn't blown the story out of proportion. Or better still, maybe the paper had decided against running it. Karen certainly hoped so. She paid for her breakfast, and carrying the brown paper sack walked quickly up the street to Boggs Ford.

As usual she was the first to arrive, and the newspaper was in front of the office entrance, where it was every morning. She picked up the paper and unlocked the door, then stepped inside and turned off the alarm. After hanging up her coat she sat down at her desk and opened the sack. She removed the top from the container of coffee and sipped some of its contents, then bit into the muffin. As anxious as she was to see what might be in the newspaper, she realized she was putting off looking at it.

Go on, you jerk—open it.

She unfolded the newspaper and scanned the front page. There were two stories with big black headlines—one about a trucker's strike, and the other about a fight over nuclear power stations that was developing in the state legislature.

But there was nothing about her role in helping the police locate little Michael Miriski's body. Karen felt a surge of relief and turned the page.

And there it was.

PSYCHIC LED SEARCHERS TO BOY'S CORPSE

With a picture of Karen and one of the Mariski boy. She felt as if she'd been kicked in the stomach.

The story carried Sally Benson's byline and ran a column and a half. Karen read through it rapidly, flinching at some of the lurid phraseology. It said she had "strange powers," and that she was unable to account for them. And that she had received information on the location of the body as if in a dream. The piece also quoted Mrs. Mariski, who said she and her husband had been struck by the peculiar way the young woman had suddenly appeared at their home "like she came from another world."

When Karen finished reading she was conscious of heat in her face. Her pulse was racing and she was slightly nauseous. It was the nightmare she'd always dreaded, and it had been laid out for the whole town of Braddock to see and shake their heads over. She was a freak, all right, and now it would be public knowledge. She read through the story again, slowly this time, and it didn't get any better. She wished she could go off somewhere and crawl into a hole.

Her picture—where had that come from? She didn't remember it, and yet it seemed vaguely familiar. The photograph was grainy and not quite sharp. As she studied it she realized it was from a group shot of the Boggs Ford staff that had been taken a few months back. The paper obviously had cropped it and blown it up, but how had they gotten it in the first place? Not that it mattered much now.

The phone on her desk rang and she jumped at the sound. She answered it: "Boggs Ford."

A male voice said, "Is Karen Wilson there, please?"

"This is Karen."

"Good morning. This is Jud MacElroy, chief of police."

"Yes?"

"Have you seen the story in this morning's newspaper?"

"I just read it."

"I'm sure you're upset by it."

"I—yes, I am."

"Karen, I just wanted to say I'm sorry the paper got hold of it, and I hope you won't let it bother you too much."

Tears welled in her eyes and her voice trembled. "Won't let it bother me too much? With what it says about my strange powers, and how it's like I came from another world? You're telling me you hope I won't let it bother me?"

"It'll blow over, Karen. In a day or so it'll be forgotten. That's the way those things are. In the meantime, just shrug it off. If anybody asks, tell them it was only a hunch and that the paper blew it out of proportion."

"I—I'll try."

"Good. I just wanted you to know I was thinking of you, and I realize how tough this is for you. If there's anything I can do to help, just let me know."

"Thank you. And thanks for calling." She hung up.

She went back to the newspaper, trying to read the rest of it but not succeeding as her eyes blurred and her thoughts kept going back to that hateful story. Breakfast was also a bust. The coffee tasted acidic and the muffin was like sawdust. She put the top back on the container and dropped the whole mess into her wastebasket.

Twenty minutes later Ed McCarthy walked into the showroom with a copy of the *Express* under his arm and a big smile on his face. His voice was cheerful. "Hey, Karen—how's the celebrity?"

For the second time that morning her face flamed. "I'm no celebrity."

He came over to her desk. "That's what you think. When people read that piece in the paper you'll be famous. You know, that's amazing, what you did. I never knew you could do stuff like that. Hey, tell the truth—is that really how it happened? You saw the kid in your head and you knew where he was?"

"No. It was just a hunch."

"Yeah?" He gestured toward the copy of the *Express* that lay on her desk. "Don't tell anybody—the paper's version is a hell of a lot more exciting. Next thing that happens is you get another story on you, this time in *People* magazine. Then Carson has you on as a guest. After that somebody writes a book about you."

Karen shook her head. Ed was like a great big overgrown kid.

He went to the rack and hung up his coat, then returned to where she was sitting. "Tell you what. You hire me as your agent, and we'll both make a bundle. After Carson, we put you on the lecture circuit."

"I don't think so. Like I said, it was just a fluke. A one-shot. So my career has already ended."

"Think I'm kidding, don't you? I'm telling you, a thing like this could be worth a lot of money."

She folded the newspaper and put it aside. "Sorry, Ed. And now if you'll excuse me, I've got work to do."

That brought her five minutes of peace, which was the last she'd get that day. The telephone rang again, and this time it was the radio station, WBDK. Braddock wasn't big enough for its own TV outlet; the only broadcast operation was this one, an affiliate of WCBS-FM. A young man identified himself as a news reporter and asked if she'd care to add to the story in that morning's *Express.* The station wanted to run a feature on her, he said. They'd record her in an interview to be broadcast later in the day.

Karen told him to forget it and hung up.

A few minutes after that Jack Morrow and Fred Guzik came in. Whenever Karen saw them, she thought of Frick and Frack. But this morning they were no joke. Both of them began teasing her about the piece in the paper, making idiotic remarks and then guffawing at each other's cleverness. Joe asked if Karen would help Fred locate his pliers, which he'd mislaid someplace in his garage. Or could she tell Joe which horse to bet in the fifth race at Hialeah? Would she like to go to Vegas with them for the weekend? They could make a killing. No? Then how about Atlantic City?

They kept it up until Boggs arrived, only then backing off and going to their own desks in an effort to convey to the boss that they were working hard.

Boggs had a strange expression on his face as he passed Karen and said good morning. She mumbled a reply and then he told her to come into his office—he wanted to talk with her. He went on in and closed the door.

For a minute or so she simply sat still. Again she wished she could just get up and put on her coat and walk out of Boggs Ford and never come back again. But that wouldn't really solve anything. As she had so many times, she reminded herself that the job paid well, and she needed every cent she could make. Finally she stood up, and squaring her shoulders walked to his office. She knocked, opened the door and stepped inside.

For once she was glad to close the door behind her before approaching his desk. She certainly didn't want any of the others to overhear whatever it was he had to say.

He looked up at her, the peculiar, wide-eyed expression again on his face. "Sit down, Karen." He indicated a chair.

She sank down onto it, holding her breath.

"That story in the paper," he said. "That true?"

She took her time before answering, telling herself to follow the police chief's advice. "It was way overplayed. I just had a feeling something like that might have happened. You know how kids take chances fooling around on ice. So I suggested the police look in the pond."

"And that's all?"

"That's all there was to it."

"So the reporter just blew it up into a big deal."

"Pretty much."

"You know what I think went through some people's minds when they read that story?"

She kept her gaze steady, her face expressionless. "No, I don't."

"You can bet they thought of the headsman. They said to themselves, if she could find the answer to one mystery, maybe she could solve another."

Which is what went through *your* mind, Mr. Boggs, she thought. "That's a farfetched idea."

"Yeah, well. You know how people are. Wouldn't surprise me a bit if the cops started asking for your help. Soon as they read the story. That reporter who wrote it—you know who she is, don't you?"

"Her name is Sally Benson."

"Yeah, and she's also the chief of police's girlfriend."

Karen was stunned. She stared at him, trying to wrap her mind around what he'd said.

Boggs didn't notice her reaction. "I'm surprised she didn't tip him to the idea. That you could help with the Dickens case, I mean. With the cops coming up with nothing, I'd expect him to jump on it."

He went on talking, but Karen didn't hear him. She felt dazed, sitting in the chair with her stomach dropping out of her.

Sally Benson is Jud MacElroy's girlfriend.

So he'd lied to her. Completely deceived her. Let her go on and on with the assurance that anything she told him was in confidence. And then he'd tipped off his sweetie the hotshot reporter that there was a hell of a story to be had. He'd even had the gall to call her this morning and tell her not to let the story both her.

The rotten bastard.

She got to her feet and Boggs halted whatever he was saying in mid-sentence. "Karen—are you all right?"

"I'm—no, I'm not."

"What is it?"

She shook her head. "All of a sudden I just don't feel well."

"You want some water or something? Want to lie down?"

"No, no. Really."

"Listen, if you're sick, maybe you ought to go home."

"I think I'll do that." She got up from the chair and waved him away when he rose and moved toward her. "Please, I'll be okay." She left his office.

When she put on her coat and walked out the front door she was aware that people in the outer office and the showroom were staring at her.

ELEVEN ··
From Out of the Past

1

Jud was at the desk talking to Brusson when the call came in. Brusson said Chief Broadhurst was on the line from Binghamton, and Jud told him he'd take it in his office.

He went in and shut the door behind him, then sat down at his desk and picked up the phone. "Hey, Chief—how are you?"

"Good, Jud. I think maybe we got something more for you on the family you asked about. The Donovans?"

Jud leaned forward. "What is it?"

"One of our guys here remembered hearing the daughter went up from New York on armed robbery. I made a couple calls to the city and found out the case was handled by the Seventeenth Precinct. I talked to a lieutenant there, and I just heard back from him. He said Joan Donovan had a long sheet for prostitution and then after that she was arrested twice in jewelry store holdups. First time she did a year and two months in Westchester, second time she got five to ten.

"She out now?"

"No, still in Westchester. The superintendent's name is Fred Wallace. You want the number?"

"Sure." Jud took it down and said, "Thanks, Chief, you've been a lot of help. I really appreciate it."

"Anytime, Jud. Glad we could come up with it."

Jud hung up and thought about what he'd learned. Then he called the number Broadhurst had given him for the Westchester Correctional Facility and asked for the superintendent.

When Wallace came on, Jud told him who he was and said he was calling about an inmate, Joan Donovan. The superintendent said he'd had another call on her from the chief of police in Binghamton and asked if this was in connection with the same case. Jud said it was, that it was a homicide investigation and he wanted to interview Donovan. He made an appointment for the next day and hung up.

Next he called Sally Benson at the *Express*.

When she answered he could hear the excitement in her voice. "Did you see my story this morning on that Wilson woman and the Mariski boy?"

"Yeah, you did quite a job."

"I told you it was a good piece. I've already had a bunch of calls complimenting me on it. Even Maxwell said he thought it was first-rate. And getting praise from him is really something."

"I'll bet it is."

"And you know what some people have said?"

It wasn't hard to guess. "What have they said?"

"That maybe Wilson could help with the Dickens murder. Maybe she could tell where Buddy Harper is. So now you don't have to get mad at me over the idea—it's occurred to others as well."

"Uh-huh."

"Well—are you going to follow up on it?"

"No. What's more, I expressly forbid you to quote me or to write anything that suggests I'm even considering such an idea. You got that?"

"Oh, Jud. You can be a real ballbuster at times, you know that?"

"Answer the question. Do you understand me?"

"Yes, I got the message."

To take some of the sting out of it he said, "You may not think so, but I appreciate hearing some of the things you come up with. It's just that I can't have anybody saying I'm feeding stuff to a reporter or cooperating with her because she's a friend of mine. You know that—we've been over it a hundred times."

"Haven't we, though."

"And now I have a favor to ask."

"A favor? Now you want me to do you a favor?"

"Will you help me?"

"Do I get something I can use?"

"Maybe later on, if it turns out to be valuable. How about it?"

"I guess so. What is it?"

"You said you have a morgue in that place, right?"

"Yeah, but it's not great. I told you, I had to do a lot of digging just to find the pieces on the Donovan murder."

"Is there a photo file?"

"Yes. Also hit or miss."

"Okay, here's what I want. Go back to the period around the middle nineteen sixties and see if you can find pictures of men who were living in Braddock and who are still living here now."

"Wait a minute. You want pictures that were taken then, so you can see what they looked like at the time?"

"That's it."

There was a pause. "Hey, this sounds exciting. You've got an angle on the Donovan case, right?"

"I don't have anything. I'm only trying to find something that might give me a direction to follow."

"I don't believe you, but sure—I'll help. Just don't get your hopes up too high."

"Don't worry, I won't."

"Now tell me who you have in mind."

"Like I said, anybody who's around today but lived here back then. And any kind of pictures you can round up. Group shots of any kind, portraits—anything. Okay?"

"I guess so. But I can tell you right now, this is a project. When do you want the pictures—tomorrow, I suppose?"

"Wrong. I want them tonight."

She groaned.

"Well?"

Her tone brightened. "If I bring them over, do I get a repeat performance?"

"Sure, do I?"

"Yes, but I didn't appreciate the way you sneaked out on me last night."

"I was just being careful not to wake you. I couldn't stay there anyway, I didn't have my uniform." Jesus, why was he making all these dumb excuses?

2

Jud left his office a little after eight. He drove over to Memorial to see the kid who'd been struck by the Cadillac and gave him the baseball he'd bought earlier in the day. The kid was in good shape, considering. He'd suffered deep cuts and a concussion, and a compound fracture of his left wrist, but the doctors had said he'd have no problem mending. The cast would come off in a couple of weeks. He was due to leave the hospital the next day, and he was tickled with the ball. After that Jud went home.

He drank a beer and then took a shower and put on jeans and an old flannel shirt and went back into the kitchen to see what he could find to eat.

There wasn't much; for dinner he had one of those frozen things in a plastic-and-foil package. He took it out of the freezer and stuck it into the microwave and by the time he finished another beer it was ready. It was a mixture of ground beef and gravy over noodles and it made him think of the stuff you got in the army they called shit on a shingle. Except here you didn't even get the shingle. Nevertheless it was hot and it didn't taste too terrible and with another beer it went down all right.

The best thing about it was that when you finished you didn't have dishes or pots and pans to clean up; you just heaved the plastic into the garbage and that was that. It occurred to him that the meal made quite a contrast with the one he'd had at Armando's the night before.

He cracked a fresh beer and went into the living room. There was still some kindling left and a few logs on the hearth and in a couple of minutes he had a good blaze going. He got out the Gibson and sat in front of the fire as he tuned the guitar.

His fingers were a little stiff and he ran some chords to warm them up. When they were limber he tried a walking rhythm he'd been practicing, one he'd heard on a Roy Orbison record and admired. Then he went into a song, accompanying himself with the new rhythm.

> Goin' down a long and lonesome road
> Carryin' an awful heavy load
> Hopin' that my trip will end
> Hopin' that I'll find a friend
> Wanna quit this long and lonesome road

Not bad, he thought. He liked the way the rhythm worked; sort of fit the lyric, too. Not that it was much of a lyric, but it was all he'd thought of so far. He kept the rhythm going, trying a variation of it by emphasizing the first and third beat of each bar. He was in F, because he preferred keys with flats over the ones with sharps. They were the traditional blues keys, for some reason or other, and he didn't know why they worked so well for R&B but they did. He stayed with it for eight more bars, then modulated into E-flat and sang the song again.

He'd been at it for over an hour when Sally arrived. She came in the front door carrying a cardboard box and an overnight bag. Jud kissed her lightly and took her coat. As he hung it in the closet she put the box on the kitchen table and carried her bag into the bedroom.

When she came out she turned to him and smiled. "How about a drink? It's the least you could do after I've been playing detective for you for hours."

"How'd you make out?"

She gestured toward the kitchen. "See for yourself. I don't know if you'll find what you're looking for, but I pulled out a lot of pictures. If nothing else they'll give you a good laugh. It's amazing to see how much people change in twenty-five years or so."

"Sure, let's look. But first I'll get you that drink." He started for the kitchen and over his shoulder asked if she'd had dinner. She replied that she had. Which was a good thing, because the only food he could have offered her was another of the frozen conglomerations. He got out a glass and poured her a bourbon over ice. Then they sat together at the table and Jud went through the contents of the box.

She was right—the photos were funny as hell. There were dozens of them, individual shots as well as all manner of group pictures, and Jud didn't recognize half the people in them.

Sally pointed to one of a young man with bushy hair and sharp features, skinny as a weasel. His eyes were peering out through wire-rimmed glasses. "Bet you can't tell me who that is."

Jud stared at the photo. It was black and white, a snapshot showing the guy standing outdoors on a flight of steps, his arms folded. There was something vaguely familiar about him, but as hard as he tried, Jud couldn't identify him. Finally he turned his hands palms up. "Okay, you win. Who is it?"

"Dr. Reinholtz."

"You're kidding." He peered closely at the print, recognizing its subject now but disbelieving what he saw. "He's got hair, and no mustache, and he's thin. Also the hair's black. No wonder I didn't know who it was."

"Isn't that something? There are lots of them like that. Sometimes they sort of look like somebody you know, but you're just not sure."

"So how'd you know who these guys were?"

"They're kept in alphabetized jackets in the photo file, and their names are on the backs of the pictures."

He turned over the shot and saw the doctor's name printed in ink along with the date: *April 16, 1963.*

Shuffling through the stack he picked out another at random. It was a color shot, the kind a cheap portrait studio turned out. It showed a smiling, heavyset youth with blond hair, and this time Jud had no idea who it might be.

"That's Gil Bishop," Sally said. "The fire chief."

He shook his head. This one was even more surprising than the one of Reinholtz. Nowadays Bishop was still burly, but he was bald as an egg. And instead of appearing heavy but fit, as he did in the photo, his features drooped, so that whenever Jud saw him he thought of a bulldog with loose jowls.

He riffled through more of the pictures, checking the backs to identify the subjects and organizing them into groups. Most of the photos he kept, but some he discarded for one reason or other. Mel Richards, a partner in the law firm of Richards &

Ward, was dying of cancer, and there were others who also were now infirm. The ones of that type he put aside.

But he still had quite a collection. A lot of them were of people he saw around Braddock every day.

Some of the men were in uniform. There was Ben Tucker, who now ran the Tucker Construction Company, wearing Marine Corps dress blues and with his arm around the girl he later married, and Bob Ormandy and Elmer Hobbs and Dieter Bloch, all in navy uniforms, and Tom Hecht in the green beret of the Rangers.

Frank Hathaway was there too, slim and clean-shaven, wearing army olive drab. Jud studied the photo of the man who was now confined to a wheelchair and teaching English at Braddock High School. The uniform Hathaway was wearing was that of an enlisted man, so the shot must have been made before Hathaway went to OCS. Seeing it reminded Jud that he'd intended to check out the man's army record and hadn't got to it. It was just one more thing he had to remember to do.

The pictures of the men in uniform had all been taken during the time of the Vietnam War, and Jud realized he was looking at photos of the lucky ones. These were the guys who'd come back. There were plenty of young men from Braddock who hadn't—at least not with their lives. They were the ones who'd returned in stainless steel boxes and whose names were now on the wall in Washington. What a total fuckup that war had been.

So intent was he on his inspection of the photo he hardly realized it when Sally got up and made herself a fresh drink, becoming aware of her presence again when she set a fresh beer down in front of him. She bent over and kissed his cheek, then sat down again alongside him.

She sipped her bourbon. "You gonna let me in on the big secret now?"

He glanced at her. "I told you, you're not to write anything that could give somebody the idea you're in on what I'm doing."

"And I said okay, I won't. But after all this trouble I went to for you, you could at least let me know what's going on."

"Sally, I can't. Don't ask me, at least not now. Later, if it goes anywhere, I'll tell you all about it."

"That means I get an exclusive interview?"

"God, don't you ever quit?"

"Nope. That's the secret of my success. One of them, anyway."

He put the pictures he wanted to keep back into the box and handed her the others. "Like I told you, we'll see where it goes."

She pointed at the box. "How long will you need these?"

"Just a day or two. I'll take good care of them."

"Please do. I can't have them out of the files too long. Not that I can imagine anybody asking for them, but I didn't sign them out."

He cocked his head. "Why not?"

"Because I figured you wanted this kept as quiet as possible."

He smiled. "Always thinking, huh?"

"Sure. As I told you yesterday, I think it's exciting, and it didn't take too much to figure out what you were up to."

"No?"

"Oh, Jud—stop pussyfooting around. I know damn well you think this is going to give you something in the Donovan case."

At least he knew one sure way to shut her up. He drained his beer and rose from the table. "Listen, woman—you planning on sitting here and arguing all night?"

She grinned and got up from her chair, pressing herself against him and drawing her arms tight around his waist. "Okay, Chief. I give up."

He led her into the bedroom, and although it was good, their lovemaking didn't have the explosiveness it had the night before. But then, even the best things in life weren't perfect all the time.

3

In the morning Jud went through the routine business he had to handle as quickly as possible. The day was slipping by and he was anxious to get on the road. There had been another two-car accident on Route 23 the night before; an old man driving an aged Buick had sideswiped a station wagon with a bunch of kids in it. Two of the kids had been injured slightly and the old man had suffered a broken leg. All three had been taken to Memorial and the kids were released after a quick patch-up in the emergency room. The old man was still in the hospital.

Jud looked at the officer's report and shook his head. This was the third accident the duffer had been in this year. In the previous one he'd slammed into another car in a supermarket parking lot and crushed a woman's pelvis. His license had been suspended, which meant last night he'd been driving illegally.

That was one of the crazier aspects of the motor vehicle laws. Here this guy, whose age according to the report was eighty-six, thought nothing of getting into his mangy pile of junk and putting people's lives at risk, and there were thousands like him all over the country. Jud believed the laws concerning drivers over sixty should be tightened, and had thought so from the time he'd become a cop. Statistically, kids were the worst drivers as far as causing accidents was concerned, but old people weren't far behind. From sixty on, he believed, they should be given an annual driver's test and a physical as well. And maybe there should be a mandatory cutoff age, say seventy-five or so.

And on the subject of drivers, Grady told him Victor Scalzo's lawyer was threatening to sue for false arrest. Jud asked if the witness who'd seen him hit the kid on the bike was willing to testify and Grady said she was. Good, Jud thought. With a trial in this county they could stick it up Mr. Scalzo's ass.

After that Jud went into Pearson's office and asked the inspector how it was going.

Pearson gave him one of his tolerant smiles. "Just a question of time now."

"You seem pretty sure it was Buddy Harper who killed the Dickens girl."

The inspector sat back in his chair. "After a while you see patterns in these things. The facts may be different, but the overall pattern is there. And that's what we've got here. The kid was fucking her, the autopsy showed that. They were together that night, and in the morning she was dead. He used the ax because he knew everybody in this town would believe that headsman crap. Then something scared him. Maybe it was the pressure I was putting on him. Whatever it was, he lost his nerve and took off. The rest of it is nothing but details."

"What about a motive?"

Pearson shrugged. "Who knows? Jealousy, maybe. Maybe something else. Far as I'm concerned, that's just one of the details. When we pick him up we'll get the rest of the answers and that'll be it."

"Where do you think he went?"

"Out of state someplace. It's obvious he even had that planned."

"How do you figure?"

"Leaving the car like that, as if he'd been working on it. That was just to throw his parents off, and they went for it. Said he'd never go off and leave his car behind. What happened was, he squirreled some money away and then he beat it. Maybe took the train to New York or whatever. From there a bus or maybe a plane. But he won't leave the country—kids never do that, they're afraid to go out of the States. So sooner or later we'll get a call from someplace and we'll go pick him up."

"Good luck," Jud said.

By the time he left headquarters it was after ten o'clock. He told Grady where he was going and drove one of the unmarked blue Plymouth sedans. He wore his uniform, however, and carried the box of photographs with him.

It was a sunny day, relatively mild for late winter, and as always his hopes came up that they'd seen the last of the snow. Which was wishful thinking, of course—the heaviest snowstorms of the year were almost always the ones that came at the end of March. They'd had some riproaring blizzards after St. Patrick's Day, and even well into April. But today's weather was pleasant compared to what they'd been having, and he relaxed and enjoyed the drive.

There was a fair amount of traffic on the roads, especially on the throughway. He kept to the righthand lane and nailed the speedometer on sixty miles an hour, noting that he was one of the few drivers who did. Most of the others blew by him as if he were standing still. Even the tractor trailers, the huge sixteen-wheelers, went pounding along at well over seventy.

On the whole trip he passed only one police car, a state trooper going in the opposite direction.

The way Jud saw it, the issue wasn't staying within the speed limit, it was staying alive. Which was another thing his years as a cop had taught him. If you wanted to avoid becoming a statistic, you drove defensively. He'd spent too much time sweeping fatalities up off the roads to ignore that rule. The only time he exceeded the limit was when there was an emergency.

It was past noon by the time he reached Bedford, and he was hungry. He stopped at a diner and wolfed down a couple of hamburgers and a cup of coffee, pondering as he did how long his stomach was going to stand for the punishment he dealt in on an almost daily basis. When he finished he asked directions to the Westchester Correctional Facility and drove to it.

At the entrance two guards checked out his shield and I.D. He told them Superintendent Wallace was expecting him. They telephoned Wallace's office and then opened the gate and waved him through, pointing to a parking area in front of the administration building.

Security here was light. There was only a single chain-link fence. No high stone walls, no searchlights, no towers with guards carrying rifles and machine guns, even though this place was classified as a maximum security institution. Nothing like Attica or Sing-Sing, some of the really tight prisons he'd visited.

He knew the reason: Westchester was for females. And even though there were some very tough cookies in these ugly old buildings, women prisoners were a breeze to handle compared to men. Male inmates often carried weapons ranging from sharpened screwdrivers to homemade knives, and even zip guns that had been fashioned in the prison shops.

Men also fought constantly with each other and with the guards, taking the resultant hitch in solitary as just another part of the routine. And if an inmate stole or ratted or made it with somebody else's punk, he stood a good chance of being found dead in the shower room or the place where his job was. To most of those guys, life inside the walls had no more value than it did outside—maybe less.

Women, on the other hand, rarely became violent, either in

their rebellions or their squabbles with each other. Sure, there was the occasional punch-out and biting fray, and once in a while even a knife rip or a gouged-out eye. But murder among female prisoners was rare. For that matter, so were female prisoners themselves. Of the thirty thousand or so inmates in the state of New York, less than five percent were women.

Jud parked the cruiser and went into the building.

Wallace was heavy and slow-moving, with a gut that must have taken years to nurture. His black hair was pasted over the top of his skull, and his eyes looked at you from under bushy brows with innate suspicion, even though you were a cop. He had a slow, deliberate way of talking as well, which Jud knew would drive you nuts if you had to listen to it every day. He indicated a chair in front of his desk. "You're here to see Joan Donovan," he said.

"Right." Jud took off his cap and unzipped his jacket as he sat down. He kept the box of photos on his lap and placed his cap on top of it.

The superintendent rested a heavy hand on a manila folder that lay on his desk. "Got her file here, if you want to look at it before you talk to her."

"Thanks, I will. I understand this is her second trip?"

"That's correct. Both times for armed robbery in New York. Knocked over jewelry stores. In the first one the guy she was with did the actual stickup, she was just a lookout. But as you know, the law don't distinguish. She got two to five on a plea bargain, served fourteen months. Second one she was with a different guy. Only this time she had a gun too. They hit a store on Madison Avenue and the manager tried to put up a fight so she shot him. Bullet lodged in his skull. He lived, but he would've been better off if he didn't."

"You said on the phone she's been here three years this time?"

"Yeah. She got five to ten, but it could've been more."

"Why wasn't it?"

"Another plea bargain."

"You must get a lot of those."

"Ninety-eight percent. That's why most of the inmates here are short-timers."

"How is that?"

Wallace shrugged beefy shoulders. "A perpetrator's got any brains, or her lawyer does, she bargains. When she does, she gets off light. She comes up here and pretty soon she's back on the street. Average term for our ladies is two years."

"What if she doesn't bargain?"

"That forces a trial. Costs a lot of time and money. Courts are so clogged now they'll never get caught up. So like as not the judge'll be pissed off and stick it to her. She winds up with a maximum sentence."

"What if she's innocent?"

The superintendent's lip curled. "Innocent? Who the fuck is innocent?"

"About Donovan."

"Yes?"

"When is she likely to be paroled?"

"Hard to say. She's eligible, but the board turned her down."

"Why?"

"She's a troublemaker, for one thing. Always running up charge sheets."

"What's a charge sheet?"

"When a C.O. writes up an inmate for a violation of rules. With her it's fighting with other inmates, giving the C.O.s shit, stuff like that. Also she's got a long record. Prostitution, drugs, and the robberies. But the worst thing is how she conned the board before and got herself paroled the first time. Gave 'em a load of crap and they bought it."

He paused, and when he spoke again there was an edge of satisfaction in his tone. "Against my recommendation. She was out for a year and then she knocked over the other store and shot the guy."

"So they remember?"

"It's all in the file. They go through it and they're not that ready to look stupid again so quick."

"What's the penalty for rule violation?"

"Depends on what somebody did. And how many charge sheets they had in the past. With her there's plenty."

"What happens, usually?"

"Restriction. That's like solitary, only here it just means in a cell, away from everybody. No work, no exercise, nothing. Not like in a male penitentiary, where they got a real hole. Here we're dealing with ladies."

Jud was tempted to ask Wallace if he'd prefer having a hole to confine his ladies in, but he held his tongue.

The superintendent was studying him. "You said you're on a homicide?"

"That's right. High-school girl was killed in her home by an intruder. Her head was cut off."

"Yeah," Wallace said. "I read about that. What's the connection?"

"Donovan's mother died the same way, when Joan was six years old. Family was living in Braddock at the time."

The bushy eyebrows lifted. "Same M.O.?"

"Yes."

"All it says in the file is her mother is deceased."

"Uh-huh. But that's what happened."

"Any suspects in the one you got now?"

"Maybe. The girl's boyfriend disappeared a few days after the murder."

"What makes you think Donovan can help you?"

"I don't know whether she can or not. I just want to question her."

"Okay." Wallace pointed to the file jacket. "You want to see this?"

"Yes, I do." Jud picked up the file and opened it. There was a list of arrests and dispositions of each count, and several reports by Westchester personnel and psychiatric social workers. The typed reports by the facility people said Donovan was a bad inmate. The pages were full of grammatical and spelling errors, and read as if a ten-year-old might have written them. In contrast, the ones by the social workers contained mostly jargon, reams of psychobullshit to the effect that the subject could be fully rehabilitated, provided she received sufficient therapy. Everybody seemed to have been writing about a different person.

There was also a set of photographs showing 82-6-74 DONOVAN, JOAN head on and in profile. To Jud's surprise she wasn't bad-looking, if you could get past the harsh lighting and the crudeness of the black-and-white photography.

He put the file back down on the desk. "Can I get a copy of this?"

"Only the arrest record," Wallace replied. "I'll have a Xerox made. You want to see her now?"

"Yes."

Wallace lifted a phone and called a number. He told whoever answered to bring Donovan to Visitor's Room D. Then he called another number and a few seconds later a Corrections Officer came into the office.

This one was a woman. She was black, about as wide as she was tall, wearing a blue uniform.

Wallace said, "Officer Tate, this is Chief of Police MacElroy. The chief is from Braddock, upstate."

"Hello," Jud said.

Officer Tate grunted.

"Take the chief down to Visitor's D," Wallace ordered.

"I suppose to stay with him?"

"Not necessary." He looked at Jud. "The C.O. who brings Donovan down will wait for her. When you're through, tell the C.O. to call here and we'll send somebody for you."

"Okay, thanks for your help."

Wallace made no reply.

Jud followed Tate out of the office, carrying the box of photographs. They went through a labyrinth of corridors and doors and wound up before a room marked Visitor's D.

When Tate opened the door to the room, she followed him inside and asked, "What you after Donovan for?"

"I'm not. I just want to talk to her."

Tate gestured toward a wooden table with straightbacked chairs on either side. The room was much smaller than the typical visiting setup in a man's facility, and there were no glass partitions to separate you from the inmates. He put his box and his cap down on the table and hung his jacket on the back of a chair before sitting down.

Tate made another attempt. "You looking for her on something she done?"

"No. I just want to ask her a few questions." It wasn't hard to figure out what the C.O. was after—any information on an inmate might turn out to be useful, one way or another. He smiled pleasantly. "She's a friend of yours?"

Tate expelled air from between thick lips. "Sheeit."

At least that put an end to the probing. A minute later another C.O. appeared. This one was also female, white this time and tall, with a prominent nose and a downy line of dark hair on her upper lip. Following her into the room was a slim young woman wearing a pale green prison dress. Clipped to the neck of the dress was a laminated I.D. card.

The tall C.O. looked at Jud. "You the visitor?"

"Yes. I'm Jud MacElroy, Chief of Police in Braddock."

"I'm Officer Geraldi." She indicated the inmate with a tilt of her head. "This here is Joan Donovan. Sit down, Donovan."

Jud said, "Hello, Joan."

Donovan fixed him with cold blue eyes and remained silent. She took the chair opposite him.

Her face was thinner than it had appeared in her file photograph, and her ash-blond hair was tied back in a bun. With makeup and her hair done she would have been quite attractive. Jud had never seen a picture of her mother, but from the way Ray Maxwell had described her, she'd probably looked much like the woman seated across from him now. Despite the baggy dress he could see that her body was trim and shapely.

The Corrections Officers continued to stand there, giving no indication they intended to leave. Geraldi leaned against the wall and folded her arms.

"You don't have to stay," Jud said to them.

Tate turned and left the room, but Geraldi kept her position against the wall.

He tried again. "I said—"

Geraldi sniffed. "I heard what you said. But I gotta stay with the inmate. Regulations."

Joan Donovan turned toward the C.O. and spoke for the first time since she'd entered the room. "Okay, bull dyke—why don't you do what the man says and get the fuck out of here?"

The C.O. flushed. "Watch your mouth, Donovan, or you get a charge sheet."

"Take your charge sheet and wipe your hairy ass with it."

Jud held up his hands. "Excuse me, Officer. I was told this could be a private conversation. If you want to call the superintendent's office, I'm sure Mr. Wallace would confirm that."

Bright with anger, Geraldi's eyes locked on the inmate. She moved away from the wall and started for the door.

Donovan returned the stare, opening her mouth and flicking her tongue from side to side obscenely.

For a moment the C.O. looked as if she was going to pop off again, but then she walked out and closed the door behind her.

Donovan turned back to Jud, a mirthless smile lifting one corner of her mouth. Her voice was no longer strident, but low and husky. "So how are things in dear old Braddock?"

"You remember the town?"

"Sure I remember it. And I know why you're here, too."

"You do?"

"Mm-hm. Matter of fact, I've been expecting you. Ever since I heard about that kid getting her head chopped off. I figured sooner or later somebody'd connect it to what happened to my mother and see if they couldn't get something out of me. And here you are."

Jud sat back in his chair. "You think you can help me?"

The crooked smile widened a notch. "It depends on the deal."

"I can't promise you anything," Jud said.

"Yes you can." There was genuine amusement now in Donovan's blue eyes, as if she knew exactly what his thoughts were and she was enjoying the little game they were playing.

"What do you have in mind?"

She tilted her head. "You guarantee me you'll go to bat with the parole board. And I don't mean you just write a nice polite letter and that's it."

"Then what do you mean?"

"I mean you help get me out of this shithole."

"I don't have that kind of clout."

"I think you do."

He raised a hand. "Look, Joan. You help me, I'll do my best for you. I'll go before the board personally, and I'll pull every string I can. That good enough?"

"Maybe. You guarantee it?"

"Yes. I guarantee I'll do my level best."

She seemed to relax a little. "Okay, so let's talk. Your name's Jud?"

"Right."

"Pretty young, aren't you, to be chief?"

She was stroking him, of course. And yet it was the damnedest thing—even though he knew it, she was projecting an animal magnetism that was almost palpable. Joan Donovan would be some handful. Again he thought of her mother.

"How old were you," he asked, "when you left Braddock?"

"Seven. We moved to Binghamton a few months after my mother died."

"How well do you remember her?"

"Very well. I remember everything about her. The way she looked, the way she walked. Even the sound of her voice. People've told me I'm a lot like her."

"How'd you get along with her?"

"Great. It was simple. She had as little to do with me as possible."

"Why was that?"

"Because I cramped her style, of course. The last thing she wanted was a kid around. But I just happened, so I guess she figured the best way to deal with it was not to deal with it."

"Then she wasn't home much?"

"Sure she was. See, she had lots of friends. And even though she spent a lot of her time out of the house, there were other times when she'd have them over."

"You're talking about men she was seeing?"

The half-smile returned to her mouth. "What else? You don't think she belonged to a sewing circle, do you?"

"I guess not."

"Yeah. So when she'd have a friend over, she didn't care whether I saw them or not. They closed the bedroom door—I don't mean I saw them that way—but she didn't care if I knew it. Afterward she'd give me candy and stuff to shut me up. And a lot of times the guy would give me money."

"So you never mentioned any of this to your father."

"What, and kill a good thing? Hell no, I didn't."

"What was he like, your father?"

Her voice took on an edge of bitterness. "He was an asshole. After a while I realized he knew what was going on too. Or at least he suspected it. But the dumb shit never said a word about it."

"They ever fight?"

"Not really. Not that I remember. He just let everything go by, and as long as it didn't interfere with his business he didn't care to know about it. At least that was the way it seemed to me."

"After you moved to Binghamton he remarried, right?"

"He sure did."

"And I take it you didn't get along with your stepmother."

"That bitch?"

"I understand she died last year."

"Should have been twenty years sooner."

Jud was quiet for a moment. "About your mother's friends."

The blue eyes fixed on him. "You want to know if I can remember any of them, right?"

Again she'd been a step ahead of him. "Yes."

"I think I can, but it's been a long time. And I can remember what some of them looked like, but not their names. I doubt if I knew their names, anyway."

He gestured toward the box. "I brought some photos. Old ones, from around that time."

"Aren't you clever."

"Maybe. We'll see."

He got out his pocket notebook and a ballpoint, placing them on the table. Then he opened the box and took out the stack of pictures. "I'm going to show you these one at a time. If you spot somebody, say so. Even if one of them just looks sort of familiar."

"Sounds like fun. Do I get a prize?" She made the question sound like a proposition."

Jud held up the first photo. On the back he'd lightly penciled a number, as he had on all of them. This one was a picture of George Demmerle, who currently ran the Gulf station out on Route 23.

She squinted at it. "No."

He put the picture back into the box and held up the next one.

She shook her head.

They went through a dozen of them before she said, "Wait a minute."

"Recognize him?"

"No. It's just that you're going too fast. You go that fast, it gets confusing. Screws up my memory."

"Sorry. I'll show you one, and then we'll wait a moment. Or if you want to take a break anytime, just say so."

"Okay."

He raised the next photo.

"That one."

"You sure?"

"I think so. Yeah, I'm sure. Let me see." She took the photo from him and peered at it intently for half a minute or so. When she handed it back she said, "That one used to give me money."

A slight sensation passed through Jud's chest. The picture was a head shot of Bill Swanson.

"You remember anything else about him—anything at all?"

"No. Just him giving me money."

Jud opened his notebook and jotted down the number he'd penciled on the back of the photograph. Then he put the photo back in the box and picked up the next one.

They went through ten more before she hit another. "Yeah. Him."

"Sure?"

"Yes." She went through the same routine, staring at the picture. "I remember his face. But that's all."

"Okay." The guy was Mark Stanton, a manager with the telephone company.

They took a few minutes' break after that, and she asked him how long he'd been a cop.

Eleven years, he told her, counting his MP time.

"You must like it, huh? Or just do it for the money?"

He knew she was needling him. "What money?"

"Only kidding, Chief. Fact is, I know what makes a cop tick."

"You do?"

"Uh-huh. It's the power, right? You get to carry a big gun, wear a badge that tells the world you're hot shit. And with you it's even better, because now you got a gold badge that says you're the hottest shit of all."

"That must be it."

"You married?"

"No."

"Bet you got a cute girlfriend, though. And I'll bet she just loves getting that big cop dick shoved into her. See, women are like that too, if you haven't noticed. Nothing turns them on like power."

She was stroking again, and he knew it, but for some crazy reason it was having an erotic effect on him, sitting here while she worked on him with that knowing look in her eyes.

He picked up another photo. "How about this one?"

She shook her head.

They kept going, and as the pile dwindled he began to wonder if this would work out. Two hits out of all these pictures wasn't overly encouraging.

Suddenly she burst out laughing, pointing at the photograph he was holding.

He peered at her, eyebrows raised questioningly.

She laughed again. "Uncle Sam?"

"What?"

"Uncle Sam. That one I even remember his name because it was kind of a joke. He said to call him that, and I used to wonder how he could be Uncle Sam without the whiskers and the top hat. But that's the guy, all right."

Jud felt excited and uneasy at the same time. "Anything else on him?"

"No, that's it. Jesus, that's funny."

He said nothing, but wrote down the number and placed the picture in the box. It was a studio portrait of a man who was now mayor of Braddock, Sam Melcher.

A half hour later they were down to the last four photos in the box. The positive pile now had four pictures in it, the maybes were five. Just as the publisher of the *Express* had told him, Janet Donovan had had affairs with many men. And as Jud had guessed, some of those men were now among Braddock's leading citizens.

Ray Maxwell's admonition also returned to his mind. Jud was charging into a very sensitive area, and it wouldn't take much for all this to blow up in his face. He'd already gathered enough information this afternoon to cost him his job if he wasn't careful.

Donovan stretched, giving him a good view of her breasts. Even in the crummy prison dress, he could see that they were ripe and full. She smiled when she saw him watching her, which had to be why she'd stuck her chest out in the first place.

She said, "You know, Jud, it can get awful lonely in this place."

"Uh-huh."

She placed her hand over his. "So I have an idea."

He said nothing. But he didn't move his hand, either.

"Long as we're alone and we know it's gonna be private"—her voice dropped into a still lower register—"why don't we take advantage of it?" Her tongue moved slowly across her upper lip. "I'll give you the best head you ever had."

For one insane moment, he felt himself respond. And then he took his hand away. "Knock it off, Joan."

Her eyes flashed. "You chickenshit prick."

He smiled. "I thought we were friends."

That made her laugh. And just as quickly as the anger had appeared, she slipped back into her seductress role. "Hey, baby, you know it'd be fun."

"Yeah." He lifted one of the last photos out of the box and glanced at it, then held it up to her.

She looked at the picture and her expression hardened. "Yeah. That's a definite."

In disbelief he turned the photo over and again looked at the man in the shot. When he glanced back at her he saw she was wearing the familiar half-smile, a cynical glint in her eyes.

"You're sure?"

"Of course I'm sure. How could I forget a cop?"

Jud studied the photograph of Joseph Grady. He wondered if she was merely being spiteful, getting back at him because he'd turned her down. Or if maybe it was a way of jeering at him, telling him cops were no different from other men when it came right down to it. Maybe it was all of those.

Or maybe she was telling the truth.

"You remember anything else about him?"

She shook her head.

He wrote down the number in his notebook and held up the last photo in the box.

She barely glanced at it. "No."

He put the stack of photos back in the box and replaced the cover. She stretched again, this time even more suggestively.

But he ignored her movements. "When your mother died—"

"Mm?"

"Were you questioned at the time?"

"Oh, yeah. For about two minutes. Nobody paid much attention to me."

"Who did the questioning, do you remember that?"

"A cop. I don't know who he was."

"But not the same one that had been seeing your mother?"

"No. This guy was old, and he smelled of booze. He talked right in my face and he stank."

"Where were you when she died?"

"In bed."

"You were in the *house* when it happened?"

"Yes."

"Tell me what you remember of it."

"My father was out. My mother gave me supper and put me to bed early. I guess I went to sleep. The next thing I knew, there was a lot of commotion downstairs. I heard her screaming. Then it was quiet, and I got out of bed and went to the head of the stairs. I was scared, of course, so I kind of peeked down there. I could see somebody moving in the living room. I looked, and . . . there was my mother's body laying on the floor, with no head." She shuddered.

"Did you see anything else?"

"I'll say I did. I saw this big man, all in black. He turned, and then I saw he was holding her head by the hair. He had an ax in his other hand."

"Could you see anything more about him?"

"No. There wasn't much light in the room, and right after

that he left the house. I just remember that big black shape. And he was wearing a hood. Later on I heard all those stories about the headsman."

"What did you do after he was gone?"

"Got back in bed and shivered until my father came home. I was scared out of my mind."

"And your father called the police?"

"I guess. I heard him yelling, and he came running into my room and he grabbed me and held me. It was about the only time I ever remember him hugging me. He told me to stay in bed, and then in a little while the house was full of cops."

"When you were questioned, you didn't tell what you'd seen?"

"No. Christ, no. When the cop talked to me—the boozy one—I just said I was asleep the whole time. I was afraid if I said anything that spook with the ax would come back and get me. I had nightmares about it for years. Once in a while I still do."

He leaned back in his chair. A moment later her bare foot came up between his legs and brushed his crotch.

He pushed the foot down gently. "You never give up, do you?"

She raised one eyebrow. "Where there's cock there's hope."

He stood up. "You've been a lot of help, Joan. I really appreciate it."

"Just don't forget our deal."

"I won't. I promised to help you, and I will."

He put away his notebook and picked up the box of photographs and his cap. Then he went to the door and told C.O. Geraldi his visit was over.

TWELVE ···
A Ghostly Trail

1

Karen Wilson twisted and turned in her bed. Light flashed before her eyes, as startlingly bright as if she were in the midst of a summer thunderstorm. An instant later there was another burst, and then another. In the lightning streaks she saw black boots and a black hood with slanted eyeholes. She saw a man's hands encased in black gloves. She saw a hulking form moving about in an area that appeared to be surrounded by walls built of stone.

The bursts of light continued, and in their blue-tinged incandescence she saw the hands pick up a wooden block that was worn and stained. The hands set the block down on a low platform, as if placing it into position. Then they lifted a great double-bladed ax and held it up as the eyes within the black hood inspected its razor edges.

The headsman stepped down from the platform, and holding the ax in one hand, went to where the figure of a man lay on the raw earth. He bent down and grasped the man by the arm and then half-dragged him to the platform. The man's face was contorted by pain and fear, and in the brief moment Karen saw it she realized the man was unfamiliar to her; it was the face of a stranger.

The headsman pushed his victim down onto the platform and rolled him over onto his back, setting his head into place on the block. Then the hooded executioner raised the ax.

There was another burst of light, and the images were suddenly gone.

Karen sat up, gasping.

God. Had this been a dream—a nightmare? Or was it another vision? And if it was, what did it mean? Who was the man the headsman was about to execute? Where was this happening, and when was it taking place?

Her skin crawled as she realized what she had seen. The headsman had been readying the man for a ritual beheading. He'd set the block into position and forced the condemned man down onto it, preparing him to receive that awful ax.

And then, unlike what she'd seen the other times, when he'd lopped off the heads of the teenage girl and boy, the images had suddenly stopped. What did that mean?

She jammed her fists against her mouth to keep from crying out again.

The house was small; as she forced herself to be quiet she worried about having disturbed her grandmother, but no sound came from the old lady's bedroom, which was next to hers. For a moment Karen tried to settle down under the covers, but that was like risking a journey back into that awful set of images that had rocked her mind. Instead she got out of bed and put on a robe, then left her room and went downstairs.

In the kitchen she rummaged around in a cupboard until she found the bottle of brandy her grandmother kept there. For medicinal purposes, the old lady said. But Karen had noticed that the contents dwindled rapidly and then the bottle was replaced by another every couple of days.

She opened it and poured herself a stiff drink. The stuff was like liquid fire. It burned its way down her throat and she choked and her eyes watered, and yet by the time it reached her stomach it became only pleasantly warm. She poured another, and this time it wasn't nearly as fiery, only soothing. She sat down at the table and again filled her glass, her mind returning inevitably to the terrible impressions she'd seen earlier.

As much as she wanted to deny them, as much as she longed to push the images away from herself, she knew she couldn't. They were there and they were real.

And face it, she told herself. A big part of this is guilt. You know that thing is out there somewhere, and that he's going to do the same hideous thing again. He was getting ready for it—you saw him. So you can't just keep your mouth shut, you *can't*. No matter how you feel about staying out of it, no matter how you've been used, you can't just let him kill again without trying to warn somebody.

A further realization suddenly struck her. She hadn't known where the headsman was in the images, hadn't been able to identify a place or even understand what kind of location he had been in. But now she understood that those images were exactly like the ones in the old painting the chief of police had shown her. There was the low platform and the block on which the victim's head would rest as the ax hurtled downward. Even the stone walls seemed the same.

You've got to go to Chief MacElroy and tell him what you've seen.

But she couldn't. She couldn't go back into the police station and open up to that man. He'd lied to her, misled her, tricked her. He'd pretended to understand, given her his word she could trust him. And like the fool she was, she'd believed him. She'd told him things she'd never admitted to another human being in her life, and all the while he'd been sneering at her from behind that calm face.

Maybe that was what was so hard to take. He'd seemed so *decent.* But in the end he'd turned out to be no different from any other deceitful bastard. Not only had he betrayed her, but he'd done it in the worst possible way. He'd given her story to a newspaper reporter—a reporter who just happened to be his girlfriend. Karen could imagine the pair of them, the ruggedly good-looking cop and his pretty girlfriend, lying in bed together and laughing about the weirdo who worked at Boggs Ford. She pulled a tissue from the pocket of her robe and wiped her eyes, then sipped some of the brandy.

So he'd lied to her. And she hated him for it. But did that absolve her responsibility? Could she just sit by now while someone else's life was in danger?

And then again, was it? She *thought* what she'd seen was another vision, but how could she be sure? Wasn't it possible it actually had been a nightmare, after all? She'd had plenty of those lately, to the point that she'd begun to worry about her sanity.

And when it came right down to it, how could she be sure of what she'd seen the time before, when she actually had gone to the police chief? She was positive she'd seen the headsman kill that boy, and yet the boy was believed to have run away. The papers and the TV had been full of stories that he'd become the prime suspect in the murder of his girlfriend, and that he'd fled to escape being charged. Police all over the country were looking for him. So there wasn't a shred of proof that what she'd seen—the struggle between the headsman and the boy, and then the boy's death—had actually taken place.

Maybe the answer was right in front of her. Maybe she'd been tripping over it all along, just as she had only a minute ago.

Maybe the truth was that she was insane.

She got up from the table and put the brandy bottle back into the cupboard. Then she rinsed out her glass and turned off the lights before going back upstairs to her room.

The air was bitterly cold. She draped her robe over the foot of the bed and shivered as she slipped under the covers and curled herself into a ball. The sheets were like ice. Outside the wind was bending the limbs of the oak tree, the tips of its branches scratching against her window. She closed her eyes, knowing further sleep was impossible, and waited for morning.

2

There were only a few cops in the stationhouse when Jud got back from Westchester. He'd stopped for some food on the way and it was late now and he was tired, but he'd resisted going straight home. He wanted to know what had happened during the day, and he also wanted to sort out what he had been told by Joan Donovan.

Joe Grady was still in the station. He walked into Jud's office, carrying a mug of coffee. "How was the trip?"

"It was okay. Didn't learn much, though."

"You talk to Donovan's daughter?"

"Yes. But she didn't remember anything worthwhile. She was only a little kid when her mother was killed."

"Too bad she couldn't help."

"Yeah, I had my hopes up. But I knew it was a long shot, anyway. Say, Joe?"

"Yes?"

"You check out that spill on the floor of the Harpers' barn?"

"Oh, yeah. Nothing but oil."

"You sure?"

"Uh-huh. I even pried up one of the floorboards and looked underneath. Just some crankcase oil, and most of it seeped away."

"I see. Anything else doing here?"

"The usual shit. Nothing out of the ordinary. I was about to leave."

"Go ahead, then. I'm going to cut out myself in a few minutes."

"Okay. See you in the morning."

After Grady had gone, Jud closed the door and locked it. Then he sat down at his desk and got out the photographs. He looked at each of them carefully, examining the definites first and after that going through the maybes. As he did, the warning Ray Maxwell had given him seemed more apt than ever. In his efforts to break this case Jud had already turned over too many rocks in Braddock. Now he was about to flip over some more.

Spread out on the desk in front of him were photographs of the town's mayor and a police sergeant who had more years in service than anyone else on the force. Also members of Braddock's best-known citizens, including Bill Swanson, the man many believed would be the next mayor, and Loring Campbell, president of the town's leading manufacturing company. Ed Dickens was there, father of the slain Marcy, and so was Peter Harper, whose son was now missing.

There was also the shot of the teacher, Frank Hathaway. Joan Donovan hadn't identified him, even when Jud had urged her to take a second look. He put that one aside to remind himself to call Washington and check the man's record with Armed Services Records and Identification.

He looked at the array of photos. Had one of these men murdered Janet Donovan? Or was all this just a hell of a reach? The only thing he knew for sure about their relationship to the victim was that they'd been screwing her. That is, he *thought* he knew it for sure. And even if it were true, he couldn't equate an illicit affair with murder.

For that matter, he couldn't even be sure Joan Donovan's identification of these men had been legitimate. She might have been running a game on him, which would make this collection of photographs just so much bullshit. He certainly wouldn't put it past her to tell him anything she thought would get him to work on the parole board in her behalf.

Except that there was one man here she'd proven she knew. There was no way she could have made up the Uncle Sam story on Melcher.

Jud sat back in his chair and let his gaze run over the photos. So maybe there was something here after all. Maybe one of them was indeed a picture of Janet Donovan's murderer. And maybe Marcy Dickens' as well. And Buddy Harper's, if in fact he was dead. Checking them out would be a dance on eggshells.

He looked at his watch and thought about calling Sally, then decided against it. All he wanted tonight was a beer or two, and then a long sleep. Maybe a little guitar before he went to bed. He put the photos back into the box, then unlocked the closet behind him. He set the box on a shelf inside, closed the door and relocked it.

It had been a long day, even longer than usual. He turned out the lights as he left the room.

Passing the office the state police detectives were using, he was surprised to see them still there. On impulse he stuck his head inside. "You guys ever go home?"

Pearson looked up from the desk. His appearance wasn't nearly as dapper as usual; his shirtsleeves were rolled up and his collar was unbuttoned, his tie pulled down. An empty paper coffee container sat in front of him and alongside that was an ashtray full of butts. "Hello, Chief. Missed you today."

He knew it was the inspector's indirect way of inquiring as to what Jud had been doing. "I was busy running around on routine stuff. We've had quite a few accidents lately."

"Same problem our troopers have in the wintertime," Pearson said. "People love to bash up their cars on icy roads."

"How's it going?"

Pearson picked up a pack of Marlboros and extended it. Jud shook his head and the detective put a cigarette into his mouth and lit it. "We don't have our boy yet, but we will before long."

"You get a break?"

It was obvious that Pearson was being deliberately casual. "Sure did. A kid answering Harper's description was spotted in Texas. Small town near the Mexican border. He was driving an old pickup truck with Pennsylvania plates. Police are combing the area for him now."

"You sure it was Harper?"

"It's him, all right. I talked to a Texas state trooper. He says the description of the kid fit the picture we put out to a T. Also Harper abandoned the truck and lit out when he realized he'd been seen."

"We ran a check on the plates," Williger added. "Truck was stolen four days ago near Scranton."

Pearson exhaled a stream of blue smoke. "Like I told you, I've worked on more homicide cases than I can count, and this one strikes me as an old story. Pair of young lovers, something happens to make trouble. They fight, boy kills girl. He tries to ride it out, but then panics and skips."

Jud had heard this speech often enough to be able to recite it himself. But he listened quietly.

Williger again spoke up. "The Barnaby case in Westlake last year. Same deal. Girlfriend threatened to break up with this guy, he choked her. Had all the same elements as this one."

"Like I also told you," Pearson said to Jud, "you work on this stuff long enough, you've seen it all at least once."

"What if Harper didn't do it?"

A tolerant smile crossed Pearson's face. "We'll worry about that when we get him."

"Sure," Jud said. "See you guys later."

They said goodnight and he left the office.

He walked out of the stationhouse and drove home. When he got there he drank a beer while he undressed, and then fell into bed, too tired to even bother with the shower he'd promised himself.

But sleep would not come for a long time. His head was

filled with ghostly faces in old, grainy photographs that faded in and out as he thought about them, one after another.

3

In the morning Jud got into his cruiser and headed out toward Route 5.

When he pulled into the driveway the Jeep was parked in front of the barn and the hound again came out to snarl at him. He left the patrol car next to the Jeep and went up the snowy walk to the house. He knocked, and Emmett Stark opened the door.

Jud was shocked by the old chief's appearance. He looked drawn and pasty, and his hand trembled as Jud shook it. But he smiled at his visitor and said to come on in. Jud followed him into the kitchen, where Stark poured mugs of coffee for them, and from there they went into the workroom.

The potbellied stove was glowing, and the area was comfortably warm. The atmosphere was as masculine as ever, with the mounted animal heads and the rifles and fishing rods in their racks on the walls, but Jud noticed that the workbench appeared not to be in use. Something was going on with Stark; Jud sensed that whatever it was, it wasn't good. Instead of sitting at the bench, the old man led him to the leather sofa and chairs along the far wall.

They sat down, and Jud peered at him. "How you feeling, Chief?"

For a moment he thought the old chief would offer up a cheerful lie, but then Stark said, "Lousy."

"What is it?"

"Heart again. I had a bad spell here a week or so back."

"Angina?"

"Yep. That quack Reinholtz wanted to put me in Memorial, but I told him to go to hell. Once you get inside that goddamn place you'll never get out. If I'm gonna die I'd rather do it here, on my own terms."

"Who's talking about dying?"

"Oh, there's one person you can't bullshit, and that's yourself. I don't have any illusions about what's going on."

"Maybe what you need is to get out of this climate."

"Maybe."

"What about going to Arizona to live with your son?"

"Yeah, well, that could be. If I get to feeling better I just might think seriously about it."

Jud didn't know what to say. Stark had always been a tough character, with a gruff way about him. To see him going downhill was depressing. But he tried to strike a note of optimism. "Be spring soon, things'll change then. Lot of trout swimming around out there, waiting to get caught."

Stark smiled. "Sure. I'll be back in shape by that time."

Jud sipped his coffee. He wanted to talk with the old man, but he didn't want to put any strain on him.

Stark seemed to know what was on Jud's mind. "How's it going with the Dickens case—any line on where the Harper kid might've got off to?"

"No. Pearson's got a dragnet set up like you wouldn't believe. They think they spotted the kid in Texas, but they haven't got him yet."

Stark grunted. "They will, sooner or later. Police procedures are pretty good these days. There's a lot better cooperation with the different agencies. Didn't use to see that until the last few years. What else is happening?"

"I've been looking into the Donovan case, for one thing."

"Kind of a cold trail, isn't it?"

"Yeah, it is." For a moment Jud thought about telling him of his visit to Westchester, but then he decided against it.

"You said there was nothing in the records?"

"No. But I've been asking around. Some people still remember Mrs. Donovan. Seems she was quite a swinger in her time. Mixed up with just about every young hotshot in Braddock."

"Not surprised to hear that. Whenever you get a good-looking young married woman murdered, it's either her husband or a lover who's responsible, nine times out of ten. You want to know what I believe happened, I'd say John Donovan's the one who swung that ax."

"He had a good alibi, Chief. Out of town when it happened."

"Maybe so. But if I'd been investigating it, I'd have worked

Donovan over plenty. He could have gone back to the house and done it, then doubled back to wherever his business was that day. Later on he goes home and yells, oh my god, what a tragedy. Now that's just a theory, but that's what I would have gone after."

"What about the lovers?"

"Same thing. If she was seeing other guys, I would've concentrated on them too, you can be sure of that."

"Not many of the old force still around from those days."

"No, I suppose not."

"Joe Grady's about the only one who's left."

"Uh-huh."

"He worked under you for a long time, Chief. What's your opinion of him?"

"Why—you having problems with him?"

"Not really. But what do you think of him?"

Stark considered the question. "I'd say he was a pretty good cop. He's got his limitations, of course. And being a thick-headed Irishman doesn't help. Got a hell of a temper, and he was always too quick with a nightstick. But by and large, okay. Now, what's going on?"

Jud smiled. "Still as suspicious as ever, eh?"

"Damn right. I was a cop myself too many years not to smell the smoke. What's bothering you about him?"

"Some of the time I get the idea Joe's going down a separate path. And he makes sure I don't know where that is. He never accepted me, you know. Never got over my getting this job instead of him."

"Human nature, isn't it? He spent all those years waiting for me to retire, and then when I did I picked you to succeed me instead. You wouldn't exactly expect him to love you, would you?"

"No, I suppose not. For that matter, I don't suppose he's overly fond of you either, under the circumstances."

"You're right about that. Joe figures I stuck it to him. I tried to make him understand, too. Had a long talk with him, explained how the job called for new blood. Pointed out he'd be retiring himself before long. But it didn't seem to make much of an impression on him. So if he's giving you a hard time now, I'm not surprised."

"What do you know about his personal life?"

"Well, he's got two grown kids, a boy and a girl. One's in Buffalo, the other lives in Detroit, I think. I forget which one is where. Both married, with kids of their own."

"How's his marriage?"

Stark pursed his lips. "Kind of a truce by now, I guess. Was a time when they used to fight like hell. Peggy's a strong-willed woman, and Joe liked to hit the sauce pretty good when he was younger."

"I didn't know that."

"Oh, yeah. In the last couple of years he seemed to quiet down a lot. But he was a hellraiser in his day. Lot of times he'd come in smelling like something died. And every now and then he'd go off on a bender. Sometimes for as long as a week. I came that close to firing him more than once."

"Ever know him to play around with the ladies?"

"Yeah, that too. Joe always had something going."

"Would you remember any of the women he was seeing?"

"Oh, Christ, Jud—that was years ago. Like I said, he's reformed with age. I'd have to think if I knew who any of his friends were. Is it important?"

"No, I was just curious."

"If I can come up with anything, you want me to let you know?"

"Yeah, if something occurs to you, call me."

"You know, Jud, it might be good if I gave you a little advice."

"On what?"

"This Donovan business, if we can get back to that for a minute."

"Yes?"

"Seems to me you could get your tit in a wringer, messing around with that one."

"That so?"

"You think about it. Your chances of cracking it are just about zero. Not after all these years, and especially with the way the original investigation was loused up. If you ever did it'd be a miracle. Or the biggest stroke of luck you could think of."

"You're probably right."

"Sure I am. So in the meantime, you go messing around in that pile of shit, some of the things that crawl out could bite you."

"Yeah, I know that."

Stark raised his coffee mug, then abruptly set it down. His face contorted, and his breath came in shallow gasps.

Jud leaned toward him. "Hey, Chief—you okay?"

The old man nodded and dug into his shirt pocket, coming up with a plastic vial. He fumbled it open and took out a small white pill, popping it into his mouth. After a minute or so his breathing returned to normal.

Jud put his hand on Stark's arm. "What was that, nitro?"

"Uh-huh. I'll be all right, soon as I rest a bit."

"You want me to stick around?"

"No, no—you get on back to work. I appreciate your coming by."

"Sure you're okay?"

"Hell, yes. I'm gonna get a nap, and that'll fix me up. Doc told me I just can't overdo it, is all."

Jud got to his feet. "Don't bother to walk out with me—you stay here and take it easy."

Stark's voice was weak. "Yeah, I'll do that. So long, Jud."

"See you later, Chief. Take care of yourself."

When he got back into the car Jud looked back at the old house, and then at the Jeep and the snarling hound. He had a feeling that one way or another, Emmett Stark wouldn't be around here much longer.

4

When the bell rang to signal the end of the period, Frank Hathaway peered out at the class. He'd deliberately waited until the last possible moment before giving them homework, because that would make it all the more annoying. They'd think they were getting away without an assignment, and here he was with the good news. "Before you go," he called out.

The rustle of gathering books and papers stopped and the students turned toward him, displeasure showing on their faces. They waited.

"Read chapters ten through fifteen," he commanded. "I'll give you a quiz on the material tomorrow morning."

To his satisfaction a collective groan rose from his pupils. They'd been reading Jack London's *Call of the Wild,* and plainly found it boring. But then, anything above the intellectual demands of a comic strip would have had the same effect. They streamed out of the room grumbling to themselves.

Hathaway touched the controls on his wheelchair, sending the machine into a turn toward his desk.

"Mr. Hathaway?"

He stopped and looked back. Betty Melcher was approaching him. "Yes, Betty?"

"Could I talk to you for a minute?"

"Of course." He indicated a vacant chair nearby.

She sat down and crossed her legs, letting her skirt slip out well past her knees. "I wanted to talk to you about my grade."

"Yes? What about it?"

"Well, with what I've been getting in the tests and on my homework, I'm about at a B level, is that right?"

"I'd have to look at my grade book, but I'd say yes, that's probably about what it is."

She sat back in her chair, arching her back a little. She was wearing a tight red sweater that buttoned down the front, and the top was open enough so that he could see the swelling of her breasts. Melcher had a nice body and a way of moving that he found extremely provocative. From the first day of class last fall she'd been teasing him, giving him little glimpses of her thighs, bending over so that he could see down the front of her blouse, looking at him with a wanton expression on her face.

"I was wondering," she said, "what it would take to improve it."

He smiled. "Why the sudden interest in higher grades?" The fact was, she'd always played up to him more than any of the others in the class. Which was why she was at the B level. Actually her test scores and her homework weren't worth more than a C.

"Oh, I just thought it'd be nice to finish the year with a good record."

"Come on, Betty—what's the real reason?"

An impish smile crossed her face. "Can you keep a secret?"

The idea of sharing a confidence with this nymphet had an erotic effect on him. "Of course."

"My father promised to buy me a new car if I made honors. An A in your class would do it."

"I might have known."

Her smile widened. "It's a good reason, isn't it?"

"Perhaps. At least you're honest about it."

"So what would it take?"

He studied her. She moved again under his gaze, thrusting her chest out a little more boldly this time and moistening her lips as her eyes locked on his. Careful, he thought. Don't read something into this that might not be there. "I guess it would take some extra effort."

She nodded. "Okay. It's pretty important to me. I'd do anything to get it."

"Anything?"

She uncrossed her legs and then crossed them again, the skirt riding up even higher. "Anything."

He felt himself respond. Despite his resolve, she was getting to him. And from the look on her face, she knew it. He let his gaze slide down to her breasts and then back up to her eyes. "Maybe we could work something out."

"Whatever you say, Mr. Hathaway."

He tried a probe. "How would you feel about my giving you some special instruction?"

"You mean like in private? Sort of like tutoring?"

"Something like that."

"Sounds great."

Maybe it was his condition. Maybe it was the idea that from the waist down he was dead—at least, she *thought* he was—that was making her bold. She could entice him because she thought he couldn't do anything about it anyway, so she was safe. Was that it? He'd have no way of knowing short of asking her, unless—

"We could meet someplace," she said. "Outside of here."

He let his guard down another notch. "I think that would be delightful."

"So do I." She tilted her head, still holding him with that knowing look. "You live in an apartment, don't you?"

"Yes."

"Maybe I could come over some day after school."

It was time to test her a little. "Might give people the wrong idea."

"Who'd have to know?"

"No one, I suppose."

She smiled and moved her body once more. "And I'd never tell." Then she stood up, her breasts now at his eye level. "You just say when. The sooner the better." She turned and treated him to a rear view as she strolled out of the classroom.

The brazen little *bitch*.

Did he dare? Well, why not? After all, it wasn't only the Betty Melchers of the world who considered him helpless; everyone else did, too. So what was wrong with a student so eager to learn that she stopped in at his home for an extra assignment or to discuss the material they were reading? That is, *if* anyone were to discover she'd been there, which probably wouldn't happen at all. In fact, there was no reason for anyone to know a thing about it. This would be just between the two of them.

The fact that Sam Melcher would never know what his daughter was up to made it all the more alluring.

But he'd have to be extremely careful. No matter what happened, she could never be allowed to guess the truth about him. After all, it was possible for him to be only partially paralyzed in the lower part of his body, wasn't it? At least, as far as she knew? Another of their little secrets?

Which would hide *his* secrets.

A bell rang signaling the next period, which he had free. He touched the controls and the wheelchair whirred its way out the door and down the hall.

5

From Stark's place Jud drove out to Empex headquarters on Old North Road. The sun was higher now, and the air was cold but crisp and invigorating. He parked in one of the spaces marked VISITORS and when he got out of the car he could hear the flag on the pole in front of the building snapping in the wind.

This was one of the more modern structures in Braddock, three stories tall, a center section with a wing off each side, all of it clad in gray glass. There was no name on the building, only a small bronze sign out front. Jud had been here once or twice before, but he'd been driving a patrol car in those days; it seemed a long time ago.

The receptionist looked up and greeted him pleasantly when he stepped into the lobby, asking if she could help him. He told her he wanted to see Mr. Campbell and she lifted a telephone and spoke into it.

Jud didn't know much about the internal workings of this company, except that it made instruments for aircraft and for boats and heavy construction equipment. Loring Campbell's father had founded it, and the old man had died some years ago, passing control on to his only son. Empex was Braddock's most important employer. There were second- and even third-generation Empex workers.

Jud's contacts with Loring Campbell had been limited to meetings of the town council. And also at a couple of semisocial events, such as dinners for the Little League or the Lions Club. He'd also met Mrs. Campbell once or twice. His impression was that she was much like the wife of a politician, good-looking in a well-coiffed, well-dressed way, always ready with a big smile and a hand thrust out for you to shake while she made a quick assessment of how important you were. Then she'd be off to meet someone else.

Stumbling across Campbell's involvement in an affair hadn't been much of a surprise, for a number of reasons. One, in a small town like Braddock it was damn near impossible to carry on without being seen if somebody was curious, and Jud was curious.

Two, the woman Campbell was involved with was enough to tempt anybody. Jean Harper was not only beautiful, she radiated sexual magnetism. On top of that, she was something of a prowler herself, always on the lookout for an interesting liaison. Jud had heard rumors about her for years.

And three, nothing that went on between men and women surprised him. If he'd been in another line of work he might not have been interested. But he was a cop, and from his first days in police work he'd known that the key to effectiveness was the ability to gather information. The trick was in knowing how—and when—to use it.

That was one point old Emmett Stark had been dead right about: know what's going on, but be damn careful of what you do with what you learn. Information was valuable, but it could also be dangerous.

"Chief MacElroy?"

He turned to see a handsome, gray-haired woman standing near him. "Good morning," she said. "I'm Mr. Campbell's secretary. He says he'll see you, but he has meetings scheduled and doesn't have much time."

"Fine. This won't take long." He followed her back through the door and down a corridor, past offices where he saw people working and then through an open area that appeared to be a secretarial pool. From there they went down another corridor to a door with a small nameplate beside it that read *L. Campbell*. She knocked on the door and opened it and Jud went inside.

The office was large and, like the rest of the building, ultramodern. There was an expansive desk and a grouping of chairs and a sofa covered in squashy gray leather. One wall was a vast window giving a view of distant snow-covered hills.

Loring Campbell was standing behind the desk. As Jud walked in Campbell stepped around it to greet him, smiling and extending his hand. He looked like the kind of guy you might see on the cover of *Fortune*, tall and slim and obviously in good shape, his skin still tan from a trip south somewhere. His dark hair and trimness made him seem much younger than Jud knew he actually was, and in his charcoal gray sharkskin suit with a white shirt and a blue houndstooth tie he had style you didn't often see in Braddock.

He was also cordial. Especially for someone who'd been interrupted in the middle of a busy morning. "Good to see you,

Chief." He waved toward the grouping of furniture. "Let's sit over here where we can be comfortable. Take your coat?"

Jud unzipped his jacket. "No, thanks." He sank into the leather cushions of the sofa.

"All right, then." Campbell dropped into one of the chairs. "What can I do for you? One of our people get into a scrape?"

"No, nothing like that. What I've come to talk about is the Dickens case."

Campbell's eyebrows arched. "The Dickens case? Terrible. I feel so sorry for Ed and Helen. Their only child. My God, what a tragedy. You know, the day you came over to Sam Melcher's house, I thought we were all a little rough on you. But I'm sure you could understand that. Everybody's been so upset about it. The townspeople are outraged, and also scared."

"You're right about that."

"Any progress in locating the Harper boy?"

"No," Jud said. "There's been no sign of him."

"That's just made the whole thing even worse. The idea that he could be responsible for something like that. It's almost unthinkable."

"Yes. Inspector Pearson's in charge of that part of the investigation, as you know. What I'm looking into is a different angle."

"Oh? And what's that?"

"As you know, there was a similar case here in Braddock twenty-five years ago."

"Yes, I know. That's what's kept this damned headsman story alive for so long. I've heard there were other cases as well. Some of them going back a hundred years or more. You know about that?"

"A little," Jud said. "But most of it's based on hearsay and old tales that've been passed down. There isn't much concrete evidence those things ever actually took place. The headsman is mentioned in some histories of the region, but as far as anything definite on any killings is concerned, it's pretty hard to find a record."

"I see."

"On the other hand, the case I'm talking about was real. That victim was also female, and she was also decapitated. She lived here in Braddock, and she and her husband were quite well known in the town." He paused, waiting to see if Campbell would volunteer any knowledge of her.

He didn't. Instead, he simply regarded his visitor without expression.

"After Marcy Dickens was killed," Jud went on, "the *Express* ran a long piece about the earlier murder. Maybe you read it."

"Yes, now that you mention it, I did."

"Her name was Janet Donovan. I believe you knew her."

Campbell's eyes narrowed. "I did, slightly. She and her husband belonged to the country club. I remember seeing them once in a while."

"You mind telling me what you remember about her?"

"Oh, Lord—that was a long time back. So if I ramble a little, forgive me."

"Take your time," Jud said.

"Braddock was a lot different in those days. Believe it or not, the town was even more insular than it is now. Everybody knew everybody's business. I was just settling in here at the company—my father was alive and heading it then—and I ran in a different crowd than the Donovans. All I remember is that they were members of the club."

"And that's where you met Janet Donovan?"

"Could have been. Although it seems to me I might have met her through her husband. If I remember correctly, he was in the insurance business. Always trying to sell you a policy."

"Uh-huh. What was she like?"

"Janet? I guess you'd call her attractive. Dressed well. Drove a red convertible around town, so you couldn't miss her."

"I understand that she had a lot of friends."

"That I couldn't say. As I mentioned, I ran with a different crowd. We were all single. A lot of us had grown up together, more or less. Kim Menager—she's married to Bill Swanson now—and Charley Boggs, a whole bunch of us."

Campbell was keeping all this as casual as possible. It was time to push him a little. "How well did you know Mrs. Donovan personally, would you say?"

There was no change of expression in the smooth features. "Not very well. Enough to say hello to, or to chat with, I suppose. But nothing beyond that."

"From what I've been able to learn, she was something of a swinger."

"Really? Well, I suppose that's possible."

It was interesting. As they'd been talking, Campbell would have been thinking about what could possibly tie him to Janet Donovan after all these years apparently concluding nothing could. So now he was feeling secure, confident that he could respond to any question this jerkwater cop might ask without worrying about his answer.

Jud watched him closely. "Did you have an affair with her?"

Instead of being shocked, Campbell seemed amused. "Chief, please. I might have been a young stud at the time, but if I wanted to get laid I didn't have to chase married women. You didn't really come all the way out here this morning just to ask me that, did you?"

"As a matter of fact, no, I didn't. When you knew the Donovans, did you ever go to their house?"

This time his eyes flickered slightly. "I don't know. I really don't remember."

"Don't you? Then let me ask you this. Do you remember that the Donovans had a daughter?"

"I'm not sure."

"You don't remember her?"

"Only vaguely."

"She remembers you."

Campbell's mouth opened and then snapped shut again. His manner changed abruptly. "What are you getting at?"

"Before Janet Donovan was killed, she had several lovers. You were one of them."

The executive tensed, the muscles in his jaw working. "Hey, what the hell is this? How dare you come in here making accusations like that without a shred of evidence? You're trying to tie me into a murder that took place years ago on the grounds that I had an affair with the victim? Jesus Christ—have you lost your mind?"

"You heard what I said. You were Janet Donovan's lover."

Campbell stood up. "All right, Chief. That's enough. You know, I was one of your supporters. There are people on the council who think you ought to be fired. But I was one who spoke up for you. I believed you were just what we needed—a good young cop who could run the department and at the same time be a decent, responsible citizen. Instead, you've turned into a fucking lunatic. The fact that there's a homicide investigation going on doesn't give you any right to make a lot of wild accusations—sticking your nose into other people's lives. Now get out of here, right now."

Jud had been expecting this. He'd been well aware of the potential explosiveness in what he'd be asking Campbell, and the executive's reaction was no surprise. He sat where he was.

Campbell stared at him. "Did you hear what I said? Get out! And I'm warning you, the members of the Council will hear about this. I find your attitude and your actions not only offensive but outrageous. You'll regret you came barging in here."

Jud said, "Sit down."

"What?"

"I said, sit down. There's more."

Campbell hesitated. His curiosity was working on him, as Jud knew it would. He sank back into his chair, continuing to hold the chief in a flinty stare. "This better be good."

"What I said about you and Janet Donovan I can prove," Jud went on. "In fact, I can produce an affidavit that'll confirm your relationship with her."

Campbell grew truculent once more. "The daughter again, right? That just shows me how stupid you are. The Donovans had a daughter, yes. I remember that. But at the time I knew Mrs. Donovan—knew her *slightly*, mind you—the kid couldn't have been much more than a baby."

"She was old enough to know what was going on."

"Maybe she was, maybe she wasn't. But just who do you think would be dumb enough to believe allegations made twenty-five years later? Do you have any idea how preposterous this is?"

"There is no statute of limitations," Jud said, "on murder."

There was another pause as Campbell thought it over. "You

know what this sounds like to me? It sounds like somebody's thinking they've found a way to capitalize on all the publicity the Dickens murder and the headsman crap has generated. Somebody's trying to cash in, right? And what's your own involvement, Chief? Are you foolish enough to let yourself be used in some cockamamie scheme, or are you trying to be one of the users?"

"Neither one."

Campbell compressed his lips. "I think you know my lawyer, don't you? Mark Peterson of Merriwell, Peterson and Ives?"

"Yes, I know him."

"You won't be surprised that a lot of what Peterson does for me is to fend off nuisance cases. Situations where somebody decides that just because I run a successful company I'm fair game for any crackpot who thinks there's a buck to be made. Throw rocks at me or at Empex and we'll pay up just to get rid of the problem. Is that what's going on here?"

This was interesting, too. Jud wasn't sure whether he was hearing a threat or a subtle pitch. Campbell was no pushover.

The executive thrust out his jaw. "Well? What about it? Is this daughter—this Donovan woman—looking for a payoff? Is that why you're here?"

"No," Jud said. "It isn't. I'm here to ask you questions about a murder. There were a lot of similarities between the Donovan and the Dickens cases. It's logical to assume that someone who knew something about one could know something about the other."

Campbell glowered. "That's all. I'm not going to listen to this shit for another minute. Either you get out of here now or I'll call security and have you thrown out. Cop or no cop, you've overstepped your bounds, MacElroy. And even though you don't seem to realize it, you've got yourself into a hell of a lot of trouble. Now go, or I pick up the phone."

It must be quite a kick, Jud thought, when you get to the point that you operate by a different set of rules than the ordinary shitbird who pays his taxes and still worries about a speeding ticket if he goes over the limit. Empex had its own police force. And in this guy's view, it was stronger than the town's.

"You hear me? Out. *Now.*"

"Tell me," Jud said. "You ever spend time in a motel?"

"What?"

"Like the Mayflower, for instance?"

Some of the color went out of Campbell's face. And along with it, some of the arrogance. "What are you saying?"

"Room Twenty-two?"

His tone changed, grew softer. "So I was right. This is a shakedown, isn't it?"

"No, it's not. It's just to let you know you're not quite as high and mighty as you think you are. You want to squash me, go right ahead and try. I know when you were there and who you were with. I also had a little chat with the manager, in case somebody tries to get to him. Anticipating you might want to deny certain things. Like being there at all, for instance. I let him know what perjury was all about. Just in case he might have to testify in court. He got the message. He'll remember you."

Campbell clasped his hands in front of him and stared at them for a time. When he looked up at his visitor he said, "What do you want?"

"Answers," Jud replied. "I want to ask you questions about Janet Donovan, and I want you to tell me the truth."

Campbell's eyes were like slits in the smooth face, but otherwise his features gave no hint of what he was feeling. He made no reply.

"How often did you visit her?"

"Wait a minute. This other business?"

"Yes?"

"Are you saying if I answer questions about Donovan, the uh—visits to the Mayflower stay quiet? You'll keep that in confidence?"

Visits, plural, Jud thought. He doesn't know it, but he just admitted there were a number of them. I wonder how long he's been seeing her. "That's right. I'll forget all about it. Provided you tell me what I want to know about you and Donovan. You used to go to their house, correct? When her husband wasn't there?"

Campbell swallowed. "Look. I saw her a few times, yes. But I was just one of a lot of people, believe me. She was a bimbo who was married to the town jerk. And I was only a kid. So yeah, a couple of times when her husband was out she invited me over and I went."

"You were seeing her at the time she died, weren't you?" That was purely a shot in the dark, but he wanted to see how Campbell would handle it.

"Yes, but I swear to God I knew nothing about her murder."

"You said you were just one of a lot of people."

"That's right."

"Who were the others?"

"I'm not sure."

"Are any of them still living in Braddock?"

"I don't know."

"You said Bill Swanson was in your crowd. He was seeing her too, wasn't he?"

That was another shot in the dark, but it went home. "Yes, I think so."

Or maybe he's trying to spread the responsibility around, Jud thought. "And Charley Boggs—he was another one, wasn't he?"

"I told you, I'm not sure who the others were."

"How did you first become friendly with her?"

"I suppose it was at one of the Saturday night dances at the club."

"Then what?"

"Then she—suggested I drop over some time. Said her husband was often out in the evening."

"And that's what you did."

"Yes."

"You ever argue with her, ever have a fight?"

"No."

"She ever threaten to tell her husband about you and her?"

"No, nothing like that."

"How often did you visit her?"

"I don't know, just once in a while."

"Ever go places with her, ever take her anywhere?"

"No. Never." His resolve seemed to stiffen. "Look, MacElroy, as soon as you get out of here I'm going to talk with Mark Peterson. I've told you everything I remember about what happened back then—probably more than I should have or needed to. Even though our chief of police had to resort to blackmail to get me to reveal something that happened years ago. A flirtation. That's practically all it was."

"Is that so? You were fucking a married woman and while you were carrying on with her she was brutally murdered. Somebody chopped off her head off. And you say that was nothing but a flirtation?"

"I said I had absolutely nothing to do with her death. I don't know anything about who killed her or why."

"You remember where you were when it happened?"

"No."

"Where were you living at the time?"

"I had a place on Lake Wachitaug."

That was a resort about fifteen miles northwest of Braddock, a springfed lake that meandered through the foothills of the mountains. It was surrounded by pine forests, and on its shores were the summer homes of people who could afford to pay a lot for what they called cottages. Some of them were residents of Braddock, but others came from as far away as New York City to enjoy the cold, clear water and the bracing air.

"You lived there year-round?"

"For a couple of years, yes."

Jud had heard about the kind of parties that went on out at the lake—not only in the summer, but especially in the wintertime, when most of the area was deserted. That was when there was a lot of heavy boozing and cocaine use, and stories of wife-swapping sometimes got around. Once about five years ago, Jud recalled, a young woman who'd been spaced out on alcohol and pills fell into the lake on a bitter-cold winter's night. She'd managed to get out of the icy waters but apparently had become disoriented and couldn't make her way back to shelter. When they found her in the morning she was frozen stiff.

"You ever have Janet Donovan visit you out there?"

Campbell's features hardened. "No. And I've said all I'm going to say. For the last time, I have no idea who killed Janet Donovan."

Jud stood up. "Thanks for your time. You'll be hearing from me. I hope what you told me was the truth."

Campbell stayed in his chair. He looked as if somebody had opened a valve and let out all his air.

On the way back to the lobby Jud waved to Campbell's secretary, who started to rise from her desk when she saw him. "Don't get up," he said. "I know the way."

THIRTEEN ··
Ahead of the Game

1

In the morning Jud went to the stationhouse feeling like the bear that woke up in mid-winter. The coffee didn't help; it was thick and bitter and made his mouth taste worse than it had before he drank it.

His visit to Joan Donovan and what he'd learned from her kept turning over in his mind. The more he thought about it, the more he felt she'd put him on a trail that could lead to the man who'd killed her mother. And Marcy Dickens? And perhaps Buddy Harper as well?

Or could it?

The trip to Empex had been galling. Loring Campbell was an arrogant, conceited son of a bitch who thought he could do any thing he pleased in Braddock because he as much as owned the place. It was a fiefdom, a village inhabited by ignorant peasants, and the rules by which he controlled them and lived were his own.

But was he a killer?

Jud didn't know. And for all his bluster, he wasn't sure how he would go about finding out. He'd backed Campbell into a corner, but that was yesterday. By now the Empex CEO would have had a discussion with his lawyers about how to deal with this upstart cop who'd had the nerve to threaten him. Jud had left Empex yesterday feeling he'd won a round. But now; in the cold light of dawn, he knew that all he'd really done was to piss in a hornet's nest.

He had to admit to himself that he'd never been up against

anything remotely like this. It wasn't a vehicular accident, and it wasn't manslaughter, and it wasn't even murder in any form he'd ever run into. Nobody had gone into a drunken rage and split somebody else's face, or had a violent quarrel with a family member and got the shotgun out of the closet or the knife out of the kitchen drawer. Nobody had done anything like what he'd dealt with over the years he'd been a cop.

Face it, you fool. Even when you're running around playing detective, acting as if you know what you're doing, you don't have the faintest fucking idea what you're up to. You think you're on to something, sure. But you have no idea what. The only thing you're sure of is that pretty soon you won't have a friend left in this town.

Which reminded him. He flipped through the Rolodex for the card on Armed Services Records and Identification. When he found it he called the number in Washington and spoke to army records, telling them to give his request priority; this was a homicide investigation. The guy he spoke to said he'd send it out in a day or two. Jud told him that wasn't good enough and to call him back with the information.

He hung up and thought about the other things he wanted to do today, feeling guilty that he'd been neglecting the routine work of the department. He looked at the pile of paper on his desk and wished he could burn it or simply push the whole thing into his wastebasket. Instead, he began going through the stuff resignedly.

An hour later A.S.R. and I. called back and read him the record of Hathaway, Frank L. Hathaway had been inducted into the U.S. Army in November 1964. As he had told Jud, he'd been in the 364th Infantry. He had spent six months in Vietnam. He had not, however, been a lieutenant and he had not been a platoon leader. He was a corporal and a headquarters clerk. And instead of being wounded in action, he had been injured in a jeep accident. He'd spent six weeks in a stateside hospital and was discharged with a twenty-percent disability rating.

Twenty percent?

That meant Hathaway wasn't just a liar. He was a liar who could walk.

Jud asked the guy at A.S.R. and I. to send him a transcript of the record, thanked him and hung up.

Jesus Christ. What kind of mind would lead its owner to hide himself behind such a mask? Not only had the man assumed this role, but he'd punished himself terribly by doing it. He lived the life of a cripple, a half-man who demanded pity from the members of the community he depended on for a living. Poor Frank Hathaway. Shot to pieces in Vietnam, has to spend his time in a wheelchair. Can't control his bladder or his bowels, can't get laid. Fine man, though. Dedicates his life to teaching our kids. Least we can do is appreciate him.

It wasn't only nauseating—there was something dark and evil going on here.

Jud sat back in his chair, thinking about what he'd do next. Confronting Hathaway before he had a plan would be a mistake. But he sure as hell would do some more checking into this guy, and he'd do it right away. Even though Joan Donovan hadn't identified him as one of her mother's lovers, the bearded teacher with the cold eyes and the condescending manner had taken on a whole new dimension—one that was staggering to contemplate.

Jud got up and left his office, going down the hall to the squad room for a fresh mug of coffee. Maybe this batch would be better than the last. When he returned he saw that the mail had arrived. A stack of it had been deposited on his desk, a bundle of envelopes and some circulars and a package.

The package was about fourteen inches square, wrapped in brown paper and sealed with tape. His name was printed on top in black marker. As he glanced at it, two things went through his mind. The first was that it looked like the kind of thing someone would send a cake in, which was a silly idea he immediately dismissed. The second was that it contained something he'd ordered from L.L. Bean or Eddie Bauer. But that didn't make sense either; he'd have had anything like that sent to his home, not here. And besides, this apparently hadn't come through the mail.

Curious now, he took a jackknife out of a drawer of his desk and cut away the paper, revealing a cardboard box. He pulled open the flaps and peered down at the contents.

What he saw inside was Buddy Harper's head.

2

It was lying so that the face was looking up at him, the eyes wide open and staring, the lips parted. The color of the skin was bluish white, and the lips were gray. The neck had been severed across the larynx, and the tissues and the tendons and the shattered vertebra were visible in the raw wound. The expression on the boy's features was a mixture of fear and horror, the bulging eyes conveying the terror he must have experienced as he saw the blade whistling down to chop away his life.

Jud felt as if he'd been slugged. His pulse quickened and the rush of blood pounded in his temples. At the same time, there was a dull pain in the pit of his stomach. He had to force himself to remain calm, to keep from yelling, to keep from shoving the hideous thing away from him.

It took several seconds for him to get himself together. Then he took a deep breath and examined what lay in front of him.

The box was lined with waxy white paper, the kind a butcher would use, and there were splotches of dried blood on it. Jud reached in to lift out the head, then thought better of it. He'd want others to see this just as it was, just as he himself had first discovered the box and what it contained.

He looked at the cardboard and at the outside wrapping. There were no markings on any of it, with the exception of the crudely printed block letters of his name. The state police would examine these materials in the lab, but Jud's instincts told him they'd have a tough time tracing any of it. And how the hell had the thing gotten here?

Again he peered into the box. Buddy's face looked so ghastly, and yet so pitiable. It was apparent that the boy had been dead for some time; the sickly stench of putrefaction attested to that. And from the appearance of the wound, the fatal blow had been delivered in exactly the same way as the one that had killed Marcy.

Jud pictured the scene Karen Wilson had described to him. What she had seen in her vision was almost surely how it had happened. He felt so strongly about that now. She was no fake, no sicko who wanted to involve herself in whatever tragedy she could talk her way into.

No. Karen Wilson and her strange powers were for real.

But why had this been sent to him?

Jud could guess the answer. The severed head was a warning made because someone knew of his poking around in the dusty corners and the back rooms and the closets of Braddock. Someone was sending a message that he should have kept his curiosity to himself.

But why had Buddy been killed? What could motivate anyone to murder a teenage kid?

Madness, of course. The murders were the actions of a diseased mind. No other answer was plausible.

The phone rang. He answered it and was told Sally Benson was on the line. He took the call, and her voice was a barely audible whisper. "Maxwell found out about the pictures and went crazy. I wanted to warn you. I'll try to call you later." She hung up.

Jud put the phone down. He looked at the revolting thing on his desk, thinking that trouble was coming in waves. He left his office, shutting the door behind him, and walked down the hall to where Chester Pearson was sitting.

3

The inspector was alone, leaning back in the chair behind the desk and reading that morning's edition of the *Braddock Express*. He looked up as Jud stepped into the office, and frowned. "What happened to you? Look as if you've seen a ghost."

"You're close," Jud replied. "Come on back here with me."

His face registering puzzlement, Pearson got up and followed MacElroy back to his own office.

Jud pointed at the package, and the inspector stepped over to the desk and looked down into the box.

"Jesus Christ." Pearson's mouth dropped open and his eyes grew wide. He stared into the box and then at Jud. "It's the Harper kid."

"That's correct."

"Where did it come from—how'd you get this?"

"It was on my desk when I got back here a few minutes ago."

"It was on your desk? You mean just sitting here like some fucking Christmas present? So how'd it get here? Who brought it?"

"I don't know."

The inspector looked down again, peering into the box for several seconds, the shocked expression still on his face. When he brought his gaze up this time he said, "I don't believe it."

Jud could guess what was going through the detective's mind. The fact that the boy had been killed, and especially the *way* he'd been killed, blew all of Pearson's pet theories out the window. The inspector had been made a fool of, proven totally wrong in all his smug conclusions. How was he going to take it?

"This may not be what it looks like," Pearson said.

"What?"

"Regardless of this, I'm not ready to say Harper didn't kill his girlfriend."

Jud kept his mouth shut, but it took an effort.

Pearson must have realized how foolish he sounded. He tugged at his shirt collar. "It could have happened a lot of different ways. Could've been some kind of a triangle."

This was too much. "You know what everybody else'll say happened."

Pearson slammed his fist down onto the desk. "Shit! Why did this have to—" He looked at the box once more, and then turned to Jud. "You better call the coroner. And I don't want anybody else knowing about what's in there until I've had time to notify state police headquarters. I want to think this out."

He strode out of the office, saying to no one in particular, "God damn it. God *damn* it. And where the fuck is Williger when I need him?"

Jud stepped to his desk. He used a ruler to push the top of the box closed, then picked up the telephone and called Dr. Reinholtz. After that he left his office and went out to the front desk.

4

The cop on duty was Brusson. He said he didn't know how the package had arrived. It had been there along with the mail when he got to the stationhouse to start his shift. The guy Brusson had relieved was Charley Ostheimer, who didn't know either. Ostheimer said he'd been in the squad room for awhile, drinking coffee and shooting the shit with other cops, and when he came back it was there. He figured it was something personal that had been dropped off for the chief. Later Brusson had taken the package along with the mail and some reports into Jud's office and put them on the desk. Nobody else knew anything about it.

Goddamn strange, Jud thought. The thing hadn't just floated into the place; somebody had *brought* it. How was it possible they'd done it without being seen? It was because Ostheimer had broken a regulation by wandering off and leaving the desk unattended while he made a coffee run, that was how. And yet . . .

"You ever leave this desk again without somebody covering, I'll fire your ass right off the force," Jud told him.

The young cop flushed. He looked at the floor and mumbled an apology.

Jud didn't say what the package had contained, but within minutes every man in the stationhouse knew something big was up and that it had to do with a box wrapped in brown paper that had been sent to Chief MacElroy. Grady asked him what was going on but Jud told him he couldn't say until Pearson gave the word. That didn't improve the relationship between Jud and the sergeant any; he could see that Grady was resentful at not being let in on it.

When Reinholtz arrived, Pearson led him into Jud's office, taking care to permit no one in there but the three of them. He shut the door, and Jud told the doctor what had happened.

Reinholtz's expression first registered astonishment, then anguish. Jud understood that; Buddy had probably been another of the Doc's kids.

There was a moment's silence, and Reinholtz's shoulders

sagged. Then he straightened up and approached the desk, looking at the package, his manner turning brisk and business-like. Jud pushed open the flaps with the ruler, and Reinholtz peered inside. He said nothing, but a low groan sounded in his throat. The stink from the open box drifted out like an invisible presence, permeating the room.

The doctor was carrying a valise. He set it down on the desk, then took off his coat and hat and dropped them over a chair. Opening the valise, he took out a pair of rubber gloves and a plastic sheet. He put on the gloves and spread the sheet on the desk next to the package. He reached into the box and carefully withdrew its contents, setting the head down onto the sheet. Clucking softly to himself, he began his examination.

Watching this, Jud saw the long brown hair fall down onto the boy's forehead, partially obscuring the eyes. This would be one time when Buddy wouldn't be able to toss it back.

Pearson was impatient. "What about it, Doc—was this done the same way as the girl?"

Reinholtz glanced at the inspector as he might have at a case of bubonic plague. "Without question. The boy was decapi-tated with an ax."

"You sure—about the ax?"

Reinholtz raised his eyebrows. "You heard what I said, Inspector. Somebody cut his head off, and they did it with an ax. What's more, I'd go so far as to say it was the same ax as the one that was used to kill Marcy Dickens."

"How can you tell that?"

The doctor gestured. "It was accomplished with one blow, which indicates the instrument was very sharp and very heavy. Unusually so. The two wounds are virtually identical. Does that answer your question?"

Pearson grunted. It seemed to Jud he'd be willing to grasp at any theory but that one.

When Reinholtz finished, he wrapped the head in the plastic sheet.

"Where you taking it?" Pearson demanded.

"Memorial. It'll be in the morgue. Refrigeration will prevent any further deterioration. If any of your lab people want to see it, they can go over there."

Reinholtz picked up the head and put it into his valise. He had to jockey it a little to get it inside, but he managed. Then he stripped off the gloves and tossed them in as well before he closed the bag and locked it.

He put on his coat and hat. "That's it, gentlemen. We can't do a complete autopsy until you come up with the rest of the body."

"I'll send Williger over there with somebody from the lab," Pearson said. "We'll want to take pictures."

"Yes, of course."

"But I want this kept under tight security. No one else is permitted to see it. And I don't want some attendant shooting his mouth off."

"I'll see to it we get the security," Reinholtz said mildly. "But may I ask why?"

"Why?" Pearson was incredulous. "When we make this public there'll be a roar going up like you never heard before."

There sure will, Jud thought. And everybody in God's creation will know what a fucking idiot you are, Inspector.

"I suppose you're right," Reinholtz said. "But they're going to know sooner or later, aren't they?"

This time Pearson made no reply. What he was thinking was obvious, at least to Jud; Inspector Dickface wanted time to come up with excuses. Or a way to dodge the bullets.

Reinholtz picked up his valise.

"You okay with that?" Jud asked him. "I could get somebody to give you a hand."

"My car's right outside," the doctor replied. "And anyway, it's not that heavy." There was a note of sad irony in his tone. "The human head weighs only twenty five pounds, you know. I'll be fine."

When Reinholtz had gone, Pearson turned to Jud. Apparently he'd thought it through and had come to the only conclusion possible, although he had to be choking on it. "I'm going to have to make an announcement about this."

"Sure. What about the boy's parents?"

"Yes. You'd better let them know first."

Thanks, Jud thought dryly. But he'd do it. "All right."

"And whatever you do, don't touch the box or the paper until the lab guys get here."

"No, of course not."

Pearson was eyeing him, the mustache twitching under his fleshy nose. "I want you to tell me something, Chief."

"What is it?"

"Of all people, why were you the one that package was sent to?"

Jud felt a quick flash of anger. It was a question he'd been wrestling with himself. But he'd be goddamned if he'd share his conjectures with this asshole. He kept his reply calm. "Beats me."

"Does it? I'm not so sure about that. I have a feeling you may know a hell of a lot more about this case than you're letting on. I shouldn't have to remind you again, but I'm in charge of this investigation. What I expect—what I *insist* on—is cooperation."

Despite his good intentions, Jud felt himself getting hot. "Since when haven't I—"

"Look, Chief. You've resented me from the minute I walked in here on the Dickens homicide. You hated like hell to have to turn the case over to a professional investigator. Okay, I understood that. This was your territory, and you didn't want it to look like you couldn't handle a major crime. But by God, if you're holding anything back from me—"

"Yeah? You'll *what*, Inspector? Huff and puff and blow my stationhouse down? Now why don't you do me a favor and get the fuck out of my office?"

Anger rose in Pearson's face like a red tide. He clamped his jaw shut and stomped out, slamming the door behind him. As soon as he was gone, Jud crossed to his desk and slipped open the telephone directory. He found the number for Boggs Ford and called it.

FOURTEEN ················

Pilloried

1

When he told her who was calling, she clamped up tight. Jud didn't get it. The last time they'd spoken she'd been so willing to confide in him, despite her anxiety. "Is there something wrong, Karen?"

"No. Everything's fine."

Everything was fine? Her manner was icy. He decided the publicity on her part in the Mariski case was probably at the root of it. "Look, something's bothering you, that's plain enough. If you'll tell me what it is, maybe I can help."

"I don't want any help. I just want to be left alone."

That had to be it. The story in the *Express* had been precisely what she'd told him she wanted to avoid. When it appeared, it must have seemed to her a plague had been brought down on her head.

"Karen, I know the attention you got when the Mariski boy was found was troubling to you. I understand that, and I don't blame you. But there was nothing I could do to suppress it. If I'd been able to stop it, I would have."

"Would you?"

What the hell could she mean by that? "Yes, of course I would. I knew you didn't want publicity. You made that clear the first time we talked."

She didn't reply.

He pushed on. "But something else has come up and I need to talk to you about it. In confidence, of course."

"Chief MacElroy, I don't have anything to say, and I'm sure I wouldn't be any help to you."

303

He was damned if he'd let her back out on him. "Do you remember the things you told me when you came to my office—the things you'd seen that were so disturbing to you?"

"Yes. But I was mistaken. I just imagined all that. It was nothing more than a bad dream."

"No it wasn't."

"It was, I tell you. I was upset and confused, and that's all there was to it. I'm sorry if I wasted your time as well as my own. Now if you'll excuse me, I have work to do."

"But you didn't just imagine what you told me, Karen. Those things actually happened. I know they did, because we now have proof."

There was a pause. "Proof?"

"Yes. Something that was missing came to light today. It proved that what you told me was real. It took place just as you said it did."

Again she was silent for a moment. When she spoke again, her voice sounded small and strained. "It must have been a coincidence."

"You know better than that. Your description was accurate. That's why it's important that we get together and talk."

"I can't see that it would serve any purpose."

"Let me be the judge of that, Karen, it could mean saving someone's life."

This time she was quiet for an even longer time. He could hear her breathing, as if she was under great stress. Finally she said, "No. *No.* Do you understand me? Don't call me again."

Before she could hang up, he said, "If I have to, I'll come over there."

"Oh, God—please don't do that. I'll—"

"All I want is to talk with you for a few minutes."

She hesitated. "But not here."

"All right, where then? Shall we have coffee?"

"No. I don't want to be seen with you."

He could understand that as well. "I'll pick you up in my car, and we can talk there."

"In a police car?"

"It's unmarked. A blue Plymouth." He looked at his watch.

"I'll be there in forty-five minutes. I'll stop just down the street from you."

Before she could change her mind he hung up. He rose from his desk and took his cap and jacket off the hook, putting them on as he left the office.

There was something else he had to do before meeting Karen Wilson, and he dreaded it.

2

Harper's Drug was one of the more expansive retail operations in Braddock. It wasn't as large as Sears or the Grand Union, but it was by far the biggest operation of its kind in the town. Originally a prescription drug outlet, it had first added stocks of patent medicines and then later a soda fountain under the aegis of its founder, Buddy Harper's grandfather. Nowadays it sold everything from books and stationery to candy and toys. You could buy T-shirts and eyeglasses and lightbulbs and cameras and a thousand other items that had nothing remotely to do with prescription drugs, although that department still flourished. The soda fountain had grown into a fast-food restaurant that competed with McDonald's and Burger King.

When Jud arrived he found Peter Harper standing in one of the aisles, listening to a harangue from a customer, an old woman. She was babbling on about how opposed she was to the municipal bond offer the town council was trying to push through. She said nobody had any respect for money nowadays, and that reckless spending could bankrupt the town and inflation could eat everybody alive and if you wanted proof just look at the price of the merchandise in this store.

Jud thought she'd never shut up. He stood to one side, watching as Harper listened patiently, as if there was nothing the store owner would rather do than hear this old crow's complaints.

When the customer finally finished her diatribe and moved off, Jud stepped closer and Harper noticed him for the first time. When he did, the expression on Jud's face must have given him away. He didn't have to say why he was there.

Harper seemed to sense the purpose of this unannounced visit. His voice was small. "It's Buddy, isn't it?"

Jud nodded.

"What happened?"

Jud told him, the words sticking in his throat.

Harper winced, as if the chief had struck him. He put out a hand and grasped a shelf to steady himself, his eyes closed tight.

It was awkward and terrible and again Jud thought of the Dickenses; it was the same horror all over again. He wished there had been some way to soften it, but he knew from bitter experience the only way to break the news of a family member's death was to break it. There was no other way. It would cause the kind of pain only the person hearing it could deal with, in whatever way that person could. You had to get it out as gently as possible and let the process begin.

When Harper opened his eyes, they were glassy and unseeing. But then they fixed on the police chief. His voice grated. "God damn you."

Jud had seen this kind of reaction before; it was a lashing out in anger and frustration. "I—"

"Get away from me, you son of a bitch."

Other customers began to notice. A few of them turned to see what was happening between Harper and the chief of police. They would have been curious anyway, but with the thousand rumors about Buddy that had been flying around the town they were virtually panting to find out what was going on.

"You'd better go home and tell your wife," Jud said. "I'll go with you, if you want me to."

"Get out." Harper's voice was rising, his face reddening. The skin on his balding pate was becoming blotchy. "You hear me? Get out, God damn you."

"I'm sorry, Peter," Jud said quietly. "I really am."

He turned and left the store. As he returned to his car he noticed that the sky was the color of lead and the air was very still. He knew what that meant; snow was on the way. The weather service had been predicting a storm. For once they could be right.

3

Boggs Ford was apparently busy. When Jud drove slowly past the front of the dealership he could see a number of customers in the showroom. He pulled over to the side of the road about fifty yards farther down and took off his cap to make himself less conspicuous. A glance at his watch told him he was a few minutes early.

It was eerie, the way Karen had described Buddy's murder. With cops all over the country on the lookout for the skinny teenager with the long brown hair, she had told Jud exactly what had happened. He pictured the scene in his mind as he had a hundred times before, just as she had described it. He saw the boy working on his car, saw the hooded man with the ax step out of the shadows, saw Buddy fighting for his life—and losing.

Afterward the killer had carted his victim away. Now the police had the head, but what had been done with the rest of the body? It must have been a bloody mess—bulky, awkward to handle, and yet not hard to hide; it would have been a simple matter to put it somewhere, in the woods maybe. Where was it now?

A detail suddenly came into focus: the oily residue on the otherwise clean floors of the barn, next to where Buddy had been working on his car. Now Jud realized how the oil had come to be there. It hadn't spilled but had been poured deliberately to cover the blood. The headsman had dumped the bucket of drain oil onto the floor, and then had tossed the bucket aside. Jud had seen it lying near the workbench.

And Joe Grady had told him there was nothing there but oil.

The passenger door opened, and Karen Wilson got into the car. Despite the cold, she wore no coat.

Jud reached across her and shut the door. "Hello, Karen."

She wouldn't look at him. "What did you want to say to me?"

"I wanted you to know that what you told me about the Harper boy was true."

"You said there was proof?"

"Yes. This morning Buddy's head was sent to police headquarters."

"Oh, my God. How? What—"

"It was in a box, addressed to me. It had been cut off the same way the Dickens girl's had been. Just the way you told me."

"That's horrible."

"Yes." He knew her emotions had to be churning. "I wanted to say how much I appreciated your coming in and telling me what you'd seen. And I thought you'd want to know that it's been confirmed now."

"Did you let anyone know you were coming over here to see me?"

"No."

"I wish I could believe that."

"You can, I give you my word."

"For what that's worth."

"I was hoping you'd be willing to give me some further help."

Now her eyes met his, and there was defiance in them. "No, I won't. I can't help. What I said to you that day was only a coincidence. I had no idea what I was talking about."

"You know that's not true."

"I don't know anything, except that I was wrong. The things I told you were all just out of my imagination."

There was no way he could force her to cooperate. The only way he could enlist her help was by appealing to her as one human being to another. "Look, I promise anything you say will be kept in strict confidence."

"Is that so? I'm sorry, but I don't trust you."

"What do you mean?"

"I mean I don't want anything more to do with you or your case or the whole subject of what I saw or didn't see. If you try to involve me I'll deny everything. I'll say you were just trying to get me to talk about things that never happened."

He felt a sinking sensation. He'd been sure she could help him. Especially now that he was convinced of her visionary powers. "But you know that whoever killed Buddy killed Marcy Dickens as well. The headsman killed them both. And nobody knows what he might do next. Maybe you could help me find him before he goes after someone else. How would you feel if you refused to help and he killed again?"

She was silent for a moment, and then she burst into tears.

He felt awkward, regretting that he'd been so rough on her. He reached out to her, but she shoved his hand away.

"No." She controlled her sobs with an effort, shuddering as she fought for breath. "I meant what I said. I can't help you. I just—can't."

"At least think about it. Will you do that?"

She shook her head and opened the door.

"Karen—"

She scrambled out of the car. "Tell it to your girlfriend. But don't call me again."

The door slammed, and she was gone.

Jud felt like a fool. How could he have been so goddamn blind dumb? She'd learned of his relationship with Sally and had concluded he'd fed her the Mariski story.

He should have figured that out long ago. And yet he hadn't. Now how was he to repair the damage? Tell her he was sorry—again? Explain that the reporter who had written the story in the *Express* was indeed his girlfriend, but that he hadn't betrayed Karen's confidences to her?

Christ, what a mess. No matter which way he looked at it, he was wrong.

But he was certain of one thing. Buddy's murder had happened the way Karen Wilson had told him it had. And what she claimed to have seen the night Marcy was killed fit as well. Maybe when she cooled off he could get her to come around. Or at least she might be willing to talk about it more rationally. She could help him, he was sure of it.

The photographs. If he could show them to her, maybe they would trigger something. Which brought something else to mind. Sally had said Maxwell threw a fit when he learned she'd taken them. Why?

In the meantime, there was another angle he wanted to check out. Where did you look for a two-hundred-year-old weapon?

One place was a museum.

He started the Plymouth's engine and pulled away. The first

flakes of snow had started to fall. They were so fine you could hardly see them coming down, and when they touched the windshield they melted instantly.

4

He swung down Main Street and then turned left on Elm, heading for the library. He'd get the keys to the museum from Mulgrave and see what he could find. The curator wouldn't like the idea of Jud snooping through the moldy old place by himself, but at this point Jud didn't give a shit what Mulgrave liked or didn't like.

Both Marcy Dickens and the Harper boy had been killed with an ax, and Doc Reinholtz was sure the weapon had been the same one.

Very sharp, and very heavy.

And very old? Jesus, could it be?

The snow was heavier now, the wind whipping the shimmering flakes along the surface of the road, some of them collecting in drifts. The temperature was falling, and there had been warnings that a massive storm could be headed toward Braddock. They were about due; for all his bitching about winter, this one had been relatively mild. Not nearly as severe as last year, or the year before.

The Plymouth was a clunker. It had a limited-slip differential like the regulation police cruisers, but that wouldn't mean much if the snow got really deep. At some point he'd switch over to his Blazer. There was a lot he needed to do, and the last thing he wanted to contend with was getting stuck.

The library looked lonely in the swirling snow, its lights gleaming weakly through tall windows. Jud parked the car in front of the building and made his way up the walk. The snow was sticking; it would be deeper than his shoetops in another hour or so.

To his surprise, the door was locked. He knocked on it, but got no response. That the library had closed with a storm coming was understandable, but why had the lights been left on?

He knocked again, pounding on the door with his fist.

Nothing.

Somebody had to be here. He raised his hand to strike the door once more when he heard the lock being turned from inside. The door opened a crack and one of the librarians squinted out at him.

Jud touched a finger to his cap. "Afternoon, ma'am."

This was the ancient one who'd been at the desk the last time he was here. The expression on her thin features was no warmer than the outside air. "Library's closed," she sniffed. "Come back tomorrow, if the roads are plowed by then."

She pushed on the door, but before she could shut it Jud wedged it open with his foot. "This is official police business," he said.

She swung the door open and he stepped into the vestibule. He took off his cap. "I want to see Paul Mulgrave. Is he in?"

"No, he's not."

"Did he leave early? Not that I blame him—this storm's getting worse by the minute."

"Mr. Mulgrave didn't come in today. We haven't heard from him."

"Isn't that unusual?"

"Yes, very. He always comes here first thing, no matter what. When we didn't hear we thought he might be sick, so we called his home. But there was no answer."

"May I use your phone? I'll try to reach him."

She glanced with distaste at the melted snow dripping from his cap and his jacket, but then said, "Very well. If you'll follow me, please."

She led him to a cubbyhole office under the stairs. There was a telephone on the desk, and she gave him Mulgrave's number. He dialed it, and stood there listening to it ring. The librarian stayed in the doorway, watching him. After a dozen rings and no answer, he put the phone back onto its cradle.

He looked at the old woman. "Did he have an appointment or anything you can think of that might have detained him?"

"Not that I know of."

"Do you know where he keeps the keys to the museum? There's something I need to see over there."

She stiffened at the question. "I have no idea, and I wouldn't give them to you if I did. That's Mr. Mulgrave's business."

The fact that Jud was a cop, and the chief of the Braddock force at that, didn't seem to go very far with her. But it wasn't worth an argument. He'd get the keys when he located Mulgrave. "Can you suggest anyplace he might be?"

"No. And now if you don't mind, I want to lock up and go home. The other librarian left just before you came, and I'm alone. I'm afraid if I don't go soon I could be stuck here."

"You have snow tires on your car?"

"I don't have a car."

"You mean you're going to walk—in this?"

"That's correct, officer. I live only a mile from here, and I walk it every day, rain or shine."

"Not today, you won't. Get your coat and I'll drop you off."

"Young man, I'm quite capable—"

"Get your coat ma'am. Now."

She did as she was told, and a few minutes later Jud deposited her in front of a tiny frame house.

He waited until she went inside and turned the lights on before he pulled away.

As he did the radio crackled, and Jud heard Tony Stanis calling him. He reached under the dash and picked the mike off its hook. "MacElroy."

"Chief, Inspector Pearson wants you to come to the station-house right away. And there's an urgent message here for you from the mayor."

"What is it?"

"I don't know. It's in a sealed envelope. But I was told to contact you and say it was important that you get in as soon as possible."

Jud broke off the call and swung the Plymouth into a U-turn. He had a feeling there was another storm on its way and that this one would be a lot tougher than a blizzard.

5

As he approached police headquarters, Jud saw that the word was out. Among the cars parked in front of the town hall were several vans with TV station call letters painted on them. Once again they had to have set speed records to get here from Albany or Syracuse or wherever, but any break in this case would draw them like flies. They'd be expecting to hear that Buddy Harper had been apprehended, as Pearson had all but promised the kid soon would be. What they'd hear instead would be a bombshell.

Jud knew how much the media loved a murder case— especially one with bizarre overtones—and from the start the legend of the headsman had been a bonanza for them. Now this second ax killing would be a lot more than conjecture about some dusty ghost story in a small town. And it wouldn't be merely regional news, either.

He parked the Plymouth in the lot behind the building then trudged through the drifting snow to the back door of the stationhouse. As soon as he walked in, a swarm of reporters descended on him, poking microphones into his face, shouting questions, firing flash cameras. He pushed through them, heading for his office.

Before he got there Chester Pearson grabbed his arm. "Been waiting for you. I promised these people a press conference, and I wanted you to be here for it."

He wanted to protest, but he never got the chance. He and Pearson became surrounded by reporters and cameramen, and it took several minutes before the inspector could quiet them down enough to make a statement.

"A couple of hours ago," Pearson told them, "the young man we've been looking for was found. At least, part of him was. Buddy Harper was decapitated, and we have recovered his head."

That triggered an uproar, and again Pearson had to wait for the crowd to let him continue. "The severed head was sent here, to Chief MacElroy. Maybe he can tell you why it was sent to him."

For the second time that day, Jud felt as if he'd been punched in the gut. He stood there like a fool as the wave of shouted questions washed over him, not knowing how he was going to handle this, his anger surging over the way he'd been set up. Pearson had sidestepped the issue of why the investigation had focused on the Harper boy as the killer of Marcy Dickens and was dumping the responsibility for this new development onto Jud.

"Why you, Chief?"

"What did you know about this kid?"

"Where's the rest of the body?"

"What haven't you told us about Harper and the Dickens girl?"

Jud fumbled his way through it, trying to answer above the noise, mouthing platitudes that made him sound as silly as he felt. "We have no information at this time." And "We don't know why it was sent here." And "We have no further leads at present." Until he wished he could find a hole and crawl into it.

Finally he held up his hands and said, "That's all we can say until we get reports from the lab." He turned and shoved his way through the mob, making his way down the hall toward his office. When he got there he went inside and shut the door behind him.

The paper and the cardboard box had been removed, presumably by the state police investigators. In the center of his desk there was now an envelope with his name on it. That had to be the message Stanis had told him about. He tore it open and withdrew a sheet of stationery with an Office of the Mayor letterhead. He scanned the contents.

A meeting of the Braddock Town Council had been scheduled for five o'clock that afternoon, it said. It was mandatory that Chief MacElroy attend.

His watch told him that was ten minutes from now. He wasn't sure what was on the agenda, but he knew that whatever it was, from his standpoint it wouldn't be good.

6

The fact that Sally was a woman meant nothing. Reporters stepped on her feet and elbowed her out of their way in their efforts to get closer to the inspector and the chief of police. Her reaction was to stomp, shove and elbow back.

Taking notes would be impossible; she'd just have to do the best she could to remember what was being said—or shouted—in this melee. Compared to this one, the earlier press conferences had been love-ins.

Which was understandable. The announcement that Buddy Harper's head had been found was a tremendous shock. It meant that all the smug state police assumptions had been total nonsense. Not only had Harper not been Marcy Dickens' murderer, but he had become a victim himself. And who—or what—had killed him? No wonder the inspector seemed shaken. After only a few terse words, just enough to state what had happened, he'd turned the floor over to Jud.

As much as she wanted this story, she felt pity as she watched Jud stand there and take it. The reporters were howling for blood, demanding to know why the Harper kid's head had been sent to the chief of police and why he hadn't leveled with them about what was really going on.

And he had no answers for them. At least none that were acceptable. He simply mumbled a bunch of cliches that added up to an admission that the police didn't know what to do next. It was awful.

But it was also annoying. Ethics and regulations were all wonderful, but damn it, this was a tough, competitive world. He could at least have given her a hint as to what was happening. The phone call from him earlier today—had he already received that hideous package?

Probably he had. Shit.

As if she hadn't stuck her neck out for him, spending hours pulling those old photos out of the files, and then letting him borrow them. Was this all the thanks she'd get?

She'd also strained her relationship with Maxwell. The old man had to be getting senile. First he'd fallen all over himself in praising her work on this story, including her initiative in digging up the angle of the Donovan murder. But then when he'd discovered her returning the photos he'd had a fit.

Of course, she hadn't told him *why* she'd slipped them out. If she had, he probably would have fired her on the spot, judging from his frenzied reaction when he saw her with them.

But what was the big deal anyway?

The press conference was on the edge of chaos. Two guys with TV camcorders were trying to outmaneuver each other and looked as if they were about to come to blows. The noise level was even higher, and Jud was trying to get the reporters to shut up.

She realized that from here on out this event would be little more than an exercise in futility. Beyond learning that Buddy Harper had been decapitated and that his severed head had been sent to the police, she'd get nothing more of value.

But what a hell of a development *that* was. Not only would the town of Braddock and every city in the area go crazy; the story of the headsman would be *national* news. She knew at once that the *New York Times* and the *Post* and *Time, Newsweek* and *U.S. News* would all send crews up here, as would the television networks.

So what was there to gain by staying here and watching these guys muscle each other? She'd do better to go back to her desk as fast as she could and bang out the story. Before the others got the same idea.

Getting out of here would certainly be easier than coming in had been. She shoved her way through the crowd and left the stationhouse via the back door.

Outside, snow was continuing to fall with the persistence that presaged a major storm. She turned up the collar of her trenchcoat and tugged her hat down, walking as quickly as she could through the cushion of white. Her boots were crunching in the stuff, and the wind-whipped flakes stung her face and her eyelids. She was grateful that the offices of the *Express* were only a short distance away.

7

The conference room in which the Town Council meetings were held was on the second floor of the city hall. When Jud went up the stairs he was trailed by a couple of reporters who had hung around, apparently hoping to glean something more on the story of Buddy Harper's murder. He ignored their yapping, going through the paneled doors and shutting them behind him.

This was an ornate room, with high ceilings and tall windows flanked by heavy, dark blue drapes. Portraits of past city officials looked down from the paneled walls, and an American flag hung from a pole at the far end. Illumination was provided by an elaborate brass chandelier that had originally supported gas lamps when the building was constructed over a century ago.

In the center of the room and running most of its length was an ancient, intricately carved mahogany table. Seated around it and eyeing him coldly were the members of the Braddock Town Council.

Sam Melcher was at the head of the table. As mayor, he was automatically chairman of this group. On either side sat three men: to the left Ed Dickens, Charley Boggs and Ray Maxwell; to the right Loring Campbell, Bill Swanson and Peter Harper. The mayor indicated the chair at the foot of the table. "Sit down, Chief."

Jud did, noting that there was none of the cozy informality he'd observed the last time he'd been together with some of them, when he'd been invited to Melcher's home for a drink. The hostility was so thick now he could almost reach out and touch it. Seeing Peter Harper here was startling; he would have expected Harper to be home after learning the devastating news of his son's death. Instead here he sat, staring at Jud as balefully as the rest of them.

"The reason for this meeting," Melcher began, "is to question you about recent events in this horrible murder case. The first thing we want to know is"—he shot a glance at Harper—"why that, uh, package was sent to you."

Jud had heard that on several other occasions today; this time he was ready for it. His manner was calm. "I don't know. It's reasonable to assume the killer sent it, I suppose. Maybe he was also sending a message to the police. Killers have been known to do things like that, especially psychopaths, as this one has to be."

"Has to be?" Swanson was peering at him. "What proof do you have of that?"

"I don't have any proof," Jud said. "But his actions would certainly convince me. No sane person kills kids with an ax."

Boggs spoke up. "So let's say the killer sent the package. He didn't just send it to the police. He sent it to you."

"As chief, I represent the police force," Jud said. "Maybe that was why."

"Maybe," Ed Dickens said, "it was you he was sending a message to."

"I don't know what his motives were," Jud said. "And I don't think anyone else does, either. Except the killer himself."

Swanson leaned forward, his heavy hands curled on the table in front of him. "Chief, I'd be interested in hearing what your role in this investigation has been up to now."

That caught him off balance. "My role? I've been doing what I can to help. Inspector Pearson is in charge, as you know."

Swanson looked at Melcher. The mayor said to Jud, "We had a talk with the inspector after this latest development. I'm going to be blunt with you, because we want all the cards out on the table. Inspector Pearson told us you've been very uncooperative throughout the entire investigation."

Despite his resolve, Jud felt a surge of anger. "I don't know how he could say that."

"Neither do we," Swanson said. "Unless it's true."

"Have you been reporting to him?" Melcher asked.

Jud shifted in his chair. "Not on every detail, I suppose."

For the first time since the meeting had started, Peter Harper spoke. "The morning you came out to our home," he said, "after Buddy disappeared. You didn't report to Inspector Pearson then. You just came out without telling him anything about it. When he got to the house he was obviously angry with you for not informing him of what was going on. After you left, he told us he was disturbed by your failure to cooperate."

Loring Campbell had also been silent up to now, holding Jud in a cold stare. He said, "We get the impression you've been poking into a lot of people's private business under the guise of working on this investigation. Yet Inspector Pearson didn't know anything about that, either."

"I've been trying to develop leads," Jud said. It sounded weak even to him. He felt foolish, mumbling half-baked excuses. But what could he say? The last thing he'd want to do would be to let on why he'd been asking questions and to reveal what answers he'd turned on—especially to this group.

Among the men who were grilling him now were several he could definitely link to Janet Donovan. Men who'd slept with her. Men who might have a motive for killing her.

"Developing leads is one thing," Campbell said. "Snooping around in citizens' private lives is something else."

"Loring's right," Melcher said. "A chief of police has a very important position in our community. A sensitive position. One of his responsibilities is to maintain law and order, of course. But another is to see that high standards are maintained. To see that citizens' rights are protected, not violated."

Ray Maxwell closed his throat. "Frankly, I was astounded by what I've been hearing. Not just today's news, but other things that have come to light recently. It seems you've been using your position—and this case—to pry into matters that have nothing to do with police business."

"Just what is it you're looking for?" Melcher asked. "I'd like to know what it is you're after, and why you think you have a right to be carrying on the way you have."

Jud looked at the faces of the seven men. Each of them was glaring at him with obvious resentment and barely controlled anger. He felt as if he were being pilloried. And yet there was no way he could defend himself without revealing information he wouldn't want any of them to have.

Despite the tension, he kept his voice steady. "I've been looking at various angles of the case, seeing if I couldn't find something that would be useful."

Ed Dickens spoke again, his voice harsh. "When my daughter died, it was clear that outside help was needed. That's why the state police were called in. Could it be you were so miffed when they were that you started working at cross-purpose? That you were deliberately hindering them?"

"Or did you see a way to use the case as a cover," Campbell added, "for whatever your real motives were?"

This was too much to take. Jud leaned forward. "That's goddamn ridiculous. I've been doing everything I can to help solve this thing, and that's been my only interest right from the beginning."

"Maybe," Melcher said. "And maybe not. Whichever way we look at it, you've contributed nothing while you've gotten a lot of people very upset. The bottom line is, you've betrayed our trust in you. It's my duty to inform you that the Town Council is giving you a vote of no confidence."

"A unanimous vote," Campbell added. There was a satisfied smirk on his face. Jud wished he could rip it off.

"We're putting you on notice as of now," Melcher went on. "The next step will be a formal hearing to determine whether you should be dismissed."

"The thing you don't seem to understand," Boggs said, "is that we're in a crisis situation here. The children of two of our leading citizens, both members of this council, have been murdered in their homes. People are in a panic, and you can hardly blame them."

"This headsman business," Swanson said. "It's got everybody hysterical."

"It's like a circus," Boggs went on. The set of his mouth looked as if he'd bit into something rotten. "All those reporters swarming around. They're tearing Braddock's reputation to pieces."

Jud was incredulous. This pack of wolves was as much bothered by the fact that the town was the subject of a lot of bad publicity as they were by the murders. As far as they were concerned, the headsman was an unfortunate problem, like a natural disaster. As if a blight had run through the town, or a fire.

And at the same time, he wondered if one of the men at this table didn't know a lot more about all of it than he was letting on.

"Do you have anything to say?" Melcher asked.

It took self-control for Jud to get the words out, but he kept his voice as steady as possible. "I'm sorry to hear how you feel about my work as police chief. When I was appointed, I took pride in your faith in me. In the short time I've had the job—just over a year—I've done my level best at all times. Now we're trying to deal with a tragedy—a series of tragedies—that's been tearing the town apart. I don't think it's right to blame me for the lack of progress in the case. I haven't been in charge of the investigation, and in spite of what anybody says, I've done whatever I could to help. I certainly haven't tried to obstruct the state police, and I have tried to cooperate. If my efforts to uncover a useful angle have rubbed some people the wrong way, I'm sorry. That was never intended, and I regret it. All I was trying to do was my job, the best I knew how. If that's so wrong, I'm sorry about that as well. You say you're putting me on notice. That won't be necessary. You want me out, I'll spare you the trouble and resign."

The faces showed no change in emotion, and all eyes continued to hold him in a hostile, unblinking stare.

"On the other hand," Jud went on, "I'd like to point something out to you. As you've said, the town is hysterical. And I agree that what the media will be saying now will make it even worse. But I think you ought to consider what effect my leaving the job would have. Seems to me it would just fan the fire. I'd give them another headline to call all the more attention to our problems."

There was silence for a moment, and then Charley Boggs turned to the mayor. "He's right about that, Sam. We got enough hooting and hollering from the newspapers and TV without having something else for them to yell about. It'd give the town an even bigger black eye. Make people think there was even more to all of this than what they knew about. As if maybe we were hiding something."

"No," Campbell said. He spoke to the others, but his gaze was fixed on Jud. "I don't agree with that at all. What the chief is doing now is squirming to find a way to hold on to his job. I think he's given us the answer by offering to resign. If he's willing to do that, we should take him up on it right now."

Melcher hesitated, his bulbous nose seeming to sniff the wind. He looked at the others around the table, most of whom didn't appear now to be quite so resolute.

"It seems," Campbell said acidly, "as if we have a division of opinion."

Melcher covered his mouth with his fist and coughed once. "Maybe we ought to hold off our discussion until we're by ourselves."

There was muttering and mumbling among them, as they turned and spoke with each other in low voices. As they did,

Jud looked out the window across from where he sat. The snow was whirling down in thick white flakes, making a ticking sound as the wind drove it against the glass. This would be one bitch of a storm.

Finally Melcher looked up at Jud. "We'll defer taking action until we've had a chance to talk about this. As far as you're concerned, Chief, there has been no change in your status. At least for the time being. Above all, you're not to discuss this meeting, or anything to do with the Council's business, with anyone. Is that clear?"

"Yes." Jud got to his feet. "That's clear. Good afternoon, gentlemen." He turned and left the room.

fifteen ·····························
Lying in Wait

1

As Sally walked back to the *Express* offices, she planned how
she'd set up the story. The problem was not merely to report
this latest development; that would be relatively easy. The
news wouldn't even be all that fresh, because TV would cover
it this evening, hours before the first edition of the *Express*
appeared. What she needed was an angle—something that
would make her piece unique.

She knew instinctively that the slant she was looking for had to
focus on the headsman. That was a given. But first came the job
of straight reporting—pumping out the news of the discovery of
Buddy Harper's severed head.

When she reached the offices of the newspaper she stamped
snow off her boots and hung her coat and hat in the closet. Her
lead was already framed in her mind, the words itching to jump
off her fingers into the word processor. One bizarre murder was
news. A second one would be an earthshaker. Especially with
the elements this situation had.

ANOTHER YOUNG LOVER DECAPITATED
YOUTH'S HEAD SENT TO POLICE CHIEF
AX MURDERER PROWLS SMALL TOWN
LEGENDARY HEADSMAN RETURNS WITH A VENGEANCE

It was enough to take your breath away.
And yet she was troubled. It was big news, all right, but a
short time from now her article in the *Express* would be

nothing more than the local coverage. A fart in a windstorm. By the time her version appeared, television and the big city newspapers and the wire services would have run away with the story. They'd get the attention because they had the audience. They were the big time, while she was nothing but a hayseed writer on a farm sheet.

It would be *their* story—not hers. Damn it, it wasn't fair.

Nevertheless she had to get this out, and fast.

As she passed Maxwell's office on her way to her desk she noticed the editor wasn't there. She didn't have time to ask where he'd wandered off to; she could catch him up on this newest break later. Blowing on her hands to warm them, she sat down and started typing.

The speed at which she knocked out the piece was surprising, even to her. In less than an hour she had over a thousand words. Her story announced the news of Harper's death in her best Oh-my-God style, with plenty of allusions to the headsman that would have readers believing the ax-wielding monster was lurking behind every bush in Braddock.

It was a first-rate job, if she did say so herself. Maxwell would want color stuff as well, but that would be mostly pickup from earlier stories on the backgrounds of the victims, a recap of the Dickens homicide, other bits of headsman lore, pictures of both kids, and so on. What she had just written was the important part, and she was confident she'd turned out a powerful piece. As soon as her draft was printed, she went back to the editor's office with pages in hand.

But he was still out.

"He's at a meeting," a voice said. Sally turned to see that the speaker had been Marge Diehl, Maxwell's secretary. Diehl had been on the staff forever, a gum-chewing doyenne in harlequin glasses. She was sitting at her typewriter, a cigarette hanging from one corner of her mouth.

"When's he coming back, do you know?"

The secretary shrugged. "Beats me. It's the Town Council at city hall."

"The meeting's about the Harper boy?"

"I guess so. The mayor called him, and as soon as he got the word he ran out of here." Diehl stubbed out her cigarette and got up from her desk. Mug in hand, she headed for the coffee urn.

Sally stepped into Maxwell's office and dropped her story onto the pile of papers on the editor's desk. She turned to leave, and as she did her eye caught sight of something in the midst of the clutter. Bending over the desk, she pushed the heap aside and looked at the thing that had caught her attention.

It was an old book, lying open, its pages yellow and crumbling with age. On them she saw spidery illustrations made from steel engravings. They depicted a tall man dressed all in black, carrying out an execution with an ax.

Sally felt a chill run through her body that was colder than anything the snowy weather outside had produced.

Where had this thing come from? Why hadn't Maxwell shown it to her?

She looked at the book's cover. It was of black leather, dull and worn, the title stamped in gold letters so faded with age she was barely able to make out what they said. Holding the cover up to the light she read,

BRADDOCK
A HISTORIE OF THE TOWNE
by
Jonathan Wells

Flipping through the motheaten pages she saw that the book was profusely illustrated with the same type of drawings. They showed views of the village in colonial times, men and women quaintly dressed, revolutionary war soldiers marching through the narrow streets. There were scenes of farmers tilling their fields, of draft animals drawing plows and stone sleds, of hunters tracking deer and turkey, of men raising a barn, and of people gathered in front of the old Methodist church on North Street that had burned down only a few years ago.

But the pictures that stunned her were those of the headsman. She turned back to them, the captions informing her that they showed the execution of a highwayman who had been apprehended in the village after he had robbed and killed a traveler.

The execution took place in the old Braddock house, the captions said. The house had been named for General Edward Braddock, as had the town itself. Braddock had been commander of the British forces for a time during the French and Indian wars in the mid-eighteenth century. Before mounting the campaign against Fort Duquesne in which he was killed, the general had spent a winter in his headquarters here. Later the house was used as the town's meeting hall. There were dungeons in its basement, and that was where the village executioner had carried out his assignments.

Sally looked at the pictures of the house, and again a chill passed through her. The house the drawing showed was the building that was now Braddock's museum.

Dungeons? In the museum? And executions had taken place there?

She put the book down, feeling that she'd discovered a hidden door into the past, opened it and peered inside.

So that was where Braddock's dreaded headsman had done his work. In the moldy old wreck of a structure that was the oldest building in the village. And she was looking for a new angle for her story—one that would be exclusively hers? She had one now. You could bet your sweet ass she did.

Maybe the snow wasn't so bad, after all. A good blizzard would tie up the roads and the airports at least through tomorrow. Which meant that the town would be isolated. All those hotshot reporters from New York or wherever wouldn't be able to get here for a day or so. Which would give her a head start.

Excitement coursed through her as she thought about it. She wouldn't let anyone else in on this opportunity. Not even Maxwell. And as she thought about it, *especially* not Maxwell. Why hadn't he shared this with her?

Whatever the reason, the hell with him. What she had to do now was get to the museum.

2

Jud was exhausted, physically drained. His head ached and his back was stiff, as if he'd strained it by carrying a great weight.

He didn't look too good, either. After going back downstairs to police headquarters he stopped in the men's room to take a leak and caught sight of himself in the mirror. There were fatigue shadows under his eyes and the eyes were bloodshot. His usually neat shirt had sweat crescents under the armpits and was full of wrinkles. He went back down to his office and shut the door behind him, then slumped down heavily in his desk chair.

This was it, he realized. The inevitable crossroads he'd been approaching ever since that fateful Saturday morning that had started out to be dull and boring and then had irrevocably changed his life. The day that now seemed to have taken place a hundred years ago.

What now, he asked himself. What do you do? Stay here and wait for that collection of turds to make up their minds about you? That was ridiculous; they'd obviously made them up before the meeting of the Town Council had been held. They'd even voted *before* he'd been called in. The meeting had been simply a formality, a step the members had to take so that everything would appear to be reasonable and proper and in accordance with the town's procedures.

When in fact they'd been salivating like wolves trailing a crippled moose, moving in for the kill. What would they do next? Accept the resignation he'd offered them, of course. They'd meet again and argue among themselves, might not even reach a decision right away. But they'd come to it. The murders were bad enough, but to have an upstart cop rooting around where he didn't belong would be seen by many of them as even worse.

So they'd hem and haw, and then they'd announce that they had reluctantly accepted Chief MacElroy's resignation. It would be in Braddock's best interests, they'd say. Because the town had to use every resource to solve this terrible series of crimes, and if that meant bringing in a more seasoned officer to head the force, then members of the council would do what was right.

What a load of crap.

But how could Dickens and Harper be part of it? For both of them to have lost kids and still be in on this witchhunt was baffling. Where the hell was their sense of values?

Or was Jud wrong? Maybe *he* was the one who was out of step with the world. Maybe the wiser course would have been to just play the game, after all. Let Chester Pearson and Williger and the rest of the state police task force carry out their investigation while he went on being the loyal, helpful young chief who minded his manners and chased traffic offenders.

But it was too late for that.

Even if he could have lived with himself afterward. Which he couldn't. Not as long as he had to look at himself in the mirror every morning.

So what was the answer? There wasn't any. At least, none that offered satisfaction or suggested a course that could bring about a resolution. That was the trouble, he realized. For once in his life, he was in a situation that seemed hopeless. He'd done his digging, had even made progress. But he had to admit he was a long way from having anything nailed down. The fact was that all he had to show for his work didn't amount to a hill of henshit.

He swung his chair around and unlocked the closet behind him. Taking out the box of photographs, he opened it and spread the contents onto his desk.

The faces in the old black-and-white pictures stared back at him solemnly. Some of them he'd seen only a short time ago, in the council meeting. If one of these men was the one he was looking for, that one would have had the best reason of all for wanting him out.

The thought sent a sudden rush of anger through him, anger fueled by frustration and self-doubt and humiliation and resentment. Goddamn it, what he wouldn't give to get his hands on the bastard who was responsible for all this.

Whoever it was, the man was his enemy. Not merely because Jud was a cop and this guy was his quarry. The killer had now singled him out on a personal basis.

The killer had sent him Buddy Harper's head.

Jud stared at the pictures for a long time. Finally he put them back into the box and returned the box to the closet, locking the door.

After that he spent another hour going over the routine stuff that had piled up on his desk during the day. There was a thick stack of reports there, and although Jud went through the papers his mind wasn't really on them. They were just something to occupy him, a way to divert his attention for a while.

Finally he pushed the pile aside and stood up. What he really needed was some fresh air and a beer and something to eat. He put on his jacket and cap and left his office, walking through the station to the front desk.

Ostheimer had the duty. He looked up as Jud approached. "There was a bad one on Route Five, Chief. Trailer truck jack-knifed. It hit a Toyota and crushed it. One dead, three injured. We got two cars out there now."

Jud nodded. "What about the injured people?"

"Ambulance already took 'em to Memorial."

"They local?"

"No. From Cortland."

"All right. Soon as you get a report on their condition we'll contact relatives. Get Brusson to help you."

"Sure, Chief."

"With this storm, we're gonna have a long night. Where's Grady? I want him to call everybody in."

"I don't know where he is."

"So find him. And in the meantime, put out the call yourself. I want all hands."

"Yes sir."

Jud went out to the parking lot, noting that the storm was getting worse by the minute.

3

One of Sally's pet peeves was her car. A three-year-old Subaru sedan whose paint was weathered to a dull gray, it was noisy, tinny and underpowered. It looked exactly like what it was: a Japanese econobox. Tojo's revenge. She'd promised herself to trade it in as soon as the loan was paid off, which was only a couple of months from now.

But there was one feature of the crappy little auto she was grateful for, and that was its four-wheel drive. "You go in snow," the salesman had said. It turned out to be the only truth he'd told her, but it was an important one. Under almost any road conditions, the Subaru went. If it hadn't been for the car's ability to take on whatever weather Braddock could throw at it and get her where she wanted to go, she would have got rid of it long ago, loan or no loan.

Tonight the small sedan was being tested as it had never been. The storm had steadily increased in intensity, until now it was even worse than had been predicted. If this kept up, Braddock would indeed be isolated. Snow was drifting across the roads, and visibility was severely limited by the wind-whipped flakes. Her headlights were almost totally ineffective; their beams bounced back into her face from the wall of white. What should have been a ten-minute trip from her office to the museum took more than a half hour.

She was barely able to make out the gloomy old place in the darkness and the driving snow. From the road it was only a vaguely outlined shape off among the trees. She parked the Subaru in front of it, got out and took with her the tire iron she intended to use to force the door. She also dug a small flashlight out of the pocket of her trenchcoat, picking her way with the narrow yellow beam.

The distance from the road to the museum was perhaps thirty yards. The drifts were deeper than her boot tops, and slogging through them was difficult. Cold moisture trickled down her ankles and soaked her feet. She kept her head down and tried to lean into the wind, but snowflakes were stinging her eyelids and her cheeks. When she reached the front step she felt as if she'd walked a mile.

Despite the gloves she wore, her fingers were already cold and stiff. She pointed the flashlight beam at the front entrance, noting that the door looked very solid, with its heavy hinges and knob and knocker all made of brass. How was she ever going to force it? She'd never done anything like this, and wasn't even sure where to start. She grabbed the doorknob and twisted it, and the door swung open.

She was so surprised that for a moment she simply stood gawking. Obviously no one was here; the building was in pitch darkness. So maybe her assumption had been wrong and the place wasn't kept locked. That didn't make sense, but she was too cold and too anxious to find shelter to give it further thought. She stepped into the hall and shut the door behind her. The air in here was icy, but at least she was in out of the storm.

The old house wasn't entirely quiet. Standing in the gloom, she was aware of the sound of the wind moaning around the windows and the roof, and of the structure's ancient joints creaking. It seemed almost to have a life of its own.

She'd been here a few times before, finding the building merely odd and quaint, but that had been in the daytime, and there had been other people around. Although the interior had been dim and shadowy then, it hadn't seemed threatening. At night, with the place dark and a storm raging outside, it took on an entirely different character. Especially now that she was alone.

Despite the cold there was a musty smell in here, the odor of dank decay, of ancient dust. It was as if every aspect of the old building were repelling her, telling her she was not welcome.

Cut it out, she told herself. Don't let the haunted-house crap get to you. If you can find what you're looking for, you'll have a terrific new slant on the story. And with nobody here to disturb you, you've got the place to yourself to snoop around in. So get going.

According to what she'd found in the book she'd seen in Maxwell's office, the dungeon was underneath the hallway. She'd have to find a stairway somewhere to get down there. Following the small beam of her flashlight, she stepped along the hallway. The kitchen, she knew, was at the south end, which was to her left. It seemed logical that she'd find stairs there; old houses used cellars for food storage.

The interior was a labyrinth of narrow, twisting passages. She made a couple of mistakes as she followed them, each time doubling back until she thought she'd regained her bearings. The cold had gone all the way into her bones; her fingers had lost feeling and her toes ached. Her breath hung in front of her in tiny faint clouds.

But she found the kitchen.

It was a large room, low-ceilinged and with a great fireplace that looked like a huge, open mouth. There were a number of doors in here and she tried one after another, finding herself peering into closets and two pantries and a wood storage room. And then she opened another door and saw a flight of steep, winding stairs leading downward.

She took a deep breath. She was pleased at having found the steps, but at the same time a sense of foreboding gripped her. Again she told herself to get it together, not to let fright get the better of her.

She was about to make a tentative step onto the first tread when she heard a sound. It was different from the noise made by the howling wind, different from the rattling of the shutters and the creak of old boards and timbers.

It was the sound of a man breathing.

Fright became terror. She spun around, but as she did the flashlight was struck from her hand and went tumbling down the yawning stairway. In the blackness she could see nothing, but she was aware of a presence. Someone—or some*thing*— was very near her.

She opened her mouth to scream, but before she could make a sound a hand gripped her face, the fingers snapping onto her jaw like a steel trap. The hand lifted her off her feet, and then there was an explosion in the top of her head and she felt nothing.

4

Billy Swanson closed the door of his bedroom and turned on the radio, rolling the dial until he hit WBDK–FM, the local station. As he tuned in, a news announcer was winding up a report on the discovery of Buddy Harper's head, breathlessly recounting how the thing had been sent in a package to the chief of police, and how the authorities were baffled by this latest development in the case. The citizens of Braddock, the guy said, were shocked by the horrifying turn of events. This was the second ax murder in recent times, and tales of the dreaded headsman were on everyone's lips.

Billy himself had been stunned by the news when he'd heard it earlier in the day, feeling an icy chill when he learned that Buddy was dead. Especially because of *how* he'd died. After all his jeering about the headsman, Billy was no longer quite so smug a nonbeliever. Like Marcy's, Buddy's head had been chopped off. And that was a bitch.

But tonight Billy had other things to think about. He had a load of homework: a problem in physics, two chapters of American History to read, a paper to write for English. And in a way that was good; it would prevent him from dwelling on the news about Buddy. He got out his books and laid them on his desk, and then turned up the volume on his radio. In the evening WBDK broadcast Top Forty records one after the other, with a few older hits thrown in. At the moment they were playing a new one by Miami Sound Machine. Outside his window the snow was falling heavily.

It took him a half hour to work out the physics problem, a dumb-ass thing involving energy loss through friction in a machine that made bowling balls, for Christ's sake. What a waste of time so much of this shit was. After that he skipped through the history assignment, two chapters describing Theodore Roosevelt's role in the Spanish–American War. According to what he could glean, the Spaniards had been willing to concede to the United States' demands to give up territory in the Philippines, but the U.S. declared war anyway, largely at the urging of the Hearst press. And also because Roosevelt wanted to be a hero. So what else was new? Sounded like the same kind of crap that went on today.

That left the paper in English, which brought to mind Mr. Hathaway. Now there was one weird dude. When the news hit school that Buddy's head had turned up, everybody flipped out. Girls had wept, guys went around looking as if they'd just lost their best friend. A lot of people had gone to the counselor, hoping to get some help for the emotional pain. And yet Hathaway hadn't so much as mentioned it, even though both Buddy and Marcy had been in his class. He'd just gone on being his usual sour self, talking down to everybody except a couple of the girls.

Which was another thing about the English teacher that was strange. He was stuck in that damn wheelchair, paralyzed from the waist down. And yet you'd have to be blind not to notice the way he always had little games going with any of the girls who came on to him. They'd bat their eyes and cross their legs and wiggle around, and Hathaway would eat it up. Every time he looked at Betty Melcher lately, she practically did a dance for him. Could something really be going on there? Billy had heard rumors for a long time that the teacher sometimes fooled around with the females in his class, but he didn't know if it was true.

The question was, what could he do with them, if it came down to it? Paralyzed meant paralyzed, didn't it? If Hathaway's legs didn't work, nothing else did either, including his dick. Wasn't that the way it was? So even if a chick was willing to play, what could he do? Maybe he was a muffdiver.

But whatever he did or didn't do was Hathaway's problem, not Billy's. He had his own appetites to think about. And think about them he did. He could imagine being with Alice Boggs right this minute, holding her body tight against his own, feeling her pushing it up to him, while her mouth opened in one of her patented sloppy kisses and he practically licked her tonsils.

Goddamn, but that was something to dream about. Seeing the mental picture and imagining how it would feel gave him a throbbing erection. Wouldn't it be great to be with her right now, instead of doing this lousy fucking homework?

Nevertheless, he tried to settle down and write the paper. It was to be on Stephen Crane's *The Red Badge of Courage*.

But how was he going to write a paper on it if he hadn't read the book?

He opened his notebook, hoping he'd jotted down something he could pull from. Nothing. The page contained only a scribbled note on the assignment and some doodles in the shape of a girl's tit.

Which made him think of Alice again. He fiddled with his ballpoint while the radio blasted more rock—Springsteen this time—out of the stereo speakers. Finally he put the pen down and picked up the telephone. He had his own line, which his father had ordered installed after his parents had all but gone nuts with the frustration of having the phone tied up for hours at a time. He touched the buttons and waited to hear her voice.

Alice had her own phone as well, for the same reason Billy did. She answered in the low tone she was affecting lately, probably because she thought it made her sound sexy. She was right; it did.

He said, "It's snowing out. You know what they call a quickie in the snow."

"No, what?"

"A coolie."

"Very funny."

"You'd have to be there."

"I wish I was."

"Me too. So why don't we get together?"

"Fat chance. The weather report on TV says it's a blizzard."

"It's all in your mind. Just a snow shower."

"You're so brave, why don't you come over?"

His dander always came up when she dared him to do anything. It was as if he was being tested. "Maybe I will."

"You serious?"

"Sure, why not? A few snowflakes wouldn't stop me. Where are your folks?"

"Oh, they're here, down in the living room. I'm doing my homework. But hey, you're kidding, right?"

"Who is?"

"Come on, Billy—you'd never make it."

"You don't think so? I got the Bronco, don't forget. Wouldn't be any problem at all."

"You sound like one of my father's salesmen."

"Well, it's true."

"Bullshit."

"Yeah? I'll be there inside of twenty minutes."

"You really are serious, aren't you?"

"Sure. Can you get out?"

Excitement crept into her voice. "No, but I've got a better idea. I'll leave the side door unlocked, okay? You come up the back stairs to my room, and they'll never know you're here."

He laughed. "Sounds great."

"Doesn't it? You think you could make it?"

"Just watch me. And don't forget to unlock the damn door."

He hung up and laughed again. This could be a hell of a lot of fun. For more reasons than one.

He left his desk and looked out the window. Tonight he'd

need something more weather-resistant than his varsity sweater. He put it on anyway, but pulled a nylon parka over it.

There was a strict rule laid down by his father that there was no going out on a school night. Which had never hindered Billy in the least. Unlike Alice's house, the Swansons' had no back stairs. So for years he'd been sneaking out via the same route: through the window of his bedroom onto the back roof, down the drainpipe onto the terrace. Nothing to it. With the radio blaring in his bedroom his parents never suspected he wasn't there. When he came home later on they were in bed, sound asleep. He just breezed in through the garage door into the kitchen, got something to eat, then marched up to his room with no concern. It had never failed him.

He slipped through the window and within moments reached the driveway. Once outside, he found the snow even deeper than he'd thought. The Bronco was sitting in the turnaround, where he'd left it when he came home for dinner, and it was already covered with a thick coat of white. He opened the door and got out the scraper, clearing off the windows and the hood. The noise of starting the engine was no problem; the snow muffled it. He rolled down the driveway and turned onto the road before switching on his headlights.

The trip took longer than he'd expected. With the Bronco in four-wheel drive he could get through the snow okay, even though there were drifts now in many places. But it was slow going. He saw several abandoned vehicles on the way and passed only two moving cars, both of them with chains clanking.

Alice was right—this was a fullblown blizzard. From the time he was a little kid he'd always been thrilled when one hit. He loved the way it turned the world into a silent, frozen place. Everything would be shut down as houses, barns, buildings and cars were all buried under the ghostly cover.

If the storm was heavy enough there would also be a power failure, which meant you had to use candles and kerosene lamps for light and fireplaces for heat. Cooking would be done on propane stoves. There was no TV, but you could still get music from battery-powered radios, which picked up stations in distant places if WBDK went off. It was exciting—kind of like camping out. Only better, because you could sleep in the comfort of your own bed. His mother would put on extra blankets and he'd wear socks and a wool stocking cap and be as snug as he could ever hope to be.

And best of all, a big storm meant no school. When he was little he could hardly wait to get outside after the snowfall so he could drag his sled over to Beacon Hill and spend the day sliding down the slopes. He'd had a Flexible Flyer, of course, with the eagle painted on the center slat, the fastest sled ever made. And the most prestigious, the one every kid wanted.

But that was then. Nowadays no school meant he could sleep in. It also meant he'd wasted an hour doing that dopey homework. But what the hell, if there was no school tomorrow, which was a sure bet, he'd have to turn it in the next day anyway. So it wasn't a total loss.

The lights were on everywhere in the Boggs house. He decided to leave the Bronco on the road. No sense taking chances by trying to sneak it into the driveway; Alice's parents might spot it there. He turned off his headlights and came to a stop, then shut off his engine and climbed out of the vehicle.

5

The headsman stood in the lee of the Boggs garage. Protected by the overhang from the driving snow, he watched the girl through the window of her second floor room.

Even the storm was helpful to him, cutting off the house from the rest of the world. His shoulders and legs were wet; the ancient black cloth of his garments had soaked through to his skin. But he paid no attention to the dampness and the cold, concentrating only on the figure of the girl as she moved about the room.

She was a pretty thing, with long sandy blond hair and a ripe body. As he watched, she lifted the telephone and smiled seductively as she spoke into it. She appeared to giggle, and then threw her head back, and from her expression it was easy to guess that she was talking to a young man. She spoke into the phone for some minutes, and when she hung up she clapped her hands once, as if she'd heard good news. Then she abruptly left the room.

He watched and waited.

A moment later she surprised him by opening the side door of the house and peering out into the night. She hadn't turned on the light, and for a moment he wasn't sure who had opened the door. But then he saw her clearly enough, even though visibility was further reduced by the swirling snowflakes. She closed the door and was again lost from his sight, and seconds after that she reappeared in her room.

Ah—he had it then. She was expecting someone to come through that door at the corner of the house. Undoubtedly the same someone she'd spoken to on the telephone.

And now she was preparing herself—getting ready for her visitor, he was sure of it. She pulled off her sweater and tossed it aside, then removed her bra. Her naked breasts were firm and full and tipped with wide pink nipples. He could see her gazing into a wall mirror, turning one way and then another, looking critically at her image. She picked up a vial of what he surmised was perfume and dabbed a little between her breasts.

The girl moved away, and seconds later returned to his view, again looking into the mirror as she drew on a clingy, ivory-colored blouse. She brushed her hair, and then applied lipstick to her mouth. When she finished she went on studying her reflection until, satisfied at last, she moved away from the window.

The headsman gripped the hickory haft in both his gloved hands and swung the mighty double-bladed ax up onto his shoulder. His gaze left the lighted window of the girl's room and swept down to the side porch. He waited.

Some time later, perhaps a half hour, he heard the sound of an engine. He poked his head around the corner just far enough to see headlights approaching from down the road, their beams shining weakly into the falling snow.

As he watched, the headlights went out and the vehicle came to a stop a short distance from the Boggs house. The figure that climbed out of the driver's seat was Billy Swanson.

The boy paused for a few seconds, evidently looking things over, and then made his way up the driveway, lumbering through the deep snow. He climbed the steps onto the side porch and slipped through the door, closing it after him. A few moments later the headsman caught a glimpse of the boy and the girl together as they passed the window in her room. Their arms were draped around each other and they were laughing.

There was no rush; he knew exactly what they'd be doing a few minutes from now. He wanted to give them time to begin.

SIXTEEN ···
A Deadly Surprise

1

Jud was lucky to get home, even with the car's snow tires and its limited-slip rear end. He had to crawl along the icy roads at a pace not much faster than walking, and twice he narrowly avoided sliding off into a ditch. When he reached his cottage he parked the Plymouth out front and decided to leave it there. For the rest of the night he'd use the Blazer. Only a vehicle with four-wheel drive would be able to move in this storm.

Once inside he kicked off his brogans, which were soaked through, and then stripped and went into the shower. The hot needle spray was restorative, helping to soothe and relax muscles stiff from tension.

When he'd toweled down he put on a fresh uniform and heavy wool socks and a pair of hunting boots that came almost to his knees. He went into the kitchen and cracked a can of beer, and by the time he'd drunk it he was feeling better. He tossed the empty into the garbage and stuffed a frozen chicken-something-or-other into the microwave. While it was cooking he got himself another beer. He didn't turn on the TV, because he didn't want to see himself being held up in front of the world as Chief Asshole in the little village of Braddock.

He thought of Sally. She'd been among the crowd of reporters at the press conference earlier, and seeing her had added to his embarrassment. He hoped she'd left her office and gone home by now, but knowing her as he did she was probably still there. He went into his bedroom and called the *Express*, and the woman who answered said she'd left some time ago. That was a relief. Then he tried her home number and got no answer. Maybe she'd stopped for something on the way. He'd try her later.

The meal was ready after a few minutes, and he ate it absent-mindedly, hardly tasting what he was putting into his mouth. When he finished he shoved the tray into the garbage pail and went into the living room, carrying his beer. He was still hungry; frozen dinners apparently had been concocted to feed dwarfs. But the hell with it. He wasn't about to heat up another one, and besides, he had to get back to the stationhouse.

Outside the storm was in full stride, the wind very strong. It rattled the roof and moaned in the tall pines that stood on the slope just beyond the cottage. This was no night to be anywhere but inside. As a matter of fact, it would be great to be able to stay right here. He'd build a big fire, get out the Gibson and play for hours, drink a hundred beers. Best way in the world to get his mind off his troubles.

But forget it. Stormy winter nights were when a cop earned his paycheck and then some. The worst times he could remember during his years on the force had been on nights like this one. There would be at least one more bad wreck, and if the snow kept falling a number of people would be stuck in their cars. One or two might be stupid enough to leave their vehicles and try to make their way on foot, and it was a good bet they'd wind up frozen stiff. The police usually had a couple of those every winter.

Reluctantly, with one more longing glance at the guitar case leaning against the wall next to the fireplace, he returned to the kitchen and tossed away his empty beer can. From the back hall closet he got out his fur cap and put it on, then hauled on his fleece-lined oilskin. He turned off the lights and clumped out to the garage where the Blazer was parked.

2

The door on the side porch remained unlocked. The headsman turned the knob slowly and silently, then stepped inside, his ears alert to catch the slightest noise. But the hallway was dark and quiet, the only sounds distant ones. From the front of the house came the burble of a television set, and from the floor above him drifted the thump and wail of rock music.

He closed the door and paused, listening. Melting snow dripped from the ax he held in his right hand and trickled down his black clothing. He placed one foot on the first tread of the stairs and began to climb, intent on moving silently. There were two people up in that room, and surprise was essential.

This was different from when he'd gone to the Dickens house. At that time he'd *wanted* to make noise, because he wanted the girl to hear his heavy footsteps on the staircase and be terrified. He saw her now in his mind's eye, recoiling from him, her hands extended as if to ward him off, her mouth working, her eyes popping. And then her features had grown even more contorted as she saw the ax rise higher and higher, until it began its journey downward, the glittering blade plunging toward her throat.

But tonight he had to move quietly. When he reached the landing he saw that he was in a hallway. His eyes had adjusted to the darkness, and he could make out that there were doors farther on, but only the nearest one had light showing from underneath it. That would be the girl's room, at the rear corner of the house. It was where she'd led the Swanson boy and where they had been when the headsman saw them through the window.

Many minutes had passed since the boy had entered the room. They'd be rolling around in her bed by now. The headsman could envision them grunting and straining, their bodies slick with sweat. He placed his ear against the door of the room, but all he heard from inside was the relentless pounding of the music.

Very gently, he gripped the knob and turned it. The door was locked. That meant he'd have to alter his plan somewhat, but not much. With what they were doing, they'd be unaware of what was happening until he was virtually on top of them. They would look up from the bed and he would be there, and they would be convulsed by fear, just as Marcy Dickens had been. And Buddy Harper.

And Janet Donovan.

And the others.

Even though his gloves were wet, his grip on the haft was tight and secure. He raised the ax, and his nostrils picked up the faint odor of oil from the polished steel. With great care, he placed one of the razor-sharp blades in the crack of the door, where the tongue of the lock met the striker. Then he flexed the heavy muscles of his shoulders and set himself.

3

By the time he got his clothes off, throwing his parka and sweater one way, his shirt another, and stumbling out of his jeans, Billy was ready to come. That actually happened to him sometimes, he'd get so excited. But when it did it wasn't such a big deal—within minutes he'd be ready to go again. The only thing was, he didn't want to *waste* any of this.

But when he stripped Alice's blouse away he thought he'd get off right then, she looked so great. Her breasts were as good as anything he'd ever imagined, even when he locked himself in the bathroom at home and made love to one of the dream girls he could conjure up in his imagination. Her skin was a creamy pink color, and her jugs had those great nipples standing there, just begging him to nibble on them. And then when he pulled off her skirt and her pants and pushed himself against her he was aware of the crinkly texture of her pubic patch and goddamn, that almost did it all over again.

They fell onto the bed together and the hell with foreplay; within seconds he was inside her, and within seconds after that he *did* come, and then he just lay there in her arms, her fingernails gently tracing circles on the flesh of his back.

Alice spoke in her throaty voice. "That was beautiful, Billy."

He had to smile to himself, hearing that. Beautiful? Christ—it was over almost before he got started. But then, maybe she'd come too. She certainly had been excited enough. And he had to hand it to her, this had been a terrific idea. In fact, the trip through the snow and then sneaking up to her room and jumping into bed had made it just that much more of a turn-on.

He rolled off her and lay on his back as his breathing returned to normal. There was a faint sheen of sweat on his chest, and his arms and legs felt as if they'd turned to rubber. Alice snuggled against him, resting her head on his shoulder. The stereo was playing a record by Tiffany, one of his favorite singers. It was funny, but he hadn't even noticed it before this. He put an arm around Alice and scratched the back of her neck.

"Mm-m. I love that."

"I loved all of it."

"Me too. I just meant I love it when you scratch my neck. I'm like a puppydog when you do that."

"Uh-huh."

"Billy, you know what I think sometimes, when we're together like this?"

"What?"

"I think how nice it would be if we were married."

Holy Jesus, where did *that* come from?

"I mean, I know we can't and we're too young and all that, but it's fun to, like, pretend—you know?"

"Sure. I think I know what you mean." In fact, he knew exactly what she meant, and the thought of it was nauseating.

She pressed herself tight against his side. "We're so close and all, and I really think you're great. You like me a lot too, don't you?"

"Hm? Oh, yeah. I sure do. Hey, Alice, you're still on the pill, aren't you? You take one every day?"

"Sure. Of course I do. Don't worry—I don't want to get pregnant." She was quiet for a few seconds, then abruptly raised herself on one elbow and looked down at him. "You didn't think I *did* want to, did you?"

"Me? No."

"I'm not one of those retards who think it'd be fun to have a baby so you could pet it and play mommy with it. Like it was a doll or something." She lay back down again. "Doris Persky did that last year. Did you hear about it?"

"Yeah, I guess so. I mean, I knew she had a kid."

"She's so awful. She got knocked up and she wasn't sure who did it. She tried to blame it on Donny Lonzik so she could get him to marry her, but Donny's father got him out of it."

"Uh-huh."

"Some kids do that, you know."

"Do what?"

"Get pregnant on purpose."

"I believe it. Hey, you don't have any grass, do you?"

"No. It's been kind of hard to get lately."

"You're telling me. But I hear there's a new guy dealing. Hangs around school after it gets out. I'll have to see if I can score some off him."

"Great. Get me some too, will you?"

"Sure."

She was silent again for a time, and he began to wonder if she'd dozed off.

But then she spoke up. "You know what I can't stop thinking about?"

He reached down and gave her buttock a squeeze. "Sure. I got the same problem."

"Not that, silly. I mean, I think about that, too. But I can't get the idea of Buddy out of my mind."

"Yeah, it was the worst."

"Wasn't it? I know I'm going to have nightmares tonight. Did you see the way a lot of kids were crying today in school?"

"Yeah, I did." He wished she'd get off it. Buddy's death was terrible—that was true. But blubbering about it wasn't going to bring him back. And besides, feeling Alice all warm and soft against his side was starting to get him worked up again.

But she kept on. "The worst thing is the way all that stuff about the headsman came true."

He drew a line down the cleft between her buttocks with his forefinger. "That's not so. I mean, there's still nothing to prove it."

She rose on her elbow once more. "Nothing to prove it? Are you serious? First Marcy gets killed, gets her head chopped off. And it happens the same day we're all talking about the headsman in Hathaway's class. Then Buddy disappears, and some people say okay, that's who did it—Buddy killed her and then he ran away. And the next thing you know, here's Buddy dead too. Killed *the same way*. So that's two people murdered, both of them with chopped-off heads. And you say there's nothing to prove it?"

Jesus, enough. "All I said was, there's nothing to prove the headsman did it. I still think the whole story's a lot of shit. People in Braddock've been passing it around forever. So yeah, Marcy and Buddy are both dead, and I agree with you, it's awful. Especially the way they died. But the headsman? That's the same old stuff I been hearing all my life. I just don't buy it, that's all."

"Oh yeah? Then what about that woman who got killed years ago—that Mrs. What's-her-name that was in the paper. She's another one. She had her head chopped off too, and you know what everybody said back then? The same thing they're saying now. The headsman came back to punish her."

"Why?"

"She was married but she was fooling around with a lot of other men."

"Where'd you hear that?"

"From my parents."

"Your *parents* told you?"

"God, no. I mean I heard them talking about it. They were discussing the whole thing about Marcy and Buddy and the headsman and that came up. My mother was saying it gave her the creeps the way it was happening all over again. She said everybody in town felt the same way about it then, too. They were all talking about how every few years the headsman comes back. And how some people were saying it wasn't true, just the way some people are saying it now. But the thing is, that murder never got solved either."

"Still doesn't prove anything."

"Jeez, but you can be stubborn. Look—if the headsman didn't do it, who did? And who killed all the others?"

"All what others?"

"The ones who died before that. Lots of people, going back over two hundred years."

"You're really hooked on this, aren't you?"

"No, I'm not. I'm just being more sensible than you are. You get this much showing you something's true, then you ought to believe it."

If she kept this up she'd be altogether out of the mood. Christ, if she kept it up *he'd* be out of it too. "Okay, I guess you're right."

She stared at him in mock amazement. "You mean you're actually gonna let me win an argument?"

"It's wasn't an argument—we were just talking."

She lay down again. "Sorry I got so riled up."

"It's okay." He resumed stroking her butt. "I know how you feel."

"That's good. It really had me upset."

He turned toward her and put his hand between her legs. "Yeah, I don't blame you."

Her voice was low, slightly hoarse. "Oh, Billy."

That was better. She was warm and wet, and he was as ready as ever. He lowered his head and kissed her mouth, then drew his lips slowly down her chin and her throat and on down to her breast. When he got there he teased her nipple with his tongue. He could feel it become erect under his touch. She'd begun to breathe hard once more, and Billy's pulse picked up. He raised his head and smiled as he stroked her.

Suddenly she stiffened, her eyes open wide. "What was that?"

"What was what?"

"I heard something out there—in the hall."

All Billy could hear was the rock pounding out of the stereo speakers. He glanced at the door, then turned back to Alice. "Your mother, maybe? Or your father?"

"No. They never bother me up here."

"Then relax, will you? Probably just the wind."

She settled down again.

There was a violent crash at the door.

And then another. Wood splintered, and the door sagged on its hinges.

Alice shrieked and tried to cover her eyes as Buddy sat bolt upright, his mouth hanging open. "Jesus Christ!" he yelled. "What's *that?*"

The upper panel of the door flew apart under the battering. There was another smashing blow, and the door burst open.

As Billy stared at the figure looming in the doorway, he thought his heart would stop.

It wasn't true. It was a joke. He was dreaming. It couldn't be. This wasn't happening.

But it was.

4

The man standing in the doorway was huge. He seemed to tower there, as massive and as tall as a great black tree. His head was encased in a hood, the eyeholes slanted, his eyes shining out from within. The width of his shoulders was startling. They flowed into arms bulging with muscle, the hands broad and covered with black gloves. And just as Billy had heard a hundred times, just as in the nightmares he and every other child in Braddock had experienced, the gloved hands held an enormous, double-bladed ax.

The headsman's black clothing was wet. Tiny wisps of steam rose from his body, and the stink of him spread through the room like gas from a dead, decaying animal. He stood motionless for what seemed a long time, although it couldn't have been more than a few seconds. But in that time Billy was unable to move, and neither was Alice. Both of them lay on the bed frozen in fear, the heat of their passion drained in an instant, their blood turning icy cold.

The headsman strode toward them, raising the ax as he came.

Instinctively, galvanized by desperation, Billy rolled off the bed and sprang to his feet. He was suddenly as angry as he was frightened. "You bastard!"

He was a big boy, over two hundred pounds, and strong. He was also an athlete, and a good one. He lowered his head and threw himself at the headsman.

The big man moved deftly, dipping the axhead and then bringing the flat side of it up into Billy's face with a violent snapping motion. The steel smashed into the boy's nose with numbing force, flipping him over backward and dropping him onto the floor.

Billy sat there with his head spinning, bells ringing in his ears, trying to get up but not succeeding. His vision was blurred, and he couldn't force the image of the man in black to stay in focus. It kept splitting into two fuzzy shapes that blurred as he stared at them. Blood was pouring from his nose and down onto his body in crimson splashes.

The headsman stepped forward, straddling Billy's outstretched legs. The huge man raised a booted foot and slammed the toe into the boy's chest, forcing him down onto his back. Billy grabbed the foot and twisted, and the man fell heavily. He was up again in an instant, and as Billy scrambled to his feet the flat side of the axblade again crashed into the boy's skull, even harder this time.

The blow knocked him flat, leaving him only dimly conscious. The boot pressed down on his chest and he tried to get hold of it, but the effort was feeble. He couldn't get a grip, couldn't make his hands and his arms do what he wanted them to do.

Out of the corner of his eyes, he caught an impression of Alice slipping off the bed. The headsman didn't see her; his back was turned as he concentrated on attacking Billy. Alice was no longer screaming. Her eyes were wide with terror, and she was moving toward the door.

As the headsman raised the ax, one of Billy Swanson's last conscious thoughts was that the fight he'd put up wasn't much, but at least it had enabled Alice to escape. He saw the axblade raised high over the head of the man in black, saw it begin its downward rush. He wanted so much to get out of the way, to roll aside, to dodge the blow.

He wanted to live.

But he was unable to move.

SEVENTEEN ···········
Grisly Visions

1

The lights flickered and Karen Wilson looked up from her desk, thinking to herself that she really should get out of here and go home. The storm was growing worse by the minute, and with nothing going for it but snowtires, her Escort wasn't worth a damn in weather like this. Everyone else had had sense enough to clear out long ago. Even the cleaning people had quit early, and now she was alone.

But there was still a stack of work in her in-box, and there would be more tomorrow. There were invoices to type, customer letters, factory requisitions; the pile seemed endless. So if she didn't get it done tonight, she'd only be loading more onto herself when she came in tomorrow morning.

What Boggs Ford really needed was more help, of course. One secretary couldn't handle all this work in a normal day, it was impossible. But if she complained to Charley Boggs, there was no telling what might happen. He just might decide he'd had enough of her failure to cooperate and fire her.

Lately he hadn't made a pass at her, which was a good sign in one sense and a bad one in another. She was relieved not to have him pestering her to go to lunch or to join him for a drink, and not to have his hand brushing against her bottom or stroking the back of her leg whenever she got too close to him. And he hadn't brought up all the opportunities for advancement he wanted to offer her, either. But that could also be an indication that he'd lost interest and was going to unload her. Men were funny that way. Once they decided you weren't receptive to the moves they put on you they often resented it. And then they turned against you.

Recently she'd become aware of an upsurge of women protesting against sexual harassment in the workplace. She'd read articles about how so many of them just wouldn't take any more of it, how they made their accusations right out in the open, sometimes even bringing charges against the offenders. But that was a laugh. For every female who could make it stick or who even had the guts to raise the issue, there had to be countless others who just went on putting up with the problem, because if they didn't they'd lose their jobs and no one would give a damn.

So the way for Karen to play it was to keep her mouth shut and hope Boggs would leave her alone. Even though she didn't trust him any more than most other men she'd had experience with.

Including the chief of police. He claimed he hadn't tipped his girlfriend off on the Mariski story, but she didn't believe that for a minute. Of course he had, no matter what excuses he'd made. But at least he'd been right about one thing: all of it had blown over, just as he'd said it would. And afterwards no one had tried to pin her down on getting involved in the case of the headsman.

Which had been a relief. She was surprised the press hadn't picked up on that angle—it would have been a natural for one of their cheap plays on people's emotions. More sensationalism at the expense of the families who'd lost those kids, and at the expense of Karen herself.

Another thing that troubled her was the news that the killer had sent the Harper boy's head to MacElroy. Why? Was it just to show contempt for the police, or was there more to it than that? Was there some entanglement, some aspect of the chief's life that he was trying to keep secret? Was there something *he* wanted to hide?

Most of all, she wished all of this would go away and leave her in peace. Having to contend with the curse of her vision since childhood had been burden enough, but now in this situation it was far worse than it had ever been. Seeing the headsman, knowing about the horrible crimes that were being committed, was like being invaded. And all of it seemed to be coming to some kind of ghastly climax. As if she'd been pointing toward this all along without knowing it. And now here she was in the middle of it somehow, swept along like a leaf in a river, unable to stop herself or to change course.

She looked at her computer screen and tried to concentrate on an invoice that had to be made out. She'd do just this one more, and then she'd print what she'd been working on and quit. If she didn't get out of here soon she'd really be stuck. As it was she was in for a tough time getting home.

The pain struck her without warning—violent, intense, as if a shaft had been driven into her forehead.

She winced and twisted in her chair, recoiling from the sudden assault on her nervous system. She knew from experience what the pain meant and what would be coming next. Fear rose in her, apprehension that something was about to happen—that she'd see some terrible image she didn't want to see, something repellent and horrible that made her privy to a dark secret she didn't want to know.

"Oh, God," she said aloud, "Please don't do this to me."

And then it was gone, and she almost sobbed with relief. With trembling fingers she shut off the computer and then sat still for a moment, struggling to control her emotions. She opened the bottom drawer of her desk and got out her purse. What she had to do now was put on her coat and leave. Snow or no snow, she'd get into her car and drive home, and when she got there she'd take a slug of brandy.

It was something, the way the brandy had become such a help to her. She wished she'd discovered it years ago—the fiery liquid that burned her mouth and her throat as she gulped it down and then magically turned to soothing warmth an instant later. It calmed her and dulled the sensations of fear and revulsion and prevented her from *thinking*. Maybe it would even dampen her ability to receive, would keep the visions from her. Tonight she'd drink a lot of brandy; she needed it.

She began to rise from her desk, and as she did the pain returned. It lanced her forehead savagely this time, a white-hot needle probing her skull. She fell back into her chair, feeling nauseous and faint.

And then she saw him.

The light exploded in her brain and he was there, tall and massive and forbidding, clad entirely in black and clutching the huge ax. She saw a door burst apart in a shower of splinters, saw two people cowering in a bed.

The couple was nude. The young man was muscular and blond and Karen had never seen him before. But to her horror, she recognized the girl at once. She was Alice Boggs, Charley Boggs' daughter. The flashes continued, and there was a struggle between the youth and the headsman. Karen saw violent blows and glittering steel and blood pouring down the young man's face, covering his chest with torrents of red. The Boggs girl had vanished.

As Karen watched, her fists pressed against her mouth, her body rigid, the headsman slowly raised the ax, lifting it high over his head, twisting his body so that the heavy double-edged weapon was poised for an instant over his right shoulder. The boy's mouth opened in a silent protest, and then the ax hurtled downward. When it struck the naked throat the great steel wedge sliced through flesh and bone and buried itself in the floor.

The headsman leaned down and grasped the boy's shock of blond hair, then straightened up and held the dripping head high, shaking it triumphantly.

The flashes diminished, growing smaller and smaller until they were mere pinpoints of light in her consciousness.

Karen fainted, her body slumping forward, her face falling onto the computer keyboard.

2

Charley Boggs was dozing in his favorite chair. It was close to the fireplace, and the heat from the blazing logs was like a warm blanket. He'd had his usual two scotches before dinner, and also as usual he'd eaten too much. Ethel had served one of the meals he liked best, pork chops with applesauce and mashed potatoes, and he'd come back for seconds, and then there'd been blueberry pie with vanilla ice cream for dessert.

He was aware that he was overweight. Doc Reinholtz had

warned him to cut down on his intake of saturated fats, telling him after his last physical that his cholesterol count was over three hundred. But if there was one thing in the world Boggs loved to do, it was eat. He preferred bacon and fried eggs and hashbrowns and muffins dripping with butter for breakfast, and at lunch he was partial to a steak or roast beef, either at the Century Club or in the dining room of the Hotel Braddock. Dinner was his favorite meal, however, because that was when he could really indulge himself. Ethel would fix meat and potatoes with plenty of gravy, and there would be rolls and butter and of course the inevitable pie or cake for dessert.

He also subjected himself to as little exercise as possible. Once in a while he took a short walk during the day, but that was usually to get to a restaurant when it was simpler than driving a car from the dealership. He also belonged to the country club, and from May through September played golf at least once a week. But he always went around the course in an electric cart.

As a result, he was at least fifty pounds heavier than he should have been. In addition to harping on his cholesterol level, Reinholtz warned him that his blood pressure had been rising steadily over the past few years. Charley should take action, the doctor said. So he did. The action he took was to stop seeing Reinholtz.

After all, what good was it to be a successful businessman if you couldn't enjoy yourself? He'd worked hard to get where he was, to carve out a good life for himself and his family. He considered himself an exceptional citizen, one of Braddock's leaders. He had no bad habits, or hardly any. His drinking was confined to a single vodka martini at lunch and the pair of scotches at dinner, and maybe a beer along with his late-night snack before going to bed. The only times he exceeded that intake were at the dinner parties he and Ethel attended and the ones they frequently gave, or when he was on vacation, or when he'd finished a round at the club and was sitting around on the terrace with his friends, playing gin and hashing over the day's scores.

And the only screwing around he did was very discreet.

He'd always had something going on the side. It wasn't easy

in a town the size of Braddock, but it could be done if you were careful. The trouble was, you didn't have much to choose from. He'd had affairs with the wives of several of his friends, but the women who'd been responsive to him were impossibly boring. Their idea of conversation was to talk incessantly about their children, or to repeat the latest gossip going around the club, which like as not Boggs had already heard in the locker room. After a short time he'd found each of them no more stimulating than Ethel, who at least had the saving grace of being a great cook. And then, they too were all getting older. Sagging tits and cellulite were not his idea of a turn-on.

This Karen Wilson, on the other hand, was something else again. Ever since he'd hired her, he'd been thinking about making her his mistress. From what he'd been able to observe, she had every qualification he could ask for. She wasn't beautiful exactly, but she certainly was attractive. With her chestnut hair and her green eyes she was striking, the kind of woman who'd turn heads anywhere.

And what a body. Just watching her move around the office was enough to get him fired up. He sometimes fantasized about what it would be like when he finally wore down her resistance, when he could maneuver her into becoming sufficiently dependent on him to be unable to say no.

He liked to imagine the little dates they'd have, slipping over to one of the nearby towns for dinner once in a while, stopping in at a motel afterward. Or maybe he'd even set her up in her own apartment. She was single, apparently with few friends here in Braddock, virtually a stranger. And she lived with her grandmother, which must be suffocating.

Sooner or later she'd say okay to a drink with him, and then he'd give her a raise as a subtle indication of the good things that would be coming her way. Inch by inch he'd get her there, easing her into it.

Lately he'd backed off somewhat, just to see how she'd react. She'd be wondering now if maybe she was no longer attractive to him, or if he'd simply lost interest in her. She'd be worried about her job, and her self-confidence would be shaken.

And then the next time he made a move, right out of the blue, she'd be relieved and even pleased. One thing Charley Boggs knew about was people and how to deal with them. He smiled to himself as he thought about her and about his plans. His eyes closed and he settled deeper into his chair, enjoying the warm glow from the fire.

A scream jolted him awake, piercing his consciousness like a hot knife.

He stumbled to his feet, sputtering. "What is it? What—"

His daughter ran into the living room. She was stark naked and shrieking as if the devil were chasing her.

Ethel Boggs had been watching television. She leaped up from her chair and grabbed the girl's arm. "Alice, what's wrong? What happened?"

Alice was screaming and shouting something unintelligible and crying all at the same time. She pointed behind her. "He's there. He's, he's—"

Her brother came running into the room. "What the hell's going on?"

The three family members surrounded the girl, all yelling at once.

Charley Boggs shouted loudest. "Goddamn it, Alice—will you tell me what it is? *Who's* there?"

She was shuddering, tears streaking her face, the words coming from her throat in choking gasps. "The headsman. He's there. In my room. He's going to kill Billy."

Charley was staggered. "The *headsman?*"

"Yes, yes. He's up there—he's going to kill him."

Boggs had never confronted physical danger in his life. Or even the threat of it. He hadn't spent time in the service, had never even so much as participated in a contact sport. But he'd always thought of himself as a pretty tough customer if it came to a showdown—a guy who could take care of himself.

"Holy Christ," Boggs said. "Holy Christ."

There was a pistol in the desk. He owned a number of firearms, mostly hunting rifles he'd collected and never used, but also several handguns. He kept one in the drawer of the table beside his bed and another down here.

He ran to the desk and pulled open the top drawer, rummaging around until he found the pistol. It was a .38–

caliber Colt Police Special. He'd owned it for ten years and had never fired it. His hands were shaking as he took it out of the drawer. He was suddenly short of breath and his chest hurt.

The *headsman?* Here—in this house?

Boggs looked at the pistol. Suppose the thing didn't fire, or he missed? Suppose it wasn't loaded? His wife and his son and his daughter were standing there staring at him, their faces expressing shock and fear. More thoughts raced through his mind. Why was Alice naked? What was Billy Swanson doing in her room?

But most of all he thought of the headsman, and his knees turned to jelly.

It was all he could do to check the cylinder of the revolver. He fumbled with it, remembering at last that it had a latch on the left side you had to push before you could swing out the cylinder. He got it open and saw that each of the six chambers held a brass cartridge. He snapped the cylinder back into place.

"Hurry, Daddy," Alice shrieked. "Hurry—he's going to kill Billy!"

Clutching the pistol in his right fist, Boggs made his way out of the living room and down the center hall to the rear of the house. There was a jog and then the corridor led to the back hall, where the stairs were on one side and the door leading to the side porch was on the other.

He was moving slowly, telling himself it was because he was being cautious, but knowing the truth was that he was scared to death. At least it was reassuring to have the pistol in his hand. As he made the turn into the back hall he stepped very carefully and drew back the hammer of the revolver. The click when he cocked the weapon sounded startlingly loud.

The hallway was empty, and Boggs felt a surge of relief. But Christ, wait a minute. That meant he had to go up the goddamn stairs to Alice's room. He gripped the pistol in both hands, the way he'd seen them do it on television, and went into a spraddle-legged crouch. A combat stance, he'd heard it called. Then he slowly approached the stairway.

From above him came the rumble of heavy feet descending the stairs fast. He froze, gulping for air, trying desperately to keep the revolver pointed straight ahead. It was nearly dark in the hallway and he wished he could flip on the overhead light. He groped for the switch, afraid to take his eyes off the stairs.

His hand found the switch and he turned on the light at the instant a dark, massive shape bounded into the hall from the staircase.

Boggs recoiled in horror.

The headsman was immense, his hulking form seeming to fill the hallway, and he was dressed all in black. The eyes that burned from within the slanted holes in the hood were fixed on Boggs. He stopped, and one of his gloved hands raised Billy Swanson's head high, the face frozen in an expression of terror, blood dripping from the severed neck.

Boggs fired the pistol. The report was like an explosion clapping his eardrums, and his eyes closed involuntarily in reaction to the muzzle blast.

He fired again and again, pulling the trigger double-action, cringing from the roar of the shots, not aiming or even seeing his target in front of him, but shooting blindly, impelled by revulsion and overwhelming fear. Only the click of the hammer on an empty shell told him he'd expended all six cartridges. He blinked, acrid gunsmoke biting his nostrils, and then opened his eyes wide, staring in disbelief.

There was no one in the hallway; the headsman was gone.

Boggs shuddered. He drew air into his lungs, and as he did he became aware once more of the pain in his chest. It was a searing sensation, sharp and very intense, in the direct center of his upper body. From there it spread its tentacles into his left arm and shoulder.

He suddenly found it hard to see. The light in the hallway was growing dimmer. He felt the revolver slip from his fingers, heard distant cries from his family somewhere behind him. Boggs was tired, terribly tired. He slumped against the wall and then slowly slid down it into a sitting position. The pain had become even worse, but somehow it didn't matter. All he wanted to do was sleep.

3

This storm was a piss-whistler. The flakes were thick and crystalline and they stung Jud's eyes and the skin on his face when he walked into the wind. It made him think of what it was like to ski when it was snowing and you were going downhill fast and it was impossible to see without goggles. He kept his face turned away as much as he could while he made his way by flashlight out to the shed behind the house. The drifts were up to his knees in places and he had to lift each foot high to take the next step.

Even in its relatively sheltered place in the shed, the Blazer had collected snow on its roof and hood and against its windows. Jud opened the door and got out a scraper, finding a coat of ice under the snow on the glass. When he had the windows clear he started the engine, then turned on the defroster full blast.

Now for the moment of truth. He shoved the floor lever into four-wheel drive and slowly backed out of the shed. The Chevy strained against the drifts, but it kept going. There was a snow shovel around someplace that he ought to take along, but he wasn't sure where it was.

Backing out of the driveway he saw that the patrol car had become a mound of white, vaguely resembling an igloo. Once on the road he found the going not much better than the driveway had been, but at least out here he'd have more room to maneuver.

The streets were deserted except for the occasional car that was stuck in a drift and abandoned, another ghostly figure in the night. Tree limbs were bent low under their burden of snow and ice. His headlights were all but useless, and even with the defroster roaring and the wipers ticking at high speed, visibility was terrible.

The storm seemed not to have abated at all from what he'd encountered earlier in the day; if anything it was worse. The only signs of life he saw were the faintly glowing spots of light that revealed the location of houses he passed. He wondered again how long it would be before the electric power failed.

Which reminded him to check his police radio. He turned it on, getting a flood of static and then squelching it as much as possible. He picked up the mike and called the BPD.

Tony Stanis responded. "Chief, been trying to reach you."

"Yeah, go ahead."

Excitement was making the dispatcher garble his words. "We just got a call from Ethel Boggs. The headsman was in their house. He cut off Billy Swanson's head and ran out the door. And Charley Boggs had a heart attack."

Holy shit—was he hearing this right? "Say again, Tony?"

Stanis repeated the transmission, this time sounding even more frantic.

"Okay, got it." He braked to a stop, then turned the Blazer around as quickly as he dared. "Send an ambulance out there, fast."

"We're trying to," Stanis went on, "but Memorial's only got one in service and it's stuck in a snowbank. They're digging it out now. Also we got Kramer on his way in Car Six. But he's not doing too good either. The snow's so deep he's just crawling."

"Where's Grady?"

"I don't know. He left the stationhouse this afternoon. We haven't heard from him since."

"Call his house, tell him to get in to the station. I'm going to the Boggses'."

Jud's heart was pounding as he drove. He wanted desperately to make the Blazer move faster, but he didn't dare. As it was, he was having a tough time staying on the snowy surface.

The headsman had been in the Boggses' house? And he cut off Billy Swanson's head? Charley Boggs had a heart attack? Jesus Christ—what next?

As well as he knew the area, he found to his surprise he'd missed the turn onto Riverside Road, the one that would take him out to the Boggses'. He had to back up and turn around, which was tricky enough, and then creep back to the place where the road divided. It seemed to him he wasn't making more than about fifteen miles an hour, and at times not even that. When he finally had the Blazer on Riverside he increased his speed a little, but he didn't dare push it for fear of going off the road.

He picked up the mike and tried police headquarters again, but this time all he got was static. Small wonder, in this storm. After a couple of tries he gave up and returned the mike to its hook on the dash.

There was a rise ahead he was familiar with, and he remembered that on the far side he'd be less than a mile from the Boggs house. When he reached the summit he slowed almost to a stop, then cautiously made his way down the incline. At the bottom he again accelerated a little, pointing the car in what he hoped was the right direction.

Something very large and very powerful crashed into the passenger side of the Blazer. The impact knocked him away from the wheel, slamming his head into the corner post. The vehicle slewed crazily on the slippery road surface and came to a stop, teetering on two wheels against a snowbank.

He couldn't see, and he had a hazy impression that he'd been hurt. There was a roaring in his ears and blood was running down his forehead and into his eyes. He pawed at his face and the noise in his ears grew louder and he slipped into unconsciousness.

4

He had no idea how long he was out. When he came to he couldn't remember where he was or what had happened to him. He knew only that he was stiff and cold and that there was a hell of a pain in his head. There were other aches here and there about his body as well, mainly in his back and his left shoulder, but the headache was the major cause of his misery.

He was also unable to see clearly. There were fuzzy green lights in front of him, but he couldn't focus on them. He tried to rub his eyes and realized he had gloves on. When he got them off he touched his face with his fingers and found them covered with blood. He wiped the mess away with the sleeve of his jacket as best he could and then explored further with his hands.

There was a lump above his left ear and the skin was broken; apparently that was where the blood had come from. His cap had been knocked off but he wouldn't need it, and getting it back onto his swollen head would be difficult anyway. He could see now, and he realized that the green lights were in the dashboard instruments of the Blazer. The headlights were still on and the wipers were continuing to sweep the windshield, although the engine had stalled when the vehicle was struck.

As he pulled himself into an upright position he saw that everything was tilted. He realized that was because the Blazer was resting on its side against a snowbank, with only the driver's side wheels on the road.

He turned off the headlights and the wipers to save his battery, and then opened the door and climbed out of the vehicle. The snow was coming down as fiercely as ever, whipped along by a relentless wind. He closed the door and put his shoulder against it and heaved, in an attempt to right the machine.

It wouldn't budge.

And the effort made his head hurt worse than it had before. He went around to the opposite side and saw that the passenger door was caved in, along with the right front quarter-panel.

Apparently the Blazer had been struck by another vehicle—a large, heavy machine at least as big as the Chevy. Why hadn't he seen it? Even with the snowfall he should have been conscious of the other driver approaching, should have been aware of the other's headlights.

Unless the lights had been turned off. And that other truck or car or whatever it was had rammed him deliberately, coming at him from an angle, intending to disable him—or kill him.

From behind him came the sound of an engine and the clank of chains. Instinctively, he put his hand on his pistol as he turned. A set of headlights was approaching, dim yellow blurs in the storm. He moved back around the Blazer to give himself protection, just in case.

But the lights slowed down and then stopped. A spotlight shot a blinding glare toward him and he heard a voice shout, "That you, Chief?"

He made his way over to the patrol car, struggling through the snow. He saw that Bob Kramer was behind the wheel. Jud averted his eyes from the glaring light and Kramer turned it off.

"You okay?"

"Yeah," Jud said, "I'm all right. Just had a little accident." He went around to the passenger side of the cruiser and climbed into the car.

"I was on my way to the Boggs house," Kramer said.

"So was I. Go ahead."

"You sure you're okay? Looks like you took a pretty good lick."

"I'm fine," Jud said. "Drive."

The patrol car moved forward, chains clanking and banging.

"You see any other vehicles on your way over here?" Jud asked.

"A couple in town, but that's all."

"What happened at the Boggses'? You know anything more?"

"Just what Stanis told me about Mrs. Boggs calling. Did you get that?"

"Yeah."

"I think Memorial's got an ambulance coming, but I'm not sure. Radio's not working too good in this weather."

"Anybody called Pearson?" Jud could have kicked himself; he'd only just now thought of it.

"I don't know. Maybe Stanis did."

"The phones may be still okay. I'll call from the Boggs house."

"Uh-oh."

"What is it?"

Kramer pointed. "The house is right over there, but I don't see any lights. Power must've failed."

"Shit. That's all we need."

Kramer turned on his spotlight again and the beam picked up the house when they drew closer. A car was parked on the road a few yards this side of it, but there was so much snow on the vehicle the cops couldn't make it out clearly.

They left the cruiser in front of the house and trudged through the drifts up to the front door, Kramer illuminating their way with a flashlight. Joe Boggs answered their knock, his face wearing a dazed expression, as if he'd taken a heavy blow. He was carrying a Coleman lantern, and in its glow the two officers could see well enough to shake snow off their clothes and their feet. They followed Joe through the foyer into the center hall and then into the living room.

There was another lantern in here, standing on a table.

Charley Boggs was lying on a sofa, his wife and daughter nearby. Alice Boggs was wearing a bathrobe. Her mother approached the cops as they entered the room. "Thank God you're here. Did you bring an ambulance?"

Jud told her one was on its way. He stepped over to the sofa and looked down at Boggs. The car dealer's face was as gray and shapeless as a blob of suet. His eyes were half-closed, and he wasn't moving. Jud knelt beside him and grasped his wrist.

For the first few seconds he could find no pulse. Then he got one, but it was fluttery and erratic. He tried to take a count but that proved impossible; he could detect only slight evidence of a heartbeat, too faint to measure. After a minute or two he gave up and placed a hand on Boggs' forehead. The skin was dry and cool, almost cold.

"He had a heart attack, didn't he?" Ethel Boggs' voice rose. "Is he going to die? Is he?"

Jud stood up. "He's going to be fine." He didn't know what the hell Boggs was going to be; dead would be a good guess. And soon. But he couldn't tell Ethel that. "Just keep him warm and quiet until the ambulance gets here. And stay close to him in case he needs anything, okay?"

She nodded dumbly, and he took Alice aside. When they were by themselves at the far end of the room he said, "What happened here?"

The girl took a deep breath. She appeared to be as shaken as her mother, but Jud knew kids were tougher when it came down to it. "Billy and I were . . . upstairs."

Jud cocked his head, trying to picture it. "Your parents were down here and—"

She shook her head. "They didn't know he was here. I let him in the side door and he . . . sneaked up to my room."

He got it then. At least she was being straight about it. "Then what?"

"Then we were in my room, and uh—"

"Where in your room?"

"In my bed."

"Go on."

"And all of a sudden the door just smashed open and *he* was there." Now there was a note of hysteria in Alice's voice as well.

"Take it easy," Jud said. "Try to stay cool and just tell me what happened. *Who* was there?"

She choked back tears, swallowing hard. "The headsman."

"Are you sure it was—"

"Yes, yes. Jesus, of course I'm sure. He was all in black and huge and he had a thing over his head. He had this big ax and he and Billy started fighting and I ran out of the room."

"Keep going."

"I went downstairs and told Daddy and he got a gun and there was shooting and then we found Daddy on the floor. The headsman was gone. I went back up to my room, and—oh, God." Now she did cry, pressing her palms against her face, her shoulders shaking.

Jud put his hands on her arms and she fell against his chest, sobbing. He waited a few moments and then gently eased her back. "You stay here," he said. "Take care of your parents and your brother. How do I get to your room?"

She took a tissue out of a pocket of her robe and wiped her nose with it. "Go down the hall to the end and turn right. It's the first door at the head of the stairs."

Jud signaled to Kramer and the two of them hurried through the house, flashlight beams showing the way. When they reached the stairs they went up them slowly and carefully, both of them with pistols drawn. Even though Alice had said the headsman was gone, they were taking no chances.

The mess in the bedroom was hideous. Blood was spattered everywhere, and a huge pool of it lay on the floor near Billy Swanson's headless corpse. The scene reminded Jud of what he'd found in Marcy Dickens' room on that Saturday morning that seemed so long ago. The one great difference was that this time there was no decapitated head with its eyes staring at him. He and Kramer searched the room as well as they could with only the flashlights for illumination, taking care not to disturb anything and staying as clear as possible of the blood on the floor. But there was no sign of Billy's head.

"He must have taken it with him," Jud said.

For answer, the young cop doubled over, holding his fist

against his mouth, struggling to keep from vomiting. He stumbled past Jud into Alice Boggs' bathroom and stood over the toilet as his stomach heaved up its contents. The acrid stink of puke combined with the sweet blood odor was nauseating. Jud decided to get out of here before he lost his own dinner, such as it was. He went back down the stairs in the dark and felt his way along the hallways until he was back in the living room.

He asked Joe Boggs where there was a telephone, and the boy showed him to a wood-paneled study across the hall from the living room. Joe placed one of the lanterns on the desk and left the room.

Jud called Braddock police headquarters first. As he waited for an answer he thought about the other calls he'd make. For one, he'd contact Karen Wilson to see if he couldn't get her to help. Maybe she could tell him something, if he could get her to cooperate.

Stanis answered the call.

Jud asked if Inspector Pearson had been notified and Stanis said he had. That was a relief; at least Jud wouldn't have to catch any shit on that count.

"But I think he's out of it," Stanis said.

"Why—what do you mean?"

"Him and Williger were in the bar at Howard Johnson's getting smashed. He said they'd get over to the Boggses' right away, but if they make it, it'll be a miracle."

Jud asked where the ambulance was, and Stanis said it should be there any minute. What about Grady, he asked next. No luck—the cops hadn't been able to locate him.

He told Stanis he'd get back to the station just as soon as he could make it through the snow.

He put the instrument down and expelled a stream of air. No electric power, and the police radios didn't work worth a shit. And sooner or later the phones would go out as well. Carrying the lantern, he went back into the living room.

Ethel Boggs was trying to comfort her husband, who looked even less healthy than he had earlier, and her daughter was trying to comfort her. Jud stood awkwardly by, noting that

Boggs was barely breathing and his skin had taken on a bluish pallor.

When Kramer returned to the room, Jud told him to stay there and wait for the ambulance. He'd take the cruiser, he said. He mumbled another reassurance to Ethel Boggs and left the house.

The storm was in full fury. He stumbled through the drifts to the car and swept off the windshield with his arm. Then he got into the cruiser and started it.

The headsman was out here somewhere. A short time earlier he'd tried to kill Jud; the chief was sure that was who had rammed the Blazer.

But how to find him? How to find a killer in weather like this in the dead of the night—a killer who might be a ghost?

He put the patrol car in gear and pulled away, chains clanking.

5

Karen pulled herself upright, her mind reeling from the impact of the images. They were back and coming in flashes, one on top of the other, at a faster rate than she'd ever experienced them. She saw the boy's head, eyes staring, tongue protruding, his blond hair held in a black-gloved fist. In another flash she saw a looming, shadowy building partially obscured by swirling snow.

Then there were striding feet shod in black boots. There was a wide, heavy door set with hammered hinges and a knob of dull brass. The hulking figure of the headsman went through the door, still clutching the boy's head.

The flashes continued, revealing stone walls and flickering torchlight. She saw a dark-haired woman being dragged to a block, her head set into place on it. She saw the dreaded man in black raise his ax, saw torchlight glinting from the great steel blade as it flashed in a deadly arc.

And the images were suddenly gone once more.

Oh my God, I've seen that building. And that's where he is. That's where the stone dungeon is. The headsman is there. And the woman is there, the one he's going to behead. Oh my God.

It was torture to admit the images into her consciousness. She pressed both hands to her temples and cried aloud from the pain. She couldn't endure much more of this—she'd pass out again, or go crazy, or . . . kill herself.

It wasn't the first time she'd thought of suicide. Many were the nights she'd curled up in her bed, telling herself that death would be the only release from the prison she was locked in, that dying would be the only way to escape the awful scenes that burned into her brain, forcing her to see things that she hated to look at, to know things she was appalled to learn. Maybe tonight she'd take the step at last.

She'd even thought about how she'd do it. She'd get into a hot bath, and open the arteries in her wrists with a razor blade. And then, warm, and relaxed in the fragrant suds, she'd simply become drowsy and slip into sleep. As the blood left her body, her miserable life would drain away as well.

She shook her head.

Stop it, you selfish fool. There are other people in the world besides you, and they could be suffering at the hands of that murderer. The woman you saw is in terrible danger, and you can help. So do it. Do it now, Karen, damn you.

She suddenly realized the office area and the showroom were dark. And the screen of her computer was blank. The electric power must have failed. In the darkness she reached for the telephone on her desk, and to her relief found it was still working. She dialed 911.

Waiting for an answer was maddening, as the instrument seemed to ring forever. She tugged at her blouse with her free hand, feeling she was about to explode. This was the number you were supposed to call in an emergency, for God's sake, and there was nobody there. No wonder she felt she was going crazy.

And then a voice said, "Police headquarters, Officer Stanis."

Her own voice sounded strange to her, as if it belonged to someone else. "I want to speak to Chief MacElroy."

"Who is this calling?

"I . . . my name is Karen Wilson."

"Yes, ma'am. What's the problem?"

God, couldn't he understand English? "I said I want to speak with—"

"Chief MacElroy is not available right now."

The voice had that superior male intonation she found so infuriating. But then intuition told her where MacElroy would be. "Is he at the Boggs house?"

There was a pause, and when the voice spoke again it was full of awe. "How'd you know that?"

So she had her answer.

"Ma'am? What did you say your name—"

She hung up.

No matter that fear was choking her, no matter that she wanted desperately to go home and if nothing else find oblivion in a bottle of brandy. And no matter that further involvement was horrifying to contemplate. She had to find the police chief and tell him what she'd seen.

She pulled on her boots and her overcoat, then tied a scarf around her head. With the electricity out she couldn't see much beyond the expanse of windows in the showroom. But she could hear the storm lashing against the glass, and could feel the building shuddering from the icy blasts of wind.

She was about to go out the door when realization struck her that the Escort would be worse than useless in these conditions.

But at least Boggs Ford offered alternatives. She stepped back to Ed McCarthy's desk, opened a drawer and picked through the tangle of keys. A tag on one of them said it was for a Ranger pickup. Good. That was a machine that could move along snowy roads.

She left the showroom, struggling through the drifts and hunched over against the relentless wind gusts until she reached the truck. She unlocked it and climbed up into the cab. It was a relief to have the engine start immediately and to see the strong white beams when she turned on the headlights.

She backed out of the parking space and turned into the street. If only she wasn't too late . . .

6

Before Jud had gone fifty feet he knew he wouldn't make it. Snowtires, chains, limited-slip differential—the whole rig was worthless in a storm like this. That stuff was made for driving in snow, and this was a balls-out blizzard. He went up the rise on the road leading back toward the village and was lucky to reach the top. On the way down the other side his ass-end slewed around, and for a moment he thought he'd end up in the ditch on the side of the road.

But somehow he managed to keep going.

The visibility was terrible, especially with the glare of his lights reflecting from the flakes back into his face, and the snow was so deep it was hard to figure out just where the road was.

There was a curve ahead of him, and he negotiated it with care, his headlights picking up a large mound just off to his right. When he got closer he realized it was his wounded Blazer, lying on its side in a snowbank and covered with a blanket of white. He slowed almost to a stop as he passed it, peering at the crippled machine. There was no question that he'd been deliberately rammed by someone who intended to kill him. He'd been damn lucky.

Lights came toward him out of the storm, startling him. But at least this time he had advance warning. He kept one hand on the steering wheel while with his other he pulled his service revolver out of its holster. He couldn't see the other vehicle, but he was aware that its headlights were mounted higher than those of the average car. Maybe the bastard was back, looking to finish him off. He thumbed back the hammer of the Smith and took his driving hand off the wheel long enough to roll his window down.

But the other vehicle continued toward him at a slow, steady pace, and as it drew near it kept to its own side of the road. It was a truck, he saw—a Ford pickup. He snapped on the cruiser's spotlight and trained its beam on the cab of the truck. To his surprise, he saw that a woman was behind the wheel.

Christ—it was Karen Wilson.

She held up one hand in an apparent effort to shield her eyes from the fierce beam of the spotlight, and the truck came to a stop. He pulled up alongside and called to her. "Karen? It's me—Jud MacElroy." He shoved the pistol back into its holster and turned off the spotlight.

Her voice sounded frantic and relieved at the same time. "I've been trying to find you!"

He shoved the Plymouth's shift lever into park and got out of the vehicle, trudging through the heavy snow to the pickup. "What is it?"

She was gasping for air as she spoke, the words tumbling out of her. "The headsman. I know where he is. I saw him. He killed that boy and took his head."

Jud felt a chill that was colder than the icy wind. There was only one way she could have known what happened to Billy Swanson. Once again she was proving to him her ability to envision events.

She waved her hands. "That's not all. There's more."

"Wait a minute." He opened the door on the driver's side of the truck, and she slid over to make room for him as he climbed up into the cab. After he shut the door he got a good look at her in the reflection from the truck's headlights. Her face was tearstreaked, her eyes wide and frightened. "There's more? What else did you see?"

"Your friend, the reporter. Sally Benson. He's going to kill her."

He felt a second jolt—this time, of fear. "Where is she? Where's the headsman?"

"In the dungeon. That's where he carries out executions. He's there now."

"He's *where* now?"

"In that old building. The museum. And she's there too."

Good God. Jud put the Ford in gear and backed it up a few feet to give him more room to turn around. It took several minutes of inching forward and backing up to get the truck pointed in the direction it had come from, back toward the road that would take him to the museum. If there was one thing he couldn't risk, it was getting stuck now.

eiqhteen ....
Rogues' Gallery

1

When they arrived at the old building, Jud could have kicked himself for his stupidity. In his haste to get here he hadn't thought to bring any kind of tool he could use to force his way into the place. There would have been a crowbar in the trunk of the patrol car as part of the standard equipment all BPD cruisers carried. A lot of good that would do him now. At least he had the flashlight.

He led the way from the truck to the front entrance, breaking a path through the snow, Karen following. Playing the flashlight beam across the facade, he noted there were no bars on the windows. If he had to he'd shatter a pane of glass and go in that way, although he certainly would prefer to enter silently if he could.

But when he reached the entrance, he was surprised to find the door unlocked. He opened it and they stepped inside, and then Jud carefully closed the heavy door behind them. It was cold in here, and eerily quiet, the only sounds coming from the moaning wind and the creak of timbers as the snow lashed and battered the ancient structure. There was also the peculiar smell he remembered from the last time he was here, a faint odor of rotting wood and decaying flesh, as if an animal had died in some remote part of the building.

He whispered, "You say you saw a dungeon?"

"Yes. It must be in the cellar somewhere. There were stone walls, and it was lit by torchlight."

"Is that where Sally was when you saw her with the headsman?"

372

She nodded, holding her hands to her mouth, her eyes wide.

"Come on, and stay close to me." He had no idea which direction to go in, aware only that he was looking for a stairway down. He wandered through the narrow halls, picking his way with the small beam of the flashlight, opening doors and finding the rooms empty, trying not to lose his bearings. In a matter of minutes he wasn't at all sure where he was. The goddamn place was like a maze.

Karen tugged at his sleeve.

"What is it?"

"I think that way." She pointed.

He wasn't about to ask her why; if she felt that was the way to go, he'd take her word for it. They moved along the passageway, and Jud found himself looking at a doorway that seemed vaguely familiar. He opened the door; there was a huge old kitchen.

The room was as he remembered it, with a low, timbered ceiling and a great fireplace that covered most of the far wall. Beside the fireplace was a slim door. The door was ajar. He stepped over to it and swung it open. The flashlight beam revealed a narrow stairway leading down.

He glanced at Karen, who nodded.

Jud put his right hand on the butt of his service revolver, its scored wooden grip hard and reassuring to his touch. Holding the flashlight ahead of him and moving very cautiously, he started down the stairs, Karen following.

2

The passageway down here was even narrower than the ones above. The walls were of stone, and the passage jogged and turned at odd angles. The ceiling was supported by handcut beams, and in places it was so low Jud had to duck to avoid hitting his head on the timbers. Again he was aware of the odor of rotting flesh and the stink of ancient dirt, the combination faintly acrid to his nostrils. As he stepped slowly along the earthen floor, he tried to keep track of the direction he was moving in, but he couldn't be sure.

He kept going, stopping every few feet to listen, hearing

nothing but the sounds of the old house. What reached his ears was a faint cracking and creaking, along with the occasional groan of twisting wood, as if the place were speaking to him in a language of its own.

And then he turned one of the seemingly endless corners in the passageway, and saw a door ahead of him. He opened it carefully, standing to one side with the Smith & Wesson ready, and poked the flashlight inside.

It was a large open space, and there appeared to be nothing in it but a scattering of crates and an empty barrel. Shelves lined the walls. On some of them jars and bottles were resting. He swept the area with the flashlight, its beam reflecting from the musty glass and the spiderwebs.

This probably was one of the rooms that had been used to store fruits and vegetables for the winter. He could even guess that the barrel might have been filled with apples at some point in the distant past. He heard a rustling noise, and the yellow cone of light picked out a large gray rat, its eyes glowing red as it scuttled away and disappeared behind the boxes on the floor.

Jud turned and looked at Karen. In the dim light her face seemed frozen in an expression of dread. With the hand holding the flashlight he touched her arm in an attempt to reassure her, thinking to himself that he probably felt as apprehensive as she did. He backed out of the room and continued to follow the narrow passageway.

A few feet farther along he came to another door. He opened this one the same way, as cautiously as possible. But what he found was much like the one he'd seen earlier, merely a storage space of some kind, its floor littered with empty crates and moldy cloth and unrecognizable junk.

He was beginning to think he was chasing shadows. As much reason as he had to trust this young woman with the strange psychic powers and to believe what she'd told him, he was finding nothing here. How much of what she had seen was accurate, and how much of it might simply be the product of her imagination?

Or even hallucinations? It was impossible to tell. In the

meantime, here he was wandering around in the cellar of this stinking old wreck of a house while a blizzard raged outside.

And a killer was on the loose.

He was sure of one thing: Billy Swanson was dead, his head chopped off in exactly the same manner as Marcy Dickens' had been and Buddy Harper's as well. And Sally? Was *she* in danger also, as Karen was so convinced she was?

Jud couldn't afford to lose faith now. Karen Wilson had got him this far, and events had proven her correct. A crazy thought flashed through his mind. If he could only find Sally safe he'd grab her and Karen and just get the fuck out of here. He'd take them somewhere that was warm and safe and be grateful they were alive. But first he had to find her.

Around a bend he came to the end of the passageway. And set in the wall, dead ahead of him, was another door. He stopped, and again gripped the heavy revolver, holding it with barrel pointed upward, his thumb on the hammer. Once more he used the hand holding the flashlight to try the door. It swung open noiselessly.

This was still another room, smaller and narrower than the others. Three of the walls had been built of stones set in rough mortar. The fourth was covered entirely with crude wooden cabinets. Apparently the space was similar to the others, just one more storage area. He stepped to the nearest cabinet and pulled open the door.

Inside was a shelf.

On the shelf was Paul Mulgrave's head.

3

Jud felt revulsion as he looked at the museum curator's features. The eyes were not merely open; the sockets where they had been were empty.

He realized the rats must have eaten Mulgrave's eyes. Jud could see bitemarks on parts of the face as well, in the tissue of the lips and the nostrils. Some of the flesh at the edges of the terrible wound in the neck had also been chewed away.

He stepped back, taking in what he was seeing and then looking down the wall. Dreading what he would find, he reached for another door and opened it. Resting on the dusty wooden shelf, its facial features contorted in an expression of agony, was the head of Billy Swanson.

This one was obviously fresh. The blood on the bottom of the neck was still slightly wet, slowly drying to a crusty black smear. The head had to have been placed here only a short time ago. What Karen had told him was the precise truth. It was sickening to look at, knowing how the boy had died, realizing the pain and the fear he must have suffered.

Jud opened another door. And then another. Inside each was a severed head. Unlike Mulgrave's or Billy Swanson's, these were not of people he could recognize. The heads were obviously old, the skin leathery and dessicated, the hair as wispy as cobwebs. The rats had evidently eaten the eyes out of these as well, and some of the flesh, but beyond that they were relatively intact. Whose heads they were and how long they'd been here he'd probably never know.

He opened another cabinet and found himself looking at the head of a woman. This one was also very old, but despite its dried-up mummified appearance, there was something about it he seemed to recognize. She looked like someone he knew— someone he could almost recall. Almost, but not quite. Despite the cold, Jud was sweating. Realization hit him. *Jesus—it was Joan Donovan.*

But that was impossible. So who—?

He got it then. What he was looking at was the head of a Donovan woman, all right. But it wasn't Joan Donovan's head. It was her mother's. This was what was left of Janet Donovan, the body part that had disappeared on that fateful night so many years ago. This was what the little girl had seen the headsman holding in his black-gloved hand after he had beheaded her mother. This was the head that had been missing—and adding to the headsman lore—for all the years since the night of the murder.

There were still other doors in this macabre wall, many of them. Jud looked at the doors, now knowing full well what lay behind each of them. Here was a black history of Braddock, a bizarre record of crime and punishment. It was as if the town were somehow rooted in the past, as if it had never progressed beyond the ignorant prejudices of the eighteenth century.

Of these people, some long dead, some who had been alive until only a brief time ago, how many had indeed been guilty of any transgression? How many had in fact committed crimes, and how many had died by the ax simply because the man who wielded it was a wanton murderer?

And what about Marcy Dickens—why had her head been left at the scene of the murder? Probably because the headsman had intended her execution to be as shocking as possible. He had *wanted* her head to be discovered.

Almost idly, Jud reached out and opened one more of the crudely fashioned doors. As well prepared as he thought he was by now for what he would find there, the sight was another blow.

Resting on the shelf in a pool of dried blood was the head of Sergeant Joseph Grady.

Jud stared at the obscene thing, horror and guilt and remorse washing over him in waves.

Even though this one had been worked over by the rats, it obviously hadn't been here very long. As Jud looked at it, he saw something fat and white crawling inside the mouth.

He moved back, resisting the urge to vomit. Then he thought of Karen, realizing suddenly that she'd be horrified as well. He turned to her.

4

The hands were not like hands at all, but more like metal clamps that crushed Karen's mouth and her ribs and prevented her from crying out, even keeping her from breathing. She tried to struggle, but she couldn't so much as move. The hands swept her up off the floor, and although she wanted to kick at whoever was holding her and to break free, it was impossible. She was held as securely as if she were a tiny child.

After a moment the lack of oxygen caused a roaring in her ears and she grew weak and then she was incapable of putting up any resistance at all. She was dimly aware that she was being carried, but she couldn't see where; it was dark in the passageway.

A moment later she lost consciousness.

When she came to, the sight that greeted her was eerily familiar. She was in a chamber with stone walls, lighted by torches set in holders. The floor was of dirt, and positioned against the far wall was a low wooden platform. Resting in the center of the platform was a well-worn chopping block.

She knew where she was. She had seen this place before, as clearly as she was seeing it now. She was in the dungeon that had appeared in her vision. The dungeon where the dark-haired woman was a prisoner. The dungeon where the headsman carried out his executions.

The woman was nowhere in sight.

But the headsman was.

Karen was half-sitting against a wall, watching the terrible scene come to life. The headsman was exactly as the images had revealed him to her, exactly as he'd looked in the old painting the chief of police had shown her. As she gazed at him, the awful truth of where she was and what was happening to her was driven into her mind with numbing force.

The headsman stepped closer and then stood over her, seeming immense in his foul black rags, the eyes burning in their slanted holes in the hood as he stared at her. He reached down, and one gloved hand seized her hair. She felt herself being dragged onto the platform, the pain causing her eyes to fill with tears.

She struggled, raising her hands in a feeble effort to grasp one of his legs, but all that brought her was a kick in the ribs that knocked the wind out of her and left her close to fainting.

But she wouldn't let this unspeakable thing happen to her without a fight. Choking, fighting for breath, she twisted and clawed at him, trying to bring her mouth close enough to bite him. This time the response was even more savage. A heavy, black-booted foot drew back, then slammed into the pit of her stomach. And while she lay paralyzed with agony and fear, the boot struck her again, this time in the mouth.

She felt her teeth splinter, and her mouth was suddenly filled with warm, salty liquid. She gagged, choking on the blood and gasping for air. As desperate as she was, she could no longer make her body respond. She lay still, totally helpless.

As she looked up, she realized she was lying on her back with her head on the block. Above her, she saw the towering black-clad man raise the ax. The blade flashed in the torchlight as it whipped over his head and descended toward her throat.

In a last, valiant effort, she managed to move just a little. But one of her last thoughts before the ax struck her throat was that it wasn't enough.

Even as dazed as she was, the impact was astonishing. The blade struck with explosive force, just below her larynx. His aim had been spoiled by her last-ditch struggle, but the blow cleaved her neck cleanly, the steel chopping through flesh and sinews and arteries and bone and biting into the wooden block beneath her head with a loud whack.

Oddly, she felt no pain. She was aware of a hand snatching her head aloft, and as it did she looked down and saw her headless body lying on the platform, a brilliant red torrent gushing from her severed neck.

In that horrifying instant, realization came to her at last. What she had seen in her vision had been accurate. The headsman had indeed been preparing to execute a dark-haired woman.

But that woman was not Sally Benson.

The woman was Karen herself.

And in that final, all-knowing moment, her mouth opened, and her larynx constricted, pouring out the last sound it would utter on this earth.

"Jud-d-d . . ."

And then it trailed off, and her eyesight failed, and her brain ceased to function as the soul of Karen Wilson was borne away to a place where it would find peace at last.

NINETEEN ···································
A Time to Die

1

The voice that called his name didn't sound human. It was more like the mournful cry of an animal, a dismal howl that a moment later was gone. Could it have been Karen? What in God's name had happened to her? He stepped back out into the narrow passageway and then moved in the direction the cry had come from.

Oddly, it had sounded as if it originated in one of the empty rooms he'd explored earlier. When he reached the first of them he went into it, sweeping the area with the flashlight beam.

Nothing.

He turned to leave, and another sound reached his ears. It was a dull thump, different from the creaking of the building's old timbers, but distinct. It might have come from behind one of the walls in here. He stepped over to it.

At one end of the wall, in a dark corner hidden by shadows, was a narrow opening. Jud went through it and found himself in another passageway even tighter than the one he'd been exploring. He moved around a bend, and the sight that greeted him was staggering.

Standing directly ahead of him, his hulking form filling the passage, was the headsman.

A jumble of thoughts raced through Jud's mind. The creature looked exactly like the man in the old painting Mulgrave had given him. And exactly as he'd been described by Karen Wilson. He wore tight-fitting black clothing, and his eyes seemed to burn as they looked out from inside the slanted devil-holes in the hood that covered his head.

In his hands was a huge, double-bladed ax.

Jud stood totally still, so startled he was unable to move. The headsman, too, was motionless, holding him in his piercing gaze. They stood facing each other for a long moment, implacable enemies in a confrontation at last.

The headsman moved first. He raised the ax chest-high and stepped forward.

Jud wouldn't waste his breath issuing a warning. He held the flashlight beam on the advancing monster, and with his right hand leveled his revolver. He thumbed back the hammer for maximum accuracy, and fired.

The headsman kept coming.

Jud fired again. And again. The pistol shots were shatteringly loud in the confined space. These were copper-jacketed .357 Magnum slugs, capable of stopping any animal on the North American continent, including a grizzly bear. But they seemed to have no effect on the thing in front of him.

The sixth shot struck the headsman in the dead center of his chest from a distance of no more than two feet. Every round had gone home; Jud could see the holes in the tunic. He raised the pistol to club his enemy, but the headsman was too quick for him. The black-gloved hands made a lightning-fast snapping motion, and the axhead flashed upward, its flat side catching Jud under his jaw.

There was a burst of light as the heavy steel weapon crashed into his face.

2

He was out for a time. The first thing he became conscious of was torchlight flickering against the ancient stone walls. Then he made out the wooden platform and the chopping block. The platform and the block were drenched with fresh blood.

Lying to one side of the platform was the headless body of a woman. Her head was nearby, resting on the earthen floor, its eyes bulging in the same expression of terror he'd first seen on Marcy Dickens' face, and later on Buddy Harper's.

The head was Karen Wilson's.

Jud then realized his hands and feet had been tied with a

length of heavy cord. He was propped up with his back against one of the stone walls, and every heartbeat drove pain into his skull. He heard a sound to his left and, with an effort, turned his head.

To his horror, he saw the headsman drag Sally into the room. She was bound as he was, hand and foot. There were bruises on her cheeks and her jaw, and she appeared to be only semiconscious. The headsman crouched over her, gripping her by the hair. The bastard must have beaten her until she was no longer able to resist. As Jud watched, the executioner looked up and caught sight of Jud.

A voice came from inside the hood, as cold and flat as a file rasping on metal. "Awake, are you? Good. You'll be a witness. First for her execution, and then your own."

The headsman dragged Sally over to the platform. He pulled her up onto it, positioning her face up on the block.

As the headsman prepared her for execution, Jud strained against the bindings on his wrists with all the strength he could muster. He twisted his hands back and forth in a desperate effort to loosen the cord, praying he could break free before it was too late.

Small whimpering sounds were coming from Sally's mouth. "Please don't. Oh, God—please don't."

The man in black stood over her, looking down at his victim and gripping the ax. He planted his feet in a wide stance, setting himself.

Jud gave a mighty heave, and the bonds seemed to give a little. He heaved again, and this time he was sure of it. Once more he strained and tugged.

The headsman looked across at him. The flat voice sounded again. "Stupid shit."

Lowering the ax, the executioner leaned it against the wall and stepped off the platform. He crossed the room to where Jud lay, bending down and tightening the bindings. The eyes seemed alight with rage as they stared into his. "You're next, damn you. And there's no way you can break loose."

My God, Jud thought. *I know that voice.*

As if in a gesture of contempt, the headsman slammed the back of his hand across Jud's jaw.

But disdain had made him careless. He's close enough, Jud thought. Do it *now*.

He brought his feet up in a savage kick, driving the toes of his hunting boots into the executioner's groin.

The big man gasped in pain, doubling over and holding his crotch. The motion brought his head down, and with his bound hands Jud made a grab for his throat. He missed, clutching the hood instead. He kicked again, this time driving the other back, and the black cloth of the hood ripped free.

The headsman continued to hold his groin, and then he slowly straightened up.

Jud found himself looking at the face of Emmett Stark.

"You!"

The old chief's voice was a harsh rasp. "That's right, me. And now that you know, what good's it going to do you? You're dead, you dumb fucker."

Stark drew his boot back and then kicked Jud in the face, stunning him.

Dazed, Jud shook his head to clear it. One side of his face was numb, and his mouth was filling with blood. He spat, railing at his own stupidity for not having seen the truth before this.

He stared at Stark. "It was all there, if only I'd had brains enough to put it together."

Stark sneered. "But you didn't. You never would have known the truth, right up until your head rolled off that block."

"Maybe so. But I knew there was something wrong with what I was getting from you. I just didn't pay enough attention to the signals, because I couldn't imagine your being involved. I was too busy trying to run down other people I thought could be the headsman. But it sure as hell falls into place now."

"Now that it's too late."

"For one thing, the Donovan case wasn't before your time, the way you said it was. That was just bullshit, a way for you to throw me off. With the number of years you had on the force, you must have been a rookie when it happened. Joan Donovan told me a cop was one of her mother's lovers. When I showed her Grady's picture she said she remembered him. But it was easy for her to make a mistake. She was just a little kid when

you were coming around. What she actually remembered was
the uniform, not the face. You were the one who killed her
mother."

Stark flushed with anger. "Janet Donovan was a slut. A
rotten, filthy whore."

"Why—because she was married and screwing you? Or
because she was also screwing a bunch of other guys and you
couldn't stand that idea?"

A strange look came over Stark's face, and a light appeared
in his eyes. "God told me to drive her from His kingdom."

"I'm right, aren't I? You were so jealous it made you crazy.
But you twisted that up in your mind so that it was all her fault.
She was to blame, she was the one who had to be punished.
And you figured that for you to become the headsman was the
perfect answer. You'd be the executioner, coming back to
Braddock to wipe out evil. I'll bet you were proud of yourself,
weren't you? You passed the sentence, and you carried it out."

"You're right about one thing—she got what she deserved."

"Uh-huh. And it worked just the way you wanted it to.
People not only believed the headsman had come back to
execute her, but a lot of them figured she was asking for it. She
needed to be punished, and the headsman punished her."

Stark's eyes gleamed. "It was God's will."

As he spoke, Jud continued to exert as much pressure as he
could on the cord binding his hands, hoping Stark wouldn't
notice. He had to keep him talking. "But it wasn't enough for
you, was it? There were still all those other guys she'd been
seeing. You knew who they were. All of them were young
hotshots around Braddock. Ed Dickens, Peter Harper, Sam
Melcher, Charley Boggs, Loring Campbell and Bill Swanson.
You hated them for it. That's right, isn't it?"

Stark spoke through clenched teeth. "You don't know what
the fuck you're talking about."

"Don't I? You also hated them because they were all better
off than you were. Came from rich families, went on to run the
town while you were just a cop. Then you got to be chief of the
department, and you thought that made you important."

"Shut your ignorant mouth, asshole."

"But then what happened? A lot of those same guys became

members of the Town Council. And last year they shoved you out of your job. You didn't retire—they fired you."

"They're scumbags, every one of them."

"So all that hatred that was inside you for so many years, all of it came to a boil. You figured the way to get back at them, the way to hurt them the most, was to strike at their kids. And that's what you did."

"Those little shits were no better than their fucking parents. They were dirty, dopesmoking filth. That's all they thought about—dope and sex."

"You decided to start with Marcy, because she was so vulnerable, so easy to get to. An only child living in a big house with a room at the opposite end from her parents'. Getting in would have been easy, especially for a cop. Come to think of it, you didn't even have to jimmy your way in. Ed Dickens told me about a bolt that was sticking on one of the doors. All you had to do was depress the tongue with a piece of plastic and then walk right in."

"It might have been like that."

"Might have been? That's exactly what happened. And instead of taking her head with you, the way you did with all the others, you left it there on the dresser. You *wanted* it to be found, because you knew it would scare the shit out of everyone in this town. You *wanted* them to know the headsman was back, and you wanted the message to be as bad as you could make it."

"They deserved to suffer."

"Buddy, on the other hand, you took out of that barn after you killed him. Because you knew his disappearance would throw the investigation off, give the cops more blind alleys to run down. You figured he'd be blamed for Marcy's murder, and you were right. So you cleaned the blood off the floor, and then just to be sure there'd be nothing left to trace, you dumped that five-gallon can of oil onto the floorboards. All Grady could find was old wood soaked in drain oil."

"Grady was another dumb shit."

"Was he? I don't think so. And by the way, he was the one you wanted for your job, not me. But he wasn't so dumb at all. He figured it out, didn't he?"

"He was a disloyal prick. Came after me."

"And you killed him. What'd you do with his body?"

The corners of Stark's mouth curved in a cynical smile. "By now it's nothing but a pile of dogshit."

A picture of the snarling hounds in the pen behind Stark's house came into Jud's mind. "That's what you did with the rest of Buddy's body too, wasn't it?"

"Of course."

"But you sent the head to me because you knew it would make more trouble for me, didn't you? You knew how casual those young cops often were, so you just watched and waited until Ostheimer left the desk for coffee, and then you slipped in and left the package on the desk. For it to come to me would be just one more reason for the council members to distrust me."

"They would have fired you too, MacElroy. You would've known what it felt like."

"And speaking of evidence disappearing, you were the one who took those old police records, of course. I was suspicious a cop might have done it, but I was looking at the wrong cop. I bought that crap about your health problems, too. The bullshit about taking nitro for your heart. What was it—aspirin?"

Stark grinned.

"In fact, your police background made everything easy for you. It was you who rammed me earlier tonight. You'd left the Boggs house in your Jeep, and you were monitoring police transmissions on your radio. When you ran that snowplow into me you thought that would take me out of it. And those shots I fired at you just now. They didn't stop you because you're wearing a vest, right? Police-issue Kevlar. That's true, isn't it?"

"The Lord protects me."

"Really? They'll get you, you know. Sooner or later the cops'll get you."

Stark grunted in contempt. "The hell they will. I forgot more about police work than those fuckers ever learned. Get me? Never. And you know why, asshole? Because after this the headsman'll be gone without a trace. And everybody in Braddock will say, yes, he came back and killed the ones that deserved it. And then he disappeared again. Just the way he's been doing for over two hundred years."

"You son of a bitch."

Stark stared at him. "You still don't understand, do you? The truth is right in front of you, and you don't understand at all. What you don't see, you stupid bastard, is that all this is not what you think it is."

"What do you mean?"

"What do I mean? *Think,* goddamn you. Can't you see it?"

"See what—what is it?"

His eyes were glowing. "I *am* the headsman. I am the headsman of Hounslow, come to the colonies on HMS *New Hope* in 1705. I am in Emmett Stark's body now, as I have been in the bodies of other hosts many times. Whenever God has commanded me to serve the people of Braddock, I have returned."

He's totally mad, Jud thought. Straight-out fucking crazy.

"Watch closely, MacElroy. I told you, you'll be a witness. Twice."

He stepped back to the platform and picked up the ax.

Sally had been silent throughout the exchange between Stark and Jud. The beating she'd taken had left her unable to move. Now she looked up at Stark. "Please don't. I'm begging you—don't do it."

For answer he bent over her and held the axhead close to her face. "Don't worry, you'll hardly feel a thing." He grinned. "Not after a few seconds, anyway."

She moaned, closing her eyes, her mouth trembling.

Stark straightened and looked over at Jud. "Takes skill, you know that? You want the ax to hit right there on the Adam's apple. That's the aiming point. You do it right, the blade goes through like the neck was warm butter."

Sally was gulping air in shallow gasps. "Oh, God. Please."

Jud had to keep him talking, had to slow him down. "Where did the ax come from?"

"Where? From England, of course."

"You mean that's the *original?*"

"Of course it is. Forged by a master armorer in sixteen-ninety."

"Did Mulgrave know it was here?"

"Sure he did. But he didn't know who was using it. He was scared shitless it'd be found and he'd be implicated somehow. Or he'd lose his pissant curator job. So he came here thinking he'd get rid of it."

"And found you."

"Found me, found the ax. And then justice found him." He raised the ax once more.

Jud gave another violent tug at the cord binding his wrists, but it held fast. Desperate, he struggled to his feet.

Stark looked at him in surprise, the expression on his harsh features rapidly turning to rage. He stepped down from the platform, holding the ax ready.

Jud half-staggered toward him. As Stark lifted the weapon to strike, Jud dropped into a crouch, then propelled himself at the big man's midsection. Stark swung the ax, but he was a second too late.

Jud barreled into him, ramming his head into Stark's gut. Stark stumbled against the edge of the platform and went over backward, losing his grip on the ax. As he scrambled to regain his feet, Jud snapped the top of his head up as hard as he could, smashing Stark's mouth and nose.

The big man cursed and slammed a clublike fist against the side of Jud's jaw.

Half-dazed, Jud turned and snatched up the ax with his bound hands. He swung the heavy weapon with all his strength, driving the huge blade into the center of Stark's face, splitting it open like a rotten melon.

Stark fell onto his back, the axhead buried in his shattered features. His hands and feet twitched, and then he was still.

Jud struggled until he got a hand free, then bent down and untied the cord binding his legs. He pulled Sally to her feet and freed her as well.

They stood huddled together for a long time, holding onto each other for support, both physical and emotional.

"You all right?" Jud gasped.

She was trembling, her body shaking. "Yes . . . I think so. Are you?"

"Yeah, I'm okay." He'd never experienced anything like

this, a feeling of having been totally drained, his mind still reeling from the shock of what had happened. The only thing remotely comparable to it was coming out of the fever when he'd been wounded in combat.

He was drenched in sweat, and becoming aware of his cuts and bruises. A terrible headache was pounding the top of his head.

Sally shuddered. "Please take me out of this awful place."

"Yeah, come on."

He turned, and guided her out the door of the chamber. There was a stairway just beyond it. He could feel her continuing to tremble, and thought he might have to carry her. How he'd manage that he had no idea. But she kept going, and he stepped behind her, supporting her as she put a foot on the stairs.

A hand seized Jud's shoulder in a powerful grip.

He twisted his head around, and what he saw was the embodiment of a nightmare.

Emmett Stark loomed there, one hand holding Jud, the other raising the ax. He'd torn the weapon away from his face, but the wound was horrendous. In the dim light Jud could see bone splinters and torn tissue, all of it dripping blood. One eye had been ripped from its socket and was hanging by a thread, dangling against Stark's cheek.

The other eye was fixed on Jud, burning with a fiery light. The big man swung the ax.

From somewhere, Jud found the strength once more. He slammed his right fist into the center of Stark's body, forgetting the bulletproof vest until he experienced sharp pain in his hand.

But the force of the blow knocked Stark back a step, ruining his aim. Jud moved sideways, and the ax missed him by inches.

A maniacal cry of rage boiled from the bloody center of what had been Stark's face. He came forward, lifting the ax.

As hard as he could, Jud poked two fingers of his right hand into Stark's remaining eye. The big man stumbled, again emitting that unearthly howl. He pawed his face, and Jud tore the ax away from him.

Holding the haft in both hands, Jud swung the heavy weapon in an arc. But this time he brought the razor-sharp steel directly down onto the top of Stark's head. The blade drove completely through his skull, cleaving it into two gory halves.

The lumbering body stood erect, its hands raised, blood pumping from the place where the head had been. Then it staggered backward and collapsed onto the floor, the ax handle poking straight up from it.

Only then was Jud sure it was over.

··
Epilogue

The media attention focused on Braddock was enormous.
Reporters from television, newspapers and magazines swarmed
over the community like flies on a compost heap, and Jud
MacElroy was held up to the world as a hero.

It was a role he refused to accept. Nor would he accept the con-
tract offered him by the Braddock Town Council, which would
have provided him with long-term security in his job and a con-
siderable increase in salary. Instead, he left Braddock to become
chief of police in Ardsley, California, an even smaller town than
Braddock. He did not choose the position purely on the basis of
the warm weather Ardsley offered, although that was a factor. A
more important reason was that the town was only a fifteen-
minute drive from Berkeley, and he enrolled in the University of
California Law School there, taking courses at night.

Sally Benson also left Braddock. The career opportunities
that opened up for her as a result of her work on the headsman
case were almost unlimited. She joined the staff of *Lifestyle*
magazine in New York and became an associate editor.

The lives of many other Braddock citizens changed as well.

Frank Hathaway was called to a hearing by the school board,
at which he asserted that after an injury in Vietnam, severe
emotional stress had incapacitated him. His claim was supported by a psychiatrist, who explained that what began as
psychosomatic illness had developed into a genuine physical
handicap. Nevertheless, Hathaway was fired by the board. He
too moved to New York, and was hired by a private school in
Greenwich Village.

The Harpers were divorced, and Jean Harper moved to
Boston. Peter Harper was awarded custody of their daughter.

Loring Campbell, not Bill Swanson, became the next elected mayor of Braddock.

Sam Melcher and his business partners were unable to attract a major industrial firm to the town.

Sam's daughter Betty enrolled at Skidmore, driving to the college in a new Mustang convertible.

Charley Boggs died of a massive coronary thrombosis.

Ray Maxwell also suffered a heart attack, but survived it. He retired, after selling his interest in the *Braddock Express* to the Newhouse newspaper chain.

Inspector Chester Pearson and Corporal Williger were awarded commendations by the New York State Police for their outstanding work in supervising the work of the state police task force as well as coordinating the efforts of the BPD.

Before leaving for California, Jud MacElroy appeared before the parole board in Westchester County and supported Joan Donovan's request for parole, stating that she had provided valuable help in the investigation. His request was denied.

To the people of Braddock, the death of Emmett Stark marked the end of a nightmarish period of terror and revulsion. They breathed a collective sigh of relief and resolved to get on with their lives, hoping the notoriety would fade and their little community would at last return to normal.

But among them were many who knew in their hearts that the tale of the headsman had not ended, that it never would. The legend was as much a part of Braddock as the fierce storms that roared down upon the town each winter, holding it in an icy grip.

They knew that at some point in the future, perhaps ten years hence, perhaps twenty, a shadowy figure would appear once more, a big man dressed all in black. Black boots, black tunic, black gloves. Covering his head would be a black hood, and from within the slanted holes his eyes would burn with a devilish light. In his powerful hands he would carry a huge, double-bladed ax. He would make his rounds, seeking out those who were living lives of sin.

Then there would be footsteps in the night, and cries of horror. The steel would flash in a glittering arc.

Oh, yes.

The headsman would be back.